Books by K.M. del Mara

Whitebeam

Willow Oak

Passage Oak

Beautiful as the Sky

Vagabond Wind

Twist a Rope of Sand

PARROT ISLAND TALES

K.M. del Mara

ISBN.PB 978-1-7348488-4-7 eB 978-1-7348488-5-4
Library of Congress Control Number 2024924816

Front cover image by Kris Kuszajewski, reworked by the author
Back cover photo by Hermon Charles, reworked by the author.

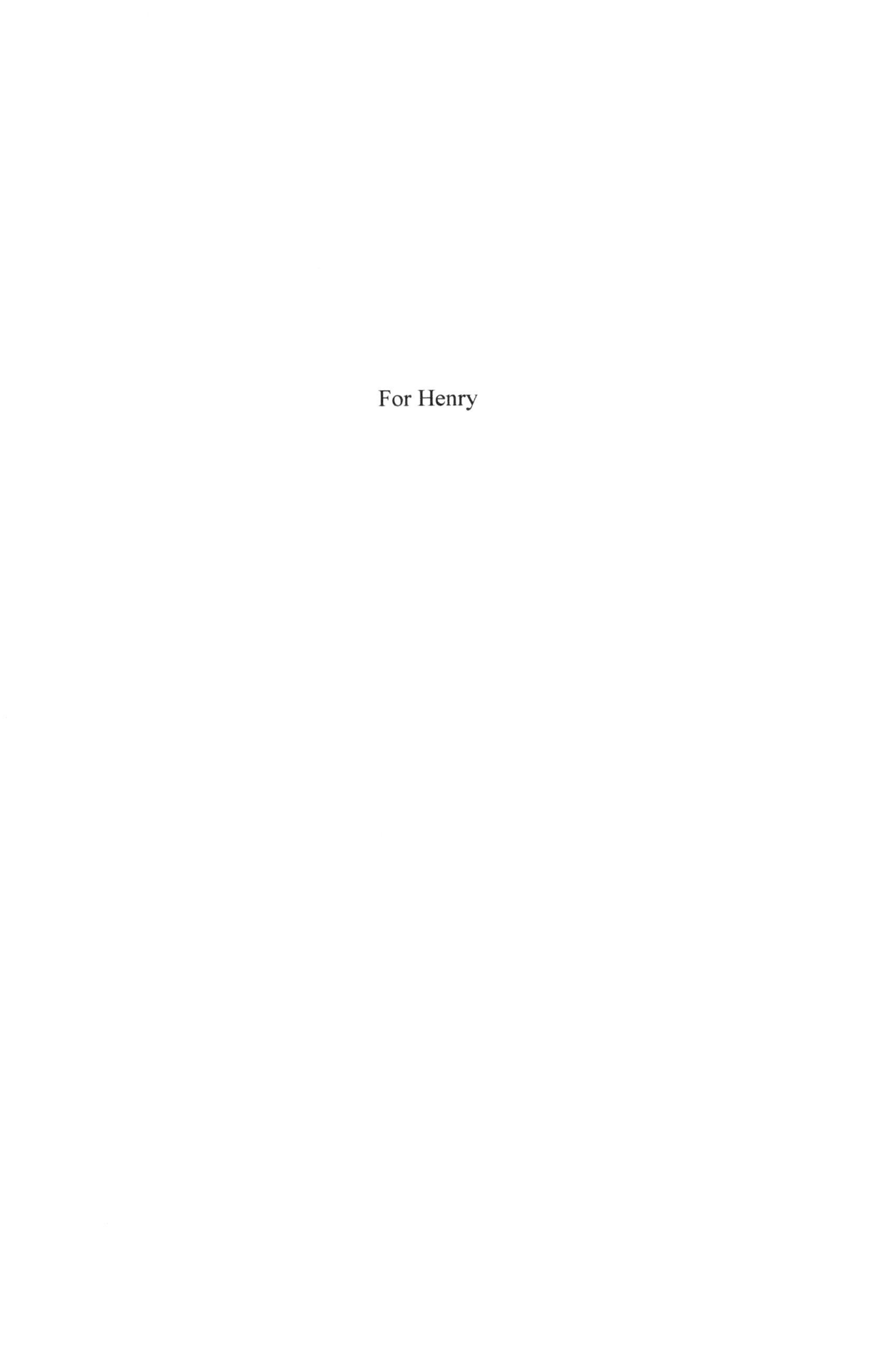

For Henry

" 'My name is Ozymandias, king of kings;
Look on my works, ye Mighty, and despair!'
Nothing beside remains. Round the decay
Of that colossal wreck, boundless and bare
The lone and level sands stretch far away."
- Percy Bysshe Shelley

"God invented [people] because he loves stories."
- Elie Wiesel

PARROT ISLAND TALES

DRAMATIS PERSONAE

LIGHTHOUSE KEEPERS AND THEIR FAMILIES

D'Inquierre

    Hey You/Anne, a mountain nomad
    Kai, her son
    Alphonse, her husband, a trader

Treyse
    Wido, a shepherd
    Ermentrude, his wife, a weaver
    Gregor, their son

Button
    Freya, an innkeeper
    Batilda, her sister, a cook
    Lisabetta, a healer

Hogar Hanon, a gardener

Teron Adante, an exiled law student

Lily, a small child

ELITE FAMILIES

Einfaldsson
    Hans-Martin, father
    Saranna, his daughter
    Soro, his son

Mynydd
    Vladimir, magistrate
    Natalia, his wife
    Dort, their son

Fairhedd
    Ruslan, factor for Mynydd
    Ludmila, his wife
    Florri, their daughter
    Gregor, her son

Ragenold, the elderly chancellor

VILLAGERS
Bobert Notting, the sheriff
Briar Tuck, a locksmith

Charlotte Russe, a village girl
Chekov, the Sunday cook
Chilperic, a boatman
Father James, a priest
Francevili
     Jozef, the harbormaster
     Irina, his wife, a landlady
Georgiana, a serving girl
Gerbert, an orphan boy
Hahri Fahri, a puppeteer
John Little, a fisherman
Magnolia, Dort's mistress
Mr. Basko, the grocer
Mr. Forman, the miller
Mr. Guntram, the blacksmith
Mr. Korsakov, the ferryman
Mr. Wunder, the baker
Nuns of St. Scholastica
     Kunegunde, a teacher
     Angelica, a teacher
     Rosemarie, an elderly botanist
     Susanna, Mother Superior
Poggio Gomoggio, a bookbinder
Radovan Weebly, the sheriff's deputy
Silvio Filvio, aka Signor Bologna, the puppet master
Sulman, a shaman
Taptoe
     Thorfinn, a fisherman
     Marie, his wife
     Bobby, their son
     Sheila, their donkey
Wohlfahrt
     Otto, the chandler
     Franz, his nephew, Batilda's fiancé

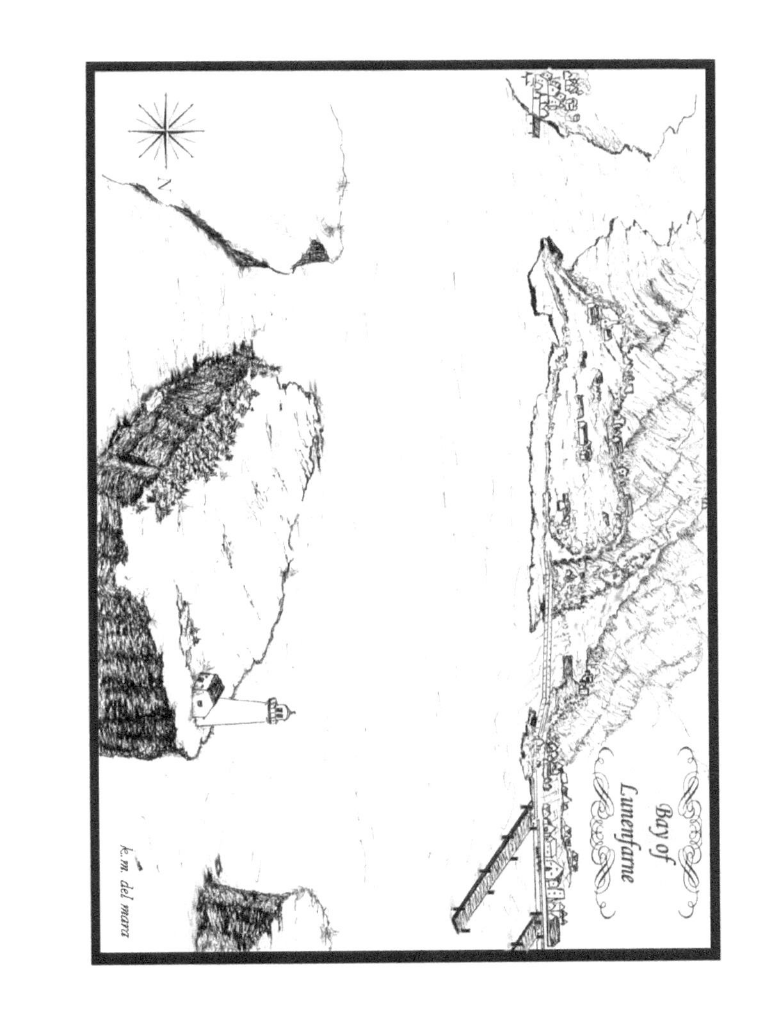

N
Bay of Lunenfarne
k.m. del mari

IMPELLER

The old cartographer had been working on the map, morning 'til night, for two full weeks. It was close to midnight when he finally finished. He was about to sprinkle the pounce that would dry the ink when inspiration jolted his tired brain. One tiny island, one little joke. His bony shoulders were shaken by a paroxysm of mirth. *Parossismo,* a good name! The Venetian would never know. He had just begun inking the name when his last candle sputtered and went out. He had to feel his way to the stairs.

Awaking to the clear light of morning, he instantly regretted adding that unprofessional bit of foolery to his carefully drawn work. Quickly he slipped on a pair of clogs and clattered downstairs in his nightshirt, determined to amend it. When his assistant announced that he had rolled up the map and handed it over to the client from Venice half an hour ago, the old man was apoplectic. By the second reheating of his Turkish coffee, though, he began to relax a little. He had invented only the smallest of islands.

What earthly difference could it make to anyone?

> I should like to rise and go
> Where the golden apples grow;—
> Where below another sky
> Parrot islands anchored lie ….
> *- Robert Louis Stevenson*

ANNE D'INQUIERRE

On ancient maps of the known world, myths, miscalculations, and sometimes outright deceptions show hundreds of nonexistent land masses. Small wonder that, from this tangle of true and false, the great adventurers of old were fond of regaling their cronies with tall tales of magical islands they claimed to have visited. Mariners love these stories and have told and retold them, but some are very little known.

There happens to be one, an old, old tale, that asks you to believe that somewhere in time, somewhere on the edge of a cold ocean in the loneliest part of the world, there once lay a small node of invincibility, an island, the Ile Par Ou. An antique French trader's map, drawn on silk long-since torn and frayed, showed Par Ou as nothing more than a dot. It sat on the brink of the infinite, a still point between the dangerous deep upswelling sea and a sparsely populated land of balsam-scented mountains.

This insignificant little island, so the story goes, cowered in the path of every storm that blasted unchecked out of Fennoscandia. The waters surrounding it were spiked with dangerous rocks and raged with cross-currents. It was a witches' cauldron for sailing vessels, such that ships' crews, stealing past the skerries off Par Ou, spoke not a word for fear of rousing its demons.

Though ships, even in those days, were plying the oceans of the world in search of markets and resources, navigation was perilous. Ports in the far north were few and far between. Landmarks were sparse or unfamiliar. A ship's navigator could only estimate his position, never certain how long it would be until he sighted a light on some distant headland, and thus assure himself that the edge of the world was not yawning directly off his port bow. So when a beacon was finally lit on Ile Par Ou, it provided the first landmark for over a hundred miles in either direction. That one pinpoint of light – no landlubber can know how sailors welcomed that telling gleam across the heaving bosom of a nightblack sea.

Ile Par Ou guarded the slim channel to a wide, deep-water harbor and protected it from all but the worst storms. The French name of the island, Par Ou, meant "which way?", because ships trying to enter the harbor had to make a choice. The passage on the south side of Ile Par Ou was deep but perilously narrow. On the north side, the wider channel hid a fathomless underwater gorge that snaked its way between rocky shoals, safe enough if the tide was high, a menace if not. Captains had to make a decision quickly. Which channel, the narrow or the wide? As often as not, devil winds made the decision for them.

On the far side of this harbor, a small village had grown up. Its ancient name, Lunenfarne, meant 'moon land', probably labeled so by a homesick voyager who found the region less than hospitable. The Bay of Lunenfarne was a good mile wide, an almost land-locked body of water fed by two rivers. Each of these rivers, in olden days, gave miners and lumbermen and traders access to different parts of the interior of a large, resource-rich continent, and that is how, gradually, this bay at the end of the earth became something of a destination. But before there were channel-markers and a lighthouse on Par Ou, the passage past the island was so difficult that few ships even attempted it.

The Bay of Lunenfarne was locked in the arms of two peninsulas that were dotted with the ruins of stone huts and an ancient longhouse built by the Tuniit people. Squeezed between these two peninsulas was the Ile Par Ou. It was less than six acres in size, uninhabited since time out of mind, its cliffs often shrouded in mist, invisible but ever haunted.

Legends about the Ile Par Ou and its reefs tell that a piece of that coastline was obliterated all in one night, crushed by the hands of wrathful gods. The waters rushed over and it sank into the ocean, save for the highest point, and that became the Ile Par Ou. When the land drowned, an ancient monastery drowned with it, thereby fittingly erasing, so they say, terrible secrets of sacrifices and pagan rituals. But the ghosts of the priests remained. Ask any villager. They had all seen them on stormy nights – and this is verifiable truth – summoning the Furies to devour the souls of shipwrecked sailors. Can a more plausible explanation be found for why no one ever set foot on Ile Par Ou – not ever, and why sailors feared being wrecked there, above all places?

Par Ou's staggering rock cliffs defended what remained of the broken land, and from the sea the island looked absolutely impregnable. It defied any possibility of a landing. But if you could stand at the top of the island and look down across it, you would see before you a lovely grassy meadow, cupping to its center, sloping gradually down to the bay, to a small hook of shifting sands. The narrow beach encircled a tide pool inhabited by an ever-changing cast of mollusks and crabs, though even these delicacies were considered untouchable by the people of Lunenfarne.

Before there was any light on Par Ou and after too many ships had foundered there on moonless nights, after too many souls had been sucked beneath the waves, then it was finally decided. The parsimonious magistrates of Lunenfarne at last agreed to pay someone to live on the island in order to tend a primitive beacon fire. They begrudged the expense, but it was necessary if they wanted the traffic of traders and merchants. The difficulty, of course, was finding someone willing to live alone on a haunted island.

Lunenfarne was a rough little port in those days, and the traders who came downriver from the interior were a callous bunch. Alphonse d'Inquierre was one such man. He heard that the town magistrates were looking for a light keeper, but he did not want the job. It would tie him down, an inconceivable restriction for someone who fancied himself an adventurer. Was he not a man who took risks other men did not dare to take, who went places most men would only dream of going? He would never consent to stay year-round in one place, not he. He would never commit to working for measly wages. He was a traveling man, was Monsieur d'Inquierre, a voyageur. He had canoed far into the northern wilderness over bottomless lakes and ice-cold rivers. He had traded iron pots for rich furs, smoked potent herbs beside the campfires of wild savages, bathed in noisy brooks with naked indigenous women, and slept in the open on beds of pine boughs. He was a real man living a real man's life, damned if he wasn't.

In this particular springtime, he had come back to Lunenfarne so he could sell his newly-acquired goods, and also to show off his wife of one month, the daughter of a chieftain of a northwoods nomadic clan. Two years before, this girl's entire family had been captured and executed by rivals. Only she had been spared. A pretty little maiden, she had caught the eye of a young buck who enslaved her to be his paramour, though she was still not yet a woman at age twelve. A year or two later, her warrior mate's new wife insisted that he abandon the girl. Alphonse was more than willing to take her off his hands. She was a mere child, he reasoned. He could mold her however he wished. He offered two decorated iron knives for her. For two knives and a string of green glass beads, the bargain was sealed and the girl belonged to Alphonse. Now he could boast that he had not wooed his wife so much as acquired her, proving that money could indeed buy anything and that he, Alphonse d'Inquierre, had the wherewithal to do so.

Even at her young age the girl was a haughty one, silent, with an aloof air that was unlike the bawds Alphonse had always preferred. He was determined to tame this wench, though, yes he was. He liked the idea of bringing a prize animal to heel, and the image he cherished of dominating a beautiful young woman was exactly why Alphonse bothered to have a wife at all. Owning this woman, breaking her like a colt, would define him, certify him as unique, a wild and adventurous man. He needed a wife who reflected his image of himself. Otherwise, why bother? If he must have a wife – and he granted that it was much cheaper and easier than the alternative – she had to fulfill a specific role: chattel belonging to Alphonse d'Inquierre, a man of significance.

After weeks together, Alphonse still had not mastered the pronunciation of his wife's name. "Hey,You!" he'd snap, when he wanted her to do something, and it was the only way he ever referred to her.

After they arrived in Lunenfarne, if you asked any white woman about Hey You d'Inquierre, you would get an earful of one opinion: you could not possibly call such a dark, unsmiling face pretty. But it was a face that men could not stop looking at, an exotic face, with some subtle quality of shrewdness that these simple fishermen found fascinating. Hey You's tilted black eyes were spaced wide apart above sculpted cheekbones. Her luxuriant black hair was woven into a half-dozen braids, gathered back and hanging to her waist. Silver charms dangled from a beaded coronet that circled her head. She spoke no English, as far as Alphonse could tell, which bothered him not a bit. "Fer crap sake," he told anyone who would listen, "I'm not feeding her and letting her share my bed just because I need somebody to talk to."

As for Hey You d'Inquierre, by the springtime that she and Alphonse arrived in Lunenfarne, she was feeling a rising sense of desperation. Raised by gentle shepherdfolk, her girlhood had been shattered by the deaths of her entire family. Her very life since the age of twelve had belonged to someone else. Her existence in an enemy clan had been miserably humiliating and uncertain. Now, as wife to a mean and stupid, not to mention wrinkled old fart, she found another reason for desperation. She told no one about it. There was no one to tell.

Alphonse was, of course, unaware of her feelings, unaware, actually, that Hey You had feelings at all. But Hey You had become convinced that she would die unless she escaped this wretched marriage.

Moving to Lunenfarne was the most recent of many shocks for her. She had been raised in verdant mountain meadows and quiet majestic pine forests. Like a dream it was, those fleeting days of her childhood. Her community had consisted of a clan of close-knit families who tended their sheep on grassy slopes and wove their wool into cloth of bold patterns. They loved poetry and song. Her people were prosperous, their lives ordered by the needs of their herds. They traveled in gaily painted caravans, whereas Lunenfarne's low cottages looked brown and dismal to her. Hey You's people were handsome, too. They stood proud and straight. They loved ornament and decoration. She saw nothing like that here.

She found these pale people, most of them, dull and unappealing. Women wrapped themselves in plain headscarves and rough brown shawls, their skin the color of root bread, their hair, wrists, and necks without a single bauble. Considering them unimaginative and uninteresting, Hey You could not understand why she was treated as strange. But as she was one and they were many, she was shunned as an outcast. Marriage to Alphonse had changed Hey You's life only peripherally, the same script with a different cast of characters.

Her husband had rented a room in a house in town that belonged to the harbor master. It took the harbor master's wife, Irina Francevili, only a day or two to decide that she needed to take Hey You under her wing. Friends warned Irina repeatedly that kindness to barbarian girls was misdirected. But when she came upon Hey You trying to start a cooking fire in the middle of the apartment floor, the look of shame on the girl's face nearly broke Mrs. Francevili's plump little heart. She told her friends that of course Hey You would need help. She was only a young girl. How could she know how to act? Her people lived in yurts and horse-drawn wagons instead of houses, according to Alphonse. Privately, Mrs. Francevili considered living in a wagon to be one hell of a sight better than living anywhere with Alphonse d'Inquierre, but life presented many crosses to bear, didn't it, and who else but womenfolk had the strength to bear them? Yes, she would help Hey You if she could.

At first, Hey You resisted Mrs. Francevili's advice. Slowly though, she began to trust that the landlady, the only friendly woman she had met, was a kind person, a person truly willing to help her understand this strange world. Hey You began to pay attention. She would have to learn how to light a stove and use a sink and an outhouse. The landlady opened cupboards and drawers to reveal mysterious items like forks and colanders, and Hey You listened, head bent, while Mrs. Francevili tried to explain their use to her. After a couple of weeks, the two women were doing the marketing and cooking together because, as the landlady told her husband, Hey You's idea of cooking was to convert any food to an ambiguous mush and throw it into a frying pan.

"She don't got a clue in the kitchen," Mrs. Francevili told Mr. Francevili, "but she's learning a few words so we can talk. What's really too bad, though," she sighed, "is that she's stuck with that miserable varmint for a husband. Her, not even fifteen years old yet, were I to guess, and she gets slapped and kicked like a dog. I told him I'd knock him into next Sabbath if I heard he was hitting her again. And I swear to you, Jozef, by all that's holy, that I meant every word!"

Jozef Francevili had not a doubt in the world that she did.

Alphonse, meanwhile, was doing a fair bit of successful wheeling and dealing down at the docks. His money passed through his hands like grass through a goose, but that is the way he had always lived. He was selling furs and skins, beadwork, and a large collection of silver jewelry and artistic little trinkets that he'd bought on his travels. He insisted that Hey You come to the marketplace with him and carry his bags of wares. His reasoning, privately, was that her presence drew the menfolk almost without fail, and Alphonse gloated when he saw the gleam of desire in their eyes. Maybe next trip he should buy another of these savage women so he'd have two, like a sultan with a harem. Then the name Alphonse d'Inquierre would mean something, damn it. No two ways about it, that was the way for a man to get respect in this world.

Yes, buying this girl was one of the smartest things he'd ever done. For the first time, he had no trouble naming a high price for his goods. Oddly, it was not with the women that he was doing the most business, but with the local men. Hey You distracted them so they could hardly think straight. She was beautiful and colorful. She was intriguing. They'd pay anything, they were that befuddled. It wasn't long before the matrons of Lunenfarne began to wonder why so many among them were receiving little gifts from their menfolk. Men who didn't know an earring from a shoe button were buying their wives silver bangles with strange markings, garnet brooches for their shawls, and dangly beaded things that, as far as the women could tell, were meant to be clipped into their hair somehow, but who knew how?

After a couple of weeks in Lunenfarne, it occurred to Alphonse that something about Hey You was different. Being a man with no more perception than your average grasshopper, he only began to realise something was wrong the night his wife punched him back when he hit her. If his nose hadn't been bleeding all over the damn place, he would have thrashed her good before she got out the door. As it was, he didn't know where she spent the night. There was another thing, too. More than once, he'd stumbled half-crocked back to the apartment to find their landlady visiting his wife. The two of them, his wife and that old snoop, seemed to be spending quite a bit of time together.

This he really resented. No, he did not like it one bit. He felt threatened, and he was not a man to back away from a threat. The next time Hey You pissed him off, he threw his big muddy boot at her, hitting her so hard in the head that it knocked her right off her feet. And, horseballs on a biscuit, not a moment later came the knock at their door.

Every friggin' time! Lately, that happened every damn time he tried to set things straight with his wife. That busybody Mrs. Francevili would hear their set-to and come a-knocking. He was fed up! He told the old battleax he was going to move to another apartment house cuz he sure as hell wasn't paying rent on some dump if he couldn't beat his own wife when she needed beating. He was too overwrought to notice the look that passed between the two women that evening, a wordless resolve.

Once resolved, Hey You needed only the smallest excuse for action.

When a trader came to Alphonse's table in the market the next day, Hey You was there as usual, weighed down with two heavy bags, their entire stock in trade. The man sidled up to her. Her eyes followed him as he circled round her speculatively. She stiffened, pulling away when he reached to touch her hair. She watched him say something to Alphonse, who sneered and nodded. The man tapped his head, in the same place where a large bruise swelled on Hey You's forehead. Alphonse laughed and shrugged. The man turned to her again. He put a finger under her chin, studying her face. She snapped her head away, frowning defiantly when Alphonse spoke angrily to her.

"Eww hew!" the man laughed, taking out a purse. "This one's pretty hot! I want her."

Hey You couldn't understand a word he said, but she panicked. She watched the man rifle through some coins. He offered Alphonse a few. And that settled it. She refused to be a commodity any longer.

Alphonse crossed his arms and answered the man with a few words. The man paused, shook his head, and reluctantly put his purse away.

Hey You stood quite still for a moment after he left. One step. She had but to take that first step. Slide the large bags she carried off her shoulders. Let them tumble to the ground, let their contents spill out. Just drop them and go.

She turned her back on Alphonse. Without a look in his direction, she walked away.

"Hey!" Alphonse croaked. He lunged and grabbed her by the arm but he pulled back as if bitten when she snatched away, baring her teeth and holding up her hands like claws. He stepped back. What was this? How dare she? How dare she do that, right out in public like this? The little tramp! It made his blood boil! His blood – ahgg, he could feel it surging in the veins of his neck. He could hardly breathe! With difficulty, he tried to rein in his anger. Women shoppers had turned. They were watching. Panting, he tried to collect himself. It would be stupid to make a scene in front of those women. He opened his hands slowly to Hey You in a placating way. There was a time and place for everything and bloody hell, she was going to get the tar whipped out of her as soon as they got home.

"Hey!" The bitch didn't even turn. "Hey! Get back here!" He put his hand on the hilt of his dagger. Oh, he'd kill her! He wanted to, he wanted to in the worst way. And he would have, he told himself. He would have, if he hadn't paid so much good money for her.

"Woman troubles?" said a voice behind him.

Alphonse turned to see another trader grinning at him. "Augh!" He wiped his mouth with the back of his hand. "Christ almighty. I am going to break her ass! She'll get such a hiding tonight she won't be able to sit down for a week!"

The other man laughed and said just the wrong thing. "Looks like you got your hands full with that one, mister."

Hands full? Did that man think this woman – this stupid cow! – had gotten the better of him? Him, Alphonse d'Inquierre?

The trader purchased a beaver pelt and purely out of spite, Alphonse charged him double for it.

Hey You went back to the boarding house and knocked softly on Mrs. Francevili's door. When the landlady opened it, Hey You gestured that she would like to come in. They stood in the doorway while Hey You, using her few words of English and many gestures, explained her predicament. She touched the bruise on her forehead, and the lady regarded her for a minute, squinting and biting her lower lip. Finally she nodded and beckoned Hey You into the house. Wide-eyed, Hey You walked slowly around the Francevili's parlor, stooping to run her fingers over the small piece of carpet, poking at cushions, putting her nose right up to some china figurines and examining them from all sides. But it was the small painting of a boy that drew her like a magnet. She touched it and pointed. Mrs. Francevili smiled and pointed too. It was an early portrait of Franz, the son she had borne by her first husband, now deceased. Hey You pointed to herself and then the painting again, nodding solemnly, trying to explain her secret.

The smile fell from Mrs. Francevili's face. "Oh dear. Oh dear love." She shook her head and sighed. "All right. Come sit down." She motioned for Hey You to sit at her kitchen table.

Mrs. Francevili made a pot of tea and gave Hey You a steaming cup.

"Wait." She put a hand on Hey You's arm. "Wait til it cools a bit."

Hey You tasted it and grimaced. Mrs. Francevili added some sugar, only a small spoonful because sugar was neither easy to come by nor cheap.

"Try it now. Go ahead." She made drinking motions.

Hey You took a sip and held out her cup. She nodded at the sugar bowl. "More."

"More, please."

"Pleece."

Mrs. Francevili added one more spoonful. Hey You sipped, smiled, chugged the rest of the tea down in one gulp, and held the cup out again.

She was on her third cup when Mr. Francevili came home for lunch. When he saw the dark-skinned girl at his table, he flashed a look of horror at his wife.

She jabbed her finger into his chest and pushed his burly frame into a chair by the table.

"Now just you stop that before you even begin, Jozef. Don't you do that! We're all God's children and you ain't being nice. No! Stay there! Sit down here a minute. Now listen to me." She put one hand on the back of his chair and leaned close to his face. "What I got is a prop'sition for you, Jozef. This girl is here cuz she's going to be living by herself from now on and she needs to earn a living. Her people are gone. She's got no one she can go back to. And just think, you been looking for someone to keep a beacon out on Par Ou, haven't you? Right? So look! She's just what you need. She would be perfect for that job."

"What? Irina! Are you crazy?"

"You could set her up in a tent til you get something permanent built. She'd be right at home out there."

"Right at home? Oh sure, like a gull on a garbage pile." Jozef grimaced. "What in hell you thinking? A woman alone tending a light on that island? You're talking about Par Ou, fer gawdsake!"

"Looks to me like she can take pretty good care of herself. Don't you see? Besides, she wants to get away from that husband of hers and believe me, I can sympathize with my whole heart."

"Now what's that supposed to mean? You starting in complaining again?"

"Jozef, I just think you should set her up out there and see how she does. Why won't you? She's just what you been looking for."

"That place ain't safe. You know that. There's ghostly things out there, so they say, and …."

"She don't know anything about those old ghost stories. So they won't scare her."

"She don't even speak our language, fer crissake, Irina."

"Who's there to talk to out on that hell hole of an island? Nobody else don't want the job anyways. You said so yourself."

"You don't even know this girl. You told me you don't even know her name, only what her husband calls her."

"Hmm." Irina pursed her lips in thought. She turned then and bent over Hey You, tapping her fingertips against her own chest. "Irina. I'm Irina." Then she tapped Hey You's chest.

"Hey You." The girl inflected the words in the same forceful way her husband did: Hey! You!

Irina tilted her head, squinting at the young woman. "That's not a name. What were you called before you married that steaming goat turd of a husband?" She shook her head and tapped Hey You's chest again.

The girl nodded. "Hey You." She paused, realizing. No one had uttered her given name for more than two winters. "Aiyanna."

"Aye –a –?" Irina tried.

"Aiyanna Petalacqua."

"What?" squealed Jozef. "What'd she say? What is that? Some gypsy name?"

Irina, one eyebrow raised, looked down at Hey You. She thought for a minute. She looked back at her husband.

"Anne," Irina finally announced, straightening. "Her name is Anne."

Jozef sighed in disgust. "Aw, geez." He hemmed. He hawed. He pressed a small pleat into the tablecloth.

"Jozef, look here. Look at me! Don't I run two boarding houses? All by myself? And also our own apartment, too? And don't I do most of your book-keeping besides?"

"Yeah yeah. Why you gotta start complaining about all this now for?"

"Well don't I do all that? And am't I a woman?"

Now that there was one tough question, and it cut close to the bone. Jozef hemmed some more haws. A potent question, though he hated that word. Potent. He shuddered. That word upset him. He re-pleated the tablecloth. Hoo, best if he left that whole question alone.

"Come on, Jozef. Just row her out there, why don't you? See how she does for a couple of weeks. What harm can that do? I betcha she'll work out better than any man you could find for ten miles around."

Jozef rocked his head from side to side. "You know I can't go to the magistrates with the name of a woman for a job like that. What'll they say?"

"Convince them. You can do it. You gotta convince them that it's in their best interest."

"Aw, Irina!" Jozef spluttered, slapping the tabletop. Damn that woman. Sharp as a tack she was. "Aw kripes!" He sighed. He scratched an itch. "Guess we wouldn't have to pay her the full freight, since she ain't a man. They'd approve of that, for sure."

"Don't you go giving me that crap! They sure as hellfire will have to fork over enough for a person to live on, the greedy pigs. She's got to make ends meet, same as anybody, buying food and whatall."

"She don't deserve that much, not the same as a man. She can't do the things what a man can do."

"What in hell you saying? Let me hear you name what things a man can do. You mean things like running into town every night? Spending hard-earned money on buying whiskey for a couple of whores? Getting so drunk he forgets to come home? Things like that what men do? That what you're talking about?"

Hastily, Jozef felt it was in his best interest to change tack. "You don't got any idea about this girl. Whether she's reliable or what!" Jozef hunkered down in his chair, breathing like a winded beast of burden. He looked across the table at the young woman sitting straight in her chair, her eyes flicking from him to his wife and back. She was so young. Kinda sorta, yeah maybe now that he looked closely, really almost pretty. Blushing, Jozef tore his eyes away and changed tack again, growling softly. "I tell you one thing, Irina, and don't you forget it. Women can be just as bad sinners, same as any man. Just as bad!"

"I take it you know this from first hand experience?"

"No!" Jozef reddened more deeply. "I hear it told."

"I hear things told too, Jozef." She squinted at her husband, watching him writhe like a snake under a boot heel. She shook her head. "Be that as it may, let me tell you what I'm going to do. I'll take her down to the harbor and point out the island to her. I'll try to explain things to her. If she wants the job, will you apply to the magistrates for her? Lordy, Jozef, she needs the work."

Jozef shook his head. "She'll never do it. Look at her. She's nothing but a savage. And I tell you," Jozef pressed, trying to drive home a point, "I still say she'll probably do like all women, casting temptations everywhere like they do."

"That's not likely."

"You mark my words. She'll be running around sinning just as bad as a man."

"Not likely, Jozef, not likely. Most women usually can't afford such carrying on. Nature don't allow it. Not if they got a baby to nurse."

That got Jozef's attention. "A baby?" For a man who had been bypassed by the miracle of fatherhood, this changed everything.

The next day, Jozef Francevili stood in the hall outside the Council Reception Room twisting his cap into a knot. His wife Irina and Anne d'Inquierre (her new name hopefully committed to her memory) sat on a bench. They'd been waiting there for half an hour when Bailiff Spittang finally came to the door and gestured.

"All righty. They're on their way. Come in, Jozef, come in. Irina, you and – and that one," he said, pointing, "sit in the back." He held the door while they slipped past.

"What kind of mood they in today, Spittang?" Jozef whispered.

Spittang's eyebrows shot up and he waggled his head from side to side. "In a bit of a snit, they is. I'd tread lightly, I was you."

Jozef groaned. "They had a full morning's work?"

"Oh Lord no. They just got here. One of them larger carriages tipped over coming down the River Road and all the rest of them was stuck behind."

"'They all live on the same road. Why don't they share the carriage ride?"

Spittang eyes bulged. "Share? They don't like each other enough to share anything." He leaned to Jozef and said softly, "They got here in some disarray."

"Yeah?"

"Yep. One of 'em's broke a fingernail."

"Ooo," said Jozef. "Pity."

"Yep," said Spittang. He straightened smartly when he heard the door to the Chamber open. "Rise!" he bellowed. "At the behest of Chancellor Ragenold, the Tribunal Extraordinaire of the Commonwealth of Lunenfarne will come to order. Vice Chancellor Vladimir Mynydd assisting."

A trumpeter attempted a flaccid fanfare.

Seven magistrates minced into the room, one, some years younger than the rest, supporting the elderly Chancellor Ragenold, who could barely shuffle. The term "pomp" did not begin to describe the spectacle they made. Jozef and Irina kept their eyes fixed on their laps. Anne d'Inquierre couldn't take her eyes off the procession. A wave of despair hit her. These were the men who would decide her fate this morning?

Seven men, everyone of them a sight to behold. All seven had heads close-shaved except for long tufts of hair spiking from various places, some from the crown of the head, some over the ears like horns, tufts here and tufts there, all bound with silken ribbons to hold them stiffly upright. Some had mustaches waxed in elaborate curlicues, and all of their fingernails, brightly varnished, were an inch long, discounting the one recently broken. Their clothing was a complex combination of restrictive wrappings and billowing clouds of fabric. Their sleeves wrapped their arms tightly in silk of gaudy colors, while loose satiny trousers puffed extravagantly above the thick gold bangles that they all wore on their ankles. But it was their shoes that most mystified Anne. How could they walk? The more elderly tripped along in thin little booties with toes that curved sharply upward. The younger men tottered precariously in boots with heels so tall they had to carry silver-worked canes to keep themselves from toppling over or twisting an ankle.

These, then, were the exalted magistrates of the Council of Lunenfarne. Their fathers and grandfathers had established fortunes by tearing into mountainsides to dig mines and trekking through heavy forests to rob them of lumber, but this younger generation was left with nothing to plunder. To give themselves a purpose, therefore, they occupied themselves with trying to squeeze what prestige and money they could from the administration of a small village of fishermen and farmers. They lived behind high walls on grand estates up in the hills above the town. They had enough time on their hands to oversee every enterprise in the community and extort every possible centavo from every living creature, even charging a fee to any villager who had the temerity to present himself as recently dead. The revenue this brought in was mere pocket change to these magistrates, but as it was into their pockets that most of the tax money went, it assuaged their neediness. They did, of course, dole out such funds as were needed to keep the town's infrastructure sound and functioning. The meaning of "sound and functioning" was left to their representatives to decide, as those terms pertained to the roads, the bridges, the fountains, and the piers of Lunenfarne. They were marvelously adept, these representatives, at saving money for the council. As a consequence, not everything that was currently functioning was truly sound.

So here came the magistrates, picking their way onto the dais. Chairs scraped. The clickclatter of needle-sharp heels and clacking canes finally diminished. The coughing and harrumphing subsided. They settled themselves and their voluminous trousers and began the meeting. They called on Jozef Francevili, as Harbor Master, to report on the status of trade. This he did as concisely as he was able. The magistrates, though, were uncomfortable with his report.

"You say," queried the young Magistrate Mynydd in a measured, deep bass voice, "that our import tariffs are down from last fall? Why is this, Francevili? It is springtime. We should already be seeing much more trade than in the winter months."

"True enough, Your Grace, but you remember that I reported two months ago that ships refuse to come into our harbor any time we got bad weather, or if it's a real dark night. It's too dangerous. They simply pass us by."

Mynydd turned to his colleagues. "Gentlemen, gentlemen. Does this make any sense? Gallston, your shipments of ore give you knowledge of boats and sea. Do you see any problem with piloting a ship into our harbor? Is it really all that difficult? It's a big harbor, wouldn't you say?"

The man he queried, Gallston, had a little bit of a cold in his nose that day. He was occupied at the moment trying to get his lace-trimmed hanky to his nostril without injuring himself, quite tricky with a handful of very long fingernails. "Ehhh, what's that?"

"I'm asking you for a judgment on Francevili's report."

Gallston snuffled loudly and dabbed carefully at his nose. "Eh ...."

Jozef Francevili raised a timid finger. "Your Grace, might I say ...."

"What is it?"

"The harbor is large, sir, but the passages past Par Ou Island are very narrow and rocky. If the tide is out and them big ships do get past the rock reefs, they many times get stuck in the south channel. And too, all up and down the coast there's not a light to be seen. On a dark night, they can't even find the entrance to the bay. Case in point is that ship what wrecked out there some three four weeks ago, and not a soul left alive to tell her story. Many a good and worthy sea captain tells us they refuse to come here at all, lessen we get a light out on that there island."

"Did we not tell you some time ago to find someone to take care of that? Clerk, did we not tell Francevili to see to that? Check your records," Mynydd insisted.

"I been trying to find someone to mind a beacon out there, Your Grace, but no one wants to live on that island." He dared to add quietly, "Not on that pay." He hurried on. "But now, today I think I finally got somebody."

"Well there you go. Problem solved – " Mynydd was stopped by the blast of a mighty sneeze. And another. Then a shriek of terror.

"Gallston? What have you done?"

Gallston's hanky was dripping with blood. "My doze! My doze! It's stuck!" he screamed.

"Is that your fingernail? Pull it out of there! Pull it out! That is ghastly! For pity sake, Gallston! Bailiff, help him. Good god, man, you've torn your nostril to shreds!"

"Ooh my arse and parsley!" wheezed the ancient Chancellor Ragenold, aghast at the sight of gore.

"Bailiff, get over here and help him. Wipe off his –" Mynydd pounded the table before him. "You're upsetting the chancellor. I'm sorry you had to see such a spectacle, Lord Ragenold. We'll get Gallston out of here. Get him out, Bailiff!"

Gallston tottered out, the bailiff supporting him as best he could without getting spattered. The clerk was making a terrible commotion, trying to mop up blood. Finally, when they were able to proceed, Mynydd was eager to wrap things up quickly.

"All right. Let's get this finished. So Francevili, we will have ourselves a lightkeeper, you say?"

"If we get money for a beacon ..."

"Fine. See that he gets something, Clerk."

"And provisions like food and such ..."

"Yes, yes."

"A rowboat ..."

"I don't think a boat will be necessary."

"The keeper can't walk to the island, Your Grace."

"If he has no boat, the keeper will be forced to stay on the island and see to his job. It's better to do without a boat."

"Well, a house, then. A small house is a necessity."

"A house? What for, I ask you?"

"Keeper has got to live somewhere, Your Grace."

Vladimir Mynydd rolled his eyes and sighed. "So be it. Write up a budget. Get it to Clerk. And don't go overboard. Are we clear on that, Francevili? Keep the costs down. All right. What name does this lightkeeper go by? Clerk, get this into your record."

"Anne d'Inquierre, Your Grace."

Mynydd looked up. "Anne?"

Jozef nodded.

Mynydd put his pen down and sat back. "A woman?"

"Um, yes. I guess she is, Your Grace."

"What kind of woman would want a job like this?"

Jozef, no words coming quickly to mind, turned and gestured to Anne to stand up. She did so. Mynydd blinked several times. "She's … she's … she's …."

"Egad! What a looker! *Gak gagh!*" A clog of phlegm nearly choked horny old Chancellor Ragenold.

Anne, appalled, confused, sat down.

One of the well-fleshed magistrates banged the table. "Enough! Mynydd, stop gawping and let's just get this settled. We give our approval." He waved a hand. "Just tell Clerk to get it in the record so we can finish up. It's past lunchtime. Let her, that ... that savage woman go live out there if she wants. How can anyone object?"

"It's actually not a bad idea," mewled a gray-tufted magistrate. "What's she doing here, anyway? We don't want her kind living here. Stick her out on that island by herself, out where she'll do no harm."

Mynydd nodded, not really hearing. He hadn't taken his eyes off the young woman. He chastised himself with the reminder that he already had a wife of many years – well, four years, in point of fact. It seemed like more.

"Vladimir! My applesauce," whined the ancient Chancellor Ragenold. He dug his long fingernails into Mynydd's arm, bringing Vladimir Mynydd thudding back to earth. "It's time for my applesauce."

"Fine. The new beacon is approved by all?" Mynydd asked quietly."So be it. Gentlemen, we have ourselves a lightkeeper."

The clerk dipped his pen and bent studiously to his book. With a clattering of canes and a clickering of heels, the magistrates rose and minced out of the room.

So the first keeper of the light on Par Ou was a woman, strange as it seemed at the time. A female keeper. Who would have thought?

It wasn't more than two weeks later, then, that Anne d'Inquierre first set foot on the island that was to be her home. It was a rare blue-sky day. Mr. and Mrs. Francevili sat beside her in the boat, both worrying silently about the girl. She was so young. And carrying a child. To their minds, she was ignorant. Could she handle the task before her? They watched her sitting very erect in the rowboat, her eyes fastened on the island.

Lunenfarne Bay. Such a large body of water, Anne was thinking, larger than any mountain lake she had ever known. Par Ou Island was that high hump of land in the distance. She leaned forward on her seat. What was she hearing? Some constant rhythmic sound that seemed to grow louder, the closer to the island they came. Waves, Irina Francevili told her. The ocean made that sound. Anne could see the waves now, water sloshing and swirling, some magical power pushing foamy water over the rocks that surrounded the island. What made the water move when there was no wind to drive it? Then Anne got her first glimpse of an even bigger lake out beyond the island. She leaned to see more of it. Irina had already explained to her that the sea was far larger than any water she would ever see in the north woods. But she had not pictured anything like this. Was there nothing out there but water? And beyond that horizon? That was the edge of the world out there. She could see it. So perilously close. She hadn't realised how close.

Suddenly this was all too overwhelming. She wasn't ready for this strange place. An island, far from any people, surrounded by vast water that swelled with mysterious, uneasy power. She sensed it, this power, some strong magic. She might be forced to confront that power someday, face it all alone. Her courage faltered.

She was the first to jump out of the rowboat, though, as soon as they touched the beach. Half-buried in the sand at her feet was something hard and white. She bent to pick it up. Beautiful, formed in a swirling shape, so like a design her people used to decorate their pottery. A shell, Irina told her. It came from the sea.

Shell. Maybe she could wear it like an amulet. Anne pressed it into her palm, a talisman.

She looked up the hill. Before her sloped a long brown meadow, grassy like the foothills where her sheep used to roam. Here was something familiar, lovely to her eye, though still in its winter drab. The land rose and rose to a high point straight ahead of her. Up there at the very edge of the cliff sat the little wooden house they had hastily built for her as the new keeper. To her right, a narrow band of spruce and hardwood trees fringed the shore.

Maybe, here on this island, she might be able to find – what? A place for herself? Where she would not be anyone's captive? No family lived here, sadly, but no gawking strangers either, no horrible iron-fingered men. No one. Alphonse would never get to her here.

Yes, she would light the beacon every evening and keep it going for the whole night. She would do everything Mr. Francevili told her to do. Hope stirred once again. Perhaps, one day, if she could get used to this place, to this kind of work, she might find some peace here.

She helped the men drag supplies up the hill to the little house. Jozef Francevili protested vehemently that she shouldn't be lifting the heavier things, but Anne didn't mind. Irina Francevili was delighted with the cottage. She helped Anne stow everything on rough shelves: pots, a few dishes, food enough for the next month, a tub for washing. She showed Anne how to make up the bed, how to pump water, how to light the woodstove that would keep her warm and cook her meals. Mr. Francevili guided her back outside to show her the enormous woodpile. It had taken the men many trips this week to bring enough logs over from the mainland. He showed her the stone platform built to hold the beacon fire, and the big red flag she was to hang in a tree as a signal that she needed help from town. Finally, Irina Francevili, her eyes glistening, wrapped her arms around Anne and told her, oh, how she wished she could stay on the island with her.

And then they were gone. Anne was alone at last.

Alone. By herself in the world now. A sad thing, but certainly a relief from her recent, hideous past. She had seen her family slaughtered, every single one– mother, father, brothers. Everyone in the clan she had grown up with was dead, torn from her by vicious enemies. She could never forget watching her family die, and she could never get them back. Where had they gone? They had apparently returned from whence they came, into the Nothingness. Gone into the Elsewhere. No matter how far she searched, she would never find them.

And she? Where she was going? She did not really know. Would she be on this island forever? She was barely fifteen years old. The thought of 'forever' was incomprehensible.

She had never spent a single night in her entire life by herself, but she wasn't afraid. She thought, as she so often had, of breezy pine-damp nights sleeping with her family in their caravan in the foothills. What a silly child she had been back then, with no idea that the world was full of filth and ugliness. Maybe that was why the murders of her entire clan had hit her so hard.

How was she to put all that behind her? How to stop seeing all those deaths, again and again in her mind? How to purge the bitter resentment that sat like a coiled snake inside her? She could not make herself believe that the horrors were over, all in the past. Aiyanna Petalacqua, once-gentle shepherdess, now Anne d'Inquierre, wary as a hunted wolf. All the more vigilant because one day she would have a wolf pup to protect.

She went into the cottage – no one but herself inside! – and brought a blanket outdoors. She spread it on the grass near the edge of the cliff and lay down. The sun was warm with the first hints of spring. The big Endless Water was fascinating to watch. It showed hardly a ripple, and yet, a brooding power lurked beneath it that she did not trust. She watched the lazy waves combing around the reef of rocks that ringed the island way, way down below the cliff. Farther out, the wrecked hull of a very big boat, bigger than any she had ever seen, had somehow become impaled on the rocks. What had happened there?

All these sights were new to her. Playful foam-capped waves, as Irina had named them, splashing rainbows against the cliffs far below. And look, on the beach across the channel, funny little birds diving into holes in the sand. Strange white birds chasing after them, then soaring aloft on arc-shaped wings. A breeze, healing in its touch, whispering across the saltwater. Waves wind water, everything moving gently around her. But this island, motionless. Solid, fixed, immovable.

Here, below another sky, she thought she had finally found a still point.

Anne rolled over on the blanket and looked up into the high blue heavens. Shining banks of cloud sat on the hilltops, brown birds raced over the meadow, and far above an eagle hunted across the winds without flapping a wing. She was that eagle.

A noise came bubbling up from inside her that she could not suppress, and she laughed out loud. Her heart swelled, and petal by petal, she felt herself opening like a flower.

For two winters past she had made herself into something hard, tough as an acorn. It was the only way she could survive, and one of these days, she would have to deal, not only her own survival, but another's as well. That was something to think about. But not just yet. She would think about that another day. For now, the important thing was to figure out where she was going. She knew she couldn't tend a beacon for the rest of her life. Maybe, when she had this little Someone beside her, she would look for a place deep in the mountains, a place just for the two of them. But anyway, that would be a long time from now, a long, long time away.

Today she was the wind, the clouds, a bird flying free.

For the first time ever, sailors on a ship coming over the horizon that night saw the light of a beacon fire on Parou Island. Black clouds had come up out of the sea. Black coastline was obscured by the dark of night for miles to the north, black to the south. But Par Ou was a new lodestar, an affirmation, a point of orientation. Not until they came abreast of the island could ships' crews see the glowing lights of the town tucked far back across a wide bay, and above the town, the dots of lights from the great hill estates. Once past Par Ou, their ship was again swallowed whole by darkness. For them, the beacon on Par Ou became a pinpoint of light astern Then it disappeared, winked out, as if it had never been.

But Par Ou's light shone forth, giving its light freely, whether anyone saw it or not.

Anne resolved to stay awake all night for her first night on Par Ou. She built a small campfire just below the beacon, wrapped herself in her blanket, and watched the stately procession of stars. Up there Polaris reigned, the Still One, the Sky Pin, the star whose rising inspired the storytellers, the bright star her people called the Central Fire. It gave her comfort, steady as a homestead fire.

Early in the night, she heard some strange sounds. The trickling sound of a little fall of stones, then another sound. She listened hard but heard nothing more. Her people told stories of small men who came out at dusk, but who would disappear in an instant if any human person turned her eyes toward them. Who would have thought she'd find them here? She told herself that they were probably glad for her company, those little men. In return, they would protect her from all harm.

The second night as she dozed on her blanket beside her campfire, she heard, just barely over the constant purl of waves, the crack of a twig. That seemed natural enough, but a few minutes after that, she heard footsteps. She was certain that she had. Was it Alphonse? Her old wariness returned.

The Francevilis had assured her repeatedly that she would be alone on Par Ou, that no one, not even the fishermen, came here. Now, her senses told her differently.

The next afternoon, Anne walked down the hill to the beach where the rowboat had landed. There was an interesting tide pool there, she remembered, and maybe she would find another shell. But when she knelt at the pool's edge she saw something strange – a footprint. The clear print of a boot with a heel, a rather large boot. She straightened and looked around. She saw no one. The print could have been made by the workmen who had been here on the day she came. Was that three days ago? She crouched to look at the print more closely. It certainly looked fresh.

Then she heard a voice.

Bend over!

She stood. A voice? Where? What was it saying? Anne didn't know those words. She whirled around. Who spoke them? Clearly there was someone close by, but where?

Then, a whistle. *Bend over. I think I love you.*

A bird came waddling over the top of a rock. Anne stepped back. A shockingly strange bird. So brightly colored blue and orange and yellow. Brilliant feathers, like nothing she'd ever seen before. A big bird, seeming almost tame. He stared at her. Anne stared back. He whistled through his curved beak. She was looking straight at him and she was certain. That whistle had come from that bird, no doubt about it.

Bend over!

Words. He could talk. If she hadn't been watching, she never would have believed it. If only she could understand his words!

Anne stood stock still, afraid to move lest she spook this strange weird thing. It raised a big wrinkled claw and, standing on one foot, vigorously scratched the back of its head. It looked up sharply when the hungry eagle glided overhead.

Damn you to hell! the bird screamed in a loud voice, watching the eagle until it disappeared.

More words that Anne couldn't understand, but they were definitely words and the bird had spoken them.

Suddenly he spread wings so big and colorful that Anne ducked, startled. The amazing bird flew away, into the woods. Anne watched it go with her mouth hanging open.

It was true, then, what she had sensed. No one had mentioned it, but she had felt it. This magic bird was proof. The island was indeed haunted.

Anne had been on Par Ou for four days before someone mentioned to Alphonse d'Inquierre that she was the new keeper of the beacon. So that's where she had gone! The cunning witch! She was not going to escape him! Then he heard that she was actually being paid for the job of lightkeeper. Paid? So much the better! Anne would have money. Fantastic! Most of his wares had been sold and he had taken in good money, but Alphonse, true to form, had blown almost all his cash.

Here was a nice piece of luck. This would work out well. His sneaky wife thought she could escape him so easily? Ha! Escape Alphonse? No, no! She belonged to him.

He waited until dark, stole a boat, and rowed out to the island. Her campfire, just below the beacon near the top of the hill, was easy to spot. Keeping low, he crept up through the meadow, close to the trees along its edge, quietly, quietly.

With owl-like senses, Anne heard someone coming, heard the sound of something sliding over the grass. She stood.

Up he rose. Alphonse! She screamed and kicked out at him but he, armed with an oar from the boat, got the better of her immediately. He twirled the oar in the air and landed a blow on the back of her head. She fell like a lifeless doll, unconscious. Grabbing her arm and a fistful of her hair, he began to drag her toward the cottage.

Suddenly he was assaulted, kicked in the kidneys, down on his knees. Who the hell? He rolled to his back and rammed his foot into his assailant's leg. A man! Alphonse had been told Anne was alone out here! Both men were down, rolling and punching. Anne lay in an unconscious heap on the grass. Now the man had gotten hold of the oar and he swung, sending Alphonse staggering to the ground. The last thing Alphonse saw before brutal punches hammered his nose and face, was a light brown beard and fierce blue eyes.

The next morning, fishermen spotted their stolen rowboat floating in the bay. Stealing a boat was a crime of the first magnitude. The thief was slumped in the bottom. When they towed d'Inquierre ashore, they saw he had been beaten to a pulp and was not in complete possession of his faculties. He could barely speak. Par Ou was haunted, he hissed at them crazily, haunted by demons. They hadn't needed his battered body to prove that to be true.

A broken collarbone, broken ribs, and a stint in jail kept d'Inquierre hanging about town for the next two weeks. He spent that time in a most furious mood. He made the excuse that he was in too much pain to seek out the man who assaulted him, but just wait until he was up and around. He would go back out there and find that bastard. He would know that man's face in an instant, if he really was a man and not a ghost. If he was a ghost, well, that was a thought too frightening to contemplate.

Alphonse, for all his evil qualities, had been blessed with a good memory. So the face he had seen once, he would see again and remember. Not for years though, not until he had made several more trips into the northern lands. And then, it wouldn't be the actual face he would see. It would be a drawing of that face, quite faded by that time. A yellowing poster, the word "Wanted" emblazoned across the top, along with another word: reward!

Aha! A reward! And, better than money, well, almost better than money, was a promise of revenge – a dish, even years later, that Alphonse would be more than willing to eat cold.

As for Anne, in the middle of the night that she was attacked, she awoke on the bed inside her cottage. She lay there, confused, trying to remember how she had gotten there. She hadn't slept inside on this bed since she'd arrived. She always slept outdoors so she could tend the beacon. Also, it felt more natural outside. She liked it out there.

The beacon! She gasped. She had forgotten it. Had it gone out? When she tried to rise, though, she felt her head swim. She fell backwards and then it all came to her. Alphonse! Alphonse had come. He had found her. She had fought him, but … where was he now? She listened. She could not hear those raspy throat sounds he made. She could not smell his fetid breath, nor even the stink of his clothes. She could not see him in the dark. Dare she try to get up? She had to. She had to check on the beacon, and she needed to know where her vile husband was. Carefully, slowly this time, she sat up. There was a large lump on the back of her head.

Then came another flash of memory. A man lifting her shoulders from the ground, cradling her against his chest. A man, speaking softly to her, holding her. Holding her gently. What a strange vision. And yet, she perfectly remembered his eyes, even though it had been dark. She had never seen eyes that light in color. But where had he come from? She was the only person here. There could be no man.

Strange, the tricks the mind plays.

She found no sign of Alphonse that night. She did find, oddly, the beacon still alight – it was burning lustily. How could that be? How long since she had tended it? She had no idea, but not long, apparently. Her head hurt. Everything seemed vague, she couldn't be sure of anything.

Morning came, and still no sign of Alphonse. The wind had picked up and it grew stronger as the day went on. Anne watched in awe as the Endless Water, so benign before, now unleashed enormous powers. Ah, here it was, revealed at last. Here was the lurking power she had sensed. This was the power she had felt when she arrived. Waves, pushing upward, growing frighteningly large, hammering against the cliffs of the island, pounding as if to destroy them. By evening, the storm was so fierce she could hardly get the beacon fire to stay lit. Spray from towering waves rose high enough that she could hear waterdrops sizzling in the beacon's flames. Lightning stabbed and thunder rocked the earth. Anne gathered her things from beside her campfire and decided she would definitely sleep inside tonight.

That was her intention, but it was not to happen. She was struggling against the wind, bent over to collect her cooking pot, trying to keep the wind from tearing her blanket out of her hands, when Hell opened wide and heaved up a sea monster of unbelievable fury. An immense wave of water plowed against the cliff. Thick, solid as a wall, higher than the house.

It bellowed a great roar, deafeningly loud even over the fury of the storm, and Anne felt the ground shake. She turned, lost her balance. A wall of dark water swept over and devoured the beacon fire. It smashed the cottage, splintering it like a toy. She wouldn't have believed it possible. Seawater cascaded toward her. She was hit by broken pieces of lumber and firewood logs. She fell to her knees, bracing herself. The wall of water was upon her. She screamed and raised an arm to fend off the wave. It knocked her flat.

She felt herself first pushed, now pulled. She dug her fingers into the grass but the wave pulled her toward the cliff edge, wanting to suck her into the sea. And then it dropped her.

Disappeared.

It was gone.

The monster wave had slithered back into the sea. Panting, drenched, overwhelmed by the roar of the storm, Anne crouched where she was, afraid to move. The wind hurled leaves and tree branches through the air. Rain sliced like knives.

All traces of her cottage were gone. She looked at the spot where it had been. There was nothing there. All her food, gone. The logs from the enormous woodpile had been scattered half way down the meadow. But nothing of hers remained. Even the red flag was gone, the signal that she was supposed to hang if she needed help. Without that, how many days would she have to wait before someone came out with more supplies?

All around her, storm winds raged. Angry waves smashed. Afraid to sleep in the open but afraid to shelter in the woods for fear of falling limbs, Anne didn't know what to do. Finally she took her sodden blanket, her last remaining possession and, leaning against the ferocious gale, her arm covering her face, she searched for a spot among the roots of a spruce tree at the edge of the woods. She settled there, protected from some of the rain at least, watching the storm writhe in fury until, finally, she slept.

The next morning was cold and she was wet. She gathered some fallen sticks and carried them back to her dead campfire. There would be no breakfast for her because all her food was gone, but at least she would have the comfort of a fire, if she could get one started.

She stopped in her tracks. She dropped the sticks with a clatter.

There, in the place where last night's fire had been, was a freshly caught fish, lying in a skillet that she'd never seen before. Under it was a pile of dry kindling and a matchstick. She looked up, surveying the empty meadow. Her eyes tracked the edges of the cliffs, the woods.

No one. Her eyes scanned the island again. No, no one there.

And yet, that fish – someone had put it there.

This island was not what it seemed. Were the horrible times beginning again, the uncertainty, the fear that made her heart shrivel? She swayed on her feet.

Not alone. Anne d'Inquierre knew she was not alone on Par Ou.

The island was haunted. Not a refuge, after all.

TERON ADANTE

Earlier that winter and farther to the south, Teron Adante had been an able law student at the university in Bellesunde when his life veered off course due to the smallest of missteps. He had considered his future to be promising, though he had lost both mother and father and it had been years since he had any family to support or encourage him. He had always been lucky, though. Money for his schooling had been lent him by a lawyer, hopefully his future employer, who had been a close friend of his father. In three more months, Teron hoped to be certified and finally earning a living, indentured, in effect, to that lawyer.

Then Chance put Saranna Einfaldsson in his path.

She came from a rich and powerful family. He was a poor student, deeply in debt. For some reason she accepted his advances. Maybe it was the novelty of flirting outrageously with a tall, handsome, but impoverished law student. Surely their class difference provided her with the excitement of a minor rebellion. Then somehow things got twisted. Saranna fell quite head over heels in love, or so it seemed to Teron Adante. So he liked to think.

On the first day of the Midwinter Fair they arranged to meet near the booth of the silk merchant, and there Teron introduced her to his friend and classmate, Prokoff. She, accompanied as always by a male relative, was with her brother Soro. This was a man from school that Teron barely knew. Soro Einfaldsson seldom made it to lectures, preferring to waste his father's money on drinking binges and carousing with prostitutes. How Saranna had found out that he was skipping classes, Soro did not know, but she threatened to tell their father unless Soro took her to the fair. Fearing Hans-Martin Einfaldsson's wrath above all, Soro had gone with his sister, only to find that it was just an excuse for her to meet this Teron Adante, apparently a classmate of his. So this was the bugger who had ratted on him! Soro resented being manipulated like this. That alone was enough to sour his mood. He didn't need the added spectacle of watching Saranna's new beau acting like a lovesick thirteen year old.

Ah, meeting your love at the Midwinter Fair, on a seductive afternoon so alive with the first breath of spring. Teron was besotted. He bowed briefly to Soro Einfaldsson and turned to brush his lips on Saranna's hand. Lips barely touching a hand – how, one wonders, can such a simple gesture entirely change the fate of three young men and a girl?

Soro, already testy, took note of this shadow of a kiss. A little bantam cock of a man, he bristled. He objected, he told Teron, to such presumptuous behavior – not from a peasant and never with his sister. Both Teron and his friend Prokoff dismissed him with a couple of barbed comments, but their words were not nearly as offensive as the meaning that Soro inferred. It didn't help that his defenses were on high alert. It didn't help that his judgment was impaired because he had been sloshed for the last two days. But even sober, he was never one to let something go. Rigid with anger, he pushed his sister aside. The three men exchanged slightly more heated insults, nothing so violent that anyone in the crowd even noticed, but stinging, very stinging to a fragile Einfaldsson ego. Provoked, Soro thrust his heavy cloak back over his shoulder and stepped threateningly close to the two men. Again, they dismissed him with a laugh. The situation didn't seem that serious, verbal parrying between reckless young men. So Teron did not see it coming.

A stiletto hidden in Soro's sleeve must have had a sinister intention of its own. Even before Soro realised it himself, his knife was in his hand. Once in his hand, Soro felt its power. A threatening lunge, nothing more, to teach that big peasant a lesson. Appalled, the two men raised their hands and counseled reason. Prokoff stepped forward to quell the antagonism, and very suddenly, it was horribly over. The argument, not even a fight, all over in half a moment. Prokoff, on the ground, his neck pierced by the stiletto, bleeding to death in the prime of his life; Teron, in shock, his tunic spattered with blood, sinking to his knees, calling his friend's name.

Seconds later, Prokoff was dead. One thrust of a knife and a young man's story diverges onto another path.

That was what happened at the Midwinter Fair. It didn't end there.

In those days, rich young men were seldom indicted for crimes, even if their crime was murder. The dead Prokoff's wealthy parents were aware of this, but after their son's burial, on principle they sued the Einfaldsson family anyway. They had no idea of the damage that would result. The compensation that they demanded meant nothing to the Einfaldssons. It was a mere pittance to them, but the public humiliation was not to be borne. Hans-Martin Einfaldsson called in a couple of favors on behalf of his son. He slipped money discreetly into the right pockets. In a matter of days, the case was brought to trial.

Whether Saranna Einfaldsson would have testified against her brother, Teron would never find out. He didn't know if she had been sequestered somewhere by her father. He never knew whether she was even in town, but in any case she did not appear at the trial. Saranna, the only other witness, had disappeared. Soro Einfaldsson's attorney asked who had seen what had happened. Einfaldsson pointed. There he is, he claimed. There was the only other person who had been close by. The murderer. With that, Teron's life slid into the gutter. He knew that he was being blamed, not for murder, but for touching his lips to the hand of a noblewoman. His words did not carry the same weight as the scion of a prestigious family, nowhere near the same weight. The trial lasted less than an hour.

Teron Adante was convicted and sentenced to hard labor in the north. They gave him a ten year sentence at Balgrim Prison which, for a young man of eighteen years, was half a lifetime. So grueling were the conditions at Balgrim that, for many inmates, even a limited conviction could easily turn out to be a life sentence. Those were the unfortunates who were worked to death, then thrown into a pit to be eaten by rats.

A ship from Einfaldsson's fleet, *Farfalla,* would soon be leaving Bellesunde, taking supplies of food to be sold to the prison. Teron, stunned and nearly out of his senses, was shackled and put aboard. They set sail for Balgrim. All his expectation of a promising profession had been instantly obliterated. He left behind a dead comrade, his young love, his home, and forever, all his prospects for respectability and happiness.

He left something else, too, something he had not had in his entire life: a bitter enemy. An enemy who knew the truth as well as Teron did, but who would do anything to conceal it.

Possibly because he was the only prisoner on the *Farfalla* or maybe just because he was so young, Teron wasn't treated badly. The ship's captain was one of Einfaldsson's henchmen and hated the sight of this prissy college student, but the sailors were decent. They slipped him food whenever they could. On a couple of sunny afternoons while they were still in the south, they even removed the iron cuffs from his wrists and ankles and let him sit on deck, until the captain found him and forbade such leniency.

Then Chance intervened once again. A vicious headwind came up, blowing out of the north. They could hardly make headway against such winds. Ice glazed the deck and rigging. The ship strained and bucked over mountains and valleys of seawater.As darkness came on and the storm only intensified, Teron Adante began to fear for his life.

"Should I let him free, sir?" Signalman Smollen yelled so he could be heard above the roar of the wind. "We could use another hand on deck."

"Are you crazy? We got the mother of all ice storms here. Don't bother with him!" hollered the captain. "Get yourself top-side now! We're abandoning ship."

The storm was unrelenting. Ice coated the rigging and caused the ship to list to port. Clinging to any handhold available, the men grabbed whatever possessions they could. Jugs of drinking water, the ship's log, the compass, all were loaded into the lifeboats.

"Smollen!" Teron begged the sailor as he passed. "The key. You've got to unlock my chains."

Signalman Smollen, frantic to get off the stricken ship, shook his head. "The captain --", he pleaded, practically in tears. "I'm sorry! Orders --"

"Please man, do me this favor. It may be your last act of kindness in this life."

This stopped Smollen abruptly. He clawed at the front of his jacket in misery. He didn't want to burn in hell.

"Do this for both of us, Smollen. I can swim. I'll be able to save us both if you'll just get these damn things off me."

Smollen, who was terrified of water, groaned and pulled the key from his pocket. He fumbled it into the lock on Teron's handcuffs. Teron rubbed his wrists. "Ah. Thanks, man. I owe you."

It was a debt Teron Adante would never have to repay.

Water was pouring in from somewhere. Gimbaled lamps were swinging wildly. The lamp by the companionway hissed and blew out.

"Smollen!" someone yelled down. "Last chance!"

Smollen thrust the key into Teron's hands. "I – gotta go. Sorry." He waded through the water and ascended the companionway. He stepped into the cockpit. Teron saw his arms flail. Smollen slipped and fell hard on his backside. His mates grabbed his arms and pulled him over to the rail. That was the last Teron saw of him.

His ankle cuffs were heavy, too heavy to lift out of the water that now swirled ever deeper. He held tight to the key. If he dropped it now, he'd be a dead man. He fumbled underwater for the lock and tried to twist it to a less awkward position. The key clicked in. He turned it. Thank God! He was free!

He lunged forward but fell onto his knees in freezing water. His legs would not work. They felt like rubber. Of course they did. He had hardly taken twenty steps in the last two days. He pulled himself up and his head smashed against the birdcage that hung swaying from the cabin roof.

"Damn!" he swore. Bou Bou, the captain's foul-mouthed parrot, rattled his wings.

Damn it all to hell! Bou Bou the parrot swore back. *Unhand me, Shit-for-brains!*

This ridiculous bird! But ah, a prisoner like himself. Teron unlatched the cage door.

"Get out of here, you obscene creature!"

The bird gave an ear-piercing squawk and flew out. But both Teron and Bou Bou were stopped at the top of the companionway. Wind tore at them. Rain beat at them. Teron could hardly see. Then the ship, with a terrible scream, came to a sudden dead stop and heeled hard to portside. Teron was thrown sliding across the icy deck. In an instant the parrot was on him, clutching, digging his claws into Teron's arm, and they both slid into the sea.

He struck hard against a rock. His shoulder was on fire with pain but he clung to that rock for dear life, and the parrot clung to him. Behind him, the ship lay on its side, impaled on a pinnacle of rock, waves bursting themselves against it, rain making buckets out of the sails. An empty lifeboat, half submerged, had smashed apart on a rock reef. There were no sailors anywhere, not a single one. The sea was a monster, sucking and pulling so hard that it took all Teron's concentration just to keep a hold on the rock. His hands were freezing, cut to pieces and bleeding. Wave after wave buried him, practically tearing the shirt off his back, and still he hung on. Suddenly he was struck from behind by something heavy. It crushed him up against the rock.

What had hit him? It was one of the lifeboats, though Teron could see no one at the oars.

He made a grab for it. The gunwale was coated with ice but he let go of the rock and clamped both hands onto the side. The boat pitched and lurched on the waves and he couldn't climb aboard. He feared it would be carried out to sea and he with it. The boat slid down a wave and carried him away from the wrecked *Farfalla*.

The lifeboat slammed into a rock and he almost lost his hold on the gunwale. All around him Teron saw his shipmates' belongings tossed on the waves, a boot, a broken lantern, a wad of blankets slowly sinking. But no survivors. He couldn't be the only one, could he?

His body could not take much more pounding. Body and mind were both dull with cold. If only he could get into the boat! Lifeboats are large, made to hold twenty men in rough seas, and not easy for one man to handle. With the strength and determination of youth though, he waited until the force of a wave favored him, then pulled himself upwards. His weight nearly tipped the boat over but he had gotten himself half over the gunwale when another wave lifted the boat free and threw him head first to the bottom of the boat. Somehow, praise be, he had managed to get aboard.

Slowly Teron raised his head, then jerked to his knees. A body! He had fallen onto the body of a sailor, a dead sailor, judging from the gaping bullet wound in his chest. There was a foot of water in the boat, turning red with blood. Teron heard a click and flinched in horror when he saw the ship's captain lying in the bow, leaning on a leather bag, a pistol in his hand. The gun's hammer clicked again. Teron recoiled. Another malfunction.

"Damn it!" The captain had one thought: to save himself and the leather bag beneath him. This prisoner Teron Adante was a serious threat. He dragged himself to a sitting position, apparently injured in some way, and flung his gun at Teron. Hurtling through the air, it tore a gash in Teron's forehead before spinning into the sea. With blood dripping into his eyes, Teron panicked. The captain lunged forward, coming at him. Stumbling, growling in fury, he came crawling over the seats and Teron crouched in terror. Just then the boat lurched and the captain fell hard and hit his chin.

He spat out a bloody tooth, still focused only on killing. He was balanced on one knee atop a seat just as a huge wave slammed the boat against a rock pinnacle. The boat spun dizzily. The captain, his face a mask of fear, flailed to keep his balance. Responding automatically, Teron reached in vain for his outstretched arms. The captain toppled backwards and he fell overboard. His head smashed sickeningly on the rocks, his life extinguished in a moment. Teron could not bear to watch his body disappear beneath the sea.

Queasy, Teron held fast to a seat to keep from going overboard himself. Cold rain soaked him. The boat scraped and jolted over a rocky reef. Bloody water sloshed violently in the bottom of the boat. And behind him lay the dead sailor. He had barely enough energy to tip the man into the sea, with no ceremony except a prayer that he rest in peace.

On his hands and knees, seawater up to his elbows, he looked for a paddle. That was when he saw Bou Bou the parrot, staring at him from the bow.

"Bloody hell! You don't give up, do you?" he gasped.

Unhand me! Unhand me, you cocksucker!

The lifeboat had one paddle remaining, lashed under the seats. Teron had just gotten it untied when a giant wave hurtled the boat against a huge cliff. He tried to use the paddle to fend himself off. Land! It was solid land!

But entirely inhospitable.

One hundred feet high, that cliff was, if it was an inch. It ran straight from sea to sky. He couldn't even find a foothold, much less a place wide enough to pull the boat up. Discouraged, too exhausted to paddle any further, he hunched in the bow and let the wind take the boat. The north wind pushed it banging along the cliff. He could see no vegetation, no place that would harbor so much as a bird's nest. As the boat skidded around to the lee side of the cliff, though, he thought he saw houses in the distance, across a wide bay. A settlement, maybe a town. What a relief!

But no. What was he thinking? He could not go there. He was a convicted criminal. He figured he was a little more than a week's sail from his home port. As soon as they got word of the shipwreck, people would come looking for him. The Einfaldssons would be up and down this coast with a monocular, looking for their ship, their captain, all their merchandise. And their convict. Could he find a place to lie low for a while and hope they would assume he was lost at sea?

Quicksilver Fate – who could trust it? Yet now it offered a spot to pull the boat up on the lee side of the cliff, if only he could get to it. That small slab of rock would provide a landing, about four feet wide, but flat enough so he could clamber ashore and possibly haul the boat at least partway out of the water.

Using the oar like a canoe paddle, Teron pulled hard to get the boat across the current. He had only seconds before he would be swept past. He would have to make a leap for the rocks. Quickly he tied the boat's painter around his waist, maybe a foolish thing to do but he did not want to get separated from the boat. He leapt for the rock. His knees and elbows hit hard. His fingernails clutched for a hold in whatever indentations they could find. The rope around his waist almost pulled him off the rock as the boat swung down with the current. It took all his strength to haul on that rope and wrap it quickly around the willow bushes that had taken root beside the rock. Weak with exhaustion and cold, he allowed himself to collapse on the rock. Land. Land, at last.

Finally, he rose stiffly, and retrieved the captain's leather bag, soaking wet, from the boat. A waterfall fell from the cliff in a thin ribbon, and he cupped his hands and drank. It was icy cold. Through the rain and darkness he thought he saw, hidden in a seam on the cliff above him, an opening in the rock. Shelter? He crawled up to it. It led to a cave. How far back did it go? It had definitely been used, maybe by smugglers in the past? He could just make out tool marks, as though an effort had been made to widen the entrance. A crude Celtic cross was incised at the opening. He crawled just inside, afraid to go deeper into the cave in the dark. The cavern seemed large and very high. He sat down inside and leaned against the wall, wet and freezing. At least he was out of the wind here. He closed his eyes and felt blessed. He heard a whir of wings and thought, with an absurd tinge of sadness, well, that will be the last time I see that parrot.

He must have slept a bit but it was still dark when he opened his eyes. He wondered what he was going to do for food, and then thought of the captain's leather satchel. It was unlikely to have food in it, probably a compass, or maybe the ship's log. No, it had neither. Delicate carvings of ivory, tortoiseshell, and jade, wads of French bank notes, colored glass beads, and a small calfskin bag full of diamonds. No wonder the captain was guarding it so ferociously. Beautiful, valuable, but no help for an empty stomach.

He sat up and realised two things. He must find out where the nearest people were. And he had to find food. The first thing would have to wait. He thought of the ship lying wrecked out on the reef. It had been bound for Balgrim with enough food to last men in the prison for two or three months. He needed to get to it. That food was his only hope. And he had to get to it quickly. Whoever found the *Farfalla* first would be all over the wreck, searching for whatever they could loot. Come the dawn, there would be townspeople out there, maybe fishermen putting out to sea from that settlement. More frightening still, there would be officers of the law, demanding first rights for the magistrates to any salvage. He did not want to meet fishermen or officers. He had to get out to that ship before anyone else did.

Teron hated the thought of getting back into the boat and paddling that stormy reef again. He hated the thought of starving even more. So he bailed bloody water out of the boat and set out. He had to paddle hard against the choppy sea. He groaned aloud with the effort, even though the wind and waves were dropping. Once out there, he tied his boat to the wreck.

The *Farfalla* lay on its side in the darkness, moaning like a wounded animal. He waded aboard gingerly, afraid it could break up at any time. Everything was tilted at a dangerous angle. One gimbaled lamp still hung, burning the last of its oil. The storeroom door was locked of course, but he found an ax and chopped it open. He pried open a few barrels, checking to see if rats or insects had gotten into anything. He chose a cask of dried beef and a barrel of pickled pork. He dragged them out and tied them so they would float behind the stern of the lifeboat. He found a tun of cheese, and one of biscuit. He filled the boat with things he thought he might need. He rolled up a thin cot mattress, a blanket, some clothing, glad now that the lifeboat was large. He rifled through seamen's belongings and collected what few coins he found.

Over rolling seas, dragging the two barrels behind the boat, he knelt in the bow and paddled like a galley slave to get back to his landing place. It took him some time to get everything ashore and pull the boat out of the water so he could hide it in the willows. His palms were sore and bleeding and his hands were shaking, but he managed to rope his supplies together and, load by load, drag everything up to the cave. The last chore was to hide the ship captain's satchel of treasures.

Day broke. The rim of the sun surfaced far out on the edge of the sea. Trembling with exhaustion, Teron opened some cheese and biscuit. Looking west from his new shelter, he watched the sun light the mountains across the bay. The trees on the slopes were still bare in this cold northern spring. He could just make out the houses clustered on the dark shore.

He had survived a shipwreck. For the time being, he was in a safe place. He had no idea how isolated this cave might be, but time would tell. Yesterday, he had been a miserable prisoner. Today, he was free. Free! He was an outlaw now, a fugitive, but free.

Damn! squawked a voice nearby.

"Well, aren't you the faithful friend." Bou Bou, the captain's parrot, sat in a stunted tree by the cave's opening. Teron offered him a piece of biscuit. "Say thank you."

Up yours.

"You're welcome. Have another."

I think I love you.

"Ah, that's more like it."

Teron slept all that day. It was evening when he finally woke and, just as he had anticipated, a flotilla of boats was nosing around the wreck. He hid in the willow bushes and watched. They didn't look like magistrates' men, just simple fishermen. Did they live near his cave or were they from that village across the bay? He couldn't begrudge them anything they took, and only hoped they wouldn't get caught. The night was clear. Wisps of cloud erased a few pinpricks of starlight. He wanted to explore, to take a look around, but he was too stiff and bruised to try to climb the cliff above him. He crawled back into his cave and slept again.

At dawn the next day, Teron watched the fishermen head out to sea before he dared hike up the cliffside that rose, nearly vertical, from the water. Not too fond of heights, it took him a long time. He finally reached the top and cautiously scanned the view before pulling himself onto flat land. He stood up and smiled at what he saw.

Empty meadow. Nothing but brown meadow grass gilded by winter-spring sunshine. He was on an island! Not a single house could he see here, no animal herd, no boat dock. From up here at the top of the cliff, the land sloped downward until it reached what looked to be a crescent of beach. Beyond that, a broad bay. To his left was a thin strip of forest that ran down one side of the island to meet the sand beach. He could not believe his good fortune. An island of several acres, about a mile from land, and he the only inhabitant! At the small settlement across the bay, he saw two ships tied to a pier. A few large estates ranged along the hills beyond the town. But up here at the top of this island, there was only meadow and what, in summer, would turn into lush grasses.

The horrors of jail, his sham trial, the dread of a long sentence in a brutal prison camp, all – all behind him.

He was the luckiest man alive. And – he laughed aloud – even better, he was dead at sea. Teron Adante would be presumed lost at sea.

Of one thing he was absolutely certain. There can be no man on earth as free as a dead man.

Teron was right about the Einfaldssons. Two weeks later, one of their ships, captained by Lord Hans-Martin Einfaldsson himself, sailed into Lunenfarne. By then, so little remained of the wreck of the *Farfalla* that they were unable to salvage anything. Lines and ropes, sails, even the masts had all been cut away. All the barrels and chests had disappeared from the galley and though the Einfaldssons questioned magistrates and villagers, everyone swore that the sea had swept everything away.

Lord Einfaldsson protested vehemently. Looting was illegal, highly illegal! This was theft! But raging at the magistrates about the injustice brought him no satisfaction. No one in the entire town of Lunenfarne had seen any looters. It had been a terrible storm, the night the *Farfalla* wrecked. Not a single sailor had been found, dead or alive. Lord Einfaldsson, a real stickler for detail, questioned the authorities carefully about that. What about a certain criminal who had been shackled to that ship? Someone in Bellesunde had drawn his face from memory. Lord Einfaldsson presented the sketch. Here, this is a likeness of him. Had anyone seen him or his body, this man who had tried to malign his son's integrity? No?

Einfaldsson ordered two of his men to board the wreck again, specifically to search for the convict. They found empty chains. They surmised that someone had released the convicted man and he had drowned with all the rest of the sailors.

Still, Einfaldsson left no stone unturned. He insisted this poster bearing Teron Adante's face must be hung where everyone in town could see it. The sheriff took the poster grudgingly and hung it in his office window. Lord Einfaldsson made it very clear that he expected to be notified if ever this man turned up, and of course there would be a reward.

When the Einfaldssons finally set sail for sunnier climes, everyone, even the magistrates, breathed more easily.

Teron recognized the Einfaldsson pennant as they sailed past his island. Oh, he yearned more than anything to blast a hole in the side of that damn ship. How he longed to see Einfaldsson thrashing in the waves. When the stern of their boat finally disappeared over the horizon, he treated himself to a mug of the wine he had stolen from the *Farfalla*. Here, safe on this deserted island, he celebrated his victory over the Einfaldssons.

In the coming days, Teron always took care that he would not be seen, not by passing fishermen, not even by a villager peering through a glass. He cooked his food only in the evening when everyone else was cooking, to disguise the smell. He busied himself doing what he could to make his cave hospitable.

Working at night, he slowly cleared a very narrow path to the meadow at the top of the cliff. He learned where to walk so he could move about in the dark. He fashioned a fishing pole from one willow stick and a net from another, and, before day broke, he often crept down to the beach's tide pool to catch crayfish for bait.

Having only the sorry company of Bou Bou the parrot, the isolation did become tedious after a while. Where could he go, though? What choice did he have? This life as a free man was turning out to have a few too many restrictions. Still, he was alive, and he told himself that, maybe after some time had passed, he would not have to hide from the world anymore. He just had to wait it out, satisfied to be free, and grateful for his amazing good luck.

Bou Bou the parrot, unlike Teron, did not consider himself a fugitive. He had no worries about being seen. He was having the time of his life. With the warmer weather, he was learning to catch bugs and worms to supplement the meals he begged from Teron. Granted, he was totally unprotected now that he lived outside a cage. A few very bad scares had made his little parrot heart pound with fear. That horrid eagle that hunted regularly over the island – what a menace he was! And the brown arctic fox – Bou Bou could not discourage that animal from stalking him no matter how much he swore at him. Watching the wild birds taught him a lot, though. He watched and he learned: always keep your eyes open and if danger threatens, fly into the tangled branches of trees.

Hiding in the spruces, he could observe the gulls diving and swooping over the fishing boats when they returned in the evenings. He watched how those birds operated. He was smart, that Bou Bou, a very smart parrot, and he could see what those gulls were after. Of course his tastes were persnickety, typical of caged birds, but he could compromise. He could adapt.

He developed a hankering for some of those slimy pink fish guts the fishermen discarded. They looked so appetizing! If they came fresh from the corpse, how tasty they would be! That is why, one day, Bou Bou decided to assume the persona of a seagull. He really thought he looked the part and could blend with the flock. Relying on his special skills, he imitated seagull cries. He dove at the returning boats, right into the thick of things, vying for some of those luscious fish guts, snapping at anything the fishermen tossed overboard.

What gave him away? He thought he had pulled off such a clever imitation of the local birds. But somehow, who is to say how, the gulls saw through his ruse. Bou Bou really could not figure out how they knew he didn't belong. He flew like a gull. He wailed like a gull. He bullied and snapped like a gull. How did they know he wasn't a gull? Maybe he was violating some arcane Waterbird Code. In any case, the gulls, every one of them, turned on him. They ganged up on him! They dove at him like a pack of hornets on a beefsteak. They cut him off in mid-flight, not the tiniest bit intimidated by his cussing.

Damn you to bloody hell!, he yelled. *Walk the plank!*

The gulls didn't listen. But the fishermen were shocked.

It's probably clear by now that Bou Bou had a significant arsenal of sailors' swear words, but nothing that he squawked at those gulls on that day made the least bit of difference.

Suck moose farts, you stupid bastards!

Curses like that, one would think, should have stopped any bird in midair, but their relentless greed made the seagulls deaf to Bou Bou's imprecations. They wouldn't let him get near the fishing boats. They mobbed him! They tormented him with their sharp beaks! They bit and they tore at his beautiful feathers!

The battle of the waterfowls raged that late afternoon and the fishermen gawked, their mouths hanging open. What kind of bird was this? What creature was bold enough to challenge a flock of seagulls right in the middle of their nightly beggars' opera? And this bird spoke! Where did a bird like this come from?

Bou Bou realised he had to give up fighting the seagulls before he lost a pin feather. He flew into the spruce trees and preened and pouted for the next two hours.

But now he had been spotted.

Men had seen him.

The fishermen had seen him, but they could not believe their eyes. Or their ears. This was terrifying! They told the other villagers about the strange, freakishly-colored bird they had seen hovering over their boat. A bird who could talk! They were horrified! They had actually heard him cursing – screaming words like a human.

A talking bird? No one among the townspeople, not one single soul, believed that ridiculous story. People could grant, perhaps, that the fishermen had possibly seen a colorful bird, though no fowl of that description had ever been known in that part of the world. But a bird that could talk? Unbelievable. Somebody was hallucinating. Been helping yourselves to a bit of the nutmeg, boys? Or some fermented apple juice? A talking bird! Absurd!

No, argued the fishermen, they were certain they had seen and heard such a bird, a devil-bird to be sure, but very real.

The fisherman stuck to their story. They had heard what they had heard. They had seen what they had seen. They thrashed through their memories of the occasion over many an evening tankard. They concluded that this bird was some omen of evil. A strange talking bird, living on haunted Par Ou Island? Yes, didn't that make perfect sense? He must be magic. He was probably the spawn of some malevolent magician-priest. He must have been living out there for a hundred years. Maybe he was the familiar of a witch. He could be a child of Satan. He could be Satan himself! It became a game, not without risk, to watch for the bird every evening on their way back to port. They spotted him occasionally but didn't hear him speak again, and for that they were very grateful. After all, how many encounters with the voice of an actual devil could a man survive in one lifetime?

It became Teron's habit to watch for the fishing fleet to pass at the beginning and end of every day. He hid in the willows, because he couldn't allow himself to be seen. But he wanted, he needed to hear them. He needed to hear the sound of a human voice. Then one morning after the fleet had gone out, when Teron had been on the island for about four weeks by his count, he heard other voices. He tensed. Men! Men were on the island. It sounded like they were right above him. Men, calling to each other. All that long day, he heard their hammering and sawing. He dared not leave his cave until nightfall, but when he finally crawled to the top of the cliff and saw what had gone on, he was seized with dismay. Now he would be even more restricted than before, even more of a prisoner. Here on his island was a pile of lumber, boxes of tools and hardware under canvas tarps, an iron stove, and worst of all, the beginnings of a small building. Was someone coming to live here? Devastating thought!

The following day even more workmen arrived. That evening, Teron saw that they had hauled a sledge of stone blocks all the way up from the little beach to the very top of the cliff. They had rolled the stones into place to make a small platform. Load after load of wood had come next, and was piled at a distance from this platform. The little building had grown taller and would soon have a roof. Teron swore in the best parrot style.

The day following that was even stranger. Among the sounds of men working, he heard women's voices. Finally, at the end of the day, all voices receded and it was quiet again. What had happened? He hid in his cave, lighting no fire.

But that evening, when he smelled smoke, he knew the danger was real. Smoke could only mean one thing: someone was still here. Someone had come to stay. He needed to ascertain the risk. He crept quietly up his cliff path and peered over the top. There was a fire, just as he had thought. A beacon fire, he realised, to warn ships about the dangerous reef. So that's what all the commotion was about. There was also a small fire near the little house. A cooking fire, and beside it was a woman. No, she looked like a girl really, a young girl. In the firelight, he could see that her skin was dark and her braided hair jet black. He had read about the dark-skinned people of the north woods but had never seen them. He hadn't imagined they would be this beautiful.

He watched the girl until it got too dark to see. She seemed to be alone. Hungry as he was for human contact, he dared not speak to her. He was drawn to her, though. Another human, an inviting fire. He could not bring himself to stop watching, perched awkwardly as he was, clinging like a foolish boy to the clifftop. A couple of times he had to change his position. He tried to do it quietly, but she must have heard him. Her head came up. She peered into the darkness. Finally, she pulled a blanket over herself and went to sleep beside her fire.

He crept back to his own fireplace and decided he could not risk cooking tonight either. Maybe she'd awaken, restless, and smell his food. He cut a hunk of cheese. Staring up at the stars, he ate his food without tasting it.

He didn't want to believe there was another person here. His refuge, breached! A beacon fire on the cliff above him! He didn't want to like the idea, and yet, somehow he was excited by it. I am a convict in hiding, in grave danger if I am found. But I'm not alone. Not alone.

For the first time in two months, another human being had stirred something besides bitterness inside him.

Teron couldn't stay away from her. Courting danger of discovery was stupid, he knew, but it was unreasonably intriguing to someone who had little else to do. He spied on the girl several times the next day but never dared approach her. He thought about little else, though. He decided that he had to reveal himself at some point, but he should choose a time that felt right so he wouldn't appear threatening. She was a sharp one. He became convinced she knew when he was near.

One night, when she had been there only a short time, Teron became aware that he was not the only one watching her. He saw a man, creeping through the shadows of the woods, carrying the oar of a boat. Suddenly the girl stood up and screamed. The man swung the oar, swung it right at her head. Teron leapt from his hiding place and attacked.

The man clawed at him like a bobcat. The fight unleashed in Teron the pent-up fury of a demon. He had been wanting to beat on someone –

anyone – for weeks. He had to force himself to stop punching the man's face and body, even when it was obvious he had knocked him out. He dragged him down to the beach, found his rowboat, literally threw the unconscious man into it, and pushed it into the bay. Swiftly, then, he went back to the girl.

She lay unmoving on the grass. Gently he raised her. Her eyes opened briefly and he smiled at her. She slipped again into unconsciousness. He carried her into the cottage, laid her on the bed and covered her. He pulled the blanket up carefully, very carefully.

He hadn't realised before, but now he began to suspect something. This young girl, all alone, or who thought she was alone, had been attacked when she was possibly most vulnerable. By and by, she might be needing help again. He knew little of such things, and he could be wrong, but it appeared that at some point she might be giving birth to a child.

The next night, a terrible storm ravaged the island, a deluge of wind and rain. Teron was spying on the girl from the woods, when he heard an unearthly sound. The roar of a gigantic rogue wave. In an instant, a wall of water rose up and crushed her cottage to matchsticks. The girl was thrown to the ground. The force of the wave blew the woodpile apart. Heavy logs rolled downhill like runaway carriages. Teron clasped a small tree trunk and hung on.

When the waters retreated, the girl was clinging to the grass, too terrified to move. He wanted to go to her. She could barely stand against the wind and rain. He watched as she made her way toward the woods and he almost went out to meet her. But something held him back. She sat down against a tree and wrapped herself in a soaked blanket.

Teron crept away. He discovered his boat had been swept into the water. It was still tied but it had nearly torn the willow bushes from the rocks. He hauled the boat ashore again and retied it. If he had been down there, he probably would have been swept away too. The cave was fortunately positioned, though. Its opening was high up and faced away from the open sea. His mattress roll was wet, everything was soaked, but he was vastly relieved to see his barrels of food were dry, standing farther back in the cave, as they were. Whatever would he have done if his food had been taken by the sea?

Very early the next morning, he caught a couple of fish and left one for the girl. He hoped it would say to her "I'm here. I won't hurt you. This is my gift to you."

Any chance of him connecting with the girl the next day was ruined. Men returned to the island with more lumber, more supplies. A few days later, there was a new cottage, back farther from the edge of a cliff. A new cookstove came a few days after that. The men gathered the logs that were strewn all over and rebuilt the woodpile. A woman was rowed out from the town, a motherly type. She brought some voluminous dresses that the girl regarded at arm's length, and a pair of ankle boots, suitable for warmer weather. Teron watched from his various vantage points. He was so relieved when they all went away again, and the island belonged to him once more – to him and to her.

It became almost a game. Teron left signs that said he was present, left them where he knew she would find them. First, a beautiful shell sitting on a rock near the tide pool that she liked to visit. He was pleased when he saw that it was gone. He hoped she had taken it. Then, a bundle of wild thyme tied with a piece of grass, left beside her fire to flavor her stew. One day, a bunch of violets; one night, he had already stoked the beacon fire with wood when she went to tend it in the middle of the night. Another day, he wove a little mat of grasses and left a piece of cheese on it. The girl sniffed it, tasted a bit. He watched, glad to see her eat it with relish.

He was hoping, he finally admitted to himself, that she would come searching for him. He was tired of being alone, not speaking, no books to read, nothing to do. The girl was his only pastime. She, however, apparently did not suffer from loneliness. She never came looking for him, at least as far as he was aware. Wasn't she even a little bit curious about him? One time when she was in the woods gathering kindling for her cooking fire, he was standing hidden quite near to her. On purpose he made a small scratching sound. He saw her straighten. She stood listening but never even turned her head. Then she walked quickly, almost running back to her fire. Only when she had a kitchen knife in her hand did she turn to look about her.

Summer drifted slowly into fall. Teron saw that the girl had begun to wear the full flowing dresses over her high suede boots. He figured her baby's birth was still a couple of months away. Her belly was not that large and she seemed as energetic as ever. He did not realise that her time was near,

He was watching one evening, as she prepared her dinner. Suddenly she stopped what she was doing and hunched over, seemingly in pain. She crouched to the ground. After a minute, she rose. Slowly she continued to add ingredients to the stew she was making. But again she had to stop, bent over, panting. Then she put the fire out, took her uneaten stew, and went into her cottage. Teron had rarely seen her go in there. She never seemed to stay inside for any length of time. Was it time for her baby to come? If that were the case, she must on no account stay on the island. But she would hardly be able to row herself to the town a mile away. And anyway, she had no boat. He did have a boat. He could take her. Yes yes, he should offer to row her over there.

He crept to her door. He didn't want to frighten her. On the other hand, it was plain she would need his help. He stood next to the door, uncertain, listening. She was moving about a little. Maybe the pain had passed. Maybe …

The door opened. Both Anne and Teron jumped. She screamed and leapt back.

"No, no. I won't hurt you!" Teron backed away too, his hands open. "I was going – I wanted to help. Here, let me do that for you." He stepped forward to take the large jug from her hands. "Do you need water? I'll get it."

She shook her head. Suddenly, she was in fighting stance. Out of nowhere, there was a knife in her hands.

"Now wait. I'm not – no. Did you think I was going to hurt you?"

She flailed her arms. She stabbed the air with her knife. A warning.

"I was going to offer to row you over to the town."

She set the jug down, never taking her eyes off him, defensive, both hands on the knife now.

"I thought you could get help in the town, if you –"

Instead of answering, she waved an arm, gesturing wildly for him to get out.

"Listen. You're going to need help. I can –"

She lunged forward with a growl, the knife threateningly close to him.

"Stop! Look, I come in friendship."

The knife fell with a clatter. The girl bent over, grimacing, small gasps of breath like soundless sobs.

Teron bent toward her. "Let me –"

Her hand came up. "No!"

He straightened. "All right." He waited, watching her closely.

After a minute, she took a deep breath and straightened also. Then she saw that her knife was in Teron's hand.

She backed away, up against the cold iron stove, moving behind it, terror in her eyes.

Teron held the knife out, handle toward her. "Here. Take it."

She blinked. She watched him lean forward. He set the knife down on the stovetop. He picked up her jug.

"I'll get you some water."

He went out. As soon as he reached the pump, she fled for the woods. He watched her go, but again she was stopped by pain, doubled over til her knees hit the ground. He left her there and took the water into the house. On his way back, he gathered an armload of kindling. The night was turning chilly. He got a fire going in the stove and filled a kettle with water. He found a candle and lit it. When he went back out to the woodpile, the girl was nowhere to be seen. She couldn't row herself across the bay. He had the only boat on the island, he knew that much. He could row over there himself and try to find a midwife or someone, anyone. But no, he was a criminal. Could he afford to take the chance that someone would become suspicious?

He took some logs up the hill to the beacon. She had laid a fire there earlier in the day. He touched the candle to the kindling and sat watching until the logs caught.

He thought of the stew the girl had been cooking. No sense letting that go to waste. He went back into the cottage, hoping she had returned. No, the place was empty. The cottage had only one room. It held a table and bench, some rough shelves for kitchen wares, a bed with a thin mattress that looked like it had not been slept on. The quilt he had seen the girl wrap around herself was folded at the end of the bed. He left the door wide open and started a fire in the stove. He put the pot of stew on the burner. When it was finally bubbling, he found a plate and sat down at the table to eat. He had not sat in a chair at a table for weeks. The stew was delicious.

He washed the plate outside, put another log into the stove, and went back up the hill to check on the beacon fire. He got it blazing, hot and bright. He moved back and watched a few sparks break free and rise heavenward, little stars, not that the sky needed anymore of them. It was so full of them tonight, it almost made him dizzy to look up. A good night, he was thinking, for a new life to begin. Standing there, head bent back, hands on hips, he tried to pick apart the mystery of where that life was traveling from. Something out there, some vibration, some connection would be made, or had been made, and there would be a new soul here on earth. He had never stopped to think about how that happened. This girl, he mused, this young girl was carrying a precious mystery.

When he turned to go back to the cottage, he saw the girl wrapped in her quilt, standing in the doorway, watching him.

He stopped. "Oh, so you've changed your mind about me?" She didn't answer. "Come on. Don't be foolish. Let me row you across the bay."

No answer. Her mouth fell open and he heard her sharp intake of breath.

"Look. I know nothing about having babies, but I do know you can't do it alone." He waited for her to speak. "Agreed? I'm an ignoramus about the whole process, but listen. I'm all you've got."

Nothing from her. Her hands pulled tight to her belly.

"Can't you admit it? You're going to need my help. I have a boat –"

Her eyes pinched closed. She gasped and Teron panicked.

"Hey, come on. Why don't we go inside where it's warm?"

She lowered her head, catching her breath and holding it tight. She put out a hand, looking ready to collapse. He strode forward, reaching for her. She tried to shrink away at first, then instead grabbed tight to his arm. He caught her so she wouldn't fall. This time, she didn't resist.

"That's right. You can trust me. Come on. Is it your time, do you think?"

Again, nothing but a small groan from the girl.

"Let's get you into the boat so you can get proper care."

How to get a baby born? He'd never even seen a puppy being born. He had to get his boat, bring it round the island, and get her into it somehow.

She groaned again and slipped to the floor on her knees.

"Are you – what do you – should we – ?" He was stammering and she wasn't answering. She dragged herself over to the bed and slowly unfolded herself upon it. "Wait, you can't stay here! Come on, we have to go. Go now!" Drops of perspiration lined her brow. "I'll go for the boat. I have a boat. We can –"

As soon as he moved toward the door, she raised herself on one elbow. "Help!"

He came back to stand beside the bed. "What do you want me to do? Tell me!"

She closed her eyes and moaned softly. Her head rolled from side to side. "Help I."

Help? He had no idea what to do. He might do something wrong. Was there ever a finer line between life and death than at birth? What if he fumbled, didn't do the right thing at the right time? Women died in childbirth all the time. He should have rowed over to that town. Damn, how selfish could he be? If this girl died, it would be his own stupid fault.

He was in a panic of nerves. She seemed resigned to her fate. But then, she had had time to plan for this. Teron felt like he was staring down the barrel of a cannon, and from that cannon was going to explode – a goddam baby! He grabbed a handful of his own hair and pulled at it in frustration. The girl gestured to the water jug, to a pot on the shelf.

"You want me me to – I should heat some water? Is that what is usually done?" he stammered.

She answered with another gesture. She had spoken only, what, two words to him? Was she deaf? Then it dawned on him.

"We don't speak – ?" He gestured back and forth. "We can't – my language – ?" Oh no. Impossible. She spoke a different language? She couldn't instruct him, tell him what to do? This thought drove him crazy. "You speak me? Talk me? You understand me?" He thumped frantically on his chest.

She shook her head and pulled her booted feet onto the bed. "No. Not many."

Teron was aghast. His shoulders slumped. He took the jug and went to get some more water, almost nauseous with fright, dreading like fire the night ahead.

The sea gave birth to the sun the next morning, and one by one the night stars went to their elsewheres. The sun labored itself high into the sky and a breeze rose, brisk and cold. Finally, finally it blew the long hours of pain away and they were forgotten.

They had cried, all three of them. But that was forgotten, too. It was over. Someone new had been brought into the light and by some magic, some inexplicable alchemy, the angels, with a kiss on his baby lips, had breathed into him a prayer that his earth journey be long and fruitful. He would never remember that kiss, but you could tell by the quiet on his baby face that he had felt it.

Teron Adante came into the cottage with an armload of firewood. It took him a few minutes to stir up the coals and get the fire going again. By the time he finished, the new mother, propped against the wall with the baby on her shoulder, was sound asleep. She roused when he lifted the infant from her arms.

"Wouldn't you rather lie down?" he asked her. He nestled the baby close to her and she encircled her little one with her arm. She looked up at the man. He stood watching her with his hands on his hips.

Who was this person, Anne wondered? Strands of light brown hair hung damp over his forehead. She could hardly help returning his proud smile, as though they were co-conspirators in some epic engagement of wit and cunning.

How had she ever thought she could birth this child all alone? In answer to a wish she had not known she made, this stranger had appeared from nowhere. In the months before this, she had been certain she was strong enough, determined enough, that she could have done this without help. Women in her clan had done it, she knew, two or three of them had, when necessity warranted it. She and her mother had assisted at a birth once, too. She believed she could have managed by herself, though she would have been as terrified as a child stumbling through a night forest. But this stranger had offered a hand to hold, an arm to lean on. He had made her pain seem less perilous. She had someone who wiped her face, who held a cup of water to her lips, who sang a little tune for comfort, though a very strange-sounding tune it was.

After a night of agony, the two of them had managed to find their way. Together, they had made this miracle. When he held her child for the first time, she had seen tears in the man's eyes. But a minute later, at the baby's first cry, how they had laughed, delighted, the two of them.

Anne's first thought, when she saw her son, was relief that the baby was going to be dark-skinned. She was glad. Alphonse would have no claim to him. She had suspected she was pregnant when Alphonse purchased her. Aside from that welcome realization, she could hardly puzzle out any other feelings. The wonder of it all – this miraculous baby boy, this man coming from somewhere – it was too overwhelming. Still wondering, Anne finally succumbed to sleep.

Teron knelt beside her bed and put his hand gently on the baby's head. What a perfect little being. A headful of fine black hair, like his mother's. He was captivated, awestruck by the wonder of this child. He even felt an inordinate pride, as though he himself had given birth.

He had been in such a panic before. He hadn't known what to do. He had never imagined the sheer terror of helping a child into the world. What if he had done something wrong? But the girl had seemed to know exactly what to do. Talking him through the whole procedure in her language, gesturing, encouraging. Putting the knife in his hand, but no words to tell him what to do with it. She had labored through so much and for so many hours, yet she was still able to help him, a clumsy ignorant man – a stranger! – to deal with those final moments. The baby's first moments. And then, cleaning the baby, wrapping him. It had all been so daunting. His hands shook the whole time, as if they had a life of their own. But he had done it. They had done it.

Slowly, Teron eased himself down onto the girl's narrow bed. Carefully, he arranged his limbs so he wouldn't wake the baby, folding his arms close to his chest. For the first time in days, he thought about his former life in Bellesunde. Imagine, if he had stayed there, how different his life would have been. He would have started his law practice by now. It would have been a good life among friends and colleagues. He would have been confident, sure of himself. Instead, he was here. Below another sky, with no idea of where he was going.

Exiled to an island. Delivering a mountain woman's baby. A baby!

For some very strange reason, and Teron did not know what to make of this, he felt he had been graced by his prison sentence, privileged instead of punished. He could not process any more than that. He too fell asleep.

A little while later, Anne stirred awake. She gazed at her infant son, still sleeping peacefully. He had been through a lot too, this little one, getting himself out into the world.

And look at this. One hand curled over the child's body, and inches from her, was this unknown man. Who was he? She watched him through half-closed eyes. Who was he, this stranger lying with his hand cradling her baby? He had been on the island all along. She had not been willing – she had been downright afraid to acknowledge his presence. But why did it seem right now? It was a relief to have him there, she had to admit.

The strangest thing of all was that she had no explanation, none whatsoever, for why this one man did not frighten her, the first man in a very long time who did not repel and disgust her.

It was about a year later that Anne saw the canoe coming across the bay, toward Par Ou. A canoe! Who but one of her people would use a canoe? She gathered baby Kai in her arms and headed down across the meadow to meet it. When she saw it was indeed paddled by someone of her race, she began to run.

In a gush of happiness, she greeted the man in her own language.

The man did not match her enthusiasm. He seemed hesitant, looking from her to the baby. Finally, he told her his name.

"This child is yours, Aiyanna Petalacqua?" he asked.

She nodded.

He seemed disappointed. She invited him to walk up to the cottage.

"No," he said, shaking his head. "Thank you, but no. I did not come for a visit. I come looking for a wife for one of my sons. I found out that you were here, the last of your clan. But I did not know another man has already claimed you." He turned to go.

"Wait! You came to take us back?"

"I thought to, yes. But now that I see this," he gestured to the baby, "it cannot be."

He was going to offer her a chance to go back? Back to her hills and her forests, to be with her own people? "Wait, wait!" she said again. "Let me assure you that my son is of noble blood on both sides. His father is a warrior who is himself the son of a chief."

"A chief from what clan? The clan that took over the river territory of your people? Vicious heathens! Those people are a blight on our race!"

"Yes, but this boy will not be one of those. This boy will grow up to be a great leader. He would bring honor to your people."

"Scion of the enemy clan? No!" The man spat. "It would be no honor to raise a son of that enemy. We do not want to mix that foul blood among our people, even if he is descended from chiefs. And you! I thought that, since you were so young, you might still be untouched. But you have allowed yourself to be defiled by the enemy."

Defiled? She had allowed herself to be defiled? Furious as she was to hear him say that, Anne was certain that she and Kai could be of value to his clan. Was this man so bound by old traditions that he could not see that?

"I am strong, a good worker. I would be a good wife. I would give your son many more children."

The man looked thoughtfully at her. "If you really want to come with me, you'd have to leave the boy behind. Then, perhaps one of the old men would take you. You would not have much status, but you would be among your own people and away from these white barbarians."

"No status?" She, a chief's daughter! This was insulting.

"How many sheep could you bring to the marriage?"

"Sheep? I have no sheep." Resentment, like poison, began to boil inside her.

"So. Worthless. You are worthless to us, Aiyanna Petalacqua. You are a beautiful girl from a noble family," the man said. "But your family are no longer among us. As the mother of an enemy's child, and with no dowry, only the lowliest man would take you. The women too would object. Your presence would cause nothing but strife and dissent. I'm sorry."

Sorry? He was sorry? Let him return alone to his ignorant clansmen then! At least here she could raise her son as she wished. The man she was living with did not care what status she had. What had she been thinking? The old ways were no longer of any use to her. She blinked tears from her eyes. It was far better to stay here. Yes, stay here for now. She watched the man turn his canoe and head back toward the mouth of the river.

What was she thinking, indeed? She and Teron were making a good life together, tending the lighthouse, working their garden. How long that would continue, she only wished she could predict. Teron probably would not stay on the island forever. Why should he? He would probably leave her, as soon as he felt it was safe for him to do so, as soon as imprisonment was no longer a threat. It had only been a year since he had escaped. Anne brushed more tears from her cheeks. Maybe even now he was wishing he could leave them, couldn't wait to leave them. He was well-educated. He would have opportunities elsewhere. He did seem to be attached to Kai, though. Would that be enough to hold him here? She looked up at the cottage they shared and realised how far from her roots she had come.

Being part of a clan and its traditions, and the security that went with it, all that had vanished long ago for her. She would need to chart a course of her own now. Make a plan. She had let too much time go by. When the day came for Teron to leave her, she must have an alternative so she and Kai could survive. Maybe then, when Teron was gone from them, when the baby was older, maybe then she and Kai would go back to the hills. Yes, they could make a living there, the two of them, raising sheep for wool.

She would buy a lamb. The next time she was in town, the very next time, she must go to the auction. She'd buy two lambs, so she could start a flock. It would be her insurance, for when the worst happened.

It was the first time in a year that Anne had thought about returning to the hills. She started back across the meadow, Kai balanced on her hip. This was a good plan, she decided. She and Kai could make their way, all by themselves. She didn't need anyone's help. It was nice, very nice, to have someone like Teron beside her, but … she stopped walking. She stood looking at the grass at her feet for so long that the baby kicked and squirmed in her arms. He patted her cheeks to get her attention. He gurgled at her and made her smile.

At least she had Kai. He wasn't going anywhere.

She walked up the hill and stood beside the beacon, looking out across a calm pale sea. She turned when Teron came up behind her and put his arms around her.

"I wondered where you two had gone."

She leaned so hard against his chest that she could hear his heart beating. And her heart? Why was her heart so full of dread? She felt desperate. Options, a plan? Yes, she needed a plan because you never knew what could happen. She had learned that long ago.

She had been foolish. She had let the island lull her into thinking she could ever have a real home here. No, she had known for a long time, hadn't she? She should not trust Par Ou to be the refuge she had hoped.

KAI D'INQUIERRE

All night long, with low and constant dirge, the inconsolable ocean moans a hypnotic basso continuo. Shackled to the bewitching moon, it swells past Parou's cliffs and plunges into the bay. Ebbing-flowing, restless, at the moon's beck and call, ebbing and flowing night and day. What is the ocean but a slave trying to break free?

Waves heave themselves against the cliffs but Parou Island holds fast, impregnable. Fog-haunted rock, tattered ghost-hazes swirling at its feet and sifting over its reefs in springtimes and autumns, or whenever icy winds from off the mountains fret the summer-warm sea. Parou, never what it seems: immovable yet appearing insubstantial, disappearing in the night haze, sometimes only its beacon-fire floating out of ethereal mists. Other-worldly but immutable, as if spellbound.

Now, out at the rim of the sea, night cracks apart and a chill grey dawn leaks slowly into the harbor. Hear the fishermen thumping their nets into their sturdy boats, loading their gear and their lunch buckets. Hear them drag their boats across the shingle, slide them into the cold chop. The creak of oars, rowers still groggy and barely awake, hardly speaking except to growl when hull bumps hull. If favored by the tide, a good start to the day.

Huddling into the canvas collars of their mist-damp jackets, rowers jostle for a place in the line. Tracing the narrow underwater gorge, they keep to the invisible passage that they have known all their lives. No need for buoys, no need for a lighthouse, not for them. Single file into the channel past Parou, men's backs swinging rhythmically as stiff muscles begin to stretch and flex, the fortunate ones having a son or brother along to help with the work. The breeze picking up, nudging away dull dreams of warm beds. The sound of the sea stirring wakefulness, the scent of the wind a prediction, though there is no turning back, no matter what the winds foretell.

No turning back, for necessity's sake. They must find fish. No turning back, for love of the ocean; a passion, glad to set sail upon her, as into the arms of a mistress, mercurial and moody though she be, and only sometimes generous with her favors. Glad for her turbulent humors, these fishermen are. And proud of having the knowledge and expertise to rise to her challenges, and the guts to master her for one more day.

Every morning, their last touch with land was Parou Island, and the fishermen always roused themselves to see what could be seen there. The woman, that brown gypsy-girl, working her garden, hanging laundry, chasing her little son and her sheep. The fair-skinned man. The one Francevili the harbormaster claimed did not exist, though they saw him every day. No one knew where he came from or why he never left the island. Maybe he was strange, maybe rowing with one oar out of the water, probably several clams short of a chowder. Imagine! A white man living with one of those dark hill-barbarians. Though if pressed to it, every man of them would admit that the girl wasn't half bad to look at. And her boy, quite the little man, he was. Dark as his mother, night-black hair down to his shoulders, always darting around as boys do, or fishing from the rocks, or helping the man pull up crab traps. His cheerful wave and shouts always made the fishermen smile, in spite of themselves. They worried when they saw that demon bird sitting on the boy's shoulder, that parrot, as they had learned the colorful bird was called. Amongst themselves now, the fishermen had made up a new name for Parou: Parrot Island they called it, after that fiendish devil-bird.

They eyed the creature with real dread. They still thought of the island as haunted. No amount of talk could change their minds about that. They had always been certain of it, felt it in their bones, convinced each morning that until they had hauled open their brown sails, until they were pulling away, away over the ultramarine blue sea, that they had not yet escaped the spell of Parrot Island.

Odd it is, that something as inconsequential as a fishermen's nickname gets a fingerhold. But the name spread with usage. Parrot Island – it was simply an easier name to remember. Navigators picked it up along with other bits of local knowledge. They passed the name on because there was a beacon fire there now, and from one mariner to another, the word spread.

Parou was transforming itself, the old name falling into disuse. Eventually, maps would have to be remade. Because Lunenfarne's harbor had never been well-trafficked, Parou Island had never been of any consequence except as a danger to navigation. But away up in those dark northern realms, that beacon-fire began to give the island some significance. A guide, a new lodestar: the Parrot Island beacon.

Growing up on the island, Kai d'Inquierre learned to call his mother "Ema", meaning "Mama" in her language. He was called Kai in memory of her father, whose name meant the willow tree that bowed before the wind but was seldom broken. As a small boy, Kai never thought to ask where his surname came from. It was the same as his mother's, and that made sense because they belonged to each other. He was always told he was the spitting image of his mother. She and only she could see in his face the traces of the warrior prince to whom she had once belonged. But the child knew nothing of this man, and nothing at all of the existence of the white man who had married his mother, and to whom, as far as she knew, she was still bound. The name Alphonse d'Inquierre was never spoken on Parou.

His mother's companion, Teron Adante was, to Kai, beloved as a father. It was Teron that Kai followed around all day. It was Teron who tucked Kai into bed at night and read him the latest chapter of the book he was writing, tales of heroes mythical and historical. Kai knew Teron had earned a university degree in Bellesunde but he had no idea that he was a fugitive from justice. Six whole years of the boy's life would pass before he ever questioned why Teron hardly ever left the island. He always assumed it was because there was so much work to do.

As almost anyone would, Teron found his exile frustrating. Maybe the only thing that kept him sane was his writing. He began working on little adventure tales for Kai but these blossomed into chapters, then epic tales, and soon, an entire book. Trained in law, he never dreamed he had a creative bent. He still did not dare to go out into the world, but he could build a world in his imagination and put it down on paper. Whether or not his book would ever be seen by other eyes was a question he refused to ponder.

Teron's writing took up every spare moment and there seemed to be too few of those. Nearly every day he trapped and fished for their dinner. He shared the duties of caring for the beacon fire with Anne. When stormy weather threatened, one or the other of them needed to check the positions of the buoys, had to stay up all night to keep the beacon fire fueled, and sometimes needed to take the boat out to rescue sailors in distress.

All three of them worked the large vegetable garden, though Kai assumed the herb patch was flourishing solely because of his tender care. They also kept a few black-faced sheep, something Anne had insisted upon and seemed to know a good deal about, though Kai and Teron were united in thinking them a smelly nuisance. And Teron didn't let a day go by without spending an hour with Anne, teaching her to speak and read the language. They were both surprised to realise that Kai, by age three, had picked up the lessons right along with his mother. He spoke two languages without accent, and he had begun to read. Though they owned very few books, Kai had paged through them all, tracing the lines of text with his finger, exulting when he found a word that he knew.

Their family functioned in the way of all working families. Kai never heard, nor could he imagine, his mother pleading feminine weakness. He thought of her as unbending in every way. He could question Teron on any issue, but his mother had rules that he must abide without question.

"We have to be gentle with her," Teron told him. "She's fiercely independent."

"What does that mean?"

"It means that she's not about to let anyone tell her what to do."

"Why not?"

"Well, it's about trust, I guess. She doesn't trust many people."

"Why, Teron?"

"Oh, things happened. Things happened to her."

"Like what?"

"Well, we told you she lost her whole family in a war. After that, it was hard for her."

"But now she has us, right?"

"She does. Yes. Of course you were her special boy the moment you were born. It took me longer to get into her good graces."

She didn't like you?"

"I had to convince her to like me."

"How did you?"

"Well, I got a lot of help from you. You came along, and that changed everything."

"It's good I did, right Teron?"

"Absolutely, son. Absolutely."

Kai was four years old when he spotted a yellowing old poster in the window of the sheriff's office. He and his mother had rowed over to the town to visit Mr. Basko's grocery.

"Ema, look! That looks like Teron." Kai pulled his mother's hand. "Come back! Look, it says 'wanted'. What do they want him for?"

Anne tried to work out the words on the poster. She could hardly decipher them. She was so shocked she could hardly think straight. A reward, money offered for Teron's capture. Was this search still going on? She felt an iron dread fall into her stomach.

"What does that mean, Ema?"

"It's just some … some old paper. It's nothing. I don't think it's really Teron."

"It sure looks like him."

"Well, it could be anyone."

They had been so careful. They had started to think they were safe, or at least Anne did. Teron Adante was supposed to be dead and forgotten –

even Soro Einfaldsson must have forgotten him by now. She would talk to Jozef Francevili, beg him to go into that office and take that poster down.

Anne and Teron had taken Irina and Jozef Francevili into their confidence long ago. Teron couldn't very well hide from them. It had not taken the Francevilis long to question the amount of food that Anne ordered every month, or to ask who had built the new bed out of salvaged lumber. Who ordered the notebooks and pens, and who read the books that Anne ordered from Bellesunde every few months? And what about Anne and Kai both learning to speak the language? They couldn't have taught themselves. So there was a lot that needed explaining. Teron never elaborated about his background but the Francevilis understood it was something they would be better off not knowing, and it made it easy for them to feign ignorance when the fishermen pestered them for gossip.

Teron continued to lie low and had almost no contact with the village of Lunenfarne. One of the few times that he went into the town was during Carnevale. He could wear a mask, as many of the revelers did, and easily blend with the crowd. But at all other times, if Anne and Kai had to go into Lunenfarne, they went without him. She rowed them across the bay to visit the Francevilis, or to poke around in the row of dark little shops along the waterfront. The iron-monger, the seamstress, the owner of the dry goods store – they all knew the d'Inquierres, mother and son. The grocer, Mr. Basko, was always eager to buy the cheese that Anne made, now that her small herd of sheep was producing milk. She and Kai were often seen, too, at the sheep auctions. She was held in very low esteem by other herdsmen. They wanted nothing to do with any savage or Egyptian or whatever the hell she was. But her animals were grudgingly admired as excellent stock, long-legged and robust. Kai found the auctions tiring and the babble of the auctioneer boring, but after his mother finished her dealings, she almost always took him to a small park to visit the puppet theatre. He loved the puppets. He loved watching the other children almost as much. He laughed when they laughed. He imitated their antics. The town had other distractions, too. Next to the rickety little puppet theatre was a playground with swings. Every time they visited, Anne could hardly drag Kai away.

It was on the playground that Kai first learned about school. School, he informed his mother, was a place where children went every day. All the children went, he insisted, and he begged to be allowed to go, too. Anne fought the idea. She didn't see the point. There was much she had adjusted to in this "civilized" life, but her love of the old ways persisted. She wanted Kai to learn to live as a herder in the wild, to be a leader of people, and yes, to learn to fight if he had to. She wanted to raise him as closely as possible, given their isolation, to the way she was raised. Teron, she knew, had a different vision. He said Kai had a good mind, and should one day pursue studies, in whatever field he chose, at the university in the south.

So when Kai continued to ask about going to school, Anne protested. "You don't need school, Kai. You know already reading. Besides, I do what all day, if no boy here?"

"You've got Teron."

"That's right. You've got me, Anne." Teron was slicing cheese for lunch. He stopped to move Bou Bou the parrot into his cage.

Squawk!

"Hush, Bou Bou. No cheese for you."

Holy crap, I gotta take a picked wiss!

"Stop that," Teron scolded but Kai laughed. "Don't encourage him, Kai. He just wants attention."

The parrot bobbed up and down on his perch.

Be a nice bird.

"That's right."

Up yours!

"Ema, I really want to go to school. All the other children go."

"Who told this to you?"

"Everyone. That kid on the swing. Gregor."

"No. Waste of time. It sound like waste of time."

"But I want to go!" Kai hollered.

"Kai, such angry voice!"

Squawk! He's madder than a witch with her ....

"Keep quiet, Bou Bou!" Teron wet his fingers and flicked a few drops of water at the bird. "Behave!"

Just keep a cool stool!

Anne ignored the bird. She did not understand most of what the parrot said, anyway. "You learning many things right here, Kai. Fish – fishing, take care of lambs."

"That's easy stuff. Gregor said they have books at school. Books for kids. And they give you paint."

"Paint? For what, paint?"

"For making pictures with, Ema."

"Pictures?" Anne looked to Teron for support. Without answering, he took a basket of bread to the table. "What pictures?"

"Pictures of whatever you want. Elephants, dolphins, crabs."

"I think that is dumb silly business."

"No. It's not dumb. Besides, I don't have anyone to play with here."

"We all play ball just last night."

The evening breeze between your knees ....

Bou Bou rhumba-ed up and down his perch.

"It doesn't count, playing with grown-ups. That's not the real kind of fun," grumped Kai. "It's not the same as playing with kids." He stomped over to the table and sat with his chin in his hands.

Teron pulled Anne aside. "If he wants to go …."

She shook her head.

"You might just think about it, Anne."

Arms tightly crossed, Anne frowned and looked away.

His mother was firm but Kai was persistent. The summer of his fifth year came to an end and on a rainy September morning, he ran joyfully downhill to the rowboat. His mother and Teron followed.

"Too bad it's raining on your big day," Teron told him.

"I don't mind! Let's go! Let's go!" Kai scrambled to his seat. His mother followed slowly, still reluctant.

Teron leaned his hands on the gunwale. "I wish I could go with you. You'll be polite to your teacher, won't you? At school you must do as she tells you."

"I will."

His mother fussed over him, neatening the tie holding his thick black ponytail until he pushed her hand away. She pulled up the hood of his coat.

"Wrap cheeses for me while I go, will you?" Anne asked Teron. "I promised cheese for grocer after school, when I go to get Kai."

"They'll be ready." He waved and Kai, gleeful, waved back.

Anne rowed them through the drizzle and across the bay. When she pulled the boat ashore in the fishermen's cove, they still had to walk almost a mile to get to the school.

Five years before, when Chancellor Ragenold still had his wits about him, he had asked the Benedictine nuns from the nearby convent to run a school. It was to be free and open to all, but the town magistrates had refused to allot funds for a building. School for fishermen's children? What was the point? One of the more grandfatherly among them came forward, though, claiming he was willing to lend an abandoned mill for the purpose. He accepted the townspeople's praise with endearing humility, somehow neglecting to mention that he received a substantial reduction of his taxes in return.

The school was run by a pair of nuns and divided into two classrooms. One sister, only a teen-ager herself, usually taught the younger children, and the other, long past her teen years, terrorized the older students. That morning, it was Sister Kunegunde who stood at the front door when Anne and Kai crossed the bridge over the old mill race. Sister had observed them, mother and son, in town on occasion. Oh, these gypsy people! Who knew what gods they served, these two from the haunted isle? Why were they here today? Good gracious, she couldn't imagine. But here they were indeed, in spite of the rain. Look at them, a pair of drowned Egyptian rats. Heaven only knew what they smelled like.

Still, Kunegunde had promised God to behave with loving kindness, even when a rejection was necessary. There was no question that she would behave properly with these two because that was the kind of person she was. She tipped her head back and scowled, then peered at her list of students and shook her head. No, she knew all the families on this list. There were no barbarian names listed here, nor was there any place for them in her school. It would hold the other children back. It would be unfair to the gypsy boy ... sad to say, very sad. But what else could she do? Gypsies were not very bright people, or so she'd heard, or thought she had heard. She'd never spoken to a barbarian, actually, or even come near to one. But she had heard things. No, that boy would never be able to keep up with the lessons. It would be kinder to send him home, and Kunegunde, it bears repeating, always did the kindest thing.

At the bottom of the steps, Kai bowed politely to her, as Teron had taught him. A flick of Sister's eyebrow was not lost on Kai and made him wonder. Had he bowed properly?

"Your name, please."

"Kai."

"I need," as should have been obvious, "your whole name. Please."

Kai turned to look questioningly at his mother. "Do I have a hole name?"

Anne gloated. Who better than a woman like this to cure Kai of his silly notions about school? "Tell the lady both your names," she said to him.

"Oh. Kai d'Inquierre."

"Beg pardon? Don – Din – ha. I don't suppose either of you knows how to spell that?"

"Sure. I do."

Kunegunde's mouth warped into a smile that faded quickly as Kai spelled out his name for her. She squinted at him. "D'Ink? Dink …?"

"d'Inquierre."

"Dinki – ?"

Kai wriggled and shuffled. He shook his head, not sure if it would seem rude to correct her a second time.

"I'm very sorry. There is no Dinki on my list."

"Here, I'll write my name on there for you."

Impertinent little beast. "Never mind. Sister Angelica will be here shortly. I'll let her … she can … deal with you."

Anne put her hand on her son's head. "I go now and wait for you in the boat in afternoon, all right?"

"Ema, I –" he murmured uncertainly, leaning against her leg.

"I see you then." Anne left, smug in the certainty that Kai wouldn't ask to go back to school for a second day.

Kai stood on the steps studying his new boots, waiting for the other teacher. He worried. Maybe he was not cut out for school. Other children came to the steps, spoke to the tall nun, and were immediately invited to go inside. They looked askance at him on their way in. He didn't feel right. This was not at all what he had imagined. Head bent, he risked a glance at Kunegunde. Holy crap, he thought, borrowing Bou Bou's vocabulary. That face would curdle milk. He lowered his eyes quickly.

He looked up again. His eyes popped. Another nun, but this one! This was a fish he would definitely not throw back.

Kunegunde was speaking to this woman, a nun much younger than herself. "This is Mr. Dinkier –" Sigh, a headshake, big sniff of air. "This is Mr. Dinker, Sister. He seems to think he should be a student here but I most definitely do not have him on my list." Her eyes, staring hard into the eyes of the other teacher, sent a message that was too unsuitably coarse for any respectable nun to say out loud. Be assured, above all, that Kunegunde did not ever allow a coarse word to escape her lips.

The young sister smiled and held out a hand to Kai. "I'll add him to the list, Kunegunde. Come with me, Mr. Dinker. My name is Sister Angelica. Would you like to see our classroom?"

Kai's heart melted. Here holy buckets right here this lady was an angel she really was a really alive beautiful angel so shining and pretty and he took her warm hand and smiled and everything was right in his world.

Halfway through that first morning, he felt a little shy approaching her. He needed to ask for her help with a small problem.

"Sister," he whispered close to her ear, "I don't know where the outhouse is and I gotta take a picked wiss."

It took Angelica a minute, eyes fluttering, to process this request.

A couple of days later, Kai made the firm decision that school was the biggest disappointment of his life. He stomped out of the schoolhouse and started the mile walk back to the cove, where Ema would be waiting beside their rowboat.

"Dinker! Dinker, wait up!"

He turned to see his playground friend, Gregor Treyse, running toward him. Kai drooped his head and walked on.

"Wait up, Dinker. I'll walk you." When Kai didn't answer, Gregor put his hand on Kai's shoulder. "Aren't you glad we don't have Kunegunde every day? What an old crank!"

"She's a witch. She didn't have to treat me like that. I never said anything wrong. I hate her."

"Well, you know how it is. Some people are just touchy, right?"

Kai sniffed.

"My father, he's got a very short fuse, too. Mother says it's not his fault."

"Hmm."

"See, what it is, prob'ly, is that Sister Kunegunde has a little trouble controlling her temper. It's just the way she is. You can't expect everyone to be patient. You have to make allowances, Mother says. We make allowances all the time, Mother and I."

"Kunegunde is so stupid! The stupidest I ever knew! I'm never going to say another word when she's around."

"Sister Angelica, though, she's nice. She smiles at me in church. How come you never go?"

"To church?"

"People say it's cuz you worship ghosts on that island. But I don't believe them."

"There are no ghosts on Parou!"

"Still, I think you must be very brave, living out there."

Kai laughed. "You do? Well, I guess that's me! The bravest of the brave! Come on! Let's run." Gregor was a good friend. He made a person feel a whole lot better.

A while later, when Anne and Kai pulled the boat up on Parou's beach, Teron was waiting.

"How was school?"

"Terrible! I hate Sister Kunegunde. She reee-ally bites the big weenie," Kai declared.

Teron winced. "Kai, I should have warned you. Don't repeat any of what you hear Bou Bou say. None of it. You can be sure it's rude. What happened with Sister?"

"She washed my mouth out with this horrible soap. I hate her."

Teron was almost afraid to ask. "You said something she didn't like?"

"Well, she was going on in class about stuff people shouldn't, you know, misbehave on. Kids were saying dumb things like 'don't hit your sister' and 'don't forget to say thank you' but my two things were real good, importanter than anybody's almost."

"What things did you say?"

"I said people shouldn't be lazy. Everybody should just shoulder their behinds and keep humping 'til all their work is done."

"Well, heh, you have heard Bou Bou say that. Fortunately it's not one of his worst."

"Then I said people should try not to get angry all the time. Keep a cool stool and it'll all work out."

"Again, Kai, that is a little rude. I wouldn't say that anymore, if I were you."

"Kunegunde said it was real rude. She got real mad at me. She even raised her voice. And she called me a name."

"What name?"

"Barbear – some kind of bear. I was sure she was gonna wallup me. So I said, 'Well, you're pretty rude yourself, calling people names! Look at you, madder than a witch with her tit caught in a winepress!'"

"Ew."

"She kinda got her panties in a twist about that. You shoulda seen her, Teron. She was raging off her nut, and her, supposed to be a grown-up and everything."

Teron hardly dared look at Anne. They both trained their eyes on Bou Bou instead, who turned in circles on his perch. "I blame you for all this, Bou Bou," Teron said. "You're nothing but trouble."

I don't give a rat's ass. Bou Bou faked a laugh, long and loud. *Haw ha ha! Who's a dirty bird?*

Teron shook his head. "What do you think we should do about him?"

"The parrot?"

"Is it time we boiled him up and fed him to the gulls?"

Bou Bou knew gulls by reputation but not by name.

"It's good he doesn't know what you're saying, Teron," Kai said, "or he would be pooping bricks."

Who's a dirty bird?

To Kai, growing up as an only child on an island, playtime with other children was something he couldn't get enough of. But having a best friend like Gregor Treyse was a gift he'd never anticipated. Steady, unflappable, ever the optimist, Gregor was salt to Kai's pepper. When Kai flew off the handle, Gregor calmed him down. He could ignore taunts and knew how to shrug off insults that would have made Kai furious. Even if Kai went off with some other boys to play at recess, Gregor never got mad. He was still there with a smile, walking Kai back to the cove at the end of the afternoon. So one morning, Kai felt a little unsettled when Gregor wasn't waiting so they could walk to school together. He wasn't there the next day either, or the next. It turned out to be two weeks before Kai saw him again.

Finally one morning, there he was, sitting on a rock near the fishermen's cove. Kai ran to him, overjoyed. Then, the shock hit him. When he watched Gregor try to stand, he was horrified. Gregor was having a hard time getting up. Once on his feet, he had to prop himself up with a home-made crutch. A crutch? This was so disturbing. And his face, how pale it was, except for a large greenish-yellow bruise on his cheekbone.

"Hey there, Dinker."

"Holy buckets! What happened to you, Gregor?" He seemed like a different boy!

"Oh. I – I fell." Gregor's voice was unnaturally subdued. He limped at Kai's side, so Kai slowed down to his friend's pace.

"How did you fall?"

"Oh, you know. I just fell." He glanced at Kai and looked away.

"These things happen."

"Yeah, but … are you gonna be okay?"

"Oh yeah. I'll be fine. I just hurt my back a little."

For the next month, Kai kept hoping Gregor would finally join their rough-and-tumble games. He must have had a terrible fall since he was taking this long to heal. And his friend was so changed. Bit by bit, he was regaining his vigor, but so slowly. Even after he gave up using the crutch, Gregor walked with a limp. The color didn't really return to his face and Kai wondered how much pain he was in. His body retained a peculiar twist. But that smile of his! It never faltered. Walking was difficult for him, running with the other children impossible, yet he never complained. Whenever the children went outside to play games, Sister Angelica would find Gregor a place to sit. She would hand him a sketch pad and she spent a few minutes of every recess looking over his drawings, pointing and suggesting.

It meant a lot to Gregor that Sister Angelica would find something for him to do. Drawing gave him something to look forward to every day. His artwork, and his friendship with Kai, their joking and horsing around, these were the things that gradually brought Gregor back to his old self. He could not explain why a boy like Kai would treat him as a valued friend, but his appreciation of their kinship colored his life forever after.

That fall was the year the ship wrecked on Parou Island. There had been other wrecks, terrifying to Kai because his ema and Teron had to row out to try to save whoever they could, even though it meant imperiling their own lives. But this wreck was the worst Kai had ever seen. The wind blew the ship scraping across the reef. It never stopped until it crashed against the island's cliffs. Kai was sure he felt the earth shake under his feet.

A terrible storm had blown up. Neither Anne nor Teron could keep the beacon fire lit. They could not even get a flame to catch. Teron tried tucking a candle under a pile of kindling to keep it out of the wind, but every time it caught, the rain and wind snuffed it out.

"Kai!" Teron yelled. "Get back inside. Look Anne! Look out there." They saw a ship floundering, trying to get into port. "We've got to warn them off, get some signal going."

She shielded her eyes against the downpour and saw the ship bucking the waves. "I'll get a lantern." By the time she struggled back to the edge of the cliff with a lantern, the ship had broached and was sliding sideways down the waves. While they watched, a wave poured over the deck and punched the ship hard against the cliff. They heard the shouts of injured and terrified sailors calling for help.

"I'll have to go out there." Teron yelled to be heard over the roar of the storm.

"You can't!"

"We can't let them drown, Anne."

"No! No!" screamed Kai, suddenly at their sides.

"Don't go!" Anne shrieked, but Teron was already running down the hill. "Teron!"

She couldn't let him go out there alone. She grabbed Kai's arm and ran with him to the cottage.

"Stay inside!" she told him.

"No, Ema! No!"

"Kai, we come back soon. You stay here!" Then she was gone, running after Teron, down to the beach where they kept the rowboat. Kai stood shivering and whimpering in the doorway, watching his mother help

Teron shove the boat into the waves. He saw Teron speaking sternly to her and pointing, saw her shake her head and set one oar in the oarlock. So Teron took the other. They pulled hard, choosing the channel that was most protected from the wind, straining to make headway against the pounding waves.

Kai forced the door of their cottage closed, crouched trembling by the fire, and waited. The storm howled. It muscled the cabin. Kai waited and waited some more, so afraid Ema and Teron would never return. Then he could wait no longer. He ran out into the storm, just in time to see the rowboat surfing back down the channel on huge swells. It was full of people. They were coming back! He ran into the house again, stoked the fire in the stove and filled the teakettle from the water jug.

Finally, the cottage door opened. Kai launched himself at Anne and Teron. "Ema!"

Teron hugged him. "Good job, Kai! You kept the fire going in the stove."

"I filled the kettle."

"We'll make tea in a minute. Can you find us some blankets, son?"

A man and a boy almost fell through the door, then halted abruptly, glancing into the corners of the humble cottage in amazement. The man, blood oozing down his sleeve, sank uninvited into the chair that faced the front of the stove and pulled the boy down beside him. Four other men followed, dripping, shivering, fearful. The faces on these four sailors were grim, stunned by the loss of the companions and workmates who had been swept away by the demons, the ghosts of this haunted isle. Seemingly by common consent, they took seats on the floor, frozen with terror, huddling near the side of the stove.

"Let me see that cut on your arm," Anne said to this man. "I have something for that." She washed the wound carefully, then took an oblong white crystalline stick from a shelf. She filled a cup with water, dipped the white stick into it, and knelt in front of him. "This is sting."

"Ye-ouch, it does!"

"Deep, this wound."

"What is that you're using? That isn't alum, is it?"

"Yes, it is."

"Where did you get alum?" Abrupt, demanding, grimacing with pain.

"My people – they use this for many things." Quickly, she glanced up at the man and lowered her eyes again. She had seen him before somewhere.

"What I'm asking is where you got it."

"I told you. From my people."

"It is not easy to get."

"I have only this piece." She rose. She didn't like his tone. "That helps bleeding. Here is a cloth."

"Can you build up the fire?" asked the boy, his teeth chattering.

"Kai will bring some blankets," Teron told him.

The boy rubbed his arms. "Thank you. We'd appreciate that, if you can manage it."

The man watched Anne bind the wound on his arm. He spoke more softly. "I must thank you also. And thank you both for rescuing us."

Now Anne recognized the oddly shaved head of a magistrate. She noted the thick gold bangles on his ankles. She remembered where she had seen him.

"I thought we'd drown for sure! What a terrible night!" the man moaned. He wiped his hands over his face. "I cannot think .... By all that's holy! Can you believe our good fortune, Dort?" he asked the boy. "I can't imagine what would have happened to us if you and your husband had not rescued us. You were very good to come out in such a storm. You deserve a reward!"

"I couldn't find enough blankets." Kai came back, struggling with an armload.

"Ah, you're a good lad," the magistrate said to Kai. He rose and took two blankets, one for him, one for his boy. The four others sitting on the floor had to share the two remaining blankets. They were working men, it appeared, from their full heads of hair. No tufts or silk cords on their heads, no gold bangles on their ankles.

Anne started a pot of tea and put some buns and cheese on a plate, some smoked fish and small apples.

"You should put on dry clothes, Anne," Teron said.

"Yes. Will you get cups?"

Teron served the tea and food.

"Grateful as I am for your assistance, my good man," said the gold-bangled magistrate, "I can't help but ask why the hell there was no beacon fire tonight? We almost missed the harbor. You people are supposed to be taking care of that. Good lord, man, it's your duty. Our captain, may God rest his soul, couldn't even find this island in the storm. Not until it was too late."

"We tried repeatedly to light the beacon, my lord," explained Teron. "But all we have is an open fire in an iron basket. It was impossible to keep it lit in such wind."

"But that is deplorable! Just when a light is most needed!"

"This is the problem with a beacon fire. Between the wind and the rain, the flame blew out every time we tried to light it."

"This is unpardonable! Something must be done! If it weren't for you and your brave wife, my son and I would have drowned tonight."

"If you don't mind me saying, my lord, what we really need is a proper lighthouse." The men by the stove nodded silently.

"Ah. Yes! Yes, I see now that is exactly what Lunenfarne needs!"

"A light in a proper tower," Teron went on. "Lamps protected by glass."

"I see. Aha. I will definitely take this up with the council. I'm Vladimir Mynydd, by the way," he held out a hand to Teron. "Town Chancellor, and this is my son, Dort." The boy Dort was probably a few years older than Kai, a good-looking boy, and very well-mannered. The chancellor wrapped the blanket more tightly around the boy and brushed his dripping hair off his forehead.

Teron was nervous. He hadn't been among strangers very often in past years, but he had just saved six peoples' lives. He hoped their gratitude would avert any questions. He introduced himself with his first name only. "And this is Anne, and her son, Kai."

"Anne. Yes. I remember you now. You came before the council and we were very skeptical about having a woman do this job." Vladimir's eyes shone as he looked steadily at her. "It appears we made the right choice after all. Not many women would do what you did tonight. I shudder to think what would have happened if you hadn't rowed out to save us. Dort and I will be forever in your debt. I mean that."

Anne smiled politely and bent to offer more food to the shivering sailors sitting on the floor. They each murmured their heartfelt thanks. "Thank you kindly, lady." Such manners she had, such manners. And her being a gypsy barbarian and all, and living on a haunted island, too. Her manner quieted some of their superstitious fears. But if they had gotten a glimpse of Bou Bou the parrot, confined to his covered cage, it is doubtful those four sailors would have accepted any food or drink in that house.

Vladimir Mynydd leaned forward and put his elbows on his knees. "My god, what a miracle this has turned out to be. We're alive. Alive! I can hardly believe it."

"You are luckier than most of the men on that ship," Teron said.

"When I think, though," Mynydd groaned, "of the cargo we lost! I had a couple of very valuable items on board that ship. Some Turkish carpets, a tapestry." He sat up suddenly. "Is there a chance we could still recover anything?"

"It's dangerous to go aboard a wrecked ship," said Teron.

Mynydd looked at the four sodden creatures sitting on the floor. "You men! You could go out there. You could, couldn't you? You could go out first thing tomorrow for me."

"You're asking a lot of these men," Teron insisted. He could see the reluctance in the faces of the sailors.

"But these people know how to scavenge. They swarm all over shipwrecks, all the time."

"They take some risks but only if they feel the profit warrants it," Teron said.

"Well, it was their fault this happened. If the passage was that dangerous, they shouldn't have taken the chance –"

The youngest of the four sailors half rose, gesturing angrily. "We ain't scavengers! And this weren't our fault! We heared you, we all did, bullying the captain. He tried to tell you he don't want to try that passage but you kept pushing and pushing him." The young man's face wrinkled with grief.

"Well I – I panicked!"

"We suffered losses, same as you!" cried another, his voice breaking. "But it's not rugs we lost. It's people. One of 'em me own kid brother, not yet sixteen years old!"

Mynydd's son Dort sat forward on his chair. "Wait just a minute …!"

Vladimir Mynydd looked horrified. He touched his son's arm. "No. No, Dort. They're right."

Dort looked at his father, then bent his head.

"I'm so sorry. I shouldn't have spoken like that. You men are absolutely right. I used bad judgement. Perhaps if I offered to pay –"

"I think it goes without saying," said Teron, "that they should be well compensated for their losses, whether they agree to recover your rugs or not. I saw how they helped you and your son."

"You're so right." Mynydd sat back in his chair. "I'm ashamed of myself. I was too hasty. What I said was monstrous and I feel terrible. Your losses are far worse than ours. I'd like to make it up to you. Could we discuss this in the morning?"

The four sailors stared sullenly at the floor, their faces still dark with anger.

"I'm afraid," Mynydd continued, turning to Teron, "that we'll have to intrude upon your hospitality tonight."

"We can't go home?" asked the Mynydd boy.

"It's too dangerous, Dort. I refuse to get into a boat until this storm is over. I hope it abates by morning."

"Of course you must stay here," Teron told him. "I only wish our accommodations were better."

"My son and I can share that bed over there. Can you hang our wet clothes somewhere, Mrs. –?"

Anne frowned at him and finally nodded. She stood and began

clearing away the food. Mynydd got up and noticed Kai staring up at him. He ruffled the little savage's hair. "Your parents are exceptionally brave, do you know that? I'm determined to see to it that you people have a proper lighthouse. Not only that, but a new home, as well. Something decent." He looked critically around the bare cottage. "This place really doesn't – " He gave his head a quick shake. "All right. We'll talk tomorrow. Come, Dort. You'll have to share a bed with me, I'm afraid."

Dort leaned to peer into the corners of the cottage. "It's … it's awfully small in here."

"We mustn't forget, son," his father interrupted, "to be grateful. Think what these people have done for us. We will be eternally beholden to them. So much so, in fact, that I believe I have never …." He hesitated, trying to get his voice under control. "I really don't think I have ever felt so grateful to anyone." He pinched his lips between his teeth to keep them from trembling. "Thank you. We owe you everything. I mean that."

"Ema," whispered Kai later as he cuddled up close under her blanket on the floor. "What is wrong with that man's hair?"

"Well, it got wet in the storm."

"Yes, but it's so weird. Isn't it a weird hairdo, Ema?"

"You should see it when it's dry.

Vladimir Mynydd was as good as his word, you had to say that for him. He wasted no time in getting the workmen together to begin on the new lighthouse and he kept scrupulous track of progress. He often employed someone to row him out to the island so he could oversee construction.

He had convinced a pair of famous brothers from Scotland, the Stevensons, to draw up designs for the new tower. These men came from a well-respected family that, for two generations, had specialized in the building of lighthouses. All the sons had taken up their father's profession, except for the black sheep of the family, Robert Louis, whose strange interest in poetry was completely incomprehensible. The Stevenson brothers insisted on a stone tower on Parou but the council of Lunenfarne, no matter how much Mynydd cajoled and bullied them, refused to spend the amount of money that stonemasons would require. They finally agreed to a stone foundation with wood shingles above.

Mynydd employed shipwrights from Otto Wohlfahrt's naval yards to build a structure that would withstand prolonged exposure to the sea. He saw to it that they worked whenever the weather permitted, through all the long winter. Mr. Wohlfahrt, the shipwright, advised them to use the same pitch-caulked oak planks that were used to build sailing ships. Defeated on the issue of construction materials, Mynydd would not back down on a schedule. Time was of the essence.

Mynydd had practical reasons for pushing the workmen so hard. Merchants from distant countries were vying for new markets, and Lunenfarne was the portal to a whole continent of resources. Lumbering and mining had already brought wealth to a few of the citizens, but Mynydd had a vision of the town as a bustling center for trade of all kinds in the north.

The town itself, except for the hillside mansions, was nothing but a shabby collection of huts and one-story edifices nestled against the bare brown foothills. But if they had a real lighthouse, Mynydd thought, Lunenfarne would be a much more viable port. New businesses, he assured the council, would spring up. Money would come pouring in. The town would begin to thrive. Mynydd had other plans as well. As soon as the lighthouse was finished, he was going to charge a fee for every ship that docked there. That new light had to be paid for somehow, after all. But he never tired of insisting it would be well worth the cost.

Mynydd could organize all that, could almost do as he pleased, now that he had attained the office of chancellor. It had taken him a long time to achieve that status, working closely with old Chancellor Ragenold for years, gradually taking over his duties when age conspired to slow the old man. Ragenold's mind was too confused to pinpoint exactly when he realised that Mynydd should take over, but he was glad it was a smooth transition, and glad the chancellorship had gone to a capable man.

Still, no matter what Mynydd's detractors said, and they did have a lot to say, Mynydd's sole purpose was not to gain power for power's sake. He had a head full of plans and a heart full of ideals. He had hopes for Lunenfarne. His hopes gave his own life a purpose, and, it must be admitted, he needed a purpose. There were possibilities in this village, opportunities. He wanted to build – yes, he was actually eager to build something here, make something better out of the place of his birth. He wanted to widen the bridge at the mouth of the Nolta River and raise it high above the rapids. They needed a new school that was more centrally located, and improvements to the ferry service on the Arum River. Lord Mynydd did not always achieve exactly what he had planned because his mind was full of more projects than he could implement. But his work excited him and took his mind off problems at home.

On one of his frequent visits to Parou Island during construction of the lighthouse, Vladimir Mynydd brought his son along. He and Kai were somewhat close in age, Dort being three years older.

"Stay away from the workmen, boys," warned Teron. "Kai, why

don't you show Dort your animal collection?"

"Sure. Come inside. You should see this new elephant Teron just carved for me." Kai motioned to Dort, who lumbered along reluctantly up the hill to the house

"Your father makes these?" Dort picked up the wooden elephant and made it run pounding across the floor.

"Hey, be careful of him. That took a long time to make – hey!"

"Let's fight them!" Dort crashed two animals head to head.

"No! No, I don't want to play fighting. You'll break his trunk! Put them back. We'll go outside, instead." He and Dort gathered the carved figures and put them back on a shelf.

"Sorry, kid. I didn't think you'd be afraid of a little fight."

"I'm not afraid. I just don't want to break anything." He knelt to gather the rest of the animals.

"They are nice animals," Dort said, changing his tone. "Your father is pretty good at making things."

Somehow, this didn't mollify Kai. He couldn't say why, but this boy Dort made him uncomfortable. "Let's go outside, see what we can find in the tide pool."

"Sure."

They walked out, but Dort stopped and said, "Hey, want to play catch? Go get a ball, why don't you. You do have one, right?"

"I'll get it." When Kai went back inside, he noticed immediately that his new wooden elephant was not on its shelf. He couldn't find it anywhere in the room. He stalked outside to where Dort stood next to Lord Mynydd.

"Dort! You forgot to put my elephant back."

"I put it back. I did," said Dort. "You must have misplaced it."

"No! It's gone!" Kai didn't mean to answer in a loud voice but he was upset.

Dort's face was all concern. "What could have happened to it?"

"You had it last!"

"I don't think I did. Gee, I'm sorry you lost it."

Kai squinted at him.

Vladimir Mynydd turned to the boys. "Is there a problem?"

"He's got my new elephant!"

"Dort?"

"Father, I swear to you. He says one of his toys is lost but I never touched it."

"You did so!" To his own disgust, tears ran down Kai's face. "That was my Hannibal elephant!"

"Well, it's only a toy."

"It is my favorite and you took it."

Teron stepped in. He put a hand on Kai's shoulder. "Let's search the house again, shall we? I'll help you. Come on." He led Kai away. When they got inside, he looked around the room. "No elephant."

"That creep took it!"

"Don't call him names. He's a nice boy."

"He's not. He is a creep."

Teron looked down at Kai. "It's going to come down to this, Kai. It's a hard choice, but I'm afraid you'll have to make it. Do you want to start a big fight, insisting another boy took your toy? Or should you keep the peace, let it go, and let me make you a new elephant? A better one?"

Kai snuffled and frowned. "It's just not fair, that's all. He took it! I know he did!"

Teron folded his arms and held them against his waist, as if he had pain there. "I know something of these people, Kai."

"Who? Dort?"

"These people who have money and power. You can't fight them and win. Believe me, I tried once."

"It's not fair! It's not!"

"No, it isn't. But sometimes, not alway but sometimes, it's smarter to let things go. You know the saying 'live to fight another day'?" Teron knelt and they wrapped their arms around each other. "I'll carve you a whole herd of elephants."

"As many as Hannibal had?" Kai asked, his face buried against Teron's neck.

"As many as Hannibal had and a dozen elephant children too." Teron looked up.

Vladimir Mynydd stood in the doorway. His face was still. He watched the man and the boy together. "I —" He started to say something. When had his own son … it had been many years … and he and his own father … never, never that he could remember ….

Teron rose. "I think we've sorted things out. Do you want to tell Lord Mynydd something, Kai?"

Kai raised his chin. Teron tensed, seeing his defiance. "Teron is going to make me a new elephant," Kai said. He reached for Teron's big hand and kissed it. He knew, without being able to put the idea in words, that he had something more valuable than any wooden elephant.

Mynydd, wordless, looked at the boy. To have such a relationship. How – how gratifying that must be.

That evening, Mynydd made it a point to go into Dort's room at bedtime.

"How about a story, son?" It had been a long time since he had tucked Dort into bed.

“I'll just read what I have.”

“You sure?”

“Well, yeah. I'm not a child.”

“True, true. Don't stay up too late, though. Good night.”

As he crossed the hall, Vladimir almost tripped on a carved elephant that lay on the floor, its trunk broken.

Vladimir Mynydd, on his visit to Parou a few days later, brought two beautifully illustrated handmade books for Kai.

“These were Dort's,” he explained. “He asked me especially to bring them to you. You can have them, if you want them.”

Kai took them hesitantly. Teron had a few books, but they owned none for children. Were these for his very own? “Thank you,” he said finally.

“I – he felt bad about your lost toy the other day.”

Mynydd looked up when he heard Anne laugh. She had just collected a basket of laundry from the clothesline and was walking toward the house. He watched her bump playfully against Teron's shoulder.

These people. They were so interesting. They fascinated him. What ... what … what kept them going? They were so poor, had so little, but, truly, they didn't seem to realise it.

Mynydd meant to spend more time in his office in town that spring, but he couldn't resist being rowed out to the island every couple of days. He made a point of discussing the progress on the lighthouse with Teron. He didn't want it to look too odd if he also took pains, on every trip to Parou, to seek Anne out. One day he found her standing by the sheepfold. Which was good. He wanted to talk about, of all things, sheep, or so he told himself. He leaned on the fence, pretending to contemplate livestock.

"I see you frequently at the auctions," he told Anne. "You're very canny."

Anne couldn't answer. She did not know whether "canny" was an insult or not.

"I'd like to purchase some of your animals. You've bred a good sturdy stock."

Anne nodded. She was well aware that Mynydd owned the largest flock in Lunenfarne. Her sheep, though, had the best wool.

"How is your workshop coming along?" Mynydd asked, trying another subject.

"Well, the looms are finally set up properly. We're starting to get some orders."

"I also have started training people here, since the duties they charge in Flanders have gotten so high. Dyers, weavers, people like you're hiring." Mynydd let a moment go by, hoping she would join him in conversation. "That reminds me," he laughed. "I have a bone to pick with you. I believe you stole one of the best women from my workshop."

"Ermentrude Treyse? I did not steal her. I just offered her more pay." Ermentrude was the mother of Kai's friend, Gregor.

"Oh. More pay. That old trick." He laughed again. "I noticed that she is doing some beautiful work for you. The colors your workrooms achieve are gorgeous."

"Thank you. My people have always had these skills."

He ran his hand over his hair, which, it appeared, was growing long. The shaved parts of his head were now covered with a fuzz of hair. The tufts had been cut off. His clothing was much more loose, too, more casual.

"Now tell me about these dyes you make. You must be using alum to set such brilliant colors." He leaned toward her with a smile. "You never told me where you really get it."

He was not going to get any secrets from her. "Alum is just one of many mordants. There are others. I use rhubarb, sumac, sometimes rusty iron. Sometimes no mordant at all, like with my dandelion dye or the boiled crab shells that I use for delicate reds." She wasn't lying, not really. She did use plants, but alum was her secret ingredient for setting the brightest, non-fading colors. It would be foolish, stupid even, to tell him – or anyone – her method of procuring it.

"Those rose colors and the oranges that you use, though. You can't get those deep colors just from vegetable dyes. But I can't figure out how you get your hands on alum, now that the pope in Rome has a monopoly on the supply."

"I dye my wools in the traditional ways of my people."

Mynydd smiled again. "Your people? Your people must be very wise."

"In fact, they are."

He moved closer to Anne. "I was thinking of having you dye a few yards for me, for a special costume I have in mind. Something really … beautiful."

She nodded.

"Maybe you can bring me some color samples."

"Was it a dark shade you preferred?"

His eyes roamed her face, her hair. "Dark, yes, dark would be most suitable." He paused. "Maybe you could get someone to deliver some samples to my office. Or you could bring them, if your husband wouldn't mind."

"Did you think Teron was my husband?"

"He's not?"

"No. And yes, I would gladly deliver a few samples."

"Good. Very good. You know where my office …."

"I'll take them right to your house. I know where it is. Your wife bought a few yards of fabric from me. I'll show her the dark rose color. I think she would like that."

"Yes." Mynydd turned away. "Yes. Natalia would love to see what you have." If only Anne knew, he thought, what spiteful things his wife called her in private.

Watching Mynydd walk away, Anne wondered if he believed her story about the alum. Alum was essential to the brilliant colors her fabrics achieved. She could never tell anyone how she procured it. It wasn't only for herself that she kept that secret. There were other women to consider. It would go very hard for them, should anyone find out what they were involved in, though as to that, she was not even sure herself how their business worked.

The winter before, everyone in the tattered village of Lunenfarne had watched a building being renovated down by the wharves. Renovations happened so seldom – well, hardly ever, really – that this one was the talk of the town. What was happening here? The place used to be a grubby old warehouse, but now the mortar crumbling between its stones was getting pointed up, second and third floors were being added, the rats drummed out of their twenty year old habitat, and soon the purpose was revealed. A new red sign hung over the front door: Bayside Inn. Lunenfarne now had an inn and a tavern, run by a pair of sisters. No one knew where these women came from. Rumor had it that one of the Button sisters had been imprisoned years ago at Balgrim Prison but had somehow managed to escape. Gossip. It was nothing but gossip. Indeed, had anyone ever escaped alive from Balgrim? There were other whispers too, wild tales, something about a feud, ongoing hostilities, something about Spanish galleons. Who knew? No one dared ask – you just didn't, that's all.

One glimpse of the inn's proprietor, Freya Button, standing in the doorway of her new establishment, and you might find yourself believing almost any gossip about her and her sister. Go on into the tavern, order a drink from her -- order two, if you want – but you would not hear a word from Freya about their past. You would be more apt to hear yourself spilling the beans about your own past – and then regret it the next morning. But Freya? Freya was a locked vault.

These two women, Freya and her sister Batilda, would stand out in any crowd, being as tall as many men. More than their height, there was something else about them, an audacity, an invisible line they drew in the sand, and certainly in Freya's case, an aloofness. Even the soggiest ruffians who patronized the Bayside Inn could tell that taking advantage of the Button sisters would not be smart. They could not put into words why this was so, the vocabulary of soggy Lunenfarne ruffians being generally rather inadequate, but it was an opinion universally accepted.

But, how to describe Freya and Batilda Button? They were imposing women, you'd have to say that much. They were smart, and ran a good business, and they were, as the men put it, easy on the eyes. You would think that such classy women would tend to leave Lunenfarne as soon as they had the chance. But these two had come to settle here. Even the nosiest person in the village could not, for the life of them, find out why.

Freya Button appeared to be the bolder of the two. She was fair-haired, blue-eyed, big-boned, and strong. If she wanted to, she could, it was rumored, make short work of almost any trouble-maker. She let the low-cut cotton chemises that she wore everyday show off a physique that was voluptuous but by no means flabby. She intimidated, while at the same time fascinating, her male patrons. More than one new customer had slopped half his beer while taking a stein from her hand. Her light sandy-colored hair was drawn back into a bun so tight that a favorite point of discussion was what effect loosening that hairdo would have on her face. A few of the more vulgar drunks wondered about loosening the rest of her. Wishful thinking, strictly wishful thinking. Freya welcomed her customers heartily, but she was never once seen to throw inhibition to the winds. Fraternization? It didn't happen. She let her employees take care of fraternization. And that hair-do of hers? Unchanged from one month to the next, every strand in its place.

Freya's sister, Batilda, was of slightly slimmer build but still tall, also blue-eyed. She smiled easily. She was gentler, quieter than her sister, or seemed so, though few customers ever got more than a glimpse of her. She wore her strawberry-gold hair in various arrangements of thick plaits and artful rolls, and covered her gown with a voluminous cotton coat while she cooked. She produced three meals a day except for Sundays. What Batilda did or where she went on Sundays was pure speculation but everyone was well aware that, out of pity, the Buttons hired a good-for-nothing writer named Chekov to do the Sunday cooking. Those in the know stayed away from the Bayside Inn until Monday. All the other days, Batilda did the cooking and kept the housekeepers and chambermaids in line. Freya kept the books and watched over the bevy of bodacious serving maids who attended the customers. Batilda turned out meals that were wolfed down as soon as the plates hit the table. Freya poured the ale. The sisters were appreciated in equal measure.

Truth be told, the inn was not the sole business endeavor of these two unusual women. They didn't make a big deal of it and only a few people were aware that they also owned a pair of ships, the two-masted *Wolf* and a lightning fast sloop, *Vixen*. Freya had hand-picked the crews of these two vessels, selecting for certain qualities that she believed were important. She paid them well so, unlike crews on other ships, hers saw very little turnover.

It was about their shipping business that Anne d'Inquierre had come to the inn one winter afternoon that year, while Kai was off at school. She had never been inside the tavern, had never met either of the Button sisters. She stood by the inn door for a minute, stomping the snow from her boots and blinking in the dimness.

Freya turned and raised her eyebrows. She had seen this dark-skinned woman around town and always took special note of the long patterned wool skirts she wore. Freya, contrary to what you might think from her somewhat stern demeanor, had an eye for such things.

"What can I do you for?" she bellowed to Anne across the room.

Anne came forward hesitantly, looking nervously at the two customers who hunched silently over their pints in front of the fire. "I'd like to speak with Freya Button, if I could."

"I'm Freya."

Anne came close and spoke softly. "Jozef Francevili said you run a shipping business."

"What do you have in mind?" Freya asked, still full volume.

"I came to ask if I could interest you in selling some of my wool in Bellesunde."

"Bales or yardage?"

"I have four bolts ready to sell now, but hope to have more soon."

"I have to see what you're offering before I do any deals."

"Patterned wool, like this that I have on."

Freya grabbed a handful of Anne's skirt. "Yeah. Nice colors. Nice hand to this fabric. Love the pattern."

"Thank you."

"You're the weaver?"

"I design the patterns and hire a woman to weave them for me."

"This is quality goods. Where'd you find somebody to do this work? Not around here."

"She lives here. Mrs. Treyse. I trained her myself."

"Who dyes the wool?"

"I do that."

"The mordant? What do you use?" She cocked an eye at Anne and now spoke more softly. "A touchy question, but I have to ask."

"I used alum for this."

Freya's eyebrows shot up. She squinted suspiciously, nearly whispering now. "You're smuggling the stuff in?"

"My people are able to get it, but they won't sell to me anymore. Alum is something else I wanted to talk to you about."

"It's not available anymore, not unless you pay through the nose and buy the Italian stuff the pope is peddling. He's got a corner on that business, all for his Holy Roman self."

"I realise that. I'm prepared to pay." Anne looked steadily into Freya's eyes.

"All right. Let's see if we can do business. Come on back to my office."

Alum had long been valued to sterilize wounds and draw them

closed. It was also the best thing for fixing ephemeral vegetable dyes and was in high demand in fabric houses throughout Europe. Because it is water-soluble, it could not be not found in wet climates but had to be brought from volcanic sites, mostly in Asia, then transported long distances to ports in Genoa, Spain, and Portugal. When the pope cornered the alum market for his own profit, it produced severe shortages in the rest of the world. Prices went sky high.

But there were ways and ways to procure alum. Pirates knew all about that. The Button sisters knew all about that. Freya drew Anne into her office and shut the door.

Kai d'Inquierre turned six in November and by the following spring, there was a new lighthouse on Parou. Also new were larger keeper's quarters. It had all been finished in record time. Parou's lighthouse looked very substantial. Its new tower held sixteen tallow candles. Thanks to the mirrors that reflected them, their light could, on a clear night, be seen for seven miles out at sea. Out there, out beyond the brink of the infinite, the Parrot Island light was a still point, a landmark to steer by. It shone across the northern ocean's heaving immensity. It represented man subduing Nature. It represented civilization, one of very few stopovers on this coast for resupplying and repairs. It marked a place of respite when seas and storms were wild. In the northern world, the Parrot Island light – after a while, the nickname had stuck – signalled a safe haven, solid and immutable.

The new light needed a great deal of cleaning and polishing every day, much more work than the beacon fire. Even Kai had to help out with the chores. One day in very early spring, as soon as he and Teron had finished with the candles, Teron took Kai down to the landing place near his old cave to check crab traps.

"Teron! Teron!"

Teron dropped the crab he had just pulled from the trap. A squabble of gulls swooped at it as if they hadn't eaten in a month and tore it to pieces. Panicked by Kai's shouts, Teron scrambled uphill to the entrance to the cave that, six years ago, had been his hide-out.

"Kai! Where are you? You all right?" Kai came to the entrance, apparently unharmed. "Ah. What's that you have?"

"Look at this! I found this box in your cave. Did you hide it there?"

"I never saw it before."

"This metal part was all rusted and it just broke when I pulled on it. But look at all this." He opened the lid of the small chest. "Look! I bet Robin Hood never had this much."

Teron scooped a handful of gold coins and ran them through his fingers. "These are – they look like – Wow, they must be!"

"Old coins! Real or just pretend?"

"Oh, quite real."

"They sure look richer than our money."

"It's gold, that's why. From all kinds of places in the world. Far away places."

"Like where?"

"Well, these are English sovereigns …."

"From King Arthur's castle?"

"Not quite that old, I'm afraid. Here's a Dutch guilder. Spanish doubloons. An English guinea. These are florins, really old, from Italy. That's where …."

"Hannibal was there! Maybe these were his!"

"I don't know about that but …."

"What were they doing in your cave, do you think?"

"I suspect they were hidden there by someone. Maybe a smuggler."

"A pirate, I bet!"

"How far back into the cave did you go, Kai? Remember I told you not to …?" He had never told Kai that he had hidden a satchel of treasure in the cave, the shipwreck captain's leather bag.

"I didn't go far back, honest. I was jumping on that big rock, you know that flat one by the opening, and it broke apart and I fell – look, I cut my hand – and this box was just under there. It was sort of hiding but the sunlight hit it just right."

"Was anything else under there?'

"All I could see was this. Can I have one of these coins to buy a sweet bun for me and Gregor at Carnevale tomorrow?"

"You could buy a lot of sweet buns with that coin. But, no. You can't spend gold like this at the baker's. We have to figure out what to do with this."

"With all this gold, we can go live in town now, can't we? We don't have to stay out here anymore cuz we've got lots of money now."

"I don't know if this is lots of money. But it's a great find. Let's show your mother."

Kai closed the casket and held his hand on the lid. "Ema will just buy sheep with it."

Teron looked at him, hesitating a moment. "Ah. Whereas it could pay for a couple of years at university for you. I mean, if you decided to go when you're older. If you decide you don't want to herd sheep."

"I don't want to herd sheep. I want to go to university like you did. But Ema – she thinks we're going to go back to live with her people."

"I know."

Kai bent his head, then squinted up at Teron. "Can we put this back in the hiding place?"

"I don't know. It feels wrong to deceive your mother." He bit his lip. "Don't you agree?"

"Okay, see but ...." Kai frowned. "I found it, right?"

"You did."

"It's sort of like mine now. Right?"

Teron tilted his head side to side. "I guess so."

"Just for a little? Could we hide it just for a little while, Teron? Til we're ready to tell Ema?"

"Why don't we take a day to think it over? Put it back for now. But find a new place to hide it. Tomorrow we'll decide what to do with it."

"C'mon! I'll show you where I found it." He beckoned Teron into the cave.

But the next day, they forgot to tell Anne about the coins. There turned out to be other more pressing issues.

Just as Teron came out of the cave, one moment after hiding the gold, a ship bearing the house flag of the Einfaldssons sailed down the south channel and past Parrot Island.

Carnevale! In the entire village the next day, nothing was done in the name of work, unless you counted filling ovens with sweet breads, or setting up booths to sell baskets or quilts or wooden toys or clay beads. Minstrels put new strings on their instruments. That was a little like work. The nuns worked and fretted and fussed through a rehearsal of the children's choir, but they got those little rascals to sing like angels. The bagpipers, well now, that was another story altogether. Their job was real work. They labored and they squeezed and they blew, and the noise that came out was what they called music. Most folks loved it. A few listeners called it hard work. In addition to their sonic bedlam, the pipers themselves could be counted on to provide a bit of a sideshow, just a moment of fun for a few tittering maidens who stood waiting for that puff of wind, that mischievous little light-fingered breeze, that gave everyone a glimpse of what was, or was not, above those hairy bagpiper thighs.

Ah, such naughty lassies! Something for everyone at Carnevale!

Expressly for the occasion, Signor Bologna's famous puppets were all dressed in new clothes and read from new scripts that involved beating on each other in all the favorite old ways. Then, too, there was that newly-widowed seamstress who made a few dozen headbands with flowery coronas and long ribbon streamers to sell to a parade of little girls. These provided targets for exasperating little boys whose new blowpipes squirted jets of water from four feet away. Made by somebody's nutty old grandpa, the blowpipes effectively wilted a many a sashaying Carnevale princess.

See that? Carnevale indeed offered something for everyone!

Traders came up from the south to sell pepper and beeswax and cinnamon. From the north came furs and antlers and falcons and silver jewelry. Because the festivities would go on into the evening, Otto the chandler raked in piles of coins selling candles in tin holders so lovesick adolescents could chase each other into dark corners and do unspeakably adolescent things to each other.

Carnevale! The best time of the year!

Of course, Carnevale attracted some rather unsavory characters, too. This year, sour old Alphonse d'Inquierre had come back into Lunenfarne for the first time in years. He was looking particularly fleabitten this spring. He had very little to sell. His winter hunting trip had devolved into one drunken bash after another. With his last bit of cash he bought some grimy taxidermy specimens and leftover skins from a more prosperous merchant, in order to have something to sell at Carnevale. He couldn't figure out why no one seemed interested in his wares. He sat glowering and alone in a far corner of the market.

But then, from a distance, he spotted Soro Einfaldsson strolling down the lane between tents and booths. Alphonse sat up. He sniffed the breeze. That was opportunity he was smelling! If only he could get Einfaldsson to give him some business. Maybe he would finance Alphonse's next trip north! He could offer to sell directly and solely to Einfaldsson. Then he wouldn't have to be stuck mingling with all this annoying market rabble.

As luck would have it, and Alphonse always had more than his share of luck, Einfaldsson walked over to his booth. He had spotted a pair of ermine skins. He flipped the skins over, ignoring old Alphonse's wolfish grin.

Alphonse leapt up. "Very nice pelts these are, my good sir," he bellowed. "Very nice. From the northern lake country. Do you see how much thicker the fur is on these? Much thicker than you usually see. Very nice pelts. Very nice."

"Whoever did the skinning must have used a butter knife. These are a mess."

Alphonse wasn't sure what a butter knife was for, but he did know how to wheedle and finagle. "Oh," he declared hurriedly, "I can get better than these, my lord! Much better. All my best pieces have sold already, see. Yes, all gone. My investors bought them all. They all value my wares. They pay me handsomely and I buy for them exclusively. I give them good deals, I do, I do." The investors were products of Alphonse's imagination. The sly grin on his face, though, was genuine d'Inquierre.

Einfaldsson began to turn away, disinterested.

"I could take on one more investor, if you're interested, my lord, but only one more," Alphonse said hurriedly. "I guarantee you'd be happy with what I bring back."

"No, I thank you."

"Wait!" He was losing the man. Alphonse's mind was going in circles. He couldn't lose this opportunity! That is when he spotted what's-her-name, that wife of his, Hey You, wandering through the market with a little boy. His own wife, bought and paid for! Alphonse's mind skipped over the little boy and leapt forward with a jolt. "Wait a minute," he urged Einfaldsson. "If you're not interested in skins, maybe I have something else you would like."

"No, I've seen enough."

"Wait! Wait! I'm talking about something you haven't seen. Not seen in a very long time, if rumors are true. I'm talking about a man."

Einfaldsson frowned.

"There was a poster in the sheriff's window, wasn't there? I seen it, I did, a while back." Einfaldsson looked puzzled. "You know the one, don't ya? That poster! Ain't I right? You put up a poster? For a man named –" Alphonse's brain shut down. What was that freaking name? Oh, this could work out perfectly, if only he could come up with the name. That asswipe hoodlum who lived with Hey You. The one who attacked him that night – what the hell was his name? He tried stalling. "I don't dare say it out loud, my lord. You know who I mean. That man you were interested in finding."

"A man?" Something clicked. "What man?" A flicker of fear flamed into life in Soro Einfaldsson's gut. Whipping the tail of that fear was a buried hatred. That old crime. Was the truth still lurking out there?

Alphonse let his tongue slide forward. He had him now. "I can tell you where that man is."

"What man, I say?"

"The man on your poster."

"You don't mean Teron Adante?"

"Yes! Adante! Yes, that's him!"

"I thought he was dead."

"No no no. Not dead. Alive. Alive and very near here."

"What can you tell me about him?"

"Well, there's a reward, ain't there? I thought there was a reward."

"That was a long time ago." Einfaldsson flipped a silver coin out of his purse. "Here. Tell me what you know."

"This is hardly the amount you were offering before."

"It's all I'm offering today."

Alphonse licked his lips. If Einfaldsson saw that he was right about Adante, maybe they could set up some kind of business relationship. The thought of revenge on Hey You – ah aha, yes! Double incentive. "See that woman over there? The one with the boy?"

Einfaldsson looked. He nodded.

"Adante lives with her."

Einfaldsson made a face. "You're making that up. Adante was an educated man. He would not take up with some gypsy savage."

Alphonse bristled, having himself taken up with that very savage. Now his ego was in play, and he would watch his mother die in a pit of rattlesnakes rather than put a scratch in that ego. "I'm telling you the truth, my lord," he spit back. "Adante runs the lighthouse out on Parrot Island."

"You are so full of shit, you liar. Adante would not stoop that low."

For his part, Einfaldsson, too, was feeling he had been hit below the belt. His own sister had flirted with Adante at one point. She would never take up with … no, Saranna would never, not ever – a lighthouse keeper? This was too insulting. This time, Einfaldsson turned away and kept going.

"You'll see!" croaked Alphonse. "You'll see! Just ask around. You'll find out that I'm right!"

By the time he arrived in Lunenfarne that day, Soro Einfaldsson had been traveling for two months. He had filled three ships with goods and was selling them in port after port on their way back to Bellesunde. Coming along the coast to Lunenfarne, he had decided to dump some of his leftover cargo in that town.

"We can't sell this junk, my lord," one of his factors had warned him. "Look at what's left. Even these northern hicks won't buy half bolts of silk and flawed gemstones. All the quality stuff is gone."

"I know the types who live here. You've met Vladimir Mynydd? He wouldn't know quality if it jumped up and bit him on the ass. We'll take one ship into their bay and send the other two home. Oh, and take those three slaves we have left. See if we can get rid of them here. They're illegal in Bellesunde." Einfaldsson considered himself to be a good judge of people. What they didn't sell to the magistrates of Lunenfarne, he was sure they could sell to some trader at Carnevale.

Pleased to be developing commerce with a merchant from the south, Vladimir Mynydd invited Einfaldsson to his home that afternoon. He escorted him into his well-appointed reception room and poured him a drink. Mynydd encouraged his son Dort to stay in the room while they talked. He was grooming the boy for a job in commerce and it never hurt to let his son see how business was done.

Soro Einfaldsson eased himself into a plush chair and looked around the room. Apparently Mynydd did appreciate beautiful things after all.

"Ah, Spanish sherry." Einfaldsson sipped daintily. "Very nice."

"It should be. It's forty years old."

"It's good of you to share it with me."

"It's my pleasure. My hope is that I can entice you to bring your ships often to Lunenfarne. We actually do have an elite class of people here. Our town is growing and we can promise you good dockage and fine accommodations. I hope you noticed the new lighthouse out there. The channel is marked now and much safer than it used to be."

Besides, thought Mynydd to himself, every ship that docked in Lunenfarne would have to pay a docking fee, not to mention taxes on whatever goods they sold. The town needed money. Mynydd had a lot of improvements planned.

Einfaldsson was not to be rushed into talking about taxes and fees just yet. Better to keep Mynydd on tenterhooks. "Speaking of that lighthouse," he said, putting his glass down, "someone just told me something about the man running that operation."

"Yes." Mynydd hesitated. "There is a man out there."

"Is he by any chance a man who has been sought by the authorities for several years now?" A man, Soro Einfaldsson did not mention, who also happened to be the only person in the world, apart from his own sister, who knew without a doubt that it was Einfaldsson himself who had murdered a young man in cold blood seven years ago.

"Someone sought by the authorities?" Mynydd felt tightness in his chest.

"A convicted criminal. I thought he was dead but I was told today that he lives on that island."

Mynydd looked away with a quick jerk of his head, not wanting to give the truth away. "Is that so?"

"What is your lighthouse operator called, do you know?"

"I'm not sure I've ever heard the man's name. He's a good man, or … or so I'm told." Mynydd felt a profound obligation to Teron Adante. Adante had saved his life and his son's life. Dort, on a sofa on the other side of the room, turned around. His father caught his eye and held it.

Soro Einfaldsson continued. "Some filthy thug in the market gave me that information. It's probably bogus. I'm sure he was just trying to make some money off me."

"Doubtless you're right," Mynydd agreed. "Besides, the town council would never have hired a criminal."

"Ah. Speaking of your council, is there anyone among your magistrates that is in need of household help? I have three slaves for sale. Young females who could be trained for household duties. Or whatever."

"Slaves?" Mynydd scowled. "No. The idea of owning another person is repulsive to me."

"These are nubile young women. Granted, they are Africans, so technically not people in the sense that –"

"No. Thank you. But no. It's not something we'd be interested in here. Now about my business proposal, …."

They spoke for an hour and parted amicably, each feeling he had gained over the other.

Mynydd showed Einfaldsson out and turned to his son. "Did you hear all that? I think we struck a good bargain here, Dort." Mynydd rested a hand on his son's shoulder as he passed. "I have to get going. I'm past due to meet Ruslan Fairhedd. I'll be at the office, if anyone asks."

Dort stood by the settee for a minute, thinking. He whirled around at the sound of a step. He had not heard his mother come down the hall. She wore her sulky look. It both made his stomach tighten and gave him the bizarre desire to bait her further.

"Where's your father going?"

He reached for her hand. "He claims he's going to his office."

"Really? His office?"

"So he said. Why do you ask?"

"He's not going out to Parrot Island again today? Pretending to deliver new – I don't know what – mirrors or candlewax or something?"

"I don't know. He might be. Or maybe," Dort suggested, slyly drawing the word out, "he's sneaking out there to see Anne d'Inquierre. He goes out there a lot." Wickedly easy it was, getting a rise out of his mother.

Natalia Mynydd bristled. "I can't for the life of me understand him. What does he see in that gypsy? Now you've upset me. Give me a hug." She drew her son close. He was nearly her height now. She brushed his hair off his forehead. "My beauty. My beautiful son." She fingered the amulet she made him wear around his neck. "Has that Einfaldsson man left yet?"

Dort gazed up into her eyes. "He's just going, I think."

"Dortie." She bent to press their foreheads together. "Do Mummy a favor? Run after Lord Einfaldsson and give him that name he was asking about."

"What name?"

"That lightkeeper. You met him. You know his name."

"You heard that conversation?"

"Mummy hears lots of things, darling. Go tell him the name."

"You tell him."

"I don't want to. Go on. Do it for me."

"Why should I do it? He'll listen to you more than me."

She kissed Dort's cheek and pushed him away. "Don't be silly, sweetheart. I need you to do this. Go catch Einfaldsson before he leaves."

"Mummy –," he protested.

"Go on. Go on."

Einfaldsson was clear across the courtyard. Dort was tempted to pretend he missed him, but then, thinking it over, he reconsidered. He didn't like those lighthouse people any better than his mother did. He had never liked them. He ran to catch up with Soro Einfaldsson.

"My lord! Could I have a moment? I have something to tell you."

"What is it, lad?" Einfaldsson kept walking.

"You were asking my father about a name."

Einfaldsson stopped. The two spoke for a minute.

"How do you know? How do you know more than your father knows?" Einfaldsson asked.

"Well, I try to pay attention," said Dort, and echoed his mother. "I hear lots of things."

What was this boy up to, claiming he knew something that his father couldn't or wouldn't reveal? "If you're trying to get me to pay for this information, you're wasting your time."

"No, no." Dort smiled, not a glimmer of guile on his face. "I require nothing in return, my lord. I just thought that if I could help you out, I would. That's all."

"Ah? I see. Well, if I send men out there and you're wrong –"

"I'm not wrong, trust me."

Einfaldsson paused, snared by the boy's earnest demeanor, his good looks. He put his hand on Dort's shoulder. Yes, here was a boy he would have to watch carefully. "How old are you, son?"

"Eleven years old, sir. Almost."

"And wise for your age, aren't you?" Einfaldsson regretted that his own son lacked this … this ... this strength of character. He wished the boy a good day. Swiftly, he turned and walked out of the courtyard, calling to his man.

Natalia had trailed her son when he crossed the courtyard because she didn't like to leave anything to chance. She had watched and waited in the garden. Now she came up behind Dort, twirling a blood red rose in her fingers.

"You told him?"

"I did."

"He believed you?"

Dort, now allowing himself a little cockiness, smirked, "I think he did, yes."

Natalia came close and stroked his cheek gently with the rose blossom, then drew him back toward the house, pressing tight against his arm. "So your father thinks highly of that woman?"

"What woman?"

"Dortie! The one out on the island."

"That barbarian woman?"

"Does he?

"Are you still talking about her? Yes. He favors her, I think." He wished everyone was this easy to manipulate.

"You think so? That savage one with the sheep?"

"Well, she is good looking, for a gypsy."

Natalia growled. "The hussy. You'd think she was something special, the way he talks about her."

"She's not so special, believe me. Compared to you, she's nothing."

Gloating, Natalia ran her hand sensuously down her throat. "He claims he can't even tell that she smells like animals. Is it my imagination? Does she smell like sheep to you?"

Dort laughed. "She smells like a barn. Why is Father so impossible, Mother? I mean, on one hand, he is so fond of this low-class woman –"

"So he is fond of her?"

" – and yet it goes against his high principles to do something smart, like allowing Einfaldsson to sell slaves here."

"Your father's ignorance surpasses understanding, Dort."

"He could be making a boatload of money from those slaves. Sometimes I think that Father is not very …."

"Your father is bloody stupid." She put her arm around Dort and squeezed him close as they walked in step. "You're not going to mention any of this to him, are you?"

"You don't want him to know that we gave away the man's name?"

"I don't think he needs to know that. Does he?"

"I'm not going to say anything to him."

"Good."

"Father really can't be trusted to know much of anything. Can he, Mummy." It was not a question.

"Your father is a brainless idiot." Dort's mother kissed him on the forehead.

They went into the house arm in arm.

Evening came, and the long spring twilight was deepening into night.

Anne and Kai were in the house, washing the dishes. Kai, still wound up from his day at Carnevale, was telling her about all the sweets he and Gregor Treyse had devoured, the games they had played.

Teron, at the top of the new tower, had polished the parabolic mirrors until they shone. The sixteen candles were lit. The lighthouse builders had agreed that the lamps on Parrot Island would not need to rotate, as this was the only lighthouse for miles and miles, and could not possibly be confused with another. That meant, conveniently, that he had no clockwork to clean and oil. That saved him a lot of work. He looked out across the empty ocean. Not a ship to be seen. He was glad that it was a calm night. Maybe he would get a chance to sleep for an hour or two before the candles had to be changed. Faint stars and a crescent moon hung above him in a dusky sky. Waves lapped gently on the rocks below. All was peaceful. He turned and began to descend, round and round, down the one hundred thirty-nine steps to the bottom of the tower.

One hundred and twenty-nine steps later he stopped in his tracks. Three men in dark military garb had weapons trained on him.

"What is this?" he asked. He felt sick. He knew. He knew immediately what this was: Fate had caught up with him once again. He had thought he was safe on this island. It had been an illusion.

"Are you Teron Adante?"

His mind grabbed frantically for an answer. Was there any way he could defeat Fate? "Who wants to know?"

"Balgrim Prison wants to know. They have been waiting for you for these many years." One man mounted the stairs and pushed Teron roughly to the bottom. Two men held him on his knees while the third chained his hands.

Anne and Kai heard the voices and came rushing to the door.

"What's going on?" she shrieked.

"The law's got a long arm, lady," one of the soldiers bawled. "This man owes ten years of hard labor to the prison at Balgrim."

"No! You're wrong! You can't – !" Anne was slammed roughly aside and Teron was almost dragged out the door. "No!" she screamed. "Stop!"

The soldiers hurried Teron down the dark slope and through the meadow.

Kai held onto his mother, sobbing. "Ema! Where are they going? Where are they taking him, Ema? They can't take him! They can't do that, can they?"

"Not if I can help it!"

Kai ran a little way down the slope from the house. "Shit-for-brains!" he screamed at the soldiers. He wiped his wet cheeks. He screamed as loud as he could. "You stupid ugly shit-for-brains!" He turned back to where Anne sagged in the doorway. "Why? Why are they taking him?"

"Get your coat, Kai. Hurry. We're going to go see Lord Mynydd."

"Now?"

"Right now." Anne grabbed a shawl, took Kai's hand, and they ran down the hill. The soldiers were already pushing their rowboat off the beach.

Anne rowed like one possessed. She tied up at the dock near the Bayside Inn and hustled Kai into the tavern. Freya Button, standing at the bar, looked up in alarm.

"Anne! What is it?"

"Will you let Kai stay here for an hour or so?"

"What's the matter? What's going on?" Freya pulled Anne to a quiet corner.

"They've got Teron."

"Who? Who's got him?"

"Some soldiers. They're taking him to Balgrim, Freya! Balgrim! I'll have to explain it all later. I can't – I can't believe this!"

"Isn't there anyone who can set this right?"

"Mynydd. Vladimir Mynydd. Maybe he'll speak for Teron. I don't know. Or maybe Mynydd made this happen because – I don't know what to do. I was going to go see him. Should I?"

"Now just calm down. Yes, go ahead. See if you can get Mynydd to speak up for you. I've got the boy for as long as you need." She touched lightly on the back of Kai's head. "Come on, Kai. Let's go see what Aunt 'Tilda has in the kitchen. Go Anne! Do what you have to do."

"Thank you, Freya. I'll be back as soon as I can." Anne ran out the door.

Mynydd! This was his fault! He must have made this happen! Where? Where to find that weasel? There! A lamp burning in his second floor office window. She ran up the stairs and pounded on his door. She didn't notice Dort Mynydd coming along the street. He stopped, seeing Anne at his father's door. She tried the door latch. It was not locked so she threw open the door and slammed it behind her.

Mynydd half rose from behind a grand rosewood desk. "Anne!"

"What in hell have you done?" She advanced on him, pounded on his desk. "What have you done, you horrible evil snake?"

"Anne, what is the matter?"

She stomped around to his side of the desk. "Don't play stupid! Why are you doing this to us? Why?"

"Doing what? I have no idea –"

"Don't treat me like an ignorant fool! Only three people know his name." That was no longer true. She knew that. But someone, someone was at fault here. "In the whole village," she broke down, sobbing bitterly, "you're the one I trust the least. You are the only one who would tell his name. You slimy son of a bitch!"

"Anne!" Mynydd took hold of her shoulders. Dort, watching from the dark street, couldn't hear them, but he could see them through the window. He could see his father put his hands on that woman.

"Don't you touch me!"

"You're talking about Teron?"

"Of course I'm talking about Teron! Don't pretend you don't know who I'm talking about. I want you to go down to that ship and get him off! Get him off! Right now!" She moved away from the window and Vladimir followed her.

"Teron is on –?"

"They took him! You know it! You know they did!"

"I know no such thing! As God is my witness, I never told anyone his name. Here, sit." He poured her a glass of whiskey but she waved it away.

Anne collapsed into his chair. Her hair tumbled out of its combs, a great mane of it falling over her wet cheeks. She thrust it back.

"Are you telling me the truth, Vladimir?"

"I swear to you, I told Einfaldsson this afternoon that I did not know the name of the lighthouse keeper."

"Einfaldsson!"

"He heard something in the market today and he asked me what I knew."

"Who did he talk to? One of the carpenters who worked on the lighthouse? Who?"

"I don't know who. But I never told Einfaldsson anything, Anne, I promise you. I swear I did not say a word."

"Then how –?"

Dort? Dort had been in the room when Einfaldsson was there. That thought hit Mynydd like a lead brick. He said, "Here's what I'll do. I'll go down to the docks and see if I can convince Einfaldsson –"

"I'm going with you."

Mynydd reached for a coat. "It would be better if I went alone. Stay here until I get back."

"No, I'm coming."

Dort slipped back into the shadows and watched them come out. His boyish imagination went wild. So they had some secret place for their little trysts? He decided not to follow them. He couldn't wait to tell his mother, give her an embellished version of their evening rendevous. A minute ago he had felt a small pang of guilt about talking to Einfaldsson behind his father's back. Now, seeing his father betray their family with that barbarian, he was glad he had talked. He would never again let guilt censor his actions.

Anne followed Mynydd down to the pier where Einfaldsson had docked his ship.

"Wait here. Please stay here, Anne. You're hysterical. Let me talk to him alone. All right?" He was gripping her shoulders again. "Here, take my handkerchief." Like a father, he dabbed at her cheeks.

"All right." She nodded, sobbing softly. "Hurry, Vladimir! Please don't let them take him away. Please. He's not a criminal. You know he's not."

"I know, I know. I'll bring him back to you."

The night was turning cold. Anne leaned against a pile of crates. Little pennants of fog from out in the bay drifted over the boats. She squeezed her arms in close to her body, her ankles together, every part of her body tight, holding everything together. Hiccoughing sobs shook her. She held the handkerchief to her face. All was quiet down here except for a faint rumble of song from the tavern of the Bayside Inn.

Anne waited and waited. She stood up to pace. Could she trust Mynydd? Believe what he said? Would he bring her Teron back to her? Ten years in prison. Ten years would kill him in that horrible place. No no no. Ten years. Why was Mynydd taking so long?

A figure moved on the deck of Einfaldsson's boat. Mynydd! She ran to meet him.

"Where is – you're alone! Where is he? Why didn't you bring him? Vladimir!"

"Anne." Mynydd's face – he looked ready to cry himself.

"Why didn't you bring him?" she whispered. He caught her arms when she started to sink.

"Come over here and sit down." He put his arm around her.

Gasping, she allowed him to lead her to a seat.

"Sit, Anne. Sit."

"No." Slowly she raised her head and looked at Mynydd. Hatred painted her face with a livid mask. She spoke softly. "You bastard. You lying son of a bitch bastard. You know what the biggest mistake we ever made was? Saving you from drowning. I wish we had let you and your nasty little son sink to the bottom of the sea."

"Anne. I couldn't get Einfaldsson to listen to anything I said. I tried! I tried to convince him but he was adamant. I can't tell you why he was so stubborn. For the life of me, I can't. There has to be a reason, but I could not find it. He would not yield, not an inch."

Anne knew why he would not yield. Teron knew that Soro Einfaldsson was a murderer. Now he was being made to pay for that knowledge. Vladimir Mynydd was capitulating to Einfaldsson. The great Lord Mynydd pandering to the rich and powerful trader from the south. Teron had always said you could get away with anything, if you had money. She loathed Einfaldsson. She loathed Mynydd.

"I tried so hard, Anne. You have to believe me."

She shook her head, answering slowly, softly. "No. I will never, never believe you. You have power. You're the chancellor. You could have done something. But you're no different from the rest of them. You're a liar. You're a monster. I will despise you as long as I live." She threw his handkerchief to the ground and turned and ran back to the inn.

Time accordions. Crescendo, decrescendo. Six good years with Teron, blown away into memories.

Time seeped through their lives, trickling, slow as an August brook. Summer days. Ocean and meadow a blur of blues and greens. Grass dotted with white daisies, whitecaps dancing on the waves, white gulls soaring, white clouds piling high, high. By night, a blank white moon tracked the flat black sky. White, so pure, and Anne was darkness, dark to her core.

The first couple of months were the hardest. Their world, their whole world, torn apart by a random blazing thunderbolt that ripped out of the sky, shattering everything. Anne went about with vacant eyes, stunned senseless. Kai clutched Teron's notebooks to his chest as though they were part of the man. He read and reread Teron's stories to himself almost obsessively, and then tucked them under his pillow for safe-keeping. On many nights, he was plagued with bad dreams. All day, day after day, he was tired and weepy. He followed his mother everywhere, climbing the tower to help her with the lights, and again in the morning, to help her with the cleaning. Wash the windows, polish the mirrors, record the weather and their official activities in the journal, clean up the wax drips, sweep the floor, move the buoys, make new candles and trade them for the old ones. They hardly spoke to one another, except to direct or acknowledge tasks. They couldn't be apart, but there was nothing they could say to one another.

The loss sat too massive upon them. It weighed too heavily, almost breaking them. Loss smothered words, blocked thoughts about anything but itself. Wash the windows, make new candles, polish the mirrors.

Between Kai and Anne, a nothingness. Teron wasn't the only one gone, or so it seemed to Kai. Ema had gone away too and Kai could not bring her back. He had been broken too, just as broken as she, but his mother didn't see. He stayed as close to her as she would let him, afraid she had forgotten all about him.

Mornings were cooler now. Patches of red showed here and there across the hills. They were up at the top of the lighthouse, out on the balcony, cleaning salt spray off the windows. Kai worked on the lower parts, Anne the upper.

"School starts tomorrow, you know."

"I'm not going."

"I thought you liked school."

Kai shook his head.

"I think you should go." Something had to change. They had to do something to break this stranglehold of grief. Kai was desperately unhappy, Anne knew that. She would have to make more effort herself, to at least pretend that things were normal. "Teron would have wanted you to go to school."

A tear slid down Kai's cheek. "What will happen to us, Ema?"

"We'll be fine."

"What if they take you away too?"

"Kai." Anne put her cleaning cloth down and knelt beside her son. "Kai, listen. That won't happen. I told you why they took Teron."

"Why do they think he hurt someone? He would never!" Kai was sobbing aloud now.

"You know what? We have to … you and I, we have to … somehow we have to …." She wrapped her arms around him and he clung to her.

"Ema."

"Somehow we have to go on by ourselves."

"Is Teron – what do you think he's doing right now? Is he at that place yet?"

"I think he's probably there by now. At the prison. I think he has to … well, they have mines there that the men … I think he has to work in the mines."

"It doesn't sound very good. What if he gets hurt?"

"It's hard work. But he's strong, remember. He's very very strong."

"I'll be seventeen."

"Seventeen what?"

"I'll be seventeen years old when he comes back." It was impossible that he would ever be that old. He would be a boy, always. He would never be seventeen and Teron would never come back.

Anne closed her eyes, then raised her face and tried to laugh. "You think seventeen is old? I'll be thirty-one."

"I'll take care of you when you get that old, Ema," he assured her quickly. "I will never leave you."

She nodded, her throat tight. She tried another pretend laugh. "I don't think I'll be a cripple by that age, you know."

"No, I'll do everything. I'll do the work up here and you can just tend your sheep. See, that's why I don't have time for school. I have to help you. I don't even want to go, anyway."

"Oh, I think I'm still strong enough to take care of everything for a little while longer. So that settles it. You can go to school."

"I don't want to go."

She pinched her lips between her teeth and thought. "Why don't we decide that in a couple of days?"

"I don't want to leave you."

Wings flared above them and Bou Bou the parrot landed with a thud. Now that nights had turned cool, he never left his perch by the stove before mid-morning.

Lady of Spain, I adore you! He inched his way along the balcony railing, screeching and bobbing.

Anne and Kai smiled a little.

Pull down your pants, I'll explore –

"Bou Bou! Stop it!" Kai scolded, knowing what Teron would have said. "Ema? Do you think Bou Bou will still be here when Teron gets back?"

"That bird? Oh, without a doubt. That bird will always be here.

Unless I smack him with a broom in the meantime."

Three days passed and Kai still refused to go to school. One afternoon he and his mother were busy pouring hot tallow into candle molds.

"This stuff stinks!" Kai said.

"We've got enough for tonight. Let's leave this. I have to figure out what we're having for dinner."

"I'm going out on the balcony for a minute so I can breathe." It was rough out on the bay that day. Wave crests wore mantles of white. Kai circled the top of the lighthouse. Down at the foot of the island, he noticed two people trying to pull a rowboat ashore. "Ema!" Kai's voice was panicked. Now what? Who were they? What were they coming for? "Ema, come here!"

Anne came out, wiping her hands on a towel. "Who is that? Some boy. He's limping. It's your little friend, Kai."

"Gregor!"

"And his mother." Kai ran down the stairs, down through the meadow to meet them. Anne followed.

Ermentrude, Gregor's mother, waved. "We thought we'd row out here to say 'hello'. We haven't seen either of you in so long."

"Come up to the house. I'll make tea," Anne said.

"Hey, Dinker! Aren't you coming to school anymore?" Gregor asked Kai as they climbed through the meadow. "You gotta see the new school building."

Anne waited for Kai's answer, then said, "He's thinking about going, aren't you, Kai?"

"I don't know. Maybe."

"We brought a cake," Gregor announced with pride.

"We haven't had cake in –" Kai stopped. They hadn't done anything pleasant lately. "Not in a long time."

"This is your house? It doesn't look haunted to me."

"We don't have ghosts. I've told you that, Gregor."

"Darn." Gregor stopped to survey the house, the lighthouse, the island. "You sure are lucky to live here."

Kai shook his head and rolled his eyes. "Are you joking? You should try it sometime. Hey, want to see some puffballs I found in the woods?"

The women sat drinking tea while the boys played outside. "I'm sorry I haven't given you any work lately, Ermentrude," Anne said.

"I wondered … should I go back to working for Mynydd?"

"No! No, don't do that! I'll get something going. Yes, it would be good for both Kai and me to get back to work. I need something to occupy my mind. You know – " Anne thought for a minute. "I wish I had more land. If I had room for a bigger herd –" She stopped to think again. "Yes. Ha! If I had a bigger herd, I bet I could put Vladimir Mynydd out of business."

"You're not serious?"

"More sheep, more wool. A bigger workshop with more looms. I could at least steal a lot of work from him. Hit him where it hurts."

"Why would you want to make an enemy of that man? He could hurt you far more than you could hurt him. He runs this town. He has a big herd of sheep, two workshops. He exports a lot of wool."

"You're right. Even if I had more land, there is no way I could handle a larger herd by myself."

"You'd have to hire someone, like he does."

"I don't know who."

Ermentrude stared into her teacup. "You've met my husband, Wido," she said to her lap.

Anne had met him once. A tense man whose face perpetually asked why life had turned on him so brutally. She nodded.

"His family raised animals. Sheep mostly. He knows how to run herd dogs." Ermentrude took a breath. "Shepherding would suit him, Anne. He'd be willing to work for you. He – it would suit him to live alone in the hills and guard a flock." She didn't say that it would make life a lot easier for her and Gregor, too. "If only you had land up in those hills."

"If only I had land."

Gregor Treyse finally convinced Kai to come back to school and time rolled on. Months unfolded, years. Chancellor Vladimir Mynydd had seen to the building of the new school. It was on the town side of the Arum River and close to the Town Hall. The two buildings shared a pretty campus planted with new gardens and painted benches. Now in his teens, Kai almost always rowed to school by himself. Mr. Korsakov, the ferryman, allowed him to tie his boat to the new ferry dock on schooldays.

A couple of years ago, Chancellor Mynydd had put forth a bill to expand the ferry service so children in the fishermen's cove could cross the river to get to the new school. He wanted the town to pay for their ferry tickets. His bill passed by one vote. Really, said the magistrates, who cares if those people go to school? They don't need an education to do what they do. But Mynydd had badgered enough people to get the bill passed. Now he was whispering here and there his plans for a wider bridge over the Nolta River, and maybe a park on Lake Arum, upriver from the bay.

"I'm going to ask the town to buy some land out there," he advised his factor. "We could make a nice park where people can picnic on Sundays. If Korsakov is smart, he'll expand his ferry business and run pleasure boats up to the lake. People are starting to get interested in building houses along the Arum River. I got three applications from those Europeans who moved here to escape the smallpox epidemic. They'll pay a hefty tax. Those river properties could turn out to be prime real estate."

Some of those Europeans were Flemish weavers. Mynydd immediately put two of them to work. Anne d'Inquierre, unwilling to let Mynydd go unchallenged, began training three more local women to help her with the dying of fabrics. Her workshop was very crowded but she couldn't afford a bigger place. She had just spent all she had to buy thirty Spanish Assaf sheep.

She spent much less time at the lighthouse. Nowadays she saw Vladimir Mynydd three or four times a week, at animal auctions, at the newly-improved market square, down at the shops along the waterfront. He never failed to greet her. She never failed to snub him.

One night, shortly after Kai's thirteenth birthday, he and Anne were at the table, just finishing dinner.

"Sheep?" Kai wailed. "Now you want more sheep? Why do we need more? We're already over-run with them."

"It's just something I have been thinking about. Don't worry, it won't happen overnight. But we have to start saving money so I can buy more land up in the hills."

Land up in the hills. Bigger herds of sheep. Two things Kai had no appreciation for. That was practically all his mother ever thought about lately. But, for the next two days, the conversation kept coming back to his mind. His mother was almost obsessed with buying land but did not have the money. One day an idea reared up inside his head, a bad idea, a terrible idea. In fact, he hated it with all his heart. But Ema was his mother. He didn't like to see her looking sad all the time, and as all the world knows, if you can do something to make your mother happy, you generally try to see that it gets done. Or die trying.

So one day after school, he sat down in the kitchen to wait for her. The solstice was a little over a month away and darkness fell early. She was up in the tower, checking the tallow candles. They burned quickly. At least twice a night, one or the other of them had to go up to the tower to replace them. It was one of Kai's least favorite jobs, lighting those dirty, horrible-smelling candles.

When he heard his mother's step on the stairs, he set a small wooden chest on the table. He felt ill. He would regret this. He knew he would regret this.

"What is that old thing?" she asked when she came in.

He sighed. "I found this a long time ago in Teron's cave."

"The cave? I forgot about that place. What is this?"

"Open it."

Anne gasped. She dropped into a chair.

"I showed it to Teron the day I found it. It was just the day before – before he left. We were going to tell you about it. Then we – I forgot."

"Did he put it there?"

"He thought pirates or smugglers hid it. I was the one who found it under a rock. He said the coins were old. They're real gold."

"Yes. I see that."

Kai hesitated. This gold would turn their fates down a path he did not want to tread. Not at all. But he went ahead. "Teron told me this gold belonged to me, because I found it. But you can have it, Ema. All of it."

He hadn't seen her face light up that way in so long. He tried to smile when she jumped up to hug him. He knew now that he would never be able to go to the university in the south. Below another sky, one faraway day he could have been studying for classes and meeting people and doing all kinds of interesting things. That was a sky that he would never see. Instead, here he would always be, day after day, here on Parrot Island. The same routines, day after day. He would be stuck on this island forever.

Antique gold coins were useless to Anne unless she could find someone to buy them. She asked Freya Button if she knew anyone in Lunenfarne who would be interested in them.

"No one," said Freya. "No one here would give you what they're worth. You'll have to take them to Bellesunde."

"But that's so far away," complained Anne. "And I don't know anyone there."

"We do some business there. Both my ships are heading for Bellesunde soon. *Vixen* will take you. One of my girls will help you find a dealer."

Freya employed a bevy of pretty young women. She claimed they were hired to wait on the customers. That claim was the truth, and if there were more to this truth, you would never hear about it from Freya.

"Georgiana!" Freya called. One of these women, pretty as a sugarplum, crossed the room now. Freya told her, "Anne wants to do some business in Bellesunde and she needs to be shown around the town. Can you escort her there before the weather turns nasty?"

"I'd be happy to. We were just saying it would be worthwhile for both *Vixen* and *Wolf* to head south one more time this fall." Georgiana smiled at Anne. "We've been hearing about a pair of Spanish galleons that are traveling together. If they are still in port, we can do some ...." She looked sideways at Freya. "Some trading. That sailor I chatted with last night was bragging about all the valuable cargo they're carrying."

"But there might be pirates," Anne said. "Everyone's been talking about pirates. If you bring back a load of merchandise and you're attacked by the Black George –"

"You never have to worry about the Black George while you're with us, I guarantee you. You'll be the safest passenger on the high seas."

"Your ship can outrun him?"

"Effortlessly."

"We'll have protection?"

"The best. The very best."

"You'll be gone for a while, Anne. What about the lighthouse?" Freya Button asked. "Do you think Kai will be able to tend it while you're gone?"

"He knows what to do. If there's a storm –"

"If there's a storm, I'll send someone out to be with him." Freya handed Anne a goblet of wine. "Have a drink. And don't worry. The *Vixen* will get you down to Bellesunde and back in three, four weeks at the most."

Kai was in a state of terror, worried that his mother would not return, that pirates would get her, that a storm would destroy the ship. But Anne was in good hands. They made good time to Bellesunde. Georgiana took her to the guild hall, introduced her to some merchants, and left her to wander about the city on her own for three days. *Vixen* and *Wolf*, Georgiana explained, had that business with Spanish traders to take care of.

Bellesunde! Anne had never seen a place like it. She had never imagined a city so large, so dignified, so beautiful. Lunenfarne seemed squalid in comparison. Here, tall buildings of golden stone were reflected in the canals that threaded the city. Boats in bright colors taxied up and down the waterways. Bells tolled from a cathedral whose windows in the evening glowed magically in brilliant colors. Anne figured she must have stared at that church window for a good ten minutes on her first evening there. Down the street, a wide market square festooned with striped awnings sold goods from far and wide, and the fountain in the square was either a necessary amenity or an excuse to display giant sculptures, Anne couldn't decide which.

To walk for three days amidst such beauty – what a difference it made to her frame of mind. She followed a walkway up to the university's noble buildings atop the hill. Teron had studied here and strolled these gracious lawns and sat beneath these leafy trees and walked under these colonnaded porticos. Anne found the library and stepped inside. She was awestruck. It was so quiet, she could hear students turning their pages and scratching their pens across paper. She stood by the entrance, afraid to step into such a place. She had never seen so many books, stacked on shelf after shelf, two stories high. A balcony circled the entire room and rows of massive tables ranged across the wide-tiled floor. How had Teron found anything in Lunenfarne at all appealing, after growing up in a place like this? Perhaps there was something after all to the vision that Vladimir Mynydd had for their town. Perhaps this was what he had in mind. If she hadn't made this trip, she would never have understood.

Anne's upbringing had been among people who did have an eye for beauty, but she realised for the first time that innovation was not something that interested them. A girl making a lovely water jug was copying her grandmother's grandmother's water jug. Her people respected tradition above all else. They vowed that, whatever their ancestors did not do, neither would they. They changed nothing. They didn't dare change anything. But how narrow that seemed to Anne now, how pointless, to refuse the chance to improve, to miss out on creating all this. These buildings, these parks, and waterways! She wished Kai could see this place.

It came to her then, that the gold she was selling could have paid for Kai to go to school here. That thought struck her very hard. Was she being foolish, or worse, selfish? She must make it up to him someday. She must and she would. Somehow, she would. It meant that she would have to work hard. She would have to double her investment so he could study in this wonderful place.

Anne sold her gold easily and three days later, she was back aboard the *Vixen*. They were home before the end of the month. They returned with a load of spices, ebony, silks, and pearls, all commodities that could be stored for the winter in Freya's warehouses until spring trading picked up again. Apparently, thought Anne, the *Vixen* and the *Wolf* had managed after all to do some business with a Spanish ship.

"Isn't is odd that Spanish ships were here in the north so late in the year?" Anne asked Georgiana when the *Vixen* returned to Lunenfarne.

"They were waiting to meet with other traders who were heading south for the winter. They feel safer traveling in groups."

"It was lucky you caught up with them."

"Not really luck. We keep an eye out for them, especially the Spaniards."

"Why the Spaniards?"

"A few old grudges, you might say." Georgiana laughed. "And they make it so easy."

"Make what easy?"

"When they pass through here, it's so easy to get Spanish sailors to talk about what cargo their ships are carrying." Getting sailors to talk. That was actually what Freya paid her to do.

"Why don't you just buy their merchandise when they are docked here, instead of chasing them all the way to Bellesunde?"

"If I told you that, my dear Anne, I'd have to kill you."

"What?" Anne paused, trying to puzzle that one out. "But Georgiana, I would think the Spaniards would avoid the north when pirate ships are lurking around."

Georgiana shrugged. "The whole world is dangerous. Not just the north."

"All the merchants I talked to in Bellesunde were saying they were petrified of the Black George. Weren't you afraid?" Anne asked.

"Us? Maybe a little."

"Did you see any pirates?"

"We did. Nothing we couldn't handle." Georgiana wagged her finger. "By the way, this alum I procured for you? Remember, if anyone asks you about it, you don't know where it came from. We don't want to have to pay taxes on that stuff."

"Where did it come from, Georgiana?" Anne asked suspiciously.

"I told you. From that Spanish ship. Ah, I wish you could have seen all those big Spanish sailors. Every one a Don Juan! Beautiful men. But black-hearted. Heartless as stones." She grinned.

"Keep that always in mind," interrupted Freya.

"I do, Freya. I do." Georgiana sobered. "I always wonder how something so nice to look at can be so evil."

"Evil?" Anne waited to hear more, but nothing else was forthcoming. "You must have paid a fortune for all that cargo," she finally said.

"Not a centavo."

"You didn't pay anything?"

"Not a centavo more than it was worth."

"You struck a good deal with them?"

Georgiana lifted her brows. "Oh, we struck! We struck, I would say, a very good deal." She laughed impudently and flounced out of the room.

By the time winter set in, Anne had purchased a hundred more acres in the hills using the money from the gold coins. Mynydd had gotten wind of her interest in the land and bid against her, but she won. Afraid, then, that she had paid too much, she became convinced that he had driven the price up on purpose. Nothing made her more angry than the thought of Vladimir Mynydd getting the better of her. In revenge, she managed to hire another weaver away from him. It meant she needed to rent some warehouse space from Freya Button until she could afford to get a bigger workshop built. But if it made trouble for Vladimir Mynydd, it was worth it.

By now, Anne's wool business took so much of her time that she left most of the lighthouse duties to Kai. Actually, he had been able to run the lighthouse by himself since he was twelve years old. Anne rowed out there to help him whenever a storm was brewing but otherwise, Kai d'Inquierre was the keeper of the light on Parrot Island.

Season followed season and Kai's loathing of the lighthouse tasks did not diminish. Summer storms saw him dragging the boat off the beach time and again, to rescue stranded sailors, to do what he could for foundered vessels, to move buoys. When winters clasped the land with iron fists, Kai rowed himself through the icy chop of the bay every morning and didn't miss a day of school. He was tall now, almost two heads taller than his mother, on a diet of fish, lamb chops, garden greens, and sheeps' cheeses. He grew broad-shouldered from rowing across the bay in all weathers. But he never got enough sleep. He carried not an ounce of fat, having to climb one hundred thirty-nine steps to the top of the tower at least twice every night. Then he was up early snuffing the candles and cleaning up wax, polishing glass, and filling the molds to make new candles before he left for school.

Spring came, the next-to-last spring of Kai's school days. After next year, he forsaw nothing for himself but endless rounds of tasks and a lonely life at the lighthouse.

At school, Sister Angelica had given them an assignment. Working in pairs, they were to take a couple of afternoons off from class to study the new local building projects and prepare to debate their value. Under the ministry of Vladimir Mynydd, there had been many improvements in the village. Some townsfolk felt they were wonderful. Some said they had no need of a better school building or a park on Lake Arum. The old Nolta River bridge had been perfectly safe. The new one was a waste of money. The people who lived in the mansions in the hills deeply resented Mynydd for emptying the town coffers on projects that cost so much money. Sister Angelica asked her students to consider both sides of these arguments.

Gregor was excited by the class's new assignment. "Let's go to the boardwalk," he said to Kai. "You can talk to some shopkeepers and write up the research and I'll make pencil sketches of all the new storefronts. We can compare them to the drawings I made a couple of years ago, before they tore down the old buildings."

The weather was mild and dry and the students were eager to be outdoors. So while Kai talked to Mr. Basko about the trials at his new grocery and Mr. Wunder about the tribulations in his bakery, Gregor sat on a bench on the new boardwalk and began to sketch. As always when he was drawing, he was absorbed completely in what he was doing.

"Hi."

He started. A girl he'd never seen before was standing in front of him.

She smiled. "Hello. Did I startle you? I – sorry to be a bother – I was just wondering what you are drawing. Can I see?"

Gregor blushed. "O – okay."

"Very nice. Wonderful! You're a real artist."

"I just, you know, just started. Just now. This is just, you know, silly stuff." He couldn't look at the girl but she smelled very nice.

"It is not silly."

"Mmm." Gregor wondered why she didn't walk away.

"I like to draw too," she said. " You wouldn't mind, would you, if I – could I – could I sit here for a minute? I'll try not to bother you."

"Oh. Sure. I don't mind."

She sat down. His pencil reacted immediately, leaping out of his fingers like a hyperactive frog who'd breakfasted on two Turkish coffees and a bar of dark chocolate. Gregor bent to retrieve it.

"Oh dear," she laughed. "I said I wouldn't bother you, but I guess I do. Sorry.'"

"No, it's no bo – bother."

"I was just wondering. Are you doing this drawing for school or what? Just for fun?"

"Yeah, school."

"So you go?" She pointed. "To that school?"

"Yeah."

"That's nice. You're lucky. I wish I could go."

"Yeah?"

"I've got this governess. She is absolutely rigid, I tell you. She would never think of assigning something enjoyable like this."

"No?"

"In fact, she doesn't even want me out here by myself. She thinks I'm at my grandma's right now."

"Oh."

"So, why did your teacher ask you to do this project? What's the purpose?"

"It's cuz, well see, the, uh, the chancellor has made all these –"

"Lord Mynydd?"

"Yeah. Him."

"I know him."

"You do?"

"My father works for him."

"Yeah?" Gregor wished he could think of a response that sounded less feeble.

"Daddy does Lord Mynydd's accounting. He has for several years now. I'm Florri, by the way. Florri Fairhedd."

"Hi."

"What's your name?"

"Uh, Gregor."

"So you were saying? You're studying some of these new building projects?" She laughed.

"Yep."

"Personally, I think the new buildings made a real difference."

"Yeah, improvements, yeah they're, they're good."

"I mean, any improvement is better than nothing, right?"

"Yeah." Gregor tried a laugh. Awkward, awkward.

"Well." Florri looked at her lap, twisted one of the rings on her fingers. "I suppose I'd better go before I get into trouble." She stood up.

Gregor did not stand. He knew he would move clumsily and end up floundering like a beached fish. But he allowed himself a brief glance at this girl. Her brown hair hung down her back like silk, her eyes dark blue, her dress mint green, her sash emerald. He painted her in his mind. Damn, she was beautiful.

"Will you be here tomorrow, Gregor? Maybe I can bring my sketch pad and we can draw together."

"Oh. Well, oh. Okay."

"You can probably give me lots of pointers, right?"

"Right."

"You're sure I wouldn't distract you or anything?"

"No. Nope."

Florri laughed. "No, I would distract you, or no, I wouldn't?"

"No. Yes." Gregor bit his lip, confused. "I don't – it would be nice to – yes, come."

"You're sure?"

He nodded.

"I will then. About this time?"

"Sure. Sure."

"Wonderful. It was very nice meeting you. See you tomorrow."

"Okay." Gregor watched her all the way down the boardwalk. He never took his eyes off her until she disappeared. "Bye Florri," he said, when she'd been long gone. Then he began to wonder if she had been just a figment of his imagination. She must have been. How could such a girl be real? Florri. Florri Fairhedd. She had actually talked to him. She sat beside him. Right here. She said she'd come –

"Hey!"

Gregor looked up. Now Kai had materialized in front of him.

"Didn't you hear me calling you?"

"Uh uh."

"You haven't gotten much done out here."

"I'm coming back tomorrow. To finish."

"I don't know if Sister will let us out of class tomorrow."

"I'm coming anyway."

"Wow. You mean Saint Gregor is going to break a rule and skip out of school?"

Saint Gregor feigned illness and left school the next afternoon. He limped, as fast as he was able, down to the boardwalk along the waterfront. He wanted to get there before Florri did, but she was already seated on the bench. She saw him and waved.

He wanted to die right then. It would all be ruined when she saw what a gimp he was. He should turn around and leave. He could hardly bring himself to go toward her, he was so humiliated. Then, somehow, he found himself there, by her bench. But he couldn't bear to look at her face.

"Hi! I got here a little early. Sit with me." She patted the bench.

"Tell me what you think of my sketch."

Hadn't she seen him? His limp? His pathetic bony body?

"Now tell me the truth, Gregor. I mean, this is not finished yet. Of course you can see that. But am I on the right track?" She looked at him when he didn't answer. She folded her arm along the back of the bench. "Gregor? You think it's awful, don't you?"

"No. I like it."

"Really? Be honest, now. Come on. I won't take it personally."

"Well, you could try varying your strokes. Use some longer, bolder strokes here."

"Ah. I see. Darken this part."

"You want to have a center of interest, right? Direct the eye?"

"You're right! I knew you'd have some good ideas. Thank you."

An hour slipped by but their pencils had been inactive for some time. Florri leaned toward Gregor, talking a mile a minute, her hand touching his arm now and then. Eventually Gregor found the courage to look into her blue eyes and felt stupid with happiness.

They arranged to meet again a couple of days later. They sketched, yes, but there was more talking than drawing. On that day, only after Florri looked up suddenly did Gregor notice Kai had joined them. He felt his insides go cold. Kai, so tall and strong, so good looking.

"Hello," Kai said.

"Hi." Florri looked at Gregor. "This is a friend of yours?" she asked.

"Yeah."

"Well? Are you going to introduce us?"

"Kai. This is Kai d'Inquierre."

"Hello. I'm Florri. I think Gregor has mentioned you."

"In glowing terms, I hope." Kai sat down. Gregor was relieved to find himself seated in the middle. Maybe he wouldn't be entirely left out of the conversation.

"I haven't heard Gregor speak ill of anyone. Maybe that's one reason I enjoy his company so much." Florri touched her hand lightly to Gregor's. "He's one of the nicest people I've ever met."

"Oh yeah, old Gregor here is a real sweetie pie. How did you two meet?"

After that, it was often the three of them, meeting after school on that bench. But the best times were when Kai had to get back to the lighthouse and Gregor had Florri all to himself. Some days they met on the boardwalk. On another day, Florri showed Gregor an arbor in the garden behind the town hall. It was a magical place back in the trees, almost hidden behind clumps of lilies and climbing roses. They went there sometimes to sketch the flowers or just talk. Lilies and roses and Florri – one always brought the other to Gregor's mind.

Gregor was waiting for Florri one afternoon when she came hurrying down the boardwalk.

"Guess what!" she gushed. "When Mummy saw the sketches I've been working on, she was so impressed she said I can come here any afternoon I want. I don't have to sneak out anymore. She really thinks my drawing has improved since I've known you. Well, to tell you the truth, Mummy thinks you're a girl. I told her a girlfriend is here with me. Heaven help me if she finds out I lied. Ha! As if I had a girlfriend."

"You don't?"

"I don't know what's the matter with me. I've never been able to find a friend, not a real one. Not among the girls who live near me. You're lucky to have a friend like Kai."

"I know. We've been friends since we were little."

Florri opened her sketch book. "I'm going to draw the lighthouse today."

Chattering on, she did not notice a carriage stop in the street above. Ludmila Fairhedd had spotted her daughter sitting on the boardwalk, not with a girlfriend, but with a boy. Ludmila rested her chin on her hand and watched them for several minutes, a smile on her face. They were joined by another boy. She watched the three of them laughing and teasing together. She could remember herself at that age, and she had a sudden memory of a certain boy, the boy she had been wild about back then. So happy in those days. Ah, but that was a long time ago. Ludmila had been worried about her daughter. She was glad now to see her socializing. Playful, laughing, enjoying the very short years of her youth. Satisfied, Ludmila sat back against the cushions and called for her driver to walk on.

Another person watched Florri that day, too. Dort Mynydd had just stormed out of his father's office in the sourest of moods. He and his father had argued bitterly. Vladimir, accusing him of wanton behavior? Furious, Dort retorted with accusations about his father's inappropriate feelings for that gypsy woman at the lighthouse. He was dredging up the past, but he could think of nothing else in a hurry. Why, why was he saddled with such ridiculous parents? Both his parents were beyond ludicrous. Natalia Mynydd had lately become infatuated with some gypsy soothsayer, probably from the same disgusting tribe as that savage, Anne d'Inquierre.

Dort leapt into his cabriolet, jerking the reins angrily. Then his eye was caught by a pretty figure. Someone new in town? Fresh meat! His interest spiked. He pulled to the side of the street. Wait. He knew that girl. What was she doing out unchaperoned? Her father had worked for his family for a long time. He also recognized one of the boys she was talking with. Kai d'Inquierre, that slob, that lighthouse creep. He had always hated that jerk. Where did he get the nerve to sit in public with the likes of Florri Fairhedd? He was actually flirting with her. He was probably in love with her. And look at the way she was behaving, leaning in a very familiar way against some other boy, the three of them laughing together. He could not believe she was associating with that low life scum. Her behavior was embarrassing. Dort resented it, tied as she was to his family. This was not right. He would speak to her father. She needed to be reined in. He would see to it.

And then a thought bloomed in his mind and a very drastic idea took shape: maybe it was time he married. Today's disagreement with his father had put him in a rebellious mood. If he were to marry, what a bombshell it would be. Vladimir could hardly call him wanton then. His father had once asked him if he had any marriage prospects and Dort had laughed about that with Natalia, his mother. Marriage, she had cried, at his tender age? What was her idiot husband thinking? Her baby, not even twenty years old yet, was too young to leave the nest. Ha, Dort had thought. If only she knew what her baby did most evenings.

He had never considered marrying. But now? The idea, radical as it was, looked more attractive the longer he thought about it. As a married man he would have an excuse for wanting to take over the reins of power in the family, or at least some of the power. That was suddenly a very attractive image.

There was the added satisfaction of pissing off that asshole Kai d'Inquierre. Dort would surely enjoy breaking up his little romance with

Florri Fairhedd.

Yes, it was decided that quickly. All he had to do was to tell Florri's father what was going to happen and it would be done. Florri was how old? Fourteen or fifteen? Too old to be flirting in public with those gutter rats! It was demeaning.

Yes. I will marry her, Dort decided. She would make an appropriate wife. He would have something nice-looking hanging on his arm. There were times when a man needed that. She was a little below his station, and probably dumb as a doorknob, but that was just as well. Her inferiority was an ace in his hand.

Marriage. He would see to it immediately.

It took surprisingly little to convince Ruslan Fairhedd that his daughter's honor was in tatters. Did Ruslan realise she was often seen in public with that gypsy charlatan, Kai d'Inquierre? That she was unchaperoned and obviously intimate, very intimate with him? Dort told Florri's father that he was deeply ashamed, for both their families' sakes. That girl should be given in marriage before she got herself in trouble and ruined all their reputations. As a business associate, and even more as a long-time friend, Dort said he cared deeply for the Fairhedd family. His advice to Ruslan was to find Florri a husband as quickly as possible. That was the only solution. Dort hated to see such a lovely girl behaving so badly. Did the Fairhedd family have the wherewithal to offer a generous dowry? Because they would have to pay well, given Florri's wanton ways. Did they know of anyone, any friend of the family who could be convinced to take this compromised girl as a bride?

Dort let Ruslan Fairhedd spend a night agonizing about his daughter.

The next day he told Ruslan that he, too, had thought the matter over carefully. He might be willing to propose himself as the best person to marry Florri, to save her reputation, to save her parents from a hideous embarrassment. Yes, he could step in to avert calamity, though if he were to offer this extraordinary gesture of friendship, the Fairhedds would have to make his sacrifice worthwhile.

To a father who was sick with worry, a large dowry seemed precious little to ask.

A bank of formidable grey clouds loomed up from beyond the mountains and came rolling down to the bay like an advancing army. Swollen with rain, they broke open with a deafening clap of thunder. Gregor hunched next to the bench on the boardwalk. Cold drops pelted his shoulders. The rain meant he would not see Florri that day. How could he last all day without seeing her? He glanced around, hopeless. Parrot Island was only a blurred smudge tossed on the waters of the dark bay. Wind blew spray off the tops of the waves and soon the boardwalk was slick with rain. Gregor, in despair, was about to turn away when he noticed a small piece of paper fluttering between the slats of the bench. He plucked it out.

A note. "The arbor"

Gregor smiled. She would come through the rain to see him? He hobbled as fast as he could to the little park between the school and the municipal offices. The roses on the arbor wept raindrops and hung their heads. He ducked inside and Florri jumped from the shadows. She grabbed him by the arms. Alarmed, he saw that she had been crying.

"What's the matter?"

"Oh Gregor." She wrapped her arms tight around him. Startled, he dropped the canvas bag he carried and embraced her. She wept into his coat and he stroked her hair. He kissed the top of her head. She raised her face to him, took his head between her hands, and pressed her lips to his. He was flooded with a joy he had never known.

She pulled away a little, then kissed him again. Finally she grasped his arm as though she would never let go. "Sit here. Sit here with me."

"What is it, Florri?"

She started to cry again and leaned her head on his shoulder. "I can't believe this is happening to me. How can this be? Just when I was so happy."

"What? What?"

She put her face close to his, her hand on his cheek. "My father. He has arranged for me to marry. He told me last night."

"What? Marry?" The world tilted. "Marry! Who –?"

"Dort Mynydd." She sobbed uncontrollably. "Oh Gregor! What can I do?"

"Marry Dort Mynydd? Why? Your father arranged this? Did you want to marry him?"

"Are you kidding? How could I ever want to marry such a person? I would rather die!"

"Don't ever say that!"

"No, I would rather die. What am I going to do?"

"You have to run away. Leave! Don't let them find you!"

"Run away."

"You could live at our house. We could even –"

"No. No, no. Run away from my parents? How could I do that to them?"

"Why? Why not, Florri?"

"My mother? I couldn't. My father – he would be so upset."

"Does that matter?"

"I've already disappointed him because I – I've been too – too loose, he said. I didn't mean to be. I embarrassed him. I didn't realise how worried he's been. He is afraid that I will never find a suitable husband."

"A rich husband.That's what you mean, isn't it?"

Florri shook her head. "He said I'm too naive. And he's right. He thinks I'll end badly unless he chooses a husband for me."

"End badly?" That was the final blow. Gregor knew exactly what her father meant. "Doesn't he care how you feel?" he asked quietly.

"Yes, I know he cares. But he wants – he wants me to marry well. It's important to him."

"What about you? What's important to you?"

"I don't know. He's probably right. I'm not smart. I'm not sophisticated. I don't know anything about the world."

"He said that?"

She nodded. "He's probably right."

"Florri, you can't marry Dort Mynydd!"

"Please, please understand, Gregor."

"I don't understand."

"More than anything, I don't want you to be mad at me. Kiss me again?"

Nothing Gregor could say would change Florri's mind. He sagged back on the bench. The air, heavy with damp, seemed too thick to breathe. Thunder rumbled away over the hills and the wet walkway shone silver.

They left the arbor holding hands.

"Florri, you won't – ?"

Florri slowly shook her head.

"I'm begging you one last time. You won't even think about standing up for what you want?"

"My parents know what's best for me." Their fingers untangled. "I'm too ignorant. I have to trust them, Gregor."

How fleeting, their time of happiness. Nothing left but memories. They stood apart, eyes fastened on the ground. Florri took a hesitant step. Gregor turned his back, unable to bear the sight of her walking away. She left him standing alone on the boardwalk.

Two months later, news of the wedding brought the whole town out for a glimpse of the young couple. Florri was a vision in lace. Dort was the most handsome man in all Lunenfarne. They couldn't be more suited to each other, everyone agreed, everyone except two or three young ladies, friends of Dort's, whose noses were distinctly out-of-joint. And except, of course, for Gregor, who rowed out to Parrot Island so he would be as far as he could get from the festivities.

The wedding reception was lavish. At first, Dort was so gallant to his new bride that half the women there burned with envy. He made it up to them all, as best he could, when the orchestra began playing. Dort danced every dance. He was so busy playing the part of enchanting man-of-the-hour, he never got around to dancing with his bride. A few elderly ladies came to make a fuss over Florri, taking her mind off Dort. A few of Dort's old girlfriends stood in a knot nearby, whispering that she was definitely a cold fish not exactly the life of the party and whatever did he see in her? Late in the evening, Florri's mother, Ludmila, looked up to see Vladimir Mynydd sitting next to Florri at the banquet table. Just the two of them. They seemed to be a having a subdued little chat. Ludmila searched the room with her eyes. Dort was nowhere in sight. When Florri's new father-in-law left her side, her daughter sat alone for several minutes. Ludmila Fairhedd excused herself to the people at her table and went to sit next to her.

Natalia Mynydd, Dort's mother, was suddenly beside them. Ludmila Fairhedd's gentle manner never failed to make Natalia prickly. "I spoke with Dort a few minutes ago," she said, all in a rush. "Florri is to come home with me."

"Well, that's a little strange, isn't it, Natalia?" Ludmila asked. "On her wedding night?"

"Dort is busy, attending to something important."

"Florri has been sitting here alone for almost the entire –"

"Business matters can't wait. You should know that, Ludmila. Florri is to wait for Dort at home."

Florri did wait. She waited in vain.

Her wedding night. How she had dreaded it. She sat alone on the end of a large richly furnished bed in a strange room. Finally, in the grey light of dawn, she rose, dropped her wedding gown to the floor, and got into bed. She was still wide awake when the bedroom door burst open. She sat up, startled, then rolled stiffly to the edge of the bed. Dort stumbled in and tore off his coat. He said not a word. Still fully dressed, he threw himself down beside her. Their backs to each other, he was asleep instantly.

My wedding night, Florri thought, the threshold of our married lives together. And I, untouched, alone.

She was still a virgin, the night that Florri left her girlhood behind.

Dort was out late most nights during the next week, if he came home at all.

He was busy, he explained, and expected her to understand, though when she said his absences didn't bother her at all, he was a bit taken aback. He had expected a tantrum, or at least a fight. He wouldn't admit it, but her indifference wounded his pride a little. He was not aware in the least that her indifference was a mirror of his own.

It took him a few days to realise that Florri had moved into a room of her own at the end of the hall.

A month after the wedding, as Gregor left school, he noticed a carriage parked by the playground. A servant in livery stopped him and handed him a note. He waited while Gregor read it. It was from Ludmila Fairhedd, Florri's mother, asking him to come for tea and bring his sketchbook. She was interviewing artists, the note said, and desired to commission someone to paint a mural on the wall of their reception hall. She had seen the sort of paintings she liked on a visit to a palazzo in Venice.

"May I drive you?" asked the servant, holding the door. Gregor mounted the step awkwardly, inside a carriage for the first time in his life.

They drove along Hill Road and he was let out in front of one of the smaller mansions. Mrs. Fairhedd was waiting for him in a comfortable sitting room. Gregor felt shaky. All he could think about was Florri. Florri had lived here. Florri had been in this room countless times. Florri used to sit in these chairs. He coudn't help but notice some of the beautiful paintings on the wall. He noticed, too, how beautiful Mrs. Fairhedd was, sitting on the rose-colored chesterfield in a soft blue gown. She looked like her daughter, so like her daughter. He noticed little else.

The lady smiled at him. "Mr. Treyse. I am told you were – are a friend of my daughter's."

Gregor hesitated, then nodded.

"She tells me you are quite the artist. Can I see some of your work?"

Gregor clasped his sketchpad. "I can't … maybe I could prepare some drawings that would be more, um, appropriate. These are not, um, not my best."

Ludmila Fairhedd held out her hand. "I don't need formal drawings. I just want to get an idea of what you do. Let me see what you have there."

"They're not very good," he said, panicking, clutching the sketchpad harder to his chest. "They're not my best."

"Let me be the judge." Her ringed fingers beckoned for his pad of paper.

He handed it over, his head hanging, sickened.

Mrs. Fairhedd opened the book to the first page. "Oh, how sweet! Hmm, nice," she smiled and sighed. She turned another page and another, slowly, poring over every drawing. Page after page, she looked at every sheet in the entire book. Gregor wished he could disappear. Without being invited, he sank into a chair.

"These are all —" She fanned the pages. "These are all sketches of Florri."

Gregor said nothing.

Ludmila Fairhedd's lips began to tremble. What had they done, she and her husband?

"May I have one of these?" she asked softly. She dabbed at her eyes with her handkerchief. "Would you mind, Mr. Treyse? This one, maybe?"

"Um. Well. All right." He really balked at giving away a single drawing of Florri. They were all he had left. But what else could he say?

"Thank you. Now, I asked you here because — I — I'd like to offer you a job, Mr. Treyse. Painting some scenery on my wall, there in the vestibule. Would that interest you at all?"

"Here?" The house where Florri lived. Used to live.

"Do you know the style I mean? A classical scene, something of that kind?"

He nodded.

"I can have some scaffolding erected. I know it's not easy for you to climb a ladder."

He didn't know what to say.

"Please. I think you might be … you might consider this a sort of … an opportunity." She watched his reaction. "I will pay you well, of course. Say you'll come to work here this summer. Please? Afternoons would be best. I won't be around to bother you, and my husband will be at his office. He'll never know – anything."

"Afternoons?" This was all so unexpected.

Ludmila smiled then. "Or any time that suits you. Can I tell Florri you'll do this for us? She likes your work very much. She will be so pleased. She's been … not quite herself lately. It's disturbing how ... maybe this will ...." She couldn't finish the sentence. What had they done?

Gregor hardly heard her anyway. Florri. It made his heart pound even harder, just hearing someone say her name.

Gregor spent the first few afternoons that summer making sketches to show Mrs. Fairhedd.

"I really like this one, Gregor. Do you mind if I call you Gregor? These colors you've chosen – so subtle. Exactly what I had in mind."

"I'm glad, Mrs. Fairhedd."

"So that's settled? We've made a decision. Now, all right." She rose hastily, suddenly flustered. "I'm sorry. Can you excuse me for a moment? I forgot to give my cook some instructions about dinner. Wait right here."

After she'd gone, Gregor heard the door behind him open, heard the rustle of a gown. He raised his head. He smelled her perfume. He turned quickly and she was in his arms a second later.

"Florri."

"Shh. Don't talk. Just hold me. It's all right. Mother won't let anyone come in."

All summer long, Gregor painted in the mornings. After lunch, Florri's carriage would appear in the drive. They would spend a couple of hours together, usually in her old bedroom, even, dangerously, a couple of times in the sitting room. Then she would have to leave and he, dizzy with pleasure, would force himself to get back to his work. Sometimes he could hardly direct his paintbrush, he was so distracted.

"Doesn't your husband wonder where you go in the afternoons?" he asked Florri one day.

"Dort thinks I'm visiting my ailing mother."

"Your mother is a wonderful lady, but I wish her a long bout of this imaginary illness."

"Besides, Dort doesn't give a fig. He has other interests. His mother questions my comings and goings more than he does."

Finally, one day, Florri moaned when she entered the vestibule and saw the work Gregor had done.

"What?" he asked, alarmed.

"Can't you paint more slowly? You're nearly finished."

Laughing, he pulled her up the stairs. "Don't worry. I haven't even started on the flowers."

"You're adding flowers?"

"Flowers everywhere. Then birds. All kinds of birds. Bugs." He wiggled his fingers. "A little snake."

But finally, inevitably, it was done. Finally the mural was finished. He had drawn its progress out as long as he could. The best times of his life were now over. He and Florri had known each other for only a few months. Now the summer was gone and it was the end for them.

One last time they parted, this time for good. Florri put her hands on her waist. "I think you've left someone in here, Gregor. Someone for me to love. I will very badly need someone to love."

"A child?" He tried to steady himself. The thought nearly knocked him over. A child of his. Then, a thought still more devastating, a child of his growing up to believe Dort was his father? "A child of mine? And I will never know him? I won't, will I?"

"We will meet now and then, you and I. We have to. At the market, at the fair. You will meet her. Or him."

"Your husband, though. It could be your husband's child. Couldn't it." The thought revolted him. Gregor was trembling.

"Well, let me just say that I had to throw myself at him a couple of weeks ago, only because I suspected I was pregnant."

"What are you talking about?"

"He hardly ever touches me. Now he'll think he's the father."

"All summer? He hardly touches you?"

She shook her head. "He's busy elsewhere. I guess he doesn't find me attractive."

He took her hand and laced her fingers with his. "I hate to think of him treating you like dirt."

"He doesn't mistreat me. Mostly, he ignores me. It's better that way."

Gregor groaned. "A baby of ours? Calling that man his father? That makes me sick."

"Someday, when she's old enough, I'll tell her about her real father and – you know, Gregor, maybe someday –"

"Yes." Not thinking, he twisted the wedding ring on her finger. "Maybe someday, Florri." Someday. He would cling to that. 'Maybe someday' was all he had. In the meantime, Florri would have a little person to be with her. He would have no one. They each considered the other to be the fortunate one.

In the next months, from Mrs. Fairhedd's recommendations, Gregor received two more commissions at other mansions in the hills. Wealthy patrons were competing for his talents. They made a great fuss over him. When he finished a project, people would invite him to their gatherings so they could show him off beside their new murals. He went to these parties always hoping for a glimpse of Florri. A couple of times he saw Dort, squiring some lady or other. He seemed to go out of his way to give Gregor the cold shoulder. But Florri never came. He did see her occasionally in town. He would feel her sad eyes holding him, but they never spoke.

In later times, a young woman could be seen on any sunny day pushing a pram along the boardwalk, and a few months later holding the hand of a swaying toddler; a couple of years after that, keeping an eye on the antics of a little boy. Passers-by might wonder why she often paused to stare out at the lighthouse on Parrot Island. It seemed a fixed point on all her perambulations. Obviously she was a woman of privilege. What did she find so fascinating about the humble lighthouse? She and the child would stop for a time. Then they would pass on, pass quietly on their way.

When Kai and Gregor's last year of school began, Kai celebrated his sixteenth birthday. It was followed by Gregor's birthday, a couple of months later. School was not difficult but it took up a lot of Kai's day. Just rowing across the bay and back took time, especially in heavy winter weather. Fortunately he had grown to be strong, so very like, if only he knew it, his warrior father. Added to his studies were the daily rounds of cleaning duties in the lighthouse and the many nights of climbing the tower to check the candles. He had recently talked to a couple of ship captains, though, who told him of improvements they had seen in other lighthouses. Gas lights, instead of candles. If only they could get rid of the horrible tallow candles, what a relief it would be. Would Vladimir Mynydd help implement this idea? Maybe he could convince Mynydd that it would be worth the money.

Kai hurried along the avenue of shops, climbed some steps, and lifted the heavy brass latch on Mynydd's office door. He entered. A man he didn't know sat at a rosewood desk. Kai felt the man scrutinise him with undisguised disapproval.

"Is it possible to have a word with Lord Mynydd?" Kai asked him.

"Lord Mynydd is out." Ruslan Fairhedd knew who this young man was. That conniving scoundrel! Dort had warned him about this barbarian, this charlatan who had preyed on his poor innocent daughter, back before she was safely married. The Fairhedd family was so very fortunate that Dort had agreed to marry Florri, tainted as she was with scandal.

"Can you tell me when Lord Mynyyd will be back?" Kai asked.

"I do not know."

"Do you mind if I wait 'til he returns?"

"I don't expect him until tomorrow, actually."

"All right. Thank you. I'll come back then."

Kai returned the next day and was told the same thing. Lord Mynydd was out and wasn't expected back for the rest of the day.

When his mother rowed out to the lighthouse later that day, Kai vented his frustration.

"I've gone to Mynydd's office twice this week and been given the runaround."

"Mynydd's office? Why? Why in the world did you go there?" Anne hissed, cat-like. "How could you even stand to be in the same room with that horrible man? Look what he's done to our family."

"You don't know for sure that he turned Teron in to the authorities, Ema."

"Of course he did, Kai. You know he did."

"Maybe you assume too much. Whenever I've needed something, he couldn't be more cooperative."

"You have spoken to that man?"

"I went to him last year about getting the tower painted and he was extremely helpful."

"You didn't tell me you made that arrangement with him."

"I knew you would be angry."

"You're absolutely right. I am angry. How could you do that? Go behind my back like that?"

"The tower was a mess. The work had to get done. He saw to it immediately. He even came out here to make sure – "

"You allowed that man to step onto this island?"

"Ema, I –"

"Kai, I forbid you to speak to him again. Ever."

"I have to speak to him. We have to get new lamps, Ema. He can get them for us."

"What lamps?"

"They make lamps now that are so much easier than candles. I am sick to death of making candles and lighting candles and changing candles – two and three times a night every single night. Then in the morning I have to clean up the mess they make, wax everywhere, not to mention how unsafe –"

"It's the job! It's part of your job!"

"It wasn't supposed to be my job! It was supposed to be your job!" He was yelling now.

Anne turned away, head bent and hands grasping her elbows. She had nothing to say in her own defense. She had used her son. She knew she had, but it was for him that she was working so hard, running her businesses all by herself. So that someday Kai could go to school in Bellesunde.

Kai picked an apple from the bowl and twirled it by the stem. "I'm sorry, Ema."

She shook her head and spoke in a near-whisper. "I don't want you to speak to him. Vladimir Mynydd has ruined my life."

"I wouldn't say that. It looks to me like you have done pretty well for yourself in the years that Teron has been gone. Big new workshops, enough money to hire a shepherd. And how many head of sheep do you own now?"

"It's been hard work. Years of hard work." She sighed. "I'm so tired of it all. I wish I'd never come to this island." Did she really mean that? She sat down and pressed her fist to her lips. "Anyway. I came out here to tell you something." She bit her lip and looked up at him. "I'm selling."

"Selling? Selling what?"

"Selling everything. I have a buyer for the workshops. I'll have no trouble selling off the herds and land. Wido Treyse, Gregor's father, has saved some money. He wants to buy part of it."

Kai sat down, stunned. "I don't believe it."

Anne straightened and put her hands in her lap. "There's another thing. I'm going to Balgrim in the spring. I'm going to bring Teron home."

"Balgrim? But you can't make a trip like that by yourself! Ema, you don't even know if he's still alive. He – he could have been dead for years."

"He's not dead. I know he's not. As soon as they release him, I'm bringing him home. He will need me. He'll need someone to be with him, in case he's – I don't know. He could be crippled or injured or something. He may need someone to help him get home."

"But Balgrim! That's a long and dangerous trip. Who will take you there? You can't go alone."

"I will find someone. I will have plenty of money. I will find someone to take me there and bring us both home." She traced designs on the tabletop with a finger. "I am only sorry to be leaving you here. I know you are not happy on this island." She reached for his hand. "When we get back, you can go, if you want."

Kai tossed the apple uneaten back into the bowl. "Go? Where would I go? Nowhere, that's where."

"You could go to university. To Bellesunde." She was squeezing his hand until it hurt. "You've always wanted to go. Now you can. As soon as we get back. I promise. As soon as Teron and I get back."

"We'll see." Kai would not, would absolutely not allow himself to hope.

The next afternoon, when he had finished cleaning the mirrors behind the candles, when he had polished the windows in the tower and swept the floor, Kai rowed across the bay and tied up at the ferry dock. He waved to Korsakov, the ferryman.

"I'll only be an hour or so, Mr. Korsakov. Am I okay tied here?"

"Don't be long. There's weather comin', ya know."

"I'll be back soon."

Kai found the heavy oaken door to Mynyyd's office locked. He looked up toward the mansions in the foothills. It would be a three-mile walk to Mynydd's villa and it had begun to rain. He would go anyway. He couldn't put it off any longer. He jogged through the market square and began to trek the twisting River Road.

It was pouring by the time the road climbed the crest and turned along the hilltop ridge, but Hill Road was paved with stone, not running with mud, as below. Still, by the time he rang Mynydd's bell, he was soaked and filthy. A servant with raised eyebrows let him in and said he would see if Lord Mynydd could spare him a minute. While he waited, Kai stepped into the doorway of the vestibule. He looked down the hall. There was a large party in progress. He looked for Florri but didn't see her. Jewels twinkled in the candlelight and silks glowed with color. Maids in uniform circulated with trays of crystal goblets. Male servants lined the walls at attention. Kai, soaked and muddy, dared not step off the tile floor of the entryway for fear of dirtying the thick Turkish carpets.

Thankfully, he wasn't kept waiting long. Vladimir Mynydd came quickly down the hall toward him, his hand extended.

"Kai, it's good to see you."

"And you, sir."

"You're wet through and through. Let me get you a warm drink."

"No, no thank you."

"A dry coat, at least?"

"Thank you. I'll be fine."

"How is your mother? Is she all right? She refuses to speak to me, even after all this time, but these rumors I've been hearing? Rumors of her selling her lands. I hope this does not mean she is unwell."

"She is quite well. A bit weary, I think, is all."

"I wish her the best, in spite of what she thinks of me." Mynydd paused. "That man, the one she – he wasn't your father, but –"

"Teron Adante?"

"Yes. Have you heard from him? Or about him?"

"We have not had a single word in ten years. If he is still alive, he will be released in the next few months. In fact, my mother is insisting she will go to Balgrim to bring him home."

"That's a long trip. Will you go with her?"

"No, I can't. Someone has to run the lighthouse."

"But Balgrim! She can't possibly go there alone! Is that what she's planning?"

"That's what she intends, sir. I am trying to talk her out of it, but so far have had no success."

"Good lord, what a woman!" Mynydd smiled. "Forgive me, Kai, I didn't mean to sound impertinent."

"I know she is one of a kind, sir."

"She is indeed. I'm not ashamed to say how much I admire her." He paused again, lost in thought. "Ah, I'm negligent. I forgot to ask what it is that I can do for you today."

"I didn't mean to interrupt your festivities but –"

Mynydd laughed. "This is not really my party. My wife hosts these salons in the afternoon. You know, all the 'best' people and so forth. I am not sorry to have a few minutes respite."

"I tried to see you at your office. I was told you were unavailable."

"You were at my office? Fairhedd said nothing to me."

"I was there twice before today. Fairhedd? That wasn't Florri's father I talked to?"

"Probably. He's my factor. He started as my accountant and has somehow wormed his way to a more exalted position. So you know my daughter-in-law?"

"Florri? Yes, we were friends before – before she married. Really, she was my buddy's friend more than mine." Kai hesitated. "How is she? We haven't seen her in a long time."

Mynydd tipped his head from side to side. "It's been difficult for her. The pregnancy and all."

"Is she here today? Could I say 'hello'?"

"She hasn't come downstairs." Mynydd moved closer and spoke softly. "Tell me something, Kai. Before – was Florri always prone to – what I mean is, would you say she was unhappy, or troubled, or – or downcast much of the time?"

"Florri? No, never. I never saw her so. Bright as sunshine. She loved to laugh. And so kind. My buddy especially was, well, he was – he was always grateful for her friendship. We both enjoyed being with her, just kind of fooling around together."

"I see." Mynydd nodded. "I see. Aha."

"Will you tell her I asked after her?"

"I will. I certainly will."

"Father." Dort Mynydd's voice, interrupting, was a rebuke. He stayed to one side of the doorway. "What are you doing?"

Vladimir Mynydd turned. "I'll be with you in a minute, Dort."

"You have guests here."

"They won't miss me unless the champagne stops flowing. You remember Kai d'Inquierre, don't you, Dort?"

Dort stepped around his father and he and Kai locked eyes. "I do. I do indeed remember." He didn't accept Kai's offer to shake hands.

"Hello, Dort." Kai put his hand back in his pocket.

"Give us a few more minutes, will you, son?"

"You should come now. Mother has that foolish man with her." Dort stared at Kai. "That fool gypsy –"

Mynydd cut him short. "Thank you, Dort. I'll be there in a minute."

Dort moved away. Kai wondered if he still lingered outside the door.

"I'm sorry. What were we saying, Kai?"

"The reason I came, sir, is to talk to you again about some improvements to the lighthouse. I mentioned a few months ago –"

"Yes, the Argand lamps. I remember. Since we spoke, I was able to get a look at some the last time I went south. We must get those installed. They'll be a big improvement over candles, or so I've been told."

"They are," said Kai. "And a Fresnel lens will make the light much brighter. Also, as you know, our light has always been stationary. But now that Kolmogory has a light, we really should establish a characteristic of our own so the two lights aren't confused."

"I'm no seaman, Kai. Tell me again what you mean?"

"A light's characteristic – it's the length of time between flashes.

Every lighthouse has its own characteristic. All different, to help sailors identify their positions at sea. Kolmogory's characteristic is fifteen seconds."

"And how does that work, the timing of the flashes?"

"Their light is turned every fifteen seconds by a clockwork mechanism. We never bothered to make our light turn because we used to be the only lighthouse for a hundred miles."

"I see. So the Parrot Island light was unmistakable."

"In the old days, yes. But now we too need a mechanism to turn our light. That and oil lamps and —"

"And one of those French lenses."

"Yes, sir."

"It will be a big expense, Kai."

"It is a big expense, I know."

"I'll have to twist some arms to get it approved."

"Still, very necessary, sir, if we want to stay up to date. The system we have now is downright primitive. And the harbormaster, Mr. Francevili, agrees with me."

"Listen, let's meet with him this week, determine what we need, and I'll get it ordered right away."

"That would be wonderful, Lord Mynydd." Kai looked up. Dort was back.

"I hate to interrupt this little tete-a-tete, but really, Father, you owe duties to your guests."

"I'm coming."

"Mother wants you. Now."

"Yes, I'll be right there. Let's make a time to meet, Kai. Saturday, at lunchtime?"

"Perfect."

"You'll bring Francevili? I'll have some food brought in. Shall we say noon at my office?"

"We'll be there. Thank you so much, sir."

Dort cleared his throat. His father ignored him.

"It's always a pleasure to see you again, Kai."

"Likewise, Lord Mynydd."

"Would you like me to call my carriage? The weather is rotten."

"No, but thank you. It looks to have stopped raining, for now."

Dort frowned. It was almost more than he could bear, watching his father clap his hand to the shoulder of that brown-faced savage. He couldn't have said which one of them, Kai or his father, he resented more.

True to his word once again, Lord Mynydd ordered the new equipment immediately and, some months later, came out to make sure it was properly installed. Though the new lamps still had to be filled with oil at least once a day and the Fresnel lens still had to be kept impeccably clean, though the clockwork had to be wound and the channel that it sat in had to be filled regularly with clean mercury, it was a most welcome modernization. Now the Parrot Island lighthouse was visible for twenty miles on a clear night.

In the light of what happened next, the improvements were also timely. Indeed, if the lamps had been ordered a couple of weeks later, the powers that be would have deemed that expense unaffordable. The list of improvements would have been scrapped. The new equipment would never have been installed at all.

Just as the town of Lunenfarne was beginning to thrive, a smudge of rot set in. Just a spot, but that was enough.

A week after the new equipment was ordered, Jozef Francevili rowed out to Parrot Island through choppy grey seas and labored up the slope to the house. Kai saw him coming and put a kettle on for tea.

"This is a surprise," he called, throwing another log into the stove. "Come in out of this weather."

Bou Bou the parrot flew to his perch near the stove and squawked resentfully at the man who brought in a blast of icy air.

Oh, they don't wear pants on the other side of France.

"Keep quiet, Bou Bou. Come in, Mr. Francevili."

"Kai, call me Jozef. You're old enough now to call me by my first name."

Kai grinned. "It doesn't come naturally. But I'll try, Jozef."

"That's better. Now," Jozef said, pulling out a chair, "I come with some very strange news."

"What has happened? Nothing about my mother, I hope?"

"No, no. So she's not here?"

"She's still in town."

"Too bad. I wanted her to hear this. Ah, thank you, a cup of tea is splendid on a day like this."

"What is this about?"

"It's about Lord Mynydd. You won't believe what has happened."

"Is he hurt? Or what?"

"He's in jail."

"Jail? What for?"

"Embezzlement. They claim he has been dipping into tax monies. More than dipping, if what they say is true. They say he stole thousands."

Kai dropped into a chair. "I can't believe it."

"Wait til you hear the rest. Not everyone knows this, so keep it under your hat."

PLLT! Who cut the cheese? Shameless as ever, Bou Bou opened his wings and did a parrot rhumba.

"Bou Bou! Stop it! Sorry, Jozef. Go on."

"You'll never guess who turned Mynydd in to the authorities. His factor."

"Ruslan Fairhedd?"

"He gave them Mynydd's account books and a load of evidence, or so I've heard."

"How do you know all this?"

"Franz Wohlfahrt, my stepson, is a magistrate now. Fairhedd brought the whole thing before the council this morning."

"That all sounds very suspect, to me."

The parrot was getting no attention. This would not do. Bou Bou knew how to mimic rude body sounds that, in certain company, never failed to put him in the limelight.

PLLT! PLLT! Speak, O toothless wonder.

"Will you quit it, Bou Bou?

Better out than in!

"This bird! I'm sorry about –"

Better out than in!

" – his language. Go ahead, Mr. – Jozef."

PLLT! PLLT! Bou Bou, once started, could not stop.

"Your bird is quite the character."

"I apologize, Jozef. Go on with what you were saying."

"Now Kai, this next is definitely for your ears only. But you won't believe it. There is already someone trying to take over Lord Mynydd's chancellor position. Want me to tell you who?"

"Who?"

"His son."

"Dort?"

"His own son. And he isn't even a magistrate. He's trying to step in and just shoehorn himself into office. It's like he thinks he owns the place."

"Is that even legal?"

"I don't know. But for some reason, it looks like he's going to push it through. My stepson was the only magistrate who objected. All the rest were too terrified of Dort Mynydd to say a word. Or else they've been paid off."

"Appalling."

PLLT! (ostensibly from Bou Bou)

"On top of getting thrown in jail, all of Mynydd's accounts have been closed. He's got no money for bail."

Kai got up. "I'm going to row across to see him."

"Maybe you should wait a bit. Look out the window."

"Oh. I thought we were finished with snow for the year."

"We're never finished with snow."

"I knew I was putting my boots away too soon."

Lady, these boots never come off.

Kai rolled his eyes and popped a cover over Bou Bou's cage.

In town later that afternoon, Kai stormed into his mother's workshop. He tugged her away from the loom she was checking. "Ema, come here." He pulled her into her office and closed the door.

"Kai, what is it?"

"Vladimir Mynydd is in jail!"

"What? Where did you hear such a thing?"

"Mr. Francevili told me."

"What did he do?"

Kai told her everything.

"I know you hate the man, Ema, but he has been nothing but helpful to me. I feel so bad for him. Do you remember his son Dort?"

"I do. You were convinced he stole your toy when you were little."

"Don't mention this to anyone, but he won't bail his father out. He's trying to take over the position of chancellor."

"His father's job? Mynydd's wife knows all this?"

"Apparently she hasn't even visited the jail."

Anne sat down at her desk and rubbed her fingers over her forehead. "Natalia must have plenty of her own money. Why doesn't she post bail for her husband?"

Vladimir Mynydd was half-way through his second day in jail. The stench in the place – the mold, the smell of dirty bodies, the crude sanitation facilities – was suffocating. He sat shivering in the cold dampness with his elbows on his knees. He pressed his cheekbones against his fists. He no longer wore the thick gold ankle rings that signified his status, because now he had no status. His associates had hardly been able contain their eagerness to remove them when they stripped him of his chancellor's position. It did not bother him so much, losing those gold rings. He had been going against the fashion of his class for a long time now anyway, and the ankle bands were starting to seem ridiculous. He had let his hair grow in the last decade and it was threaded now with a few strands of silver. He wore it in a long tail tied at the back of his neck. Three or four of the younger magistrates had followed his lead and also rejected the shaved and tufted heads of their peers. They had given up, as well, the very tight silk shirts the rest wore, in favor of loose cotton tunics. The absurd inch-long fingernails had become a thing of the past, for the younger men, at least, and so were the precipitously high heels on their boots.

Vladimir Mynydd knew that the older magistrates, as well as many people of their class, had been muttering darkly about him for some time now. Why, they begged to know, was he putting on the airs of a commoner? He had made a mockery of the exalted position of chancellor. And all these wild ideas of his? His strange notions about making changes to traditions and practices that had worked well, and filled their pockets, for decades? Was it necessary to make all these changes? He tried to explain that he wanted to see Lunenfarne function efficiently as a town, for everyone, not just for the wealthy. There was enough money, he had said, given the amount of revenue that came in from duties and taxes, to make the village a very pleasant place.

Well, where did he think he was, in Bellesunde or somewhere? A "beautiful" market square? What a waste! Their biggest objection, and Vladimir had offended many with this one, was the elimination of traditional "inspector" positions. To be sure, those jobs paid little more than chump change, but a few months later, he also did away with the annual bonuses, undisclosed amounts of money that had always gone straight into the purses of worthy citizens. Mynydd and his radical ideas! He truly did not know which side his bread was buttered on. Let the man sit in jail for a while, they said. Make him think about the mess he had made of everything.

When the sheriff came to haul him away, the magistrates' smug looks were not lost on Mynydd. Yes, he would admit to taking pride in the new projects. It was the part about his job he had come to like best. Thanks to his efforts in the last ten years, the town now had a new and wider bridge over the Nolta River, a bigger school, a wonderful park out by Arum Lake. New and broader piers jutted into the harbor. There were pleasant walkways along the waterfront, and a cleaner, less-crowded market square. He was proud of the lighthouse modernizations that allowed safer access to the harbor for traders and merchantmen, and he was, until yesterday, in the process of designing a new bandstand and an outdoor puppet theatre that would replace the rickety old thing they had used since Noah was a boy. It was silly, how much that particular project pleased him. Now it would be up to someone else to finish it, whoever the new chancellor was to be.

He had not always been so completely independent of the views of others of his class. As a young man he had been content to conform, to uphold the status of the elite, to believe that the reason he had been born to wealth was simply because his family deserved to be wealthy. That is what he had been taught. What had changed him? When had he first swerved away from the old traditions of careless idleness for the privileged class?

Growing up in a mansion surrounded by other mansions, he had certainly never heard of anyone needing money. He had never realised that there were people who worried about having enough money to buy food. Then, on a long ago night when he had feared for his life, he walked into the lighthouse keeper's cottage. Images came to his mind now. A storm raging over a grassy island meadow high above the sea. A small house with bare wood floors, lit by a wood stove. The novelty of talking to people who took their work seriously. The surprise, another time, of seeing Teron coming through the rain to offer him a box of lobsters pulled fresh from the sea. It had been simply a gift, a gift out of friendship, for him, Vladimir. Friendship! He couldn't have said why these memories had stayed with him. He only knew, with all his money, he could buy none of those things.

It was the island, he reflected. Parrot Island. That was it. His visits to Parrot Island had changed him, ever since that night those island people had risked their lives to pull him and his son from the cold sea. That had changed him.

He sat up and rubbed his arms to warm himself. Was anyone ever coming to see him in this god-forsaken place? Was no one coming to get him out of here? He had been here for two days now. He had seen no one but the sheriff, his old friend the sheriff, who could not even look him in the eye.

Mynydd knew that his independent ways were not approved by all of his associates. Was that how he ended up here, he wondered, here in the darkness of a filthy cell in the local jail, with a stinking bucket of excrement in the corner? Had Ruslan Fairhedd plotted for weeks to get rid of him?

Someone had altered his books, of that much he was sure. Someone had used false information to turn him in. He longed to explain to Natalia and Dort that he had been unjustly framed. He had to assure them that he had done nothing dishonest. What must they think of him? Neither his wife nor his son had responded to the one note he had been allowed to send. Had they not received it? Where were they? Did they actually believe the lies about him?

He heard voices in the outer office. Here they were! At last they had come. He stood and pressed himself against the bars of his cell, wishing he could fly to them.

But no. It was not Natalia, nor Dort. He knew it was certainly not

Ruslan Fairhedd.

Anne d'Inquierre stood in the doorway.

He walked backwards until he bumped into his cot. He sat down. Anne was staring. He couldn't tell what she was thinking. Slowly she came up to his cell and wrapped her fingers around a bar.

She didn't speak.

"You've come to gloat?" he asked softly.

"No. No, Vladimir. Don't you realise that I, more than anyone, know very well what you are going through in here, in this – this horrible cage?"

"You have no idea what I'm going through."

"You're so wrong. Prison? I've thought of little else for the last ten years."

"Ah." He dropped his head. "Kai tells me he is getting out this spring."

"We hope so."

"And that you are sailing to Balgrim to meet him."

"Yes. I am. I leave very soon."

Anne would be sailing the cold, troubled seas to find her man. He said, "My wife can't even be bothered to come down from the hill to see me."

"She hasn't visited?"

"Nor my son."

"Are they are having trouble getting money together for your bail?"

"She has more than enough money to get me out of here. I didn't need to spend a single night in this place." He finally put words to his fears. "Maybe she just doesn't care enough to bother."

"What about your own money?"

"My accounts have been frozen. Probably confiscated."

So it was true, what Kai had told her. Anne gripped the bars of the cell. This man was her enemy. For ten years, he had been her enemy. Now he was sitting there helpless, in a cage. She had expected to feel indifferent, if not downright glad, to see his freedom torn away.

"Vladimir?"

He looked up.

"Do you remember the night of that storm? The night Teron and I saved your life?"

"Of course I do, Anne. How could I ever forget?" He thought he knew what she was going to say next. "No doubt that is something you'll always regret."

She laughed a little. "Well, you were pretty arrogant back then."

"And look how the mighty have fallen. I hope it makes you happy."

"It does not. No, it does not." Her voice caught and her eyes welled with tears. "Somehow I feel that there must have been some reason we dragged you out of the sea."

"If you're making a prophecy, I guess I won't be fulfilling it now."

"Oh, one never knows." She thrust a fat purse of money through the bars. "Come on. Let's get out of here."

"Mother! Mother!" Dort Mynydd stormed into the room where his mother was painting her nails and Florri, her pregnancy beginning to be obvious, was sitting by the window, working on her embroidery.

Natalia blew on her nails and patted the seat next to her. "Come here, my sweet."

Her son was in no mood to be cuddled. "Mother," he fumed, pacing and glowering. "The sheriff was just here. You won't believe what has happened."

"Is it good news? Your father choked to death on a dry bread crust?"

"No!" Dort roared. "Someone posted bail for him. He's free."

"Free?" Natalia stood, panicked. "Impossible!"

"It's true! It is!" he raged. "Mother, I can't have that jackass running about. Not until they've approved me for chancellor. He's going to ruin all our plans."

Florri put her work down. "Plans?"

"Shut up, Florri," Natalia ordered. "Where the hell did Vladimir get the money?"

"You're not going to like this, Mother. From Anne d'Inquierre. That gypsy woman."

"No!" Jealous rage seized Natalia. She raised clenched fists, manicure be damned. "No! I won't allow it!"

Florri sat forward, her heart like a lead weight. "You wanted your father in jail?"

"Keep quiet! We don't need to hear from you!" Natalia's smudged red nails dug into Dort's arm. "You've got to get him back!"

"Dort?" Florri reached a hand to her husband. "What is –?"

"Florri." He bent over her, answering slowly, as to a child, in a supreme effort to be patient. "Florri. Listen. You don't understand what's going on and I don't have time to explain."

"You put your own father in jail? How could you do that?"

"I wasn't the only one! Your father was in on this! Your father was right there with me! He's the one who provided the evidence."

"My father? Evidence of what?"

"Swindling! Stealing!"

"Make her shut up, Dort!"

"Listen. We had to make it look like Father committed a crime, all right? It had to be done."

"But he didn't?"

"Not per se."

"And my father?"

"He did the damn dirty work! He's in this up to his neck!"

"My father?"

"Do you get it now, Florri?"

"What?"

"Are you satisfied now? You asked for it! You made me tell you!" Dort yelled. "Your father was in on the whole thing. Stop looking like I just fired a cannonball at you!"

Florri's mouth hung open. She couldn't breathe. She rose awkwardly. Her sewing fell to the floor. "I – this is –"

"This is none of your business, you little shitepoke!" Natalia bellowed.

Somehow Florri got herself out of the room and slammed the door.

Natalia pulled Dort around to face her. "You go out there, Dort! You go out there right now and get him back!"

"I don't have any idea where he is!"

"Find him! Bring him here! I'll kill him!"

"Here?" he shrieked. "I don't want him here! I don't want to see him!"

"Then have him chained in the fruit cellar and lock the door. If we can't trust that stupid sheriff to keep him under lock and key, we'll have to take matters into our own hands. I'll starve him to death, the bastard!" Natalia flung away from Dort and pressed her hands to her head. She whirled back to face him. "Did she take him back to her cursed island? Did she? Did she?"

"Who?"

"The slut! That savage woman! Who do you think?"

"I'll send some men out there right away. He's got to be locked up, Mother. He's no longer fit to run this town. Shit shit shit! That bastard screws up everything!"

"Oh, you've no idea," snarled Natalia. "You've no idea!"

Dort's men saddled up quickly to begin the search but they did not have to look far. Vladimir Mynydd, coatless in the pouring rain, was walking up the River Road, heading to his own house because he had nowhere else to go. He looked up, glad to see a small troupe of horsemen come thundering down the hill. Help at last! They had even brought a horse for him. They pulled up short in a splatter of mud, told him to mount up, threw a bag over his head, and bound his hands. They circled up and down some side roads, just to confuse him before dragging him into an underground room somewhere and locking the door.

Wet and freezing.

Locked in a cold subterranean room.

Vladimir Mynydd was too shocked to move at first. Gradually, a growing fury brought him new resolve.

In complete darkness, Vladimir managed to work the bag off his head by bending so he could anchor it between his knees and pull. It was still too dark for him to see anything at all, but at least he could breathe. He stumbled against a barrel of some kind and tore his sleeve on its metal hoop. This gave him an idea. He manoeuvered so the cords binding his wrists were in contact with the sharp metal. The cords had just enough give so that, working them against the barrel's iron edge and nearly scraping his skin raw, he was finally able to free his hands. He could hear muted voices. People moving about? Where was he? It smelled better here than in jail, of that much he was sure.

He was trying to feel his way around the room when, suddenly, someone rattled the latch on his door. He froze. Footsteps went away. They came back. He felt around some more, frantic to find a club of some kind. His hands fell on several round objects. Apples! He heard a jingle of keys. He turned toward the sound. A piece of well-aimed fruit might give him a moment's advantage, but only a moment. He poised, ready to throw. A key scraped in the lock. He aimed. The door opened, a candle flared, and a pretty arm in a ruffled sleeve reached to touch the flame to the wick of a lamp on the wall. Mynydd covered his eyes, squinting in the sudden light.

"Oh! My sakes in heaven!"

"Mattie?" Vladimir beheld the maid who lit the fire in his library fireplace every morning. He was in his own house.

"Lord Mynydd! What are you doing – sorry, sir. I don't mean – but oh my suds – you surprised me, is all."

"I imagine I did." It was nothing, compared to his surprise.

Mattie wasn't really that sorry. She had always liked her master. "I just come to get some, uh, – were you, uh – ?"

"I was just leaving. I'll get out of your way."

"Oh, no problem for me if you want to stay, sir."

"No, no. Duty calls, I'm afraid. This way to the kitchen?"

"Well – yes. Sure. Down to your right. Is there – is there anything I can help you with?"

"No, thank you, Mattie. You've already been of enormous help."

"I have?" Why did he have to leave so quickly? Too bad! She stood there for a good half-minute with a pleased smile on her face and her candle in her hand.

Mynydd left by the servants' entrance and cut through the garden under a line of spruce trees that shielded him somewhat from the windows of the house. He circled behind his neighbor's high wall and came out on the road that took him down the south side of the mountain. The rain continued to bucket down and he still had no coat. The road meandered about until it reached the Bay Road. He followed it until he came near the Nolta bridge. Had they figured out yet that he was gone? If so, they would surely be coming for him.

It was nearly dark now and he had met no traffic on the roads at all. Still, he hid under the bridge and waited. He watched and listened. He did not want to start across the bridge, only to be trapped by horsemen. His teeth were practically chattering with cold. If there was foot traffic on the bridge, he wouldn't be able to hear it over the pounding rain. But if there were horsemen, he'd surely hear them. When it was fully dark, he couldn't wait any longer. He leapt up to the bridge and ran across, his heart pounding more from fear than from exertion.

He made it across. No one, he wanted desperately to believe, had seen him, but he ducked under the bridge again to be certain, and waited while he caught his breath. Finally, he could no longer put off making a move. He went swiftly down to the waterfront and turned left along the boardwalk. He was not the only one out tonight, after all. A couple of seamen were jogging through the rain, coming toward him. He moved to hide in a doorway. But they were not seeking him. Laughing, they turned under the red sign of the Bayside Inn and disappeared inside.

Vladimir stood a moment longer in the shop doorway. The inn was his destination as well. There he would either find safety, or meet with worse trouble. He had never set foot in the tavern in his life, nor, he was fairly certain, had any of the people he normally associated with. But Anne d'Inquierre had convinced him that, if he found himself in need of help, this place was his best hope. He screwed up his courage, mounted the steps, and went inside.

His first impression was of wonderful warmth. Huddling by the wall with rainwater dripping from his hair and down his face, his second impression was of an atmosphere of pleasing conviviality. Men talking and jostling each other and extremely pretty maids laughing with customers and serving food and ale and a crackling fire and loud banter. How had he, in all his days, missed out on this kind of homey camaraderie? Food and ale! Vladimir realised then that he hadn't eaten since a meager breakfast of a crust of bread and water. The third thing that struck him was the imposing lady who was leaning over the bar, watching him. Was this the remarkable Freya Button? He had heard her name for years, seen it on documents and deeds and applications for inspections, but he had never met her. She looked intimidating. She frightened him. He desperately wished he could melt into her arms. He did not know which impulse to trust.

He took a step forward. She cocked her head and didn't take her eyes off him. Ensnared, his feet moved toward her through no intention of his own.

"Can I help you?"

"I'm looking for Freya Button. Anne d'Inquierre sent me."

"That's me. I'm Freya. You got a name?"

"Vladimir Mynydd."

"Ah. So. You got yourself out of the clink, I see, Mr. Mynydd?" Freya assumed that in all his life, he had never been addressed as 'mister'. She watched his reaction. He didn't bat an eye.

"Anne posted bail for me."

"Anne d'Inquierre? You mean your wife –?" Freya bit back the rest of her question.

"My wife, it's beginning to dawn on me, may have been the one to put me in this mess. For what purpose, I do not know."

"Don't suppose it's got anything to do with your son slipping you out of the chancellor's seat so he can slip into it?" Again, she watched his reaction. He stared with his mouth open.

"Dort? Dort did that?"

Freya nodded. "That's the word going about." She watched Mynydd pull out a stool. He sat down heavily. So he hadn't suspected. This would be an evening to remember. She opened a jug and poured him a glass of red wine.

He didn't touch it, but sat there motionless, his mind racing. Imprisoned in his own fruit cellar. Dort taking his job away from him. His wife, plotting against him. And Ruslan, his factor, betraying him. So that's what happened. He just never dreamed ….

"So you got a reason for coming to see me?"

He couldn't remember why he had come. He had just never dreamed that ….

Freya suddenly took rough hold of his arm. "Get up. Don't argue. Get up now, Mr. Mynydd." She jerked him off the stool and around to her side of the bar. "Georgiana!" she hissed. "Make a fuss!" Freya's eyes rolled toward the uniformed men coming through the door. Immediately, Georgiana the serving maid dropped a tray of mince pies in their path. Half the men in the place saw an opportunity for some good scenery – Georgiana leaning over – and they were at her feet to help her clean up. The men in uniform were caught in the tangle.

"What's going on?" cried Mynydd.

"In here. Keep quiet." A panel in the wall opened. Frey thrust him into a tiny space between the wall studs next to the fireplace. She closed him in and leaned against the panel. Oh, look at the floor! Mynyyd had come in soaking wet and his footprints led right to the hiding spot. A stein of beer accidentally emptying itself over the floor took care of the footprints, and Freya turned to face the four large men who were now clomping through her tavern. They were armed. They looked angry. The two in front were still wiping mince pie from their boots. The others craned their necks, eyes searching the room.

"Oh, dear. Look at this. I'm so sorry."

Four pairs of eyes shifted. Freya was a bit of a distraction herself, leaning to swipe invisible bits of pie from pantlegs here and there. She rose, watching them watch her as she straightened. "I'm sorry. It's not usually this chaotic in here, gentlemen," she told them. She straightened her bodice, a move that never failed to give a man pause. "I apologise for the mess." She moved closer to the leader and met him eye to eye. "Have a seat. One of my girls will be with you momentarily. Can I offer you something to drink?"

"We won't sit and we don't want nothing to drink," he growled. Freya glanced at the three men behind him and noticed regret flash across their faces.

"You don't want drink? What do you want?"

"We're looking for someone."

"Oh. Well, that's easy." She gestured to the room. "If you don't see him, he's not here."

"What's upstairs?" barked the leader.

She tilted her head. "Rooms." She leaned close to his ear and spoke confidentially. "You were aware, sir, that this is an inn?"

He backed away a little. "I knowed that. So … we're gonna search up there."

"Listen." Freya pressed a finger lightly against his breastbone and continued to speak softly. "Search all you want. Georgiana will take two of you up. The others wait here. But bother my guests or mess up my place, and your ass is grass." She held his eye for a long moment.

He had to force himself to turn away so he could beckon to his aide. They followed the maid upstairs.

When they came down, Georgiana was chatting gaily with the second in command. He was hanging on her every word, a look about him like a child with a face full of pudding. The leader motioned to collect his men, clicked his heels and gave Freya a two fingered salute. They stomped out the door without finding the man they sought.

"Come again when you can stay longer," Freya said softly to their backs. The front door slammed. "Or don't. It's all the same to me."

It was hours before the tavern emptied for the night, giving Freya a chance to open the secret panel and release Vladimir Mynydd. He nearly fell into her arms.

"Oh my goodness. You are a basket case, aren't you?"

He was pale and shaking, damp, distraught, and disillusioned. She was sure he was half-dead on his feet.

"Let's see about some dry clothes."

Freya led him to a room upstairs. She stripped off his wet garments and wrapped him in a robe. She built up the fire for the hot water tank. She ordered up a tray of meat pies. They sat to eat and together they emptied an entire jug of wine. There was dessert. Mynydd leaned back in his chair while Freya teased him with sweet dainties. By then, the bath water was hot. She saw personally to the soap and sponge, and finally bundled him into bed. Turns out, Mynydd was not a total basket case after all.

He slept like a baby til noon the next day. Freya woke up early, playful as a kitten, and knotted her hair in an artful new style. Her staff was quite stunned, seeing her like this. Her sharp-eyed sister was relieved. So! Finally!

One day a few weeks later, when spring was on the cusp of summer, when the shortest night of the year gave seamen only the briefest view of the North Star, Kai d'Inquierre watched his mother's ship disappear over the horizon. He was, as always when they were apart, terrified that she would never return, but she had been almost giddy with anticipation. Freya Button had urged her, for her own safety because she traveled unescorted, to dress as a man. And carry a knife. Anne was surprised how much safer that made her feel. She promised Kai she would get to Balgrim and bring Teron back as quickly as she could. He wanted to believe her but was not reassured.

Nowadays, he was not always alone on Parrot Island. Gregor Treyse came out for a couple of nights a week to keep him company. Kai knew that Gregor liked the island. He felt that, actually, Gregor was much more suited for living out here than he himself was. Many times Gregor followed Kai around as he went about his chores, and seemed to enjoy lending a hand. It made Kai's days go faster. And he hoped it did as much for Gregor.

His friend had not been himself for some time now. Kai was a little worried about him. It wasn't anything he could put his finger on, and maybe it was all his imagination. Maybe it was just that they were grown boys now, nearly men. Public school had just come to an end and, while Kai had a job to keep him occupied, Gregor as yet had nothing planned for his future. He spent part of every week up in the foothills, helping his father with the sheep, an existence that, in Kai's estimation, had to be ten times worse than operating a lighthouse.

From one day to the next, you never know what will happen. Most of the time the days tick by and the same duties come round and round again, the same tasks, the same rituals. The weeks slid away. Kai wandered through a kaleidoscope of summer days, patterns forming and re-forming from the same random shards; cold grey days dark with leaden clouds, bluesky days high-piled with white vapor-mountains, a long tableau of days. His work was the same, a drudgery of tasks, day after day.

He did not know – how could he? – that there would come one day that would offer him a flash of joy, fleeting as a phantom unicorn leaping away into the eaves of a wood.

So, one day, a ship sailed into the bay, and shortly after, Kai saw a man making his way up the slope of Parrot Island, up through the pungent summer meadow where the greening wands of goldenrod had yet to unfurl and the grasshoppers sang in the afternoon sun. Up through the meadow a stranger came walking. Then, not a stranger after all. Older by far, thin and taut as a sloop's forestay, but home at last.

Teron Adante.

Kai flew down the hill and nearly knocked the man over. They embraced and would not let go.

"Look at you! I wouldn't have known you, Kai!"

"You're well? Everything is good with you?"

"I survived. You have no idea how happy I am to be here."

They hugged each other again. Then, both spoke at once. "Come on, let's go find your mother." "Where's Ema?" They laughed. And stopped.

Teron froze. "Kai. No. Please."

"Ema –?"

"Don't. Don't tell me she's gone. Don't break my heart."

Kai could hardly say the words. "She is gone."

"She's –?"

"She left in the spring."

"Left? Left to go where?"

"To Balgrim."

"To prison?"

"Gone to get you. To find you and bring you back."

Teron dropped to the grass. "She wasn't there," he whispered, incredulous. "Anne was not in Balgrim. What – what happened?"

"She left over two months ago. She must have arrived by the time you got out. She must have!"

"No. She wasn't there."

Kai crouched beside him. "You're sure, Teron? How long ago did you leave?"

"Three weeks ago."

"You're sure you didn't miss her somehow?"

Teron nodded. "There's nothing in Balgrim, nothing but a prison. A couple of houses, one pier. Anne was not there. I would have seen her."

"What could have happened? Just when you return, she disappears?"

"This can't be happening."

"This place is cursed. This godforsaken island is cursed, Teron. I know it is! Everyone says so."

They sat staring at the turf. "Where is she? Where could she be?"

GREGOR TREYSE

The festival of Lunasa begins Harvest Month and even before the wheel of the sun rolls out of the sea that morning, the people of Lunenfarne are up and about. Little Gerbert the wharf rat crawls beneath the boardwalk, searching its length for dropped coins so he can buy a cake at the fair. Ferryman Korsakov, dreading a long day of poling back and forth across the river, holds an iron knife against his sore shoulder and mutters a charm that he was assured will draw out the worms that are obviously, terrifyingly, eating his bones. The air has been scented with baking bread for an hour already, and outside the bakery women are standing in line, hoping to be early getting their own loaves into the ovens, just as soon as Mr. Wunder's loaves come out. All week long, the smell of crushed apples has hung heavy over the town and at the mill upriver, Mr. Forman is loading jugs of cider into his cart. The day promises to be warm and his cider is always the favorite drink at the Lunasa Fair.

On Fair Day, the looms are idle in the workshops, grapes up in the convent vineyard glisten unpicked in the sun, and scythes are locked away in barns. Canvas awnings are pulled open above market booths to make shade for jars of honey, bolts of wool and linen fabrics, for crocks of pickled cucumbers and pickled beets and pickled what-have-you. The old fishermen have made nets to sell for hunting season. The nomadic mountain men, with their earrings and necklaces of silver, have come down from the hills to sell their hawks and prize hunting dogs. Minstrels wander, humming quietly, saving their bawdier tunes until dusk, after the nuns have gone home for the day. It is so deeply ingrained, this fear of offending the nuns, that hardly anyone dares trespass. Soon the Bayside Inn will disgorge sailors groggy with hangovers. They come from far away Saxony and Frisia and Lombardy, probably making their last trip to the north before the Wind Month ices the land. They offer to trade exotic peacock feathers and almonds and raisins and nutmeg and a few precious books and manuscripts, in exchange for jerkins of stamped leather, deadly iron knives and, from deep under the Tomgat Mountains, blood-red garnets set in silver.

From the villas in the hills, carriages full of dressy children and languorous women roll toward the river for a day's outing. Hoping to avoid the unruly crowds at the fair, they will be poled up the river to Lake Arum in pretty pleasure boats decorated with flowers and bright canopies. A couple of husbands, unable to stomach such folksiness, might manage to slink away on slippery excuses to pursue their own pleasures. Servants have already gone ahead to set up picnic tables in the park and tend to baskets of food and drink.

This particular Lunasa Fair would be Kai d'Inquierre's last in Lunenfarne. His passage was booked on the *Vixen* and any day now, as soon as the winds favored them, he would travel south to begin his studies at the university in Bellesunde. He and Gregor Treyse strolled idly through the square and stopped for a cup of cider at Mr. Forman's booth.

Gregor watched as Kai took the cup of cider. "Are you feeling all right?"

"Yeah. I'm okay."

"Your hands are shaking."

"Yeah. Lately, for some reason … I don't know what it is."

"You don't feel sick or anything?"

"Eh, not great. But I'm all right." Kai leaned to look over Gregor's shoulder. "Oh no. Don't look now, but Dort Mynydd is over there," he said softly. "I said don't look."

Gregor looked anyway. "Is Florri with him?"

"He's with a woman but she doesn't look like his wife to me."

"The bastard."

"He doesn't even pretend to be discreet. What a prick! This is our honorable new chancellor. I feel so bad for Florri."

"I'd like to punch his face in," Gregor hissed.

"He'd have you hung as a traitor if you did. He's already thrown one magistrate in prison."

"Not to mention what he did to his own father."

"Know what I think? I get the feeling that his father is actually happier now than when he lived in his big villa on the hill."

"Florri must feel like she's in hell up there."

"Yeah. But anyway, it's none of our business. Promise me you won't do anything rash while I'm away, Gregor."

"Like what?"

"Like punch Dort Mynydd's face in."

"I couldn't take him on. I barely have the strength to haul this crippled body around all day."

"You could try mental anguish through psychological torture, but he's probably impervious."

Gregor rubbed his head. "Oh, I'd wager that rats like him are more pervious than you realise."

Gregor, with more reasons than anyone to hate Dort Mynydd, probably came closer than most with this assessment.

Meanwhile, up in the park on Lake Arum, Florri Mynydd sat in a gazebo in close conversation with her mother, Ludmila. Her little one-year old son was asleep on her lap. Natalia Mynydd, her mother-in-law, sat some distance away, drumming long nails on the tablecloth. She was seething, watching Florri and Ludmila Fairhedd. She knew what they were talking about. Florri was surely, Natalia fumed, regaling her mother with stories and lies and complaints about Dort. Probably about herself too. Oh yes, that little witch was a troublemaker. Lord, what she needed, what Natalia needed badly right now, was a good hit of Sulman's elixir. As soon as she got home ….

Then Natalia spotted Ruslan Fairhedd arriving at the park by water taxi. She stood up abruptly, craning her neck.

Ruslan cringed inwardly when he saw Natalia Mynydd coming swiftly down the hill toward him. She looked ready to chew him up and spit him out. She stopped Ruslan at the end of the dock. He groaned to himself. One single day! He'd hoped to have just one day without having to speak to this woman.

"Why isn't Dort with you?" Natalia demanded. "Where is my son?"

"I do not know, Lady Mynydd," Ruslan responded, though he had a rough idea of the kind of day that Dort had arranged for himself.

"You came all the way up here and you didn't bring him with you?"

"He was gone by the time I left. He had business affairs, he said."

"I've heard that story more times than I can count." Natalia's shoulders hunched. Then she straightened and marched over to the gazebo. Florri stopped in mid-sentence and put her hand on her mother's wrist. Ludmila Fairhedd turned and mother and daughter looked at Natalia with identical expressions of apprehension.

"Dort told me he was coming to join us this afternoon. Where is he, will you please tell me?"

"I do not know, Lady Mynydd," said Florri.

Like father like daughter, Natalia growled to herself. "Dort is your husband. I would think you would make it your business to know why he isn't here."

"Dort does not tell me –"

"This is supposed to be a holiday. A family holiday. What kind of a wife does not know where her husband is on a holiday?"

"He never –"

"Don't you care about him? Don't you care about the father of your child? It's your responsibility –"

"Lady Mynydd," Ruslan Fairhedd interrupted. "My daughter is telling you that Dort has not shared his whereabouts with her. This is not untypical. He often goes off on some impulse without –"

Natalia exploded. "Impulse? Don't you dare accuse him of impulse! Dort is never impulsive. I will not hear criticism of my son!"

"I am not criticising. I am merely saying –"

"Do I want your opinion? You are not part of this family, Mr. Fairhedd. I will not have you butting in when I am trying to bring this hapless daughter of yours into line!"

People heard the raised voices and stopped what they were doing. Florri's child stirred awake.

Ruslan didn't reply, but bent his head in deference.

Natalia rounded on Florri again. "Is it asking too much of you to take some wifely responsibilities?"

Ruslan's head came up abruptly. "My daughter, Lady Mynydd, cannot be faulted for –"

"Your daughter can't even hold on to her own husband. If she were any kind of wife at all, he wouldn't have to seek love and affection elsewhere!"

"Ah, so you are aware that he has been unfaithful?"

Oh. Caught. Lady Mynydd scanned the crowd of gaping faces. "It's her fault!" she spluttered, pointing at Florri. "My son has no choice!"

Ludmila Fairhedd stood. "Ruslan, I think it's time we went home," she said to her husband. She reached for Florri's hand and pulled her to her feet. "Why don't you and the baby come visit with us for a little while, Florri?"

"No," pronounced Lady Mynydd. "No. She'll do no such thing."

"I won't be gone long, Lady Mynydd," Florri assured her mother-in-law.

"We don't get much chance to see each other," said Ludmila. "Surely a short visit –"

"*She*," declared Natalia Mynydd, "will return to my house. Her place is in my house. With her husband."

Ruslan saw his wife staring into his eyes. He saw his daughter watching for his response. He opened his mouth, then shut it.

Lady Mynydd turned to Florri. "She knows what will happen to my grandson if she doesn't stay where she belongs. Don't you, Florri?"

Ruslan bowed. "I'll see that they get there safely, my lady. Come along, Florri." Ignoring the looks on the faces of his wife and daughter, he started down the hill toward the water taxis.

Dort heard all about this little clash, several versions of it actually, later that afternoon at a private party. Consequently, hoping to avoid a prolonged scene with his mother, he decided he had better get the worst over and grace her dinner table with his presence that evening.

"Dortie!" his mother crooned when he entered in the middle of the soup course. "Come here, darling!" She beckoned sloppily.

Dort went around the table to kiss his mother.

"Are you happy to see your mama, sweetheart?"

"Yes, Mother." He backed away, regarding her. "Did you take a little too much of your medication tonight?"

"Where were you all day, darling? You were going to come to the – the thing with us."

"I had business. Affairs I had to attend to." Affairs. Not actually a lie.

"What affairs? You didn't tell me about any affairs."

"I was trying to find a place for the auction. I expect the first slave ship sometime soon."

Florri looked up from her plate. "Slave ship?"

"Yes. That's right." Dort went to sit beside her and take her hand. "Look, Florri, my pet. I haven't mentioned this because I don't want you to distress yourself. My little business ventures are just the way I make money. It's nothing you have to worry about." He smiled and shook his head. "You must understand that it shows how much I care for you and my family."

"Dortie darling," his mother interrupted, "Listen to me. Come here beside me. I must tell you something important. My dear Sulman was here this afternoon. You know how much better I feel when he comes. So what I did, Dortie, was that I asked him to come live with us."

Her son stared. "That witch doctor? Living here?"

"I need him, Dortie. I need him every day. I'm not well and he makes me feel better."

"No! I will not have him here."

"He's preparing special treatments for my pain. I have to have him near me."

"No, Mother. That quack will not spend one night in this house."

"Yes he will. This is still my house and my darling Sulman does me a world of good. Just look at me now, pain free! I'm like a new woman again. You can't understand how good he makes me feel and soon –"

"Mother, stop. This is not your house. It is my house now –"

"It is not!"

"It is my house now and I will tell you who can and cannot stay here."

"No you won't. I will cut you off. I will disinherit you." Dort rolled his eyes. "Please don't be mean, Dortie. You know I have to have my medicine. As soon as Sulman can get some – what is the stuff called? – quicksilver, he is going to make me a special elixir." She raised her hands, exultant. "A whole ritual we're going to perform, to draw off the obstructions."

Dort put his elbows on the table and rubbed his brow. He knew ways to calm his mother, ways to convince her to change her mind. Learning to manipulate his mother had taught him everything he knew. "All right, Mother, I'm not going to argue with you. Take whatever medications you want. I don't care." That last barb was the ultimate weapon.

"No wonder I'm not a well person!" Natalia banged her spoon into her soup bowl. "My own son doesn't even care about me!"

Thrust and counter-thrust, the accusations raged on and they hadn't even gotten through the first course yet.

The day after the fair, the bay sparkled with sun diamonds and crickets sang requiems to summer love. Teron Adante shaded his eyes and looked out toward the island. He saw Kai's rowboat heading toward him and sat down on a bench to wait for him. At Kai's insistence, they had both booked passage for Bellesunde, leaving today. Kai would start classes at the university. He was so eager to see Bellesunde and begin his studies that he could hardly wait to leave, but Teron did not have a good feeling about his own visit there. He had fond memories of the town he had grown up in and of his days at university. In Bellesunde, however, was the judge who had sentenced him to ten years at Balgrim Prison. In Bellesunde was the person who had accused him of murder. He would never again feel at home there.

He had served his ten years in prison. He had been worked to exhaustion every day. Only one thing kept him alive for all that time. His one thought had been to return to Parrot Island and take up his life with Anne and Kai again, tending the lighthouse and working on his writing, and no longer needing to hide his identity. For ten years he had never allowed himself, not even for a minute, to consider that Anne might not be there, waiting for him. Finally coming home and discovering that she was missing had been a terrible blow.

She wasn't there and, what was worse, they had no idea what had happened to her. It was almost more than Teron could bear. Their days together had been so brief.

Balgrim Prison had not defeated him. Parrot Island without Anne, that had defeated him. Now Kai would be leaving, too. Teron had planned to stay at the lighthouse. Kai was going to use the money Anne had left him to enroll in school. It was what he had wanted since boyhood.

Why don't we take this trip together, Kai had suggested. He couldn't leave Teron all alone on that island, not in the state he was in. Both of them could go to Bellesunde. Maybe Teron could find some work there, something, anything, to take his mind off his misery, his loneliness. But Teron did not want to leave the island. What if Anne came back? He wanted to be there, just in case. Besides, he argued, he could not afford the cost of the trip.

Only then did he remember the bag of treasure he had hidden years ago in the cave on the island. When he had first come to Parrot Island, he had hidden a satchel that had belonged to the dead ship captain. He had told Anne about it, but that was sixteen years ago. Was it still there? Had Anne needed to make use of it? Had she told Kai about it? For that matter, who knew whether the cave was still intact? It could have collapsed and buried the satchel in a pile of rubble. Bad luck had bedeviled Teron these many years. He was certain, he said to Kai, that it would be useless to even look for something he had left behind so long ago.

"No," Kai said. "Let's go have a look. Listen! Let this hoard of yours decide your fate. If it's there, you won't have to tend a lighthouse for the rest of your life. You could invest in some trade, or pay someone to print your book, or any number of things."

Teron shrugged.

"It might be the best thing for you. If it's not there, well, go ahead and be a hermit on Parrot Island for the rest of your life, if that's what you want. Come on, I'll go to the cave with you."

The path Teron had once worn down the side of the cliff was completely overgrown. He and Kai scrambled down the south side of the island. So many of their familiar landmarks had changed. They hunted through weeds and bushes and finally found the opening to the cave. There was the small Celtic cross roughly chiselled into the edge of the doorway. It looked like no one had been there in a long time. They went inside and

Teron found the spot near the opening where he had hidden the bag. Just as he had predicted, there was nothing there.

Teron hadn't anticipated the sharp, sick feeling of disappointment that flooded him. He sat down on the floor of the cave and rested his elbows on his knees. Kai dropped down beside him, alarmed.

"Hey. Remember the day I found that pirate gold?"

Teron nodded.

"Remember how happy we were? We thought that was such a great day. But we were wrong. You were hauled off to prison the next night."

"Wait! I just thought of something! I moved that satchel the day you found the chest!"

"You did?"

"I was afraid, if some pirate had hidden your gold coins, he might come back to retrieve them and find my bag of treasure as well. So I moved it."

"Where? Do you remember where?"

"I don't know. Farther back. We should have brought a lantern. It's so dark in here, I can't see a thing." Teron got up and felt his way along the wall. "There was a ledge. I remember a ledge, just here, yes. And a rock. I had set a rock to mark the spot." He ran his hand along the ledge.

He let out a long sigh. His legs nearly buckled. He bent his head and leaned his arms on the ledge.

"It's not there?" Kai got up.

Teron shook his head. "I can hardly believe it."

"No?"

"It's here." He pulled the leather bag from its hiding place and dusted it off. He cradled it in his hands. "Lady Luck, you fickle charmer, you. You winsome beauty, you."

Now Teron stood as Kai's rowboat reached the dock. He helped him tie up. Bou Bou the parrot's cage sat in the bow on top of Kai's belongings.

"I'm going to leave my baggage here while I go meet Gregor," Kai said. "I shouldn't be long. Whatever happens, don't let the *Vixen* leave the harbor without me."

"You act like you won't miss this place, but you will. I bet you will. I know I did while I was gone."

"I'm not going to miss it. I can't wait to get to Bellesunde."

"I can still remember the day you started school with the nuns," Teron said.

Kai laughed and shook his head. "Sister Kunegunde. Remember how I hated her? What a witch."

"It won't be any different when you get to school, you know. You will run into some real characters there, too."

"Yes, but at least it won't be Parrot Island. I hope your bookseller friend is still in Bellesunde."

"He may not have any work for me. If not, I'll come back to Lunenfarne."

"Don't be foolish. You don't want to waste your life here, Teron."

"If your mother comes back, though —"

"If Ema comes back, someone will tell her where we are."

"I guess."

"Of course they will. All right, I have to meet Gregor so he can finish getting himself moved permanently out to the island. Remember, don't sail without me."

Kai rowed for the last time to the fishermen's cove. He felt only a touch of nostalgia. It was his last day in Lunenfarne, and he couldn't get through it fast enough. Gregor was waiting for him on the shore, next to a pile of his own belongings.

"You've got good weather, it looks like, Dinker."

Kai laughed to hear his old nickname. "You're getting stuck with the bird unless Teron comes back, which he does threaten to do." Hearing the word "bird", Bou Bou gave a raucous squawk and paced nervously in his cage.

Is that a gun in your pocket?

Kai shook his head. "I can't say I'm going to miss this creature while I'm gone. Let me give you a hand with your stuff." They piled Gregor's bags into the boat.

"Lord have mercy, what is in this bag, Gregor?"

"Sheep manure."

"Haven't you had enough of sheep?"

"It's for the garden I'm going to plant."

"Our vegetable garden is more than big enough. There is only one of you."

"It's for my new flower garden."

"Flowers? Oo-kay." Kai dusted off his hands and extended one for a handshake. "So this is 'good-bye', old friend."

"I hope not for too long. I expect they'll throw you out of school for wanton debauchery and you'll be back in about a month."

"A little debauchery would please me greatly about now. I have to admit that I wish you were coming with me. I really do. Whose homework am I going to copy?"

"I'm happy to be staying right here. I can't afford university anyway."

"You'll change your mind. You've only been climbing those lighthouse stairs for a few weeks so far."

Gregor smiled. "What other work am I fit to do? At the lighthouse, I'll be making a bit of money and still have time to myself. Besides, anything is better than working up in the hills with a father like mine."

"You're wearing another badge of honor, I see." Kai pointed at the bruise under Gregor's eye.

"He never lets up on me. I finally let him have it the other day."

"You really did? Good for you."

"I'm kind of looking forward to being by myself on the island. I'll get some painting done. It'll be great."

"I'm looking forward to being away from the island. So we're both happy."

"Try not to flunk out."

"Don't forget, I'm the intelligent one here."

"Yeah. The first thing you have to do with all your intelligence is to find another sap as big as me who will do your homework for you."

"Write to me now and then, you booger, and let me know how things are here. And, you know, if you hear any news about Ema ...."

"I'll send word somehow, Kai. Of course I will."

"I left the cart by the beach so you can haul your stuff up to the house. Oh, one more thing. I didn't get that trough of mercury cleaned this week. Sorry to leave you with that."

"Not a problem. I like doing all that stuff."

"Better you than me, man."

They clapped each other on the back and parted ways for the first time in their entire boyhood. The first and last.

The *Vixen* made good speed down to Bellesunde. The farther they got from Lunenfarne, the better Kai felt. He had been reluctant to admit that he had been feeling lousy lately. Now his hands hardly shook anymore. The headaches were gone. He took it as a sign. Parrot Island simply did not agree with him. He had made the right decision in leaving.

Bellesunde, beautiful city beside the sea, laced with canals that twisted among stately houses. The university buildings rose on the hill above, their porticoed walkways already bustling with students. It was everything Kai had hoped, at least in appearance. He fell in love with the place and knew immediately that he had made the right choice in coming here.

Teron had almost forgotten how beautiful the campus was, but the memory was soured by thoughts of Soro Einfaldsson, the man who had murdered his friend and, so heartlessly, had arranged for Teron to be packed off to Balgrim Prison. Teron feared to meet him, but trusted that neither he nor Soro would recognize the other by now. He knew he himself had certainly aged, his hair greying, his body a wiry remnant of what it once was.

Aside from seeing that Kai was well-settled, aside from selling his bag of jewels and carvings and French francs, his main purpose in coming back to Bellesundewas to visit an old Italian, the printer Gioachino Rossini. He hoped to convince Rossini to take him on as an apprentice. When he was a student, Teron had spent many an afternoon pouring over the books in Rossini's shop, though at the time, he could afford to buy very few. Now, standing in front of the shop and looking up at the FOR SALE sign in the big front window, his heart sank. More bad luck.

He saw someone moving around inside so he knocked on the door. A young man answered. Thin as a willow sapling, he spoke politely. No, the shop was in no position to hire anyone. In fact, the young man was himself out of a job now. Tragically Signor Rossini, he explained, had passed away. His printing press was for sale, and all the tools that went with it.

They chatted for a while. Teron could not believe his luck when he heard the price they were asking for the printing press. He bought it without a second thought. What a boon this would be to Lunenfarne – he wasn't clear why he felt this would be so, but he felt certain it was. He didn't know how to operate the press or cast type or bind a book or make paper. He didn't know how he would use this press to make money. He only knew that he finally felt excitement again, in love with the idea of making books.

The young man, a bookbinder whose name was Poggio Gomoggio, pushed a hank of fine hair out of his eyes. He looked at Teron doubtfully. "You've never run a press before?"

"Never," said Teron, completely undaunted.

"There's a lot to learn, you know. Do you have someone who knows the business?"

"No one. But you said you're in need of a job. Why don't you come with me and teach me? I can pay you for at least a few months of work, guaranteed."

Poggio's face lit up. "I'm definitely interested."

"Will you help me crate up the tools and get everything loaded onto the ship?"

"Ship? Oh. You're not staying in the city?"

"I'm taking this to Lunenfarne."

"Lunenfarne? I don't think I've ever heard of it."

"Well, you will, someday."

"How far away is it?"

"With luck? A week up the coast. Okay, maybe a week and a half."

"Up the coast? North?"

"That's right."

"But there's nothing up there. No. Thank you, but I'm looking for something – more dependable."

"And something dependable is looking for you, Mister Gomoggio."

Poggio blinked. The lips in his small heart-shaped face puckered with doubt.

"Come with me, Poggio. You'll at least have employment for a few months."

Poggio shook Teron's hand reluctantly, but during the trip north, when they began to piece together some plans, his interest was caught. They would start the business with a small project, printing inexpensive readers for school children. Teron thought of the notebooks full of stories that he had written for Kai when he was a boy. They could offer them one chapter at a time. Maybe they could get them illustrated, Teron said. Maybe they could, Poggio agreed, maybe some simple line drawings.

Thus, finally, did Teron Adante discover his new calling. Up the hill behind the market square in Lunenfarne, he was lucky enough to find a shop that was vacant. There was a decent apartment upstairs with a view of the bay. He installed Poggio rent-free in a small room behind the shop. They moved the press and all its equipment into the front room. Teron hung a cage for his parrot near the wood stove. He splurged and had a sign made, naming the shop for the place he had been happiest: Parrot Island Books.

Meanwhile, out on Parrot Island itself, Gregor was thriving in his new job. Since coming to the island, he had never felt healthier or happier. He was putting a little money aside each week so he could order new paints. His weak leg was challenged with laboring in his garden and climbing the lighthouse stairs several times a day, but he actually fancied himself getting stronger. He worried privately about a slight tremor that had developed in his hands lately, but convinced himself it was nothing major. His mother had given him some small rose bushes and day lilies and lily bulbs, and these he planted along the walkway. That first summer even brought blooms to a few of the new plants.

In the afternoons, he often had time to get some painting done. Some days, Teron Adante took an hour or two away from his printing press to visit. He often said the island had never looked more beautiful. Once a week, Gregor rowed over to the shops across the bay and visited his mother in her work room. Then, if he had enough time before dusk, he would hike along the steep trails above the Nolta River. He sketched whatever caught his eye, to be rendered in paint when he got home. Climbing up through the rocky terrain was not easy, but he took his time and often managed to get a mile or two up into the wild country, almost up to where the convent perched on the side of the mountain.

The light on Parrot Island's lighthouse turned and turned on its new clockwork mechanism. August slipped away like a spooked trout, as August seems to do, and autumn blew in. Gregor's life had fallen into a pattern that he loved. He had time to paint almost every day, and the lighthouse chores fit into a comfortable schedule. Gregor had begged the town to install some daymarks to warn ships off the rocky reef and he was proud, relieved as well, that there had not been a single shipwreck all fall. So the light at the Parrot Island lighthouse, a faithful guardian that kept the forces of chaos in check, turned and turned and turned again.

The wealthy barons of the mining and lumbering trades, on the other hand, kept chaos at bay in another way, the only way they knew how: through wanton spending. In October, when night-frosts enameled the brown hills above Lunenfarne, the mansions in the foothills sparkled with candles and jewels and silk gowns and satin slippers. Big-toothed smiles peeked over flirtatious fans. Shiny bald heads, a last vestige of the old tradition, bowed over manicured lace-gloved hands or, in more clandestine moments, over insouciant inches of porcelain cleavage. Menservants stood unseeing near the draperies unless summoned to replace champagne flutes that were frosted with flakes of gold. Maids served delicate patés of hummingbirds' livers in thimble-sized brioches and *amuse-bouches* of heart of sparrow cunningly studded with eye of newt.

In the little brown cottages down along the shore of the bay, firewood dried on porches, fish and sausages and cheeses hung in smokehouses, and a wealth of potatoes filled innumerable barrels. Cellars smelled of apples and attics of mushrooms and garlic, kitchens of rosemary and black-market cinnamon. Lavender-scented quilts were pulled from armoires and tubs for bathing were brought in from the garden to hang beside the woodstove for the winter.

To Wido Treyse, Gregor's father, the first frosts signalled the time to bring his herds down to lower pastures. These animals belonged solely to him now, no longer to Anne d'Inquierre. Besides her sheep, she had also sold him her small herd of special cattle. He grazed these cows in select wildflower pastures all summer. Theirs was the milk Wido used to make his small batch of Arum River Cheese. As a cheese-maker, Wido Treyse excelled. He made this particular cheese only in autumn, when the milk was full of rich fats. Then he wrapped it in spruce cambium, the tree's inner bark layer. He aged it just until the start of the new year. His best customer, also his secret favorite, was Batilda Button at the Bayside Inn. She bought as much of Wido's cheese as he would sell to her. Come winter, when her back door slammed open and a rush of frigid air threw a chill over her freshly-baked pies, she would spy the top of Wido's snow-covered cap behind a crate of the best cheese in the land. After she stowed the crate behind a locked door, she would sit Wido down and serve him an apple tart with a warm hunk of his own cheese. Batilda could boast, though she never did, that she was one of few who knew how to make Wido Treyse smile. For the crotchety old hermit shepherd, one smile a year was about all he felt up to, but that one smile he gave freely to Batilda Button.

January seized Lunenfarne in its sharp fangs. Snow that had sugared the hills behind the town for the last three months now deepened into drifts. Bitterly cold seawaves the color of slate beat at the cliffs on Parrot Island and salty spray regularly froze on the balcony around the top of the lighthouse. Women trod carefully along the icy paths to the market, and older children dragged their small siblings to school on sleds. The town piers were mostly empty of ship traffic and on market day, only a handful of traders stood in the square, stamping in the cold.

These days, the once-drab little brown town of Lunenfarne was looking less like a cultural backwater. With the improvements to the town square and waterfront that Vladimir Mynydd had put in place when he was chancellor, new shops and businesses had opened. Older shops had moved to nicer quarters. Now freshly painted signs were swinging above their doors. It's generally accepted that civilization feeds on money, and more money was changing hands in Lunenfarne than ever before. The new workshops were humming with activity. A couple of families of artisans from the south had moved into cottages up behind Fishermen's Row. Weavers were stockpiling as much fabric as possible to get ready for the traders who came in the spring. The gristmill on the Nolta River ran all day long now, even in winter. Ferryman Korsakov had commissioned Otto Wohlfahrt to build him a second ferry boat, and hired Chilperic as boatman. Mr. Basko fretted that the barrels of nuts and dried beans in his grocery were already half empty, and spring still far away. Just down the lane, under the red sign with the foaming tankard, Freya Button kept her steps swept of snow and every afternoon, even in January, her sister Batilda sent for whatever catch the fishermen had brought in that day.

In winter, the Bayside Inn saw few customers who weren't local. That meant that Freya's girls had more time for gossip between themselves, instead of eavesdropping on other people's conversations, which, though not generally acknowledged, was an important part of their duties. Not only did every morsel of news in Lunenfarne pass through this inn, but also much of the news of the faraway world, especially the world of traders and shippers. It was shipping news in particular that most interested Freya Button. It was what made the tavern integral, in certain unspecified ways, to the Buttons' shipping company, an enterprise which, being on the shadier side of legitimate, was unorthodox, to say the least.

For her business to thrive, it was imperative that Freya keep her finger on the pulse of things. She had managed to do so for several years; but now that the town was growing, now that the harbor was busier in the warm months than it had ever been, now that she and Batilda ran several business ventures, Freya was finding it a challenge to stay on top of things. They were bringing in good money. In addition to their inn and the tavern, they owned three dockside warehouses, a small but busy shipping company, and four buildings that they rented out as workshops. They also still owned their old house in Bellesunde and a warehouse there that was so closely guarded it was virtually impregnable. They had plenty of cash, even enough to lend out on occasion. As well, deeply secret, were the funds that the Buttons hid for safe-keeping on behalf of a few unidentified individuals. What they needed especially, though, was someone to help manage all this.

That was the reason, or one of the reasons, why Freya Button turned over the management of her shipping and warehouse enterprises to Vladimir Mynydd. She needed an agent and he badly needed a job. On occasion, he crewed on the *Wolf*, and sometimes even on the *Vixen*, the first male ever to work on board, because there were times when simple brute strength was needed to seal negotiations of a certain – how does one say? – indelicate type. Vladimir's wife Natalia had gotten a court order forbidding him to set foot in his own house or gain access to any of his savings and his son had commandeered the rank of chancellor right out from under him. If it were not for the Button sisters, Mynydd would have had no means of making a living. For ten years he had directed the town council from the highest office in the land. Now he was forced to do whatever Freya Button asked of him. He always complied. Except for a dark regret about his only son, Vladimir Mynydd was happier than he had ever been.

It was during that winter that Ruslan Fairhedd, Florri's father, was called into Dort's office.

"Come in, come in. Sit down, Fairhedd." Dort waved him to a seat. "Would you care for a drink? We're almost done for the day."

"No, thank you."

"All right." Dort idly moved some things around on his desk while he considered his next move. "All right. Now. Some good news. Listen. That park up on Lake Arum. I want it closed off to the public."

"The park? Closed, sir?"

"Yes." Dort leaned back in his chair and swivelled it back and forth.

"I assume … closed temporarily?"

"No. No, you will love this idea, Fairhedd. That whole area up there is going to be put to more profitable use. I have been approached by the Botia people."

Ruslan Fairhedd winced inwardly. "The mining company?"

"They have discovered a vein of copper west of there, or they think they have, and they're very excited about it. So am I. They are hoping it runs right through the park. We are negotiating a deal. If it goes through, I'll have a little cash to disperse to my own people. Including you, of course, Fairhedd."

"But sir! Botia Mining will rip up the whole park. Have you seen the mines they own in the mountains?"

Dort smiled and scratched his eyebrow. "I hardly have time for sight-seeing, Fairhedd. But you know," Dort stretched his arms wide, "what must be done, must. Botia is a good company. We will all benefit from this, I assure you."

"The park is such an asset to the town, though."

"A new mine will be a bigger asset, won't it? You can't deny the benefit, at least to the people who count in this town."

"I don't know. The ferry company has invested quite a bit of money in boats that take people up –"

"I'm talking about people who count. I'm sorry for Mr. Korsakov. He made an ill-considered investment, but I don't know what I can do about it."

"And people have come to like picnicking –"

"How can that be a problem? People can take their picnics somewhere else. It's not the only scenic spot around here, is it?"

"They will want some kind of explanation, sir. People will be asking questions. That park is public property."

"It was. Not any more."

"It's not – ?"Fairhedd paused, then shut his mouth.

"I own it now. Or, well, I will soon. I put an offer on it and can buy it from the town as soon as I get the money together. This can be a real godsend to us, Fairhedd. All I have to do is grease a few palms and the park at Arum Lake will be mine."

"But – what do we tell people? Is it wise to tell them the real reason for the closure?"

"I'll leave that to you. You'll know what to do. You always do. Tell them anything. Tell them we're building public baths, a spa. Make something up. You'll think of something, Fairhedd. Botia wants to get in there fast and start digging right away. Once the pit is open, there will be nothing anyone can do to stop the project."

"I see." Ruslan slumped in his chair.

"Don't look so glum. People will find a new place to eat their sorry little picnics."

"If that's what you want, sir, consider it done. So." Ruslan sat up. "One last thing to do this morning, sir. Some paperwork for you to sign. Payments due by the end of the month." He gave Dort a sheaf of papers. Dort ran his finger down columns of expenses.

"Look at this. What the hell is this?" he asked. "That much mercury for the lighthouse?"

Ruslan looked. "Yes. Apparently they need that much."

"That stuff is bloody expensive. What do they need it for?"

"The light turns with a clockwork mechanism, I'm told."

"Yes? So?"

"So, the clockwork has to sit in a trough of mercury. The mechanism is very heavy and it turns more easily or – I don't know why, but it's standard, they tell me, or so your father once explained – or rather, it's just – it's standard."

Dort thought for a minute. "All that quicksilver? Right here under our noses, when all this time I've had to scour Spain and Italy to find tiny bottles of it. Interesting." He sat back in his chair. "You know what I need you to do? I want you to go out there, Fairhedd, and bring me back a bottle of the stuff."

Ruslan paused. "Mercury from the lighthouse, sir?"

"A few ounces. One bottle. My mother needs it for her pain. She says it helps her. She gets quite desperate and when she gets like that, she drives me nuts. I mean, surely the lighthouse can still operate minus one bottle."

"I assume so. Surely it can."

"Get out there as soon as you can. This afternoon."

Winds were relentless and rain blew in sheets that day. Even in the bay the waves were nearly two feet high. Gregor was in the tower, making sure the lamps were filled when he saw a boat rowing out from town. The oarsman could hardly make headway. Gregor finished his task and made his slow way down the stairs.

He met two men at the door, one in a dark cloak, one in uniform, both of them soaked to the skin. They pushed inside.

One of them spoke. "I'm Ruslan Fairhedd."

And he said more. Gregor knew he was saying more. He saw the man's mouth moving but all that registered was that name. Ruslan Fairhedd. Florri's father, the man who had been informed he must give his daughter away in marriage. Then did as he was ordered. Against his own daughter's wishes. This man standing here had done this thing to his daughter, because his employer demanded it.

Gregor looked up. "I'm sorry? I – I – You were saying?"

Fairhedd frowned. What a simpleton! But what can you expect? This is this is the kind of person they get to run a lighthouse. "I repeat. Chancellor Mynydd has asked me to procure a bottle of mercury. You look confused." He handed Gregor a bottle. "Take this and fill it for the Chancellor."

Chancellor? That would be Dort, Florri's husband. Gregor had to make an effort to keep his mind on the matter at hand. "Mercury. Yes, I suppose I can spare a bottle. Will you come back for it?"

"We'll wait here. He wants it right away."

"It will take me a little while. Negotiating the stairs is –" He gestured to his legs.

"We'll wait by your fire, if you don't mind."

While Gregor labored up to the top of the tower, Ruslan stepped into the house and strolled over to the easel that stood in a corner. It held a work in progress, a pencil drawing of a girl's face. He would have recognised the image as his daughter, if Gregor's skills were what they had once been.

"The lightkeeper drew this? Looks like he has the palsy," laughed the soldier. "Guess he has more than just a gimpy leg."

"He can't even hold a pencil steady."

"People shouldn't try to do things they ain't no good at," the soldier pontificated, because he knew how the world worked. "Any idiot knows that."

A few minutes went by.

"What's he doin'?" asked the soldier. "Sure is takin' his own sweet time."

It took Gregor as long as ever to get to the top of the tower. One hundred thirty-nine steps. Then it took him a couple of minutes to remember what he came up for. Going down was even harder for him.

Three more times that winter, Ruslan Fairhedd was asked to return to Parrot Island. On his last trip, it took Gregor so long to fill the bottle that Fairhedd grew tired of waiting. He shouted to him from the bottom of the stairs, and finally, calling repeatedly, he climbed up himself.

He found Gregor lying on the floor, pushing little buttons of mercury around like a child.

"Hey! Didn't you hear me? I've been calling you!"

"Oh. I'm sorry."

"I don't have all day to wait for you while you mess around. Where's my bottle?"

"I – "

"What's the matter? Are you all right, man? You look a bit off." Gregor's face was dull and pale. He looked confused. His hands shook when he handed Ruslan the bottle.

"Let me help you down the steps." Ruslan held tight to Gregor's arm. "Easy. Go easy. One step at a time." This young man is not well, Ruslan thought. The jerk's been into the sauce, thought the soldier.

Spring came round again and eased into summer. It had been eighteen years since the first beacon fire was lit on Parrot Island. The past winter for Gregor had been long and a bit lonely. His mother rowed out to see him after mass on most Sundays, bringing groceries, but the only time he saw his old school friends was when he rowed over to the shops, or occasionally, took an hour off to have a pint at the tavern. He couldn't confide to any of his friends that he had often felt a little depressed this winter. He couldn't even say why he felt that way. He had expected to be more content, living on Parrot Island. It might have had something to do with his painting. He had been forced to give it up entirely. His hands shook so much he could hardly hold a brush.

On this bright May Saturday, he decided it would be a good day to prune his roses, but as he looked out over the town from the balcony at the top of the tower, he realised there was something going on in Lunenfarne. People were preparing for Carnevale! He had forgotten that it must be Carnevale time again. I should go, he thought, heading inside for the stairs. It would be nice to stroll around a little, see some people. I can prune roses tomorrow. Oh, woops, he laughed, the steps! I almost missed them. He grabbed the railing. Whew, that was close. Carefully now, he descended one hundred thirty-four steps and then, thinking he was at the bottom, he stepped into space and landed face down. Stunned, he lay there for a minute. When he finally got up, his legs were shaking but then, his legs shook a lot lately. Remarkably, he was sore but unhurt.

His plan to go to Carnevale was forgotten until the music of bagpipers came floating over the island. Oh, yes, Carnevale! He changed his shirt and rowed across the bay. He was happy to be outside. It cleared his head to be in the fresh air, or he imagined it did.

"Mr. Korsakov!" he yelled to the ferryman.

"Gregor! It's good to see you, laddie! Sure, tie up right there. That spot's reserved for you, even on holidays. Going to the fair today?"

"Yep."

"Whoa! Here, wait, lad. Let me help you get out. You okay?"

Gregor clambered onto the dock. "Sure. Thanks. I'll only stay for an hour or so."

"Stay as long as you like. As long as you like. Gregor! Wrong way, my lad. It's this way to the fair." With narrowed eyes and knitted brows, Korsakov watched Gregor limp away.

Gregor immediately cursed himself for not bringing a sketchbook, then remembered he was no longer any good with a pencil. There were so many things to see! Ladies in pale-rainbow dresses and children ducking in and out among peoples' legs and a pipers' band blowing their lungs out and, look at this! A man juggling paper balloons in all colors and sizes!

He bought a bag of toffees and sat on a bench to watch the people going by. Carnevale, something for everyone and everybody so happy!

Until he heard the child screaming.

A large man dragged his little boy out of the crowd. The man glared threateningly, eyes rolling in fury. Disturbed, people turned away. The child, no more than three years old, was shaking his head furiously, pulling back and trying to brake with his feet. Instantly, Gregor's mind reeled away. Angry fathers. No, he couldn't watch this, he couldn't. He felt sick. People nearby stopped what they were doing, frowning. Right in front of Gregor's bench, the man yanked the child's pants down to spank his bare bottom. Mothers covered their children's faces and people hurried away from the area.

The little boy sobbed piteously, trying to get his pants pulled up and falling to the ground. The father snatched him up by one arm, the child's feet flying through the air, and dragged him to the bench where Gregor sat. He threw him so hard onto the seat of the bench that Gregor trembled with anger. He wanted so badly to punch the man's face in. That was the problem with being a cripple. He couldn't punch anybody, even if he wanted to. He had hit his father that one time, but had only managed to land the blow because it was unexpected and completely out of character.

This man in front of him was snarling at his little boy. "I don't want to hear another sound out of you! You sit there until I come back. Sit there. And stop that blubbering! Stop it! Do you hear? Do you hear?" With fists on hips and crazy eyes, he glowered until the child nodded. Then he stormed off through the crowd.

The little boy cried quietly for a couple of minutes. Gregor couldn't bring himself to get up and leave him sitting there alone. After a few more minutes, the crying subsided into quiet snuffling. What had become of the child's father?

The little boy's face was so dirty his tears left trails on his cheeks. Gregor handed the boy a handkerchief. "Here. Blow," he said softly. "Will you let me dry your face?"

The child looked doubtfully at him while Gregor gently wiped his cheeks.

"There. That's better, isn't it?" Gregor glanced around, afraid of seeing that father return. "Why don't you keep the handkerchief, just in case." The boy took it and wadded it into a small damp ball. He stared soberly at Gregor, seeming to find him fascinating. My own little boy, Florri's and my little boy, Gregor mused, would be about this age.

Again Gregor scanned the crowd, watching for the father. "Would you like a toffee?"

The boy paused, then took the toffee, unwrapped a little of it, and tried a small lick. He looked questioningly at Gregor.

"Go ahead. Eat it. It's good." He smiled when the boy put it cautiously into his mouth.

Another few minutes passed. The boy perched on the edge of the bench, letting his feet swing back and forth. Gregor couldn't imagine how the father could leave such a small boy for this long.

"Well. I'm getting hungry," said Gregor. The boy looked up at him. Gregor rose. "Are you hungry? Shall I ask Mr. Basko for a couple of sausages?"

The boy opened his mouth, then nodded. Gregor doubted he would still be there when he got back, but he was there, leaning out and watching for Gregor, wiggling until Gregor handed him a hot sausage in a roll.

"These are good, aren't they?" They ate in companionable silence, and still the boy's father had not returned.

The man with toy musical instruments went by honking on a whistle, carrying drums and flutes and tambourines. The child practically fell off the bench, watching. The lady twirling batons passed, and the man with all sorts of toys on wooden wheels. The child's eyes lit up when the man went by juggling paper balloons.

"Would you like a balloon?"

The child looked, nodded.

"Do you want to pick it out?" The boy slid off the seat and took the hand that Gregor offered him. "What color?" While the child decided, Gregor spotted the boy's father not far away, laughing and joking. He was not returning to his son, that man. He was giving no thought to his boy at all. He was standing in line to see the three-breasted woman.

"My third time!" he bragged. "Hey! Didya see that Mata Hari show yet? She got tits on her like a pair a whale bladders, I swear to ya!"

Gregor couldn't stand to hear more. He paid for the balloon. "Be careful. Don't crush it." Then, turning the boy away so he wouldn't notice his father, he spoke softly to him. "How would you like to go for a boat ride?"

Gregor smiled at the look of amazement on the child's face. He took him by the hand and walked away with him. He just walked him right out of the festival, and why shouldn't he? Was it so odd for a man to take a child for a boat ride? He didn't see anyone he knew, though why should he worry if he did? Some inkling of caution swam through his muddled brain like a quicksilver minnow, but Gregor couldn't catch hold of it.

Ferryman Korsakov, standing on the far bank of the Arum River, was sure he saw Gregor Treyse putting something into his boat. What was it? He couldn't trust his old eyes anymore. Maybe it was a new puppy. Maybe it was a sack of flour. For sure it was not a lovely maiden. Poor Gregor. Never in a month of Sundays would that boy ever find himself a maiden.

Gregor rowed across the bay and pulled the boat ashore on Parrot Island. He helped the boy get out, then stood there for a minute, his fingers pressing his forehead. The child stood next to him, looking around, finally looking up at Gregor as if waiting for instructions on what to do next.

Gregor was wondering the same thing. Not only what to do next. What had he just done? People might think he was kidnapping this boy. Was it strange, what he'd done? Wrong? It had seemed perfectly right at the time. Was it right or not? His mind went back and forth. Right or wrong? It was very confusing. He felt the child's hand slip into his and he looked down at him. The poor little soul. He would have to take him back, give him back to that awful man. That was the right thing to do.

"We'll have to go back now. Your father will be worried about you." Gregor wasn't so sure that was true. But the boy belonged with his father. Now, how would he play this? How was he to go about returning the boy? Confront the father and risk his horrible temper? Tell the man, oh sorry if I worried you, I just thought your little boy would enjoy a boat ride? After the man finished beating Gregor to a pulp, he would turn on his son.

No! He couldn't allow that! That thought turned Gregor's stomach. He had suffered that too many times himself. Maybe he could take the child to the priest and say … well, he had found this boy … yes, he had found him … where? Not on the island.

No no no. He couldn't handle that, not today. Tomorrow. Gregor cackled in relief. Tomorrow! He would think of something tomorrow. One night wouldn't make that much difference.

"Would you like to see the lighthouse?" The child skipped beside him all the way up the hill.

Gregor made cheesy-potatoes for their dinner. While that baked, he said he'd have to light the lamps in the tower.

"You stay here," he told the boy. "It's a long way up there. You would not like it."

By the time Gregor lit the lamps and wound the clockwork mechanism and turned to go back down, the child had crept to the top step and sat there waiting for him.

"Were you lonely? You weren't afraid, were you?" The boy gripped Gregor's hand and they went down together. Gregor filled the hot water tank on the stove. After they ate, he took the bath tub from its nail on the wall.

"You're going to need a bath, my man," Gregor told him. "We'll throw your trousers and shirt in there too. You'll have to wear one of my shirts to bed."

It was while he helped the boy out of his clothes that he realised the real nature of his crime. Perhaps a slightly more serious crime than he had thought, or anyway, if misconstrued, it would seem more serious. Perhaps a lot more serious. What he had done was quite bad, actually. He had worried he would be blamed for being a kidnapper? Yes, he had. But this? This made him a kidnapper of the worst kind. People would think he was whacked in the head. They put people in jail for this. How could he ever make this right?

Awkward now, he handed the child a washcloth. "Here. Scrub yourself. I'll ... I'll help you with your hair."

While the child towelled off, Gregor rinsed out the little trousers and shirt and the dirty handkerchief he had lent. The water turned almost black, the clothes were so filthy.

Now Gregor's stomach was in knots from worrying. He was in trouble up to his neck. Was he crazy? He must be. People in the town would loathe him for what he had done, that's for sure. Walking off with someone's child? The father would hate him. He'd probably kill him. Oh misery.

He had to keep this a secret. He couldn't let anyone find out, no, oh god, never. He would be whipped. Thrown into prison. He could not tell a soul. But when Gregor thought about that wild-eyed father, that horrible man – no child should have to live with someone like that. No. Gregor could not bring himself to undo what he had begun. He had done the right thing. No one knew better than he about abusive fathers. He had done the right thing.

Gregor tried to stop his mind from running in circles. In all the confusion, he realised he had not heard this child speak a word all day. He knelt down and rolled the sleeves of his big shirt back over the narrow wrists. He took the little hands in his.

"You never told me your name. What is it?" he asked. He got no answer. He sat down on the bed that used to be Kai's when he was a boy. The child hopped up and curled up next to him. Gregor played with a damp golden curl and smiled. "I'm Gregor. Did I tell you that? So now, won't you tell me your name? I'm Gregor and you are …?" A little frown puckered the forehead. "Are you Cinderella? No? Are you Goldilocks?" Well, that got a little smile and a shake of the head. "I know. You're Snow White! No? Are you sure? Come on, tell me. I won't tell anyone."

He wanted to erase the worried look on that little face. "Here's what we can do. I can give you a name. Would that be all right with you?" He thought for a minute. "I think maybe I'll call you Lily." He looked down at her. "Do you like that name? It's the name of a flower. Lily. It's pretty, don't you think? Just as pretty as you."

The next morning, Gregor went upstairs at dawn to turn off the lamps in the tower. Again, the child was waiting for him at the top of the stairs.

"You can come in, Lily." Gregor beckoned. "Come on. Look out here. You can see the whole town from up here. Do you want to go out on the balcony? It's awfully high. I don't want you to be afraid." He opened the door and the wind blew Gregor's big shirt up around Lily's waist. Gregor patted it down, laughing, and she giggled.

"Let's sit over here, out of the wind."

They put their legs through the railing and sat beside each other, looking across the bay.

"So that's Lunenfarne, Lily. Can you see your house from here?"

Lily shook her head soberly.

"Usually you can watch all the fishermen taking their boats out to sea in the morning. But not today because it's Sunday. Oh! Sunday! I almost forgot. Quick, Lily, get up! My mother is coming for a visit. See her, in that little boat coming this way? We have to hide. I don't want anyone to know you're here. Be quick. Down the steps."

Descending was not easy for Gregor. When they finally reached the bottom, Gregor opened the door to a closet. "Come on! Quick! In here! Yes, come on, it will be okay. You have to hide." Gregor stopped. "What is it? You're afraid?"

Lily started to wail.

"Don't cry! Don't cry! All right. You don't have to go in there. You choose a place to hide. We can't let my mother see you. How's this, under the bed? I'll be right near you. But be very very quiet."

"Yoo hoo!"

"Good morning, Mother." Gregor draped a quilt over the edge of the bed. "I'm – oh! Let me help you with all that."

"Did I come too early? I thought you would come down – oh, these are heavy – to help me carry the groceries." Panting, she dropped a basket onto the table. "And here's the shirt I mended for you and ..." She looked at the clothes on the drying rack. "Who do these little things belong to?" She held up the damp shirt and tsk-tsked at a hole that needed mending.

"Oh. These? These clothes?"

Ermentrude Treyse looked around. There was a paper balloon on the floor. "Did you have visitors?" Her cheeks reddened. "Oh! Oh, I'm sorry,

Gregor. Did you … are you having company? I can go back. I don't need to stay."

"No no, Mother. Don't go. Here. Sit down and I'll make tea."

"Are you sure? I don't want to interrupt …."

"You're not interrupting."

"I brought a nice little pastry. And a cake for later in the week for you. As long as I'm not …."

"No, you're not – not anything. There's no one here but us chickens."

Choo!

Now, if you think about it, if you picture a small person, clad only in someone else's big linen shirt, and imagine her stuck cramped and shivering under a bed, can you really expect her to stay still, not give a wriggle or a sneeze? Especially after hearing those delicious words? Pastry? Cake? Pastry *and* cake? What child could hear those words and not react? It would be a punishing challenge for anyone, but especially for a little girl who has developed, through life-long deprivation, the appetite of a horse when it comes to sweets. Lily pulled her knees up to her chest and half-smothered her sneeze. But it was a pretty big sneeze.

Gregor stopped with the tea kettle in his hand. Ermentrude stopped and turned from her basket of groceries. She looked at Gregor. She looked at the unmade bed. She could see into the other room. Another unmade bed. She looked back at Gregor.

Now, to be clear, Ermentrude was a lovely person, an accommodating person. She abhorred saying anything that would embarrass someone. She was not assertive by nature, not by any stretch of the imagination. But the humiliating experience of putting up with a husband like Wido Treyse through thick and thicker had given her an acute sensitivity to being ridiculed as a fool. Wido had often accused her of that and she did not like it. Ermentrude was no fool. So she wanted to face the present conundrum head on.

"Who ... sneezed?" she asked in a mousy voice, admittedly a little mousy. Audacity was a new thing for her.

"Well!" Gregor replied. He swung the tea kettle in small arcs and tapped his toe on the floor. He pulled his lips in between his teeth. He nodded. "Who sneezed."

"Who sneezed?"

Gregor sighed. He clapped the kettle back down onto the iron stove. He limped slowly over to the bed and crouched. He bent his head. His mother almost thought he was praying. He'd been acting strangely for weeks now, so it was possible, barely possible, that he actually was praying. She watched him lift the quilt and peek under the bed. She bent to peek under the bed. She straightened. She frowned, her eyes wide. Gregor's shirt was under there. With a child inside it.

"It was Lily who sneezed. And here she is. This is Lily." Gregor helped her crawl out. He straightened her shirt. Lily blink-blinked, one finger in her mouth. Ermentrude melted into a chair.

"Is she yours, Gregor?" Ermentude squeaked.

"Well, no. She's not *mine.*"

"I mean, are you the father?"

"Her father? No! Mother! No, of course not. I never ..." Well, not never. But not for a long time. "No, I'm not her father."

"How did she get here?"

Gregor sat down. Lily nestled onto his lap and he told his mother the whole story. He tried to refer to Lily and her father using terms that Lily would not understand, but he told it exactly as it happened – from his viewpoint, anyway.

"But Gregor! This is illegal what you've done. This is terrible! You can't keep —" She looked at Lily. "You can't keep someone else's ..."

"Look at her, Mother. I told you what it was like for her. Can you imagine someone abusing this little girl, mistreating her the way that man did?" He saw his mother's face crumple, yet he pressed on. "Yes, you can imagine it, can't you? So can I. Haven't we seen enough of that? Both you and I? Haven't I suffered most of my life because of a man who could not keep his temper?"

Ermentrude started to cry. "I know, Gregor. I know."

"You say what I did is wrong. Maybe it is. But if I can keep a child safe from that kind of man, I would consider myself to have every right to let her stay here. Every right." He ran his hands through his hair. "Could you take her back, Mother, now that you've seen her? Could you dress her in filthy boy's clothes and put her back in that situation? Return her to such a man? Could you?"

Ermentrude shook her head. "When you put it that way, I don't think I could. No."

Gregor turned Lily's face to his. "Lily? Do you like it here? Do you like this house?"

She nodded, her eyes fastened on his.

"Would you like to stay?"

She grabbed hold of the front of his shirt.

"Yes? Would you? Tell me the truth, Lily. Would you like to stay?"

She nodded, never loosening her grip on his shirt.

Ermentrude joined the two of them on the bed. "Lily?" She put her hand on Lily's head. "Do you know what we should do? We should get you some proper clothes. How would you like me to make you a frock? You know." She held out her skirt. "Like this? Would you like that?"

Lily nodded.

"What color would you like?"

Lily bit her lip and looked away.

"I'll make two frocks and you can choose your favorite." Ermentrude looked up at Gregor with a watery smile. "And now, do you know what I think? I think we should have that pastry that I brought."

Lily jumped to the floor and clapped her hands. Gregor and Ermentrude sat perfectly still for a long moment, watching, admiring, and smiling.

"Look at her, Mother. It takes so little to make her happy."

Ermentrude came back after work three evenings later with frocks for Lily and a white pinafore and a blue hooded cloak.

"Look what grandma …." Ermentrude stopped and looked at Gregor. "Can I pretend to be her grandmama?"

Gregor laughed. "Were you up all night working on these clothes, Mother?"

"Well, I got started and I couldn't stop. Look how pretty she looks."

Ermentrude brought some stockings and shoes that fit pretty well. She brought cookies too. It wasn't until these came out of the basket that she got a hug from Lily.

"Lily, can you say 'thank you, Grandma'?" Gregor asked, but Lily lowered her eyes with a sulky look and turned away.

Later, Ermentrude asked quietly, "Doesn't she ever speak?"

"Not a word so far. Not a word."

Gregor was not often seen around town, but when he was, almost everyone who knew him voiced private concerns about him. Look how his hands shake. Look how often he stumbles. Maybe his limp is worse? Or is he drunk? He doesn't seem drunk. He's confused, sometimes. Maybe sometimes he's confused, but usually he's pretty clear-headed. He keeps himself neat and clean. His friends say he never has more than one pint when they meet him at the Bayside Inn.

After Lily came, though, Gregor was rarely seen in the village. He relied on his mother to keep him and Lily supplied with groceries. Mr. Korsakov noticed that Ermentrude was rowing out to the island two and three times a week. Maybe something was wrong with Gregor. If so, Ermentrude said nothing to anyone about it. She never mentioned it, so of course everyone in town came to a different conclusion for what was wrong. He was lonely, too much solitude. It's that island, full of ghosts, as everyone knows. Gregor must be what? Twenty years old? And he has never had a girl, has he? Well, what girl would ...? But Gregor is a fine young man, nicer than a good many, and not bad-looking, either. Still, it is strange, and no one is saying what the problem is, so that in itself makes you wonder, doesn't it? Oh yes. It makes you wonder.

On one thing they all agreed. Something was not right.

Gregor's mother knew that he was having nightmares but he told no one, not even Ermentrude, when the hallucinations started.

One night, in the middle of the night, he awoke screaming. Lily ran to his beside, shaking him and sobbing.

"Gegga! Gegga! No no no, Gegga!" She crawled into his bed and pressed her hands to his face. "No no, Gegga. See Lily, see Lily."

Gregor sat up, wiping his forehead on his arm. He was drenched with sweat. Oh, what a terrible dream. Lily threw her arms around his neck. "Shh shh shh," she crooned.

He hugged her and fell back to his damp pillow. "I'm all right now, Lily. Everything's all right. Did I frighten you?" He stroked her head. "Oh my Lily. My little Lily."

"My Gegga, my Gegga."

Fortunately Gregor spotted the boat rowed by two soldiers before they landed on Parrot Island. He bumbled his way down the steps as fast as he could.

"Lily! Men are coming and I don't want them to see you. Please, you have to hide in this closet. It will only be for a short time. Please Lily!"

"No!"

"Lily, you must. You must stay in there until I come for you. And don't make any noise."

"No, Gegga!"

He prodded her inside. "Look, you'll be perfectly safe in here. It's just a bunch of brooms and brushes and – here. Let's turn this bucket over and you can sit on it."

"Nooo!"

There was a loud knock on the door. Gregor put his fingers to his lips and shut the closet door.

"We're here for more quicksilver, Mr. Treyse."

"I've given you all I can spare."

"The chancellor wants all of it. He says it belongs to the town and he can take it if he wants."

"What, the whole trough?"

The soldiers pointed to a cart they had brought, loaded with scoops and buckets.

"The clockwork can't run if you take it all."

"Yeah well. That's the way it goes. He said to take all of it."

"If the clockwork doesn't work, the light won't turn. Ships won't be able to tell that this is Parrot Island."

"Not our concern, Mr. Treyse. Ships came into the harbor before there was a lighthouse. They'll manage just the same way they did in the old days." The men shouldered past Gregor and marched up the stairs with their buckets. They took all the mercury they could lay their hands on, every drop, almost every little button.

After they left, Gregor opened the closet door. Lily was crouched on her bucket, desolate. She looked up at him with a red face. Her eyes were swollen from crying. She turned to face the back of the closet.

"Come here, honey."

She shook her head and punched his arm when he reached for her.

"Come on. You can come out now. They've gone. And look how brave you were." He picked her up and took her to a rocking chair next to the stove. "Now tell me what I can do to make you happy again."

She punched him in the shoulder. "Cake."

Gregor laughed. "One piece of cake or two?"

Lily held up three fingers. "Swee."

"You're a little pig!" He tickled her til she laughed.

Gregor did not know what to do about the clockwork that turned the lights. The mechanism was too heavy to turn in an empty trough. But sailors relied on seeing that light flash every twenty seconds. He had quizzed the soldiers while they filled their buckets. What was the chancellor going to do with that quantity of mercury? Sell it, they said. Some shaman or somebody had agreed to buy it all for a great deal of money. Dort Mynydd had told them to take it whether Gregor protested or not.

Gregor, if he had known the truth about the properties of mercury, should have thanked them for taking it. But actually, it was too late for that, much too late. If they had taken the mercury away weeks before, things might have turned out differently. Now the trough was empty. The quicksilver was gone.

All gone, but not gone soon enough to save Gregor.

By now, it was early autumn. Gregor finally had to admit it. He was not getting better. He did not know what was wrong with him. He had grown thin this summer because he couldn't keep food down. His hands shook constantly. Many times he could barely make it up to the top of the tower. His biggest fear wasn't for himself. He almost didn't care what happened to him anymore. He was terrified when he thought about what would happen to Lily.

His mother, Ermentrude Treyse, had watched his decline. She could not, would not lose her son. Her husband Wido was little more to her than a living ghost, so Gregor was all she had in the world. She had failed him many times in childhood. But she was going to fight to keep him now.

She went to the only person she could rely on for help, Father James at the church.

"I've seen Gregor a couple of times this past month," he told her. "I've been worried about him, too. I'll tell you what I can do. I have a duty to perform at the convent in the mountains. Let me speak to Sister Rosemarie while I'm there. She has a great knowledge of remedies and healing. I'll try to convince her to come back with me. Though I don't know. Rosemarie is getting on in years, Ermentrude. It would not be an easy trip for her. Say a prayer with me, and maybe I'll be able to convince her to come see Gregor."

Father James left the very next day for the Saint Scholastica convent. Being hale and hearty himself, it took him less than three hours to make his way up along the Nolta River to the summit of Gorm Mountain. Sister Kunegunde, now the Mother Superior, welcomed him with a list of dreary complaints and urgent needs. He had to put off asking to see Sister Rosemarie until after Nones. When he finally found her in the library, he was struck by how frail she had become. But she greeted him warmly.

"Father! It's so wonderful to see you!"

"And you, Rosemarie. I was just speaking with Kunegunde."

"Did she mention my ink? I don't have much left."

"She told me. I'm going to send to Bellesunde for everything you need. Is this the book you're working on?"

"This is my latest. Not flowers this time, but fungi."

"Your illustrations are absolutely beautiful. As are all the herbologies in your collection. What a treasure this one will be."

"All to the glory of God, James. There is much lore here that needs to be preserved." She closed the book. "Ah, the bell for vespers is ringing already. The hours fly by when I'm working up here."

"Sister, I must beg for a moment of your time before we go to the chapel. There is a young man in Lunenfarne who is quite desperately ill. We have no physician anywhere near us, so I wondered if there was any chance you could come see him? He's a boy I've always held in high esteem."

"Oh, James. Much as I would like to help, you surely must see that my old legs would never make it down the mountain. I'm afraid I'm good for little else now except working here in the library."

"I was worried you would say that. I wouldn't even have asked if he weren't such a special young man. A very artistic young fellow."

"But you know James, I could recommend someone. I have been tutoring a woman since she was a child. Lisabetta, she is called. She probably knows more than I do about healing by now. She has never taken holy orders, but you know, I truly feel she has been worth her weight in gold to us. She has nursed so many sisters back to health. However, her presence here has become a bit of a sore point. Sister Kunegunde, well –" Rosemarie smiled ruefully. "Kunegunde says we can no longer afford to keep Lisabetta at the convent since she refuses to take the vows. She threatens to send the girl away. The new chancellor has raised our taxes, as you know, and the convent is not receiving the funds from the faithful that it used to. I can understand Kunegunde's dilemma. Lisabetta does need to find another home. Oh, James. I hate to burden you with all this. I'm sure you've already had an earful of our problems."

"Two earsful from Kunegunde, Rosemarie."

"Well, we could talk to Lisabetta, couldn't we? Maybe there can be a place for her in your village."

Two days later, Lisabetta and Father James started back down the trail to Lunenfarne. James had wanted to leave on Friday but Lisabetta had so many things to pack that she could not leave until Saturday. Kunegunde reluctantly loaned a donkey to carry Lisabetta's bags and boxes and bottles of potions, of which there were a great many. Father James promised that the boy Gerbert would bring the animal back within the week.

Their progress down the mountain was slow. Lisabetta was delighting in finding wild sage, oregano, and mushrooms of all kinds to add to her basket. When they finally reached Lunenfarne, Father James had to leave her.

"I'm sorry I can't go with you to see Gregor. However, Mr. Korsakov will find someone to row you out to Parrot Island," he told Lisabetta. "I must hurry away. It's Saturday. I have confessions to hear and I'm late already."

"I understand, Father. I'll talk to this man at the lighthouse and see if I can give him any help. You'll come back for me later?"

"I'll have time before vespers to row out and bring you back. Perhaps Gregor's mother can give you a place to sleep tonight."

Gregor was working clumsily at the woodpile. He couldn't get the axe to bite into the logs. The thing seemed much more intent on trying to lop his foot off. He was leaning on the pile, frustrated and panting, when he saw a boat heading out to the island. He knew it could not be his mother, but who was this? A woman. Instantly, he thought the worst: Lily's mother? She had found him. Was she finally coming for her daughter? He wobbled into the house.

"Lily." He knelt down and took her by the shoulders. "Someone is coming. I don't know who it is. Could it be your mother?"

Lily looked mystified.

"Do you have a mother, Lily?"

She had no answer.

"Well, just to be safe, I must ask you to hide again –"

"No closet!"

"Someone is coming. We don't want her to see you, do we? Please, Lily. Be quick. Into the closet."

"No, Gregga! No no! I'm not!"

"It won't be for long, I promise you. Remember, we have cake for dessert tonight. You'll have a nice big piece. Quick now. Be very quiet. I'll come for you soon. Very soon." He closed her into the closet and went to the door. A young woman was coming up through the meadow. He was certain she was coming for Lily. Gregor's heart sank.

"Hello," called the woman. "You must be Gregor."

"Can I help you with something?"

"Father James sent me. He is worrried about you and thought maybe I could help."

Gregor stood in the doorway, confused. "Worried?"

She wished she hadn't put it like that. "I'm Lisabetta. May I come in?"

"I – I'm a little busy. I have some work to do up in the tower." He didn't want her to find Lily.

"Can we talk while you work?"

"What do you want to talk about?"

"Well, how are you feeling? I – I have some herbs with me. I brought Golden Flower. It's a soothing mix of herbs that might settle your stomach. Lavender, camomile, raspberry."

"Father James sent you?"

"He did. He worries that you are not eating."

Gregor tried to collect his thoughts. Anything out of the ordinary confused him uttterly. "I have things to do." He pointed. "Up in the tower."

"Well, it looks like a long climb," said Lisabetta, craning her neck to see up the winding staircase. "Should we get started?"

Gregor shuffled toward the stairs. "I have to fill the lamps and do some cleaning and – and fill the lamps. Oh, I said that already." He tripped on the first stair.

"Here, let me help you," Lisabetta offered. She offered her arm and was surprised that he gripped it so tightly. Slowly they made their way up the stairs.

"Look at the view!" she said, when they finally entered the lamp room. She went from window to window.

"You're not afraid of heights?" Gregor asked.

"I've spent most of my life living in a convent on the edge of a cliff. No, heights don't bother me. You said you have to do something to the lamps?"

"They have to be filled." He put out a hand to steady himself. "With oil." Shaking, he tried to remove a glass chimney.

"I can help with that."

Handing her the chimney, Gregor suddenly bent forward at the waist, his hands on his knees.

"Are you going to be sick, Gregor?"

He shook his head. "I hope not."

"Tell me what to do here."

He leaned against the wall, his face pale and damp, and gave her instructions.

"Wait!" he cried in panic. "Who's that? Who is that?"

Lisabetta whirled around. She looked back at him. "There's no one here, Gregor."

He pointed. "That man —"

"There is no one." She touched his shoulder and studied him carefully. He wiped his brow. "Do you still see someone?"

"No. No. He's gone."

"You did see someone, though?"

"I thought so."

"Does this happen often?"

"I don't know."

"I'm almost finished filling these. Then we should go down so you can rest. Should I wipe these chimneys clean?"

"There's a brush there."

"Gregor, what is this trough for?"

"Doesn't work. Not anymore."

"There's a drop of mercury in here."

"They took it all away."

"Took what away?"

"The mercury. Every last drop. Or I thought they took it all."

Mercury. Aha. She began to understand. "Was there mercury in here for a long time?"

"Always."

"I don't like that stuff. I once knew a woman who actually drank – Where are you going? Gregor?"

"Just need some air."

"Wait for me."

"It's very beautiful. Look how beautiful it is out here tonight." The door closed behind him.

"Let me just finish up here and we'll go down and make some tea, shall we?"

Lisabetta finished cleaning the chimneys. She called out the door, "Do we light the lamps now, Gregor?" She hung the brush on a nail. "Is it too early?"

"It's time. The stars have already been lit, some of them. Did you see? Look at them." Gregor was leaning on the railing, looking out across the quicksilver ocean. "Quite a few of them have been lit already. Little lighthouses. The evening star. There. See it? I've always wondered what it's like out there, haven't you?"

"I'll come out in just a minute."

"You hear it? The music?"

Gregor placed his foot on the railing. The night wind was sharp and cold. He hung there, one foot dangling. So, he thought, that's where the music comes from. The wind carries it from far over the sea. From way out there on the edge. Or maybe, yes, maybe it falls from the stars. Gregor rose slowly to stand on the railing. Listen, listen. That is where the music comes from. From the stars! So beautiful, all of it. So beautiful.

"Almost done here." Lisabetta rummaged around until she found matches for the lamps. She lit one. When she moved to light the next, she noticed Gregor swaying dangerously, trying to keep his balance atop the railing.

"Gregor?" She blew out the match. "Gregor! What are you doing?"

Fear terror can't breathe. Move move. She couldn't. Legs frozen immobile. Shouting no, Gregor, no! Reach, reach for the door and get out there, trying to get out there, out to Gregor where he teeters in the wind.

Gre-e-e-go-o-r!

His clothes and hair like feathers, all caught, caught by the wind. She would never forget that moment. Never.

Nor would he. Ah. That north star, gleaming so bright bright bright on the indigo sky. He could almost, yes he could. It was so near. So near tonight, he could touch it, take it down to show Lily ….

"Gregor!" Lisabetta reached for the leg of his trousers.

But up, up into the sunset air Gregor soared. Into the violet twilight. Flying, like a bird.

Gregor spread his wings and flew away.

Sick. A nightmare. Everything that followed was a nightmare. Gregor, nowhere. He was nowhere to be found. Where had he landed? Somewhere over the cliff. So dark, it was getting so dark and nothing could be seen of him. Lisabetta running stumbling down through the meadow to meet Father James. Come! Come quickly! Horrible horrible.

She couldn't stop Gregor. She had tried to stop him and failed oh how terribly she had failed. She had been no help to this person at all. In a panic of fright, weak and nauseous, she collapsed into Father James's arms.

People came out from the town, came out with lanterns. She did not know who they were, how they got there. She crumpled, devastated. So full of shame, she could not speak. She could not answer their questions. She was no healer. She had let a boy die on her first day in their town. How they would hate her.

Thick darkness, wind keening. Lisabetta sat crouched in the doorway of the house, shaking uncontrollably. A older man came to speak with her. Jozef. He said he was the harbormaster.

"You mustn't blame yourself, Miss," he told her. He knelt before her and pulled a quilt around her shoulders. "We've known for a while now that something was terribly wrong with Gregor. His mind, his poor body. He wasn't right anymore. He wasn't what he used to be."

She shivered under the quilt.

"Folks are down there, still looking. Do you have somewhere to sleep tonight?"

She shook her head.

"Why not stay here? I'll sleep in the other room. You won't be alone."

She nodded.

The next day, someone told her, and told the mother. They had found the ruined body.

Cold silver rain pelting the gunmetal sea. Heavy bronze church bell tolling, tolling all morning. But silenced now. Silence everywhere, oppressive, blanketing the town. In the chapel, a damp cold. Feet shuffling across the stone floor. Then, a leaden quiet, impenetrably dense. Peoples' breath in clouds of white. White faces staring up at Father James, beseeching him for an answer.

For the dead boy, the path is clear now, straight on, no more questions. It is his mourners who are the lost ones. It is they who search. Why, they ask? Why would a young man go and leave like this? Leave his mother? Leave all of us? Had their caring, their comforting arms meant nothing to him? There must be an answer. Why? But this secret is Gregor's. It is his secret forever.

They file out of the church and walk in silence, uphill to the cemetery that was pressed close under the lowering sky. The grave yawns there. The sea booms and mists blow. For some margin of comfort, people pull their damp cloaks close about them. If only, they are thinking. Oh, if only.

Their eyes avoid the open grave. No one wants to look Death in the face.

But Death is there. Death is sentient. He stares into their downcast faces.

Do you not know why I am here? I do come for the boy, yes, but not for him only. No, I come for you too, with words for you, the living.

Who in the village will understand?

The boy's father? Far up the hill beyond the edge of the cemetery, regarded by no one, Wido Treyse leans on his shepherd's crook. He is shaking, partly with cold. He is wearing only his dirty old sweater and trousers full of holes. He keeps to himself, as bent as his crook, shutting himself in close because on this day, guilt has finally pierced the heart of Wido Treyse. Guilt has stunned him. It has crushed him. He reels and puts his hand on a gravestone to steady himself. He does not feel the biting wind, does not hear the distant dirge of the sea. There is only that yawning grave. And his wife. So, twice broken, is Wido. He sees his son's grave. And he sees her, Ermentrude, his Trudy. She is not afraid. She is the brave one, brave enough to stand, acquitted, beside that deep dark hole. Far far down the hill, Trudy, his wife. It is Father James who gives her his arm. Death, Wido weeps silently, can break the living.

Freya and Batilda Button stand next to the grave, clinging to each other, hands hard-clasped. Full of dread, their eyes search the crowd of people. Someone had told them a name, the name of the person who was last with Gregor. Freya is nearly sick with apprehension.

They spot her. There she is, looking right at them.

Lisabetta Button sees her sisters and she longs to bury herself at long last in their embrace. Finally, this time, she will give in to that longing. She circles the edge of the crowd and comes to stand shaking before them, her eyes streaming tears. Though she is much younger than they, she admits that it is up to her, that she must be the one to put things back in balance. She has but to reach one hand. That is all, that one small motion, and the three sisters embrace for the first time in a dozen years. Death can be a reconciliation.

Ludmilla Fairhedd holds tight to Florri. She alone knows her daughter's secret. She mustn't let go or Florri will collapse, ill, limp as a rag doll. Ruslan Fairhedd stays back at the edge of the crowd. Among all the people around him, he is aware only of his wife and daughter. He does not know why they moved apart from him. A young man is gone, he does know that, and the boy's parents, damaged beyond repair, have been left behind. He can't even imagine their terrible grief. Ruslan does see how deeply Florri grieves. She accepts only her mother's comfort. That troubles him, but he blocks it. He shrinks from knowing why. Death asks him to face terrible, difficult questions.

Teron Adante sees Vladimir Mynydd entering the cemetery alone. He recognizes a dispossessed person when he sees him. People in the crowd pass Mynydd by and don't look up. Some never liked him and were glad to see him fall from grace. Some have learned regret, some are ashamed. Once an important man. Now, a nobody. Vladimir spies Ruslan Fairhedd, the man who betrayed him, and he moves away to the other side of the crowd. Teron goes to stand beside Mynydd. Without a word, they nod to each other. At the end of the ceremony, when Ermentrude Treyse sinks into a faint, it is Teron Adante and Vladimir Mynydd who help her home and see to it that some women will stay with her. Then, by silent assent, they end up at the Bayside Inn, where Freya pours them a couple of stiff drinks. Coming from different worlds, with mutual respect they begin to talk.

Someone tells Lisabetta that of course she could stay at the lighthouse again tonight. Did she know how to light the lamps?

Yes. Yes, she does. Gregor had shown her. Yes. A painful job, to light those lamps again after last night, but the very least she could do for the lighthouse keeper, she says, heartbroken. The very least she could do.

That night, a ghost came to stand beside a bed, Gregor's bed. Where was Gregor? Where had he gone?

Lisabetta was awakened by a sound. She listened but heard no more. She couldn't get back to sleep, here in Gregor's bed. She wished she had never come to Lunenfarne, to Parrot Island. She felt so lost tonight. If she had never come, would Gregor still be here? Thoughts of him in flight haunted her all night long.

Old Mr. Francevili, the harbormaster, rowed out to the island again the next day.

"Father James mentioned that you have nowhere to live," he said to Lisabetta.

"Well, I don't know. I'm not sure. I don't want to impose on my sisters ... it's partly pride, I guess ...."

"Did Father tell you we need a light-keeper now? The town pays a little bit of money. You'd have at least part of every day to yourself. If you want the job, you can have it."

This was something she had never considered. Out here, she could be alone to study her books, and could deal in solitude with her guilt at failing Gregor. She wouldn't have to see anyone, feel their eyes blaming her. Besides, she really had nowhere else to go. "A job?" she asked Mr. Francevili. "Well, maybe for the time being, yes, I might be interested."

"You know, Gregor's illness – some say it was loneliness, some say it was the island's old ghosts." He watched her from the corner of his eye. "Of course, none of us can know for sure."

"It might not have been loneliness. Or ghosts. I think he had a real illness. I saw symptoms similar to his once before."

"Did you?"

"I should have known. I suspected, but I didn't have time to think it all through. I should have kept Gregor close that day. I shouldn't have let him go out onto that balcony by himself. I should have –"

"Wait a minute. You couldn't have prevented anything. He was in pretty bad shape before you ever came, Miss Button."

"I wish I'd gotten here sooner. I know it would have made a difference. I came too late."

"No, it was no fault of yours." Mr. Francevili bowed his head. "But be careful while you're here. Be careful." He had known all along, hadn't he? He would not tell Miss Button but he had known, before ever there was a beacon on Parrot Island, he had known the danger of building a lighthouse here. Consider: Anne d'Inquierre, disappeared; Teron Adante, nearly dying in prison; Gregor Treyse, dead before his time. Only Kai d'Inquierre had escaped, but his day would come. That lighthouse wasn't protecting anything. Jozef Francevili knew. The island was plagued with an ancient and terrible curse.

LISABETTA BUTTON

The howling north wind battered its way down the coast. The fields had no sooner been harvested and autumn had hardly begun before Lunenfarne was iced in a thin shroud of white. The colorless world already smelled of winter cold and woodsmoke. The arctic fox, having donned only recently its winter white morph, crept almost unseen through the woods. Black wraiths blowing across the sky were marauding eagles that stole fish right off the fishermens' hooks or swooped, with only a shadow of warning, to clutch panicked white hares or mice emerging from their snow tunnels. The dark spruce woods were eery sentinels, moaning, tossing their branches and toppling their light snow mantles in cascading showers. Out at sea, the inky nights grew longer and blacker. The Parrot Island lighthouse remained a still point on the far edge of black seawater mountains, a lone fragile beam, shining even when there were no ships out there to see it.

Lisabetta Button had been alone on Parrot Island for three days now. The wind blustered across the island. Maybe it was her imagination, but it seemed more powerful than any she had known before, though she had lived in a stone convent that clung to a windy gap high in the mountains. The lighthouse's low wooden cottage responded to the battering with wraithlike creaks and groans. If Death hadn't visited there so recently, Lisabetta assured herself, the urge to look over her shoulder might not seem so compelling. Maybe if the wind would slacken, the empty house would not feel so threatening.

By the light of day, she felt easier. She found she could get the chores done and still have time to pore over the old manuscript that Sister Rosemarie had lent her. The nun had been helping her with the identification and application of healing plants. Sister Rosemarie had tried to reassure her that she had gained enough skills to make a living as a physician. Had Rosemarie been giving her false hope, Lisabetta wondered, only as preparation for her to leave the convent?

Lisabetta could not figure out a way to build a reputation for herself as a medic. She couldn't make a living without patients but no one knew her here. Yet where else could she go? She had no knowledge of the outside world. She had lived at the convent since she was six years old. In her last couple of years up there, she had often thought about moving down to Lunenfarne. Her sister Batilda would welcome her, she was sure, but Freya, no. They would make each other miserable. She hadn't seen her eldest sister for twelve years and during that time, for all Lisabetta cared, another twelve years could go by and she still would not miss Freya. Or so she had told herself, folding the bitterness away, locking the poison in.

Soon after the terrible misfortune of Gregor's death though, things began to change, first with her sisters, then with her prospects for making a living. The sudden ending of Gregor's young life had made her think again about a reconciliation with Freya. Perhaps they had both begun to soften.

Then came the opportunity of working at the lighthouse. Perhaps the little bit of money she earned as a lighthouse keeper meant she would be able to keep body and soul together while she gained some experience as a healer. It might be worth staying here after all, using the lighthouse as a refuge. Her sister Batilda had assured her that no physician lived anywhere near Lunenfarne. Maybe it wouldn't take long before the townspeople learned to trust her healing skills. Of course, the downside was that she was stuck on this island and had no way of getting off without help. That go-to-hell rowboat! It tossed and bucked and spun in circles whenever she took the oars. She could get nowhere in it. She hated the thing. That was a problem she would have to work on.

Another problem developed, as well. The lighthouse, which she had hoped would serve as a refuge, as the sanctuary she needed right now, was turning out to be just the opposite. The damn place was haunted.

She'd known nuns who believed in ghosts. Some of them claimed they saw holy spirits. Some described spirits that were alarmingly unholy. Privately, Lisabetta used to laugh at them. Those nuns were loopy, all of them, just loopy old ladies. Now here she was, acting like one of them. I'm not used to spending days and nights all alone, she told herself. I'll get accustomed to it, but right now it's nerve-wracking.

Twelve years in a convent, surrounded by women at all times, had not prepared her for the solitary life of a lighthouse keeper. She could not remember being completely alone in all her years at Saint Scholastica, even for a minute. Taking meals with the nuns, going to mass with them, foraging for mushrooms and herbs in their company, listening to a couple of them snoring for half the night – such proximity would have been suffocating if it weren't for dear Hogar. Her duties, at least in the warm season, meant she could be outside, away from the other nuns during all the daylight hours, working beside Sister Hogar. Hogar was the gardener who had grown the convent's vegetables for years. She did miss Hogar. None of the nuns smiled as mischievously. None had that devil-may-care flippancy.

And the singing! Oh, Hogar sang, all the livelong day. While hoeing, while watering, all day the garden rang with renditions of entire Handel oratorios. Soprano, alto, tenor, bass parts – Hogar knew them all. As well, Lisabetta knew no one who had quite such a mouth, as Kunegunde liked to put it. Hogar was reprimanded any number of times for swearing. It made not a whit of difference. Hogar actually encouraged Lisabetta, when in the garden, to let loose with a cuss word now and then herself. It showed she had backbone, so important in this world, or at least, that is what Hogar claimed.

How Hogar persevered at the convent was a mystery, being highly unconventional, being everything most nuns were not. Compliance was certainly not a strong point with Hogar. Lisabetta was the only one, she hoped, who knew how effectively the robes of a nun could conceal a flask of whiskey, especially if those robes were voluminous enough to cover a particularly ample girth. As for piety, well, crossing oneself twice whenever the Mother Superior approached was more for protection than piety, especially when Kunegunde became Mother Superior. Lisabetta realised only now, that it was probably Hogar's wordless influence that had persuaded her not to take the veil. She followed the rules that the nuns laid down in the convent, but it was Hogar who remained her guiding light.

She missed the convent, too, a little, because this cottage, now that she lived on Parrot Island, gave her the creeps. It wasn't a fear of being alone. Something was strange here, and Lisabetta did not think it was her imagination. Something was weird about the place.

She tried to reassure herself that odd things happened to people who were not used to being solitary. Is that what had happened to Gregor? No, Gregor had a sickness. She was convinced of that. She had seen the very same symptoms in a nun she once knew. That woman had believed, as many did, that mercury could cure illnesses. Someone had told her it would help. It did nothing to relieve her symptoms. The poor woman was finally driven to suicide. Lisabetta knew there had been mercury in the lighthouse. Had Gregor been drinking it, believing it would cure his limp? Gregor had been hallucinating the day that he fell, thinking he saw someone when there was no one there. Could this be blamed on mercury, or was it something else? She did not know for sure.

But this island. Something about this island was definitely odd.

She might as well admit it, ridiculous as it sounded. She had been hearing things. Little sounds. She kept hearing them in the night. A door creaking. Soft footsteps. Something rattling in a cupboard. She tried to convince herself that it was the wind. Or maybe her imagination was playing tricks. Last night she had finally gotten up and lit a lamp. If there were ghosts, she wanted to see them. She sat curled up in the rocking chair beside the stove for the rest of the night.

While sitting there, she noticed notebooks of some kind, a pile of them on a shelf. She had heard that Gregor had been a painter at one time. Lisabetta pulled the notebooks onto her lap and started to leaf through them.

Watercolors of landscapes, mountain scenes, brooks, views from Parrot Island. The recent notebooks showed alarming signs of Gregor's growing lack of co-ordination. As she turned back through the pages, though, she began to recognize parts of faces. An eye here, a child's face there. In an older notebook, nicely done portraits of a young woman. Page after page, always the same woman, from all angles. She was beautiful. Who was she? A painter's model?

Yawning, Lisabetta finally put the books back and, ghosts be damned, gave up and went to bed.

The next day brought a new sign from the Other World. A pie Batilda had sent her had shrunk overnight. Things like this had been happening for three days now. First there was that piece of bread she had cut the other day. She left the room for a minute and it was gone when she came back. Three apples remained in a bowl of four, and she had eaten none. The apple pie – yesterday she'd had a piece, but surely she hadn't eaten a whole quarter of the pie? This morning, only half was left. Did she have mice? She looked around. Aha! Piecrust crumbs on the floor there. And there. And over here by the linen closet.

Quietly, Lisabetta turned the knob on the closet door. She opened the door a crack. She braced herself and peeked inside. Nothing in here. She opened the door wider and listened. No sounds, no sign of mice. Blankets, lots of blankets in case of emergencies. Towels, piled on shelves. She bent down to the lowest shelf. More blankets, and ….

A small bare toe.

She jumped back. She stared. A toe? Her heart was pumping and goosebumps ran in waves over her arms. This was creepy. What had Gregor hidden here? Maybe … maybe he was crazy after all, driven insane, doing dreadful things. Was this a dead person? Lisabetta clutched her throat.

She stared hard. It looked like a toe. Should she – yes, it had to be done. Damn it all to hell.

She reached out. Crap, how could she bring herself to touch something cold and dead? Gingerly, very lightly, she touched the toe.

Hastily, it was retracted.

Lisabetta snatched her hand back, gasping, dumbfounded. She stood there, frozen, listening again. Not a sound. She had seen something, hadn't she? Yes, she had seen a toe. Maybe – maybe she was the crazy one. No, she had seen it.

She knelt down. Slowly she pulled the blankets off the shelf. She fell backwards and screeched in terror. Someone cried out.

There, curled up on the back of the lowest shelf, impossibly, a child.

Lisabetta sat up. "What are you doing in there?" Her voice wobbled. "Come out of there."

The child pulled her knees up to her chest.

"Come out of there this instant. Come on." It occurred to Lisabetta that she did not know how to talk to a child. It had actually been years since she'd even seen a child. "Please come out?"

She stretched out a hand. The child shook her head, panic-stricken.

Lisabetta sat back again. The child was not dead. That was a huge relief. And she, Lisabetta, was not seeing a ghost.

This was manageable. She could handle this. She got up and went to the sideboard, picked up two forks and what was left of the pie her sister had baked, and sat on the floor again in front of the linen closet. She took a bite of pie.

"Want some? No?" Another few bites. "You'd better come out. This will be gone soon because I'm going to eat it all and you'll have none." She turned her back on the closet and kept eating. She was actually quite full, stuffing it in now. "Mmm, good pie. Delicious!"

Less than a quarter of the pie was left when she was aware of someone standing at her shoulder. A small blonde girl in a badly wrinkled frock, no stockings. Lisabetta chewed thoughtfully and regarded the child without smiling. "If you want some of this, just tell me."

The girl pulled a long face.

"No? Well, I guess this is all for me." She had really had enough pie. She took tiny bites. Chew chew chew.

"Pie?" said a small voice.

Lisabetta looked up at the crumpled face, so full of longing."Oh. I see. So. You do want pie?"

The girl nodded. Lisabetta cut a slice and handed her a fork. The child sat on the floor and lit into that pie as though she hadn't eaten in a week.

What the hell is going on? And who the hell is this girl? Lisabetta wondered. Had she been living with Gregor? Was she his child? When she reached a hand to touch her sun-bleached curls, the girl flinched as though struck. Lisabetta pulled her hand back. A troubled girl, this one. Maybe she had been abandoned here. Abandoned, just like me. She understood that. She knew very well how that felt.

She spoke more gently. "What's your name?"

The girl's eyes slid sideways. A small pout.

"Can you tell me?"

A frown, the lower lip stuck out, but no answer.

"My name's Lisabetta." She waited. Oh, how well she remembered herself on the day she had been deserted. So full of fury, full to overflowing. So full of hurt that she could still feel its force, could summon it instantly, to this day. She looked sternly at the child. All right. A connection had to be made here, even forced. That was how she herself had been won over. Sister Rosemarie had refused to treat her with kid gloves, not at first, not until they bonded. "If you don't tell me your name," she said to the child, "I won't give you any more pie."

A snap of the head, then the face lowered. The frown deepened.

"Come on. What is your name?" Lisabetta waited.

Finally, a whisper. "Lily." Brown eyes came up and looked at her, beseeching.

"Lily who?"

"Lily Treyse."

"Lily Trace. That's a nice name."

Lily's eyes slid toward the nearly-empty pieplate.

"I can heat up some soup. Would you like that? Hot soup and a nice piece of bread?"

Lily Trace shook her head. "Pie."

Some peoples' hearts are so easily won. Whether or not Lisabetta had won her heart, Lily seemed to need to be close to someone, physically close. After she had eaten, Lily crawled into Lisabetta's lap like a kitten, curled up, and went to sleep.

Children, they knew so little of the world. She had known so little herself, as a child, and what she had known had been skewed by childish ignorance. That pretty house they had in Bellesunde when she was little. At the time, she had not understood why it had to be deserted, all in one day, because it was no longer safe. Memories of that time, the regrets and confusion, did not go away. She often wished they would.

She had lived in town with her two sisters and Mopi, her big black dog. Ah, sweet Mopi, her supremely best friend. How brief their time together had been. Lisabetta had never known her mother, but in Freya and 'Tilda, she actually had two mothers. Their father had been gone for a time now, betrayed by a Spanish sea captain into a life of bondage. He was probably never coming back, or so they told her. At the time, she didn't know what a galley slave was, but she overheard them say those words. Freya had warned her to "never trust a Spaniard". Lisabetta didn't know any Spaniards but believe you me, she kept a wary eye out for them at all times.

One day, soon after their father disappeared, Freya had gathered her little sister close. She whispered that Papa had once told her a secret. Even though they had no father to care for them, they would never have to worry. Worry about what? Lisabetta had asked. She hadn't been worried about anything, until she heard that. Well, Freya was trying to reassure her that there wasn't anything to worry about. They would be well cared for. So don't worry. But never, Freya insisted, never say a word about this secret to anyone, even Uncle Virn, Father's brother. Especially not to Virn.

Uncle Virn liked to cause trouble. Lisabetta had been aware of that much. He was nosy, Freya said. He always wanted to know how they were managing, by which he meant to find out, Freya explained, where they were getting the money they lived on. Where are we getting our money, Lisabetta had asked? Never mind, she was told, we have enough and we'll take care of you always. You don't have to worry. This of course only ramped up her worrying, trying to understand what Freya was talking about, but she couldn't persuade her sister to say more. She was like that, Freya. Secretive, bossy just because she was the eldest, pretending she knew more than anybody, and always, always insisting they do everything her way. Their sister Tilda usually went along with Freya, but there were times, as Lisabetta often confided to her dog Mopi, that she wished she could tell Freya to just shut up. She never did. You couldn't, could you, if you were six years old and your sisters were grown, almost women?

Then came the day when everything changed. She had not been prepared for that because the morning had started out well enough. Tilda said she would make pancakes if Lisabetta would go to the dairy for milk. "Take Mopi with you, why don't you?" Tilda got the big pitcher down. "Is this too heavy? Try not to spill."

Lisabetta took the pitcher, called Mopi, and headed out. Across their street, she saw a carriage parked. When she and Mopi came down the front steps, Uncle Virn opened its door and stepped out. She had never liked their uncle and today, since he wasn't smiling even one little bit, he disturbed her more than usual. A chill ran up her spine.

"Good morning, Uncle," she murmured, trained, as she had been, to be polite.

"Where are you going, my little poppet?"

"The dairy."

"I'll drive you. Come on. We can take my carriage. Come for a ride with me."

"No thank you. Mopi wants to walk."

Uncle took rough hold of her arm. "I suggest you come – hey, you nasty little – Get in that carriage!" He was hurting her, her own uncle!

"Let go!"

Rarr raaarrr! snarled Mopi. Lisabetta had never seen her look so mean.

She struggled to loosen Uncle's grip. "Let me go!" She kicked him in the shins and backed off in terror when she saw the hate in his eyes.

Raaarrrarrrarr! Mopi leapt at him.

He fought the dog and tried to reach for Lisabetta again. She screamed. The dog knocked Uncle to the ground. Lisabetta banged the pitcher against her uncle's forehead. His head fell back. Again she smashed the pitcher down hard right on his nose and blood, eww! Blood! Blood ran all over his face and all over everywhere. Look what she had done, puddles of blood. Uncle went limp.

"Tilda!" she screamed. "Freya!" Mopi barked and barked.

Her sisters flew from the house, shocked to see Uncle Virn on the ground. Batilda swept Lisabetta into her arms.

"What happened?"

"He's dead! He's dead!" She had killed him. "I didn't mean to kill him!"

Freya bent over Uncle. "Stop wailing. He's not dead." She plucked an envelope that was sticking out of his breast pocket because it had her name on it.

"What is it?" Tilda asked.

Freya gasped. "A note. This bast – this horrible man! It's a ransom note." She looked at Batilda. "He was going to kidnap 'Betta and make us pay to get her back. He knows, this says, he knows Papa hid a lot of money somewhere."

"Oh, Freya!"

"There's more. It says he deserves Papa's money more than we do, and blah blah, oh lord, and now he wants us to give it to him or else he'll …." She looked down at Lisabetta. Tilda, reading over Freya's shoulder, stopped and looked at Lisabetta. They both stared at her, shocked.

"He wouldn't dare! He wouldn't." Tilda was livid.

"You know, we've put this off long enough, Tilda. It's time," Freya said, glancing at Lisabetta. "We have to try, at least, to find Father."

Lisabetta gaped back at them. Look for Father? Where? How? What had she started? It was bad! The looks on their faces! She was hardly able to speak. "Wh-where are we going to look?" she asked. Freya folded the note and didn't answer, refused to answer. Uncle's coachman carted him off to a physician.

So yes, that was the day. The day that everything changed for Lisabetta. They had to leave Bellesunde. Freya knew of another place where they could live. Father had built a warehouse somewhere. Mr. Songer the cartman came and immediately Freya started bossing everyone, telling everyone what to do. Pack this, take it to the cart, put these in storage, no, we can't take that. That goes to the storehouse too. Everything,

everything had to go. They had to leave so early the next morning that it was still dark as night outside. Mr. Songer filled the cart with trunks and drove them down to the harbor.

After all the fuss of the day before, Lisabetta felt a little better this morning. They were going somewhere! By ship! A little trip, Tilda had said. Lisabetta curled up in the cart with her arms around Mopi. This was going to be fun! Neither she nor Mopi had ever been on a sailing ship before but she assured her dog, as they drove down to the wharf, that they would have a wonderful time.

Then, like a knife to her heart, Freya told her the worst part, the absolute worst. Mopi, her darling Mopi would not be allowed to come. You couldn't have dogs on board a ship. But look! Lisabetta had cried. They are putting a calf and lambs aboard! No, Freya and Tilda had enough to worry about. Mopi would be too much trouble. Mr. Songer would take care of her. Lisabetta screamed, screamed her lungs out, a real tantrum. She cried and sobbed but she couldn't make Freya change her mind. Tilda held her tight and tried to comfort her but nothing, nothing could make up for losing Mopi. They were abandoning her dog, her best friend in all the world.

They sailed north for days, tacking back and forth against the wind. Finally they spotted a lighthouse in the distance, a lighthouse high on a cliff. Their ship turned there and squeezed down a narrow channel and they docked at a little town. Lunenfarne, it was called.

"There is no hotel here," said Tilda, tired. "I asked."

"There's not much of anything here," said Freya.

"But we can talk to the harbormaster's wife, a man told me. She might have a room to rent by the month."

"I'm hungry," complained Lisabetta.

"And I smell bread baking." Tilda looked at Freya. "Let's get something to eat before we … before we do anything else."

"We don't have a lot of time," insisted Freya. "I want to get there before dark tonight."

"The bakery is right here, Freya. Oh, let's just get a bite before we see about the apartment. Then we'll go."

"Go where?" Lisabetta asked.

"Up into the mountains."

They stood in line at the bakery. Two boys came in. Lisabetta turned to smile at them. They were odd boys, both of them, but friendly. One had a limp. One had brown skin.

"Going to the show?" the brown one asked her.

"What show?"

"The puppets. The puppets are today."

Lisabetta took a bun from Tilda's hand. "A puppet show! Can I go, Tilda?"

Tilda looked at Freya. She said, "Freya, why don't you go see about the apartment? I'll take Betta to this puppet show." Freya sighed and gave Tilda her distressed look. "Come on, Freya. Betta needs a little – this will work out fine. We can meet you in about an hour."

It was called Signor Bologna's Fabulous Puppet Show and it was really the best. They all laughed so hard, even Tilda.

Then the confusion began again. It seems they had to be somewhere and it was far away. They would have to walk and someone was going to show them the way. Up, up into the mountains they were going, far from everything. It wasn't an easy hike. Why they were going there, no one would say. It was very far away and Lisabetta was exhausted.

Finally, high above them, they saw a cluster of gray buildings perched on a cliff above a raging torrent of water. It was a beautiful place, the Saint Scholastica convent. They stayed overnight there, listening all night to the voices of the river below.

The next morning, Freya and Tilda took Lisabetta into a garden where a couple of nuns were tending the plants, one of them small and stiff-looking, one very tall and quite broad in the beam. Lisabetta and her sisters sat on a bench in the garden. Lisabetta sweetheart, Tilda had said to her, wrapping her in her arms. It was time for them to go. Tilda and Freya were leaving and Lisabetta was staying.

"No. Oh no."

"I'm sorry but we've decided …."

"I'm not staying here. I'm going with you to look for Father."

"The thing is though, Betta, we would rather you stay somewhere safe."

"Safe from what?"

"Well, we worry, you know, we – we worry about Uncle Virn, for one thing. He's a greedy old miser and we don't want to have another incident like in Bellesunde, do we? He'll never find you here. You will be much safer here than you would be anywhere else. Tilda and I will have to be away so often that we would be always worrying about you."

"Going away where?"

"Here and there. It won't be for long. Just for now, Betta. This is just until Uncle Virn, you know, until he gives up searching."

"I don't care about Virn." Lisabetta was yelling. "I can smash him and ... and I can bite him. I want to be with you. You can't leave me." She started to cry. "You can't just go away and leave me here."

Tilda was crying too. "But it's nice here, honey. It won't be forever. Just for a while. We're going to introduce you to a nice lady who will look after you."

"I don't want a nice lady!" She sucked in a raggedy breath. "I want to stay with you!"

"Please, Betta? Can't you go along with this for now? I'm begging you –"

"No, Tilda! I won't! I won't! You made me leave my dog behind. You can't leave me, too!"

"You don't want Uncle Virn to come troubling you again, do you?"

"I don't care!" Lisabetta wailed. "I don't care about stupid old Virn!"

"Betta." Freya was stern. "Stop this crying. Stop it right now. We've decided that this will be for the best. You're only a little girl and there are some things you don't understand. Tilda and I have a lot of work to do here and we don't have time –"

"You don't want me! That's what it is! You just don't want me!"

"Shh, shh. Of course we want you." Tilda took her in her arms again. "Betta honey, of course we do, but we want you to be safe. The only problem is, we won't have any time to spend with you right now. Not until we get some things settled. Please honey, don't cry."

Freya sighed. "Stop being such a baby, Betta."

"I'm not a baby!" Lisabetta screamed. She was, though. She was the baby of the family, and she had always enjoyed being the baby. When that thought crossed her mind, it made her angrier than ever. "You're just – you're just – just stupid!"

"Listen, Betta. It's time you learned to cope with problems like a grownup. We didn't want it to be this way, but we have no choice."

"If you don't take me with you, I'm going to hate you forever."

"I hope you don't mean that."

"I do mean it! I hate you I hate you!"

Freya crossed her arms and frowned. How could they explain this?

You could tell your little sister that you were planning on starting a business that included investing in a small ship and a sailing crew. That was not problematic. It was tricky, though, to explain that Freya and Tilda were going to try their fortunes on the high seas and their ship would be a pirate ship. They were going to board every Spanish ship they could find, take what booty they could, and search every crew until they found their father. How could they explain this to a six-year old who would worry for their safety? Who hadn't been told that her good and noble father had been made a slave, and that slavery on a Spanish ship meant he felt the lash of a whip on his bare back whenever he faltered in his work?

"Look," Freya said finally, "we're doing the best we can right now. You can understand that, can't you, Betta?"

"No!" wailed Lisabetta. She stomped her foot.

Freya stood. "You are so difficult! All right. Come, Tilda. We might as well get this over and done."

Tilda pulled Lisabetta to her feet. "See that lady in the garden, Sister Rosemarie? She'll take care of you. And we'll visit you every chance we get, honey. Let's go meet Rosemarie, shall we?"

Lisabetta screamed louder than she had ever screamed in her life. "Don't come visit me! I don't care! I don't want to see you ever again!"

"Please, Betta – "

"Come on." Freya pulled on Tilda's arm. "She'll get over it."

"I won't! Not ever, Freya! I'll never get over it! Never never!"

And for twelve years, she hadn't. Batilda hiked up the mountain to see her on many Sundays, and Freya came with her the first couple of times. But Lisabetta treated her so monstrously that she gave up. They had abandoned her, so she abandoned Freya.

The life that Lisabetta never wanted at St. Scholastica, though, turned out to be richly rewarding, at least for a girl with her studious bent. Sister Rosemarie discovered in the child an insatiable curiosity much like her own, and their twice-daily sessions were rigorous explorations in medicine, chemistry, and botany that pleased them both. When she wasn't with Sister Rosemarie, Lisabetta worked in the garden with Hogar, receiving instruction in the use of tools of all kinds, and planting, and soil. Lisabetta grew in good health and strength. Once, when she was nine years old, Tilda visited with good news. Lisabetta could leave the convent and come to live with them now. Their work had been only partly successful. They didn't say that they had never found their father, but she and Freya had just finished building their new inn. Now there was a place for Lisabetta, and what was more, Uncle Virn was no longer a threat.

"Is he dead?" she asked, heartless.

"Yes, Betta. He can't hurt you anymore."

"Well, hmph," grumped the little unwanted sister. Lisabetta crossed her arms tight over her chest.

"Come on! Aren't you happy?"

"I don't want to go live with you."

"Betta!"

"I'm not going to leave here."

"What are you doing, Betta? After all the fuss you've made? After upsetting Freya whenever she tried –"

"I don't care if Freya is upset! What about me?"

"Betta, you're being stubborn. Let's get your things packed. Come to Lunenfarne with me and see the nice room we made for you."

Lisabetta scowled and snapped her head aside. "I'm staying here. Everybody likes me here." It was true. The nuns always made a fuss over her. She liked being petted and babied by them.

Lisabetta refused to be persuaded. No, they had deserted her a long time ago. Her sisters, her own sisters had gone away without her! She hoped that now they would be good and sorry that they had abandoned her.

So Tilda had gone home alone. She broached the subject again every once in a while, but Lisabetta had taken a stance. Once you did that, once you insisted you would never change your mind, you had to stick to that, didn't you? The best you could hope for was that someone would force you to do what you really deep down wanted. But no one forced Lisabetta. So she had to live with it. Which she did, for nine more years. A ridiculously long time, now that she came to think on it, but a stubborn streak forges mighty strong fetters. Mighty strong.

Lisabetta sat in Gregor's rocking chair, thinking about her childhood. She had relived it, every detail, so many times, the pain of it like a claw raking her heart.

She looked down at Lily, curled up in her arms, sound asleep. What tales did this little girl have to tell? Where had she come from, and why had no one even mentioned that she lived in this lighthouse?

Lisabetta started to get up so she could carry Lily to the bed.

"Gregga." The child, not even fully awake, murmured Gregor's name. She rubbed her eyes and then looked up at Lisabetta. "Gregga?"

"No, sweetie. Gregor is not here anymore."

"Gamma?"

"Gamma. I don't know who that is."

"Gregga? Gone?" The brown eyes shone with tears. Her troubled face begged to understand.

"Yes, he is. Gregor is gone."

"Where?"

"Where has he gone?" Lisabetta thought for a minute. "I don't know, Lily. Someday we'll find out. But no one knows."

"Want Gregga. Want Gregga!" Lily whimpered softly.

"Gregor is … he's not coming back, sweetie. No, he's not. We're sad about that, aren't we?"

Lily was sobbing aloud now.

"He didn't want to leave you. He would come if he could, but he can't. I'll be here with you, though." She kissed the top of the white-blonde head and made the best promise she could. "I will never never leave you, Lily Trace."

Tilda had asked Lisabetta to come to the inn for Sunday dinner. She, and for the last few months, she and her fiancé Franz Wohlfahrt had made that trip up the mountain almost every Sunday to see her little sister. "Now it's your turn to come to us."

"I can't row a boat," Lisabetta had protested. "No, I'd like to come, but I'd end up out in the ocean. Or drowned."

"Come on, all our girls here learned to row. You can make it."

"Your girls?"

"The girls who work in the dining room. You'll meet them when you come."

"Eh, not this week, Tilda."

Tilda smiled and put her arm around her sister. "Chekov cooks on my day off. He is making pierogies this week. You used to love those things when you were little."

"Pierogies? With cheese? Ooo."

Tilda nodded. "They're not the finest, but they're pretty good. Come in the morning so we can have the day together."

On Sunday, Lisabetta helped Lily into her favorite dress and pinafore. She looked so cute in her warm hooded coat and boots. They walked together, down through the brown meadow to the narrow beach at the bottom of the island. Lily skipped down the hill. Lisabetta lagged behind, steeling herself for an ordeal with that damned boat. The day was gray and heavy, with moderate winds. She managed to get the boat off the beach, but the west wind kept insisting they go toward the channel. They would end up out in the ocean! Lily clung to the gunwales. Lisabetta wailed in fright. In the end, Mr. Korsakov noticed her floundering out in the bay and sent Chilperic to tow her to the wharf. She thanked him profusely, having no idea how she would get home.

She wished she could preserve for all time the looks on her sisters' faces when she walked into the Bayside Inn holding the hand of a little girl.

"Betta? Who is this?"

"This is Lily Trace."

"Hello, Lily." The older sisters smiled and Freya helped her take off her coat. Catching Betta's eye, their eyebrows arched in question.

"Lily has been living at the lighthouse, apparently. Umm, she lives there with me now. She loves pie, and I would tell you more but that is about all I know."

"Pie!" said Lily.

Batilda bent to speak to Lily. "I have pies. We can warm one up in the oven. Would you like to help me with it?"

Lily looked up at Lisabetta, got a nod, and cautiously took Tilda's hand. As soon as the door closed on them, Freya turned to Lisabetta.

"She was living at the lighthouse when you got there?"

"She wasn't there when I first met Gregor. At least, I never saw her. I was there for three days before I found her hiding in a closet."

"Is she Gregor's child?"

"I have no idea. She speaks only a few words. So you never heard of a child living out there?"

Freya shook her head slowly. "Never heard a word about a child."

"Who would know about her? Isn't there someone?"

"How about Gregor's mother?"

"I would think she would have mentioned Lily to someone when Gregor died. Wouldn't she be worried about who is looking after her?"

"The woman has been very ill, apparently, since her son died. You should go see her, Betta. Maybe you have some remedy that would help her. Take the little girl with you."

"Does she live far from here? Do I have to row that bejayzus boat to get to her house?"

Freya laughed. "You can walk to the ferry dock and Mr. Korsakov will take you across the river. Go now, before lunch. Then after lunch you could take Lily to the puppet show."

"That puppet theatre is still there? I remember that! All right. I'll go to see Gregor's mother now. I don't have my bag of remedies with me, but I'm dying to ask her about Lily."

"She might not be well enough to tell you anything."

"Tell me where she lives. What's her name?"

"Mrs. Treyse."

Lisabetta raised her eyebrows. "Lily said her name was Lily Trace. Maybe she meant Treyse. This should be interesting." She paused and turned back. "What if this woman wants to take Lily to live with her?"

"She might."

"Then maybe I won't go, after all."

"But the poor woman –"

"I know, I know. I'll go."

"Take an apple pie with you. Tilda has a couple in the larder."

Mr. Korsakov took them across the river and Lisabetta asked directions. He told her how to find Mrs. Treyse near the fishermen's village.

Watching them go, Korsakov wondered how he had missed such a juicy bit of gossip. No one had told him that Lisabetta Button had come to Lunenfarne with a little daughter as blonde as herself.

There was a garden out in front of Ermentrude Treyse's house. It had been neatly mulched and was now tucked under a thin dusting of snow. The canes of an old rambling rose, climbing all the way up over the porch roof, rattled in the wind. They pushed the gate open and followed footprints that led to the porch.

"Have you ever been here, Lily?" Lisabetta asked.

Lily gripped her hand and shook her head.

"We're going to visit a nice lady. But she is very sick so we must be quiet if she is asleep."

They knocked but got no answer. Lisabetta opened the door and called. Again no answer. They stepped inside and took off their boots.

"Hello?" Lisabetta heard a faint moan and crossed to the door of a bedroom. A woman lay on the bed, pale, hardly responding.

"I'm sorry to bother you, Mrs. Treyse but –"

"Gamma!" Lily shrieked.

The woman in the bed sat up partway. She flung her arms wide open. "Lily! Oh Lily!"

Lily clambered up onto the bed, quick as a monkey. She threw herself onto Ermentrude Treyse with kisses and a big hug. Ermentrude wrapped her arms around the child and rocked her back and forth.

"Oh! Thank God! Thank God! I was so worried. I'm so happy to see you, sweetheart!"

Lily knelt beside her on the mattress and pointed elvishly. "Pie!" She poked Mrs. Treyse in the chest. "You, pie!"

"You brought me a pie? Let's have a piece, shall we?" Mrs. Treyse threw back the covers.

"I can bring it to you – you don't have to get up, Mrs. Treyse. Please, you can stay in bed." Lisabetta feared this invalid lady would fall over if she tried to get up.

"No, I'm fine. Ooo. A little dizzy." She sat back down on the bed. "If you'll just hand me that robe." She took Lily's hand. "Let's make some pearl tea, shall we?"

"Pie!" Lily demanded.

"And pie. We will have pie." Ermentrude stopped and smiled at Lisabetta. "I'm so sorry. I haven't even asked who you are. I was just so happy to see this little scamp." She kissed the top of Lily's head.

"I'm Lisabetta Button. I –"

"Oh." Ermentrude's face fell. "Miss Button. Oh yes. They told me you – you are taking over the lighthouse duties. You were with my son –" She pressed a handkerchief to her lips.

"I was with Gregor. I'm so sorry, Mrs. Treyse. I can't tell you how terrible I feel about what happened."

"You know, I knew for a long time that there was something wrong with Gregor." Her voice wobbled.

"I think he was very ill. Still, I am mortified that I couldn't – I tried but – I – I couldn't stop him."

Mrs. Treyse looked down at Lily. "Talking about him is difficult," she hinted. "Come, let's go into the kitchen where it's warmer. Bring that pie with you, Miss Button."

"Please call me Lisabetta."

"How many pieces should we cut, Lily?"

Lily fumbled with her fingers and held them up. "Sree."

"That's right, darling. Very good! Now you sit right up here next to me."

"Shall I put the water on?"

"Oh, thank you, Lisabetta. Use the big pot, dear. We have a lot to talk about. I imagine you must have some questions."

An hour later, they had both shared their stories while Lily played with some old toys that had belonged to Gregor. Lisabetta explained that she had promised to take Lily to the puppet show after lunch, but they would come the next day to see how Mrs. Treyse was feeling. She would bring her bag of remedies. Perhaps a little wintergreen would be soothing.

"You've given me the best medicine right here." Ermentrude put her hand on Lily's head. "I didn't have the strength to row myself to the lighthouse after the funeral, but I was in agony, wondering what had happened to her. I couldn't trust her story with anyone. It would sound so sordid, if I tried to explain it. And I was afraid it would tarnish Gregor's image. No one would understand why he did what he did. His kind heart –" She choked on the words. "He had such a kind heart."

"I understand completely, Mrs. Treyse."

"I'm so relieved." She hugged Lily, and then, with a little laugh, hugged Lisabetta. "I'll look forward to seeing you both tomorrow." She stood in her doorway and watched them til they were out of sight.

The next day, Ermentrude Treyse must have imagined she heard them coming up to the porch at least five times before she actually heard a knock. She took off her apron, put the plate of freshly-baked cookies on the table, and smiled on her way to the door.

She opened the door and stepped back in surprise. "Oh. Can I help you?" she asked the young woman who stood there bundled in furs. Then she looked at the little boy in her arms. She stared. A puzzled frown crossed her face and she paled. She put her hand to her head. "I – I'm sorry. I'm a little – forgive me. I think I'd better sit down."

The woman pushed through the door and followed Ermentrude to a chair. She set the little boy on the floor and knelt by Ermentrude's chair.

"Can I get you a glass of water or some tea?"

"No. I just need a minute. I was just reminded … of something. Very odd, I just –" Ermentrude tried to hold herself stiffly erect but tears leaked out of her firmly closed eyes. She groped for her handkerchief.

The young woman stood, her face full of concern. Her little boy began to look around and she took his hand to hold him by her side. "I've come at a bad time, I think," she said.

"You'll have to forgive me. I haven't been well this past week or so. Can I help you? What is it you wanted?" Ermentrude made an effort not to look at the little boy.

"Are you – I'm looking for Mrs. Treyse."

"I'm Mrs. Treyse." Her eyes slid down to the child again and back to the woman.

"I know this is a very difficult time for you, Mrs. Treyse." The young woman took a breath. "I'm Florri Mynydd. I knew – I knew your son Gregor."

"Ah."

"And – I wondered – I thought you might like to meet –" Flustered, she knelt down beside the child and turned him to face Ermentrude. Ermentrude finally settled her eyes on him. This child, this little boy. Impossible for one child to look so like another. Her face wrinkled again. Then she frowned and studied Florri's face.

Florri, her voice shaking, said, "This is my son. He's called Gregor."

Ermentrude collapsed against the back of the chair. "Gregor? He – this is so strange." She covered her mouth with her hand. "This is so odd. I don't really understand. Why did you say you are here? Did you tell me already? I've forgotten."

"It's not easy to explain."

"You knew my Gregor?"

"Quite well."

"Quite well?"

Florri nodded. "Very well."

"Very well?" Ermentrude raised her eyebrows. "Very well?" Then her face sobered. She sat still, not even breathing. When she tried to talk, she could hardly get the words out. "If this is what I think, it is a lot to take in."

"I know."

"You're wearing a ring. Are you married?"

"Yes."

"To ...?"

"His name is Dort."

"But …."

"I don't know how to explain. I never – except for my mother, I haven't told single soul. I can't. I can't find the words."

"Ah. Aha." Ermentrude sat up and bent toward little Gregor. She longed to take the child in her arms. "Dear me. Dear dear me. He's the spitting image. Did you realise that?"

"Is he?" Florri asked quickly, a quiver in her voice.

"I almost thought he was my own little boy. Come back somehow."

"That makes me very happy. To know he looks like Gregor did." She dropped her eyes and bit her lip. "I suppose you have figured out –" She raised her head and looked directly at Ermentrude. She forced herself to say the unsayable. "Gregor and I were lovers. For a time. Too short a time."

"Then, this child is …."

"He would be your grandson, wouldn't he?"

Ermentrude broke down and sobbed. Little Gregor was so obviously distressed by this that she tried hard to pull herself together. She stood with Florri's help.

"Let's have a cup of tea. I don't want to pry but whatever you feel like telling me about my son would be very much appreciated. You can't know how I long to hear about him. And this little one." She touched his head tentatively. "Gregor? Little Gregor?"

"Yes, I know, Mrs. Treyse. I want so badly to talk about him too. Finally."

The women were deep in conversation and Gregor, unobserved, had helped himself to a third cookie when there was a knock at the door. Florri stopped talking abruptly. "Someone is here?"

"Oh my goodness. I forgot all about them." She started to the door, then turned suddenly. "I should warn you, Florri. My visitors. They have a – a story too. I feel I can trust you enough to hear it. But be prepared. Since you knew the kind of person Gregor was, you'll doubtless find it – most interesting."

Florri smiled uncertainly when Lisabetta and Lily, swathed in coats and scarves, came into the warm, fragrant kitchen. Their cheeks were pink from cold. Lily clung to Ermentrude's arm and stared at the interloper, the little boy at the table. He took a cookie from the plate and held it out to her.

"Good cookie!" he assured her.

Shy, hesitant, Lily slowly crossed the room and reached for the cookie. The little boy instantly handed her another and with that, they became fast friends. Shared cookies, it is established fact, are the basis of the most enduring friendships, and this would turn out to be that kind of friendship.

As for Lisabetta, she hesitated, a questioning look on her face, then introduced herself. "I'm Lisabetta Button."

"I'm Florri Mynydd. That's my son Gregor. And this must be your little girl?"

"No." Lisabetta bit her lip. "No."

"You have the same coloring."

"Well. Her name is Lily."

Florri tilted her head and smiled, expecting more. It dawned on Lisabetta that explaining her relationship to Lily was going to be endlessly complicated. She wasn't married. And no one knew who Lily really belonged to. A little niggle of worry planted itself in her mind.

"Lisabetta has just come to Lunenfarne," explained Ermentrude, hurriedly filling in the awkward pause. "She is taking over the lighthouse duties."

"I've seen your face before," Lisabetta blurted, staring at Florri.

"You have?"

"Yes. Many times. There must be a hundred drawings of you in some sketchbooks that were left at the lighthouse."

"Oh." Florri blushed. "Gregor's sketchbooks."

"Oh," echoed Ermentrude. "Oh dear. Well, let's sit down. Maybe the children can play in the other room while I make some more tea. Another big pot." She looked from one young woman to the other and shook her head. "There are some rather – complicated issues here. I don't know how much you want to share with each other. It all connects to my son Gregor, I guess, connections that may surprise you both."

Lisabetta and Florri looked at each other. "Our children are about the same age?"

"I can only guess at Lily's age."

"She is – not your daughter?"

Lisabetta shook her head. "Maybe you can explain, Mrs. Treyse."

Florri was shocked, at first, to hear Ermentrude tell how Lily had come into Gregor's life. But when she thought more about it, it made sense. It was something Gregor Treyse would definitely do.

"I'm happy that he had Lily with him, you know, in his last months," Florri said. "Aren't you, Mrs. Treyse?"

"After I got over the shock, yes, I was happy for him. He and Lily adored each other," said Ermentrude, softly.

Florri turned to Lisabetta. "You must be wondering about Gregor and I."

"All those drawings of you. And your son is called Gregor, too. But you –" She glanced at the ring on Florri's hand.

Florri stared at the table, then looked up into Lisabetta's eyes. "I am married, but not to Gregor. You may have guessed what no one else knows."

Florri's confession of her romance with Gregor, once she started, came pouring out of her in a flood that surprised even her. Two bright spots of pink glowed on her cheeks. She confided, as well, the story of her terribly unhappy marriage to Dort Mynydd. She certainly had not meant to be so forthcoming. She had never realised how badly she needed to tell all this. It was foolish, wasn't it, to share such a private thing with two women she had only just met?

Ermentrude covered Florri's hand with hers. "To think that my Gregor had someone like you, Florri, is such a relief to me. Such a relief! And that you had each other, even for such a little time. It feels almost like a miracle now."

Florri nodded and blinked hard.

Her face had looked so sad when she came in, thought Ermentrude. It was good to see she had taken on a little color.

"It is a relief to talk about him, isn't it?" Ermentrude asked.

"But now," began Lisabetta, then stopped. "Now what are you going to do, Florri?"

"About what?"

"Well, about things. Your life."

Florri sighed. "What am I going to do about my life? It is a shambles. My father and I barely speak. My husband prefers any other woman to me. And don't get me wrong. I don't resent that, really. I do not care even a little bit. But this is not the life I wanted. I tell you, if it weren't for my son, I would go crazy."

"Have you ever thought about, well, making some changes?" asked

Lisabetta. Florri looked confused. "You know. Looking at your options?"

"Options. I don't have any options."

Lisabetta ran her finger over the tablecloth. "Can I tell you something I'm wondering about? Do you mind?"

Quickly, Florri nodded. She had never in her life had someone she could talk to.

Lisabetta took a breath. "You know, I have studied plants for a few years. Wild plants, mountain plants. One thing I've learned. A plant might manage to grow in a difficult spot, but it won't thrive. The first drought, or snowstorm …." She shook her head.

Florri pressed her hands to her cheeks and stared at Lisabetta.

"Do you have to go on like this, Florri?"

"I don't have much choice."

Lisabetta leaned forward. "Yes you do!" She backed off a bit. "I'm sorry to be so blunt. I sound like my bossy sister." She shook her head. "I mean, we barely know each other. But you do have a choice. And for Gregor's sake …."

Florri hugged her arms to her waist. "I know. But Fate has dropped me here, like a stone. I don't think I'll never get any farther than this."

Ermentrude cleared her throat. "As long as we're being frank with each other," she said in a warbly voice, "I think Lisabetta might have a point. Don't make the same mistake I did, Florri. I did terrible damage to my son because I was afraid to stand up to his father. Or, not afraid, so much as thinking it was wrong for a wife to go against her husband." She reached for Florri's hand again. "No matter what, though, I want you to know how happy you have made me today." She looked at the children playing on the floor. "You both have. There might be difficult times ahead, but you have saved one old woman from despair."

The autumnal equinox was not long past and the world was already ice-hardened. There were still occasional sunny days and even a blossom or two, rimed with frost, that held on in the more sheltered gardens. But generally the land had been stripped to its bare bones. The hare, the ermine, some of the birds, had already garbed themselves for winter. The rest retreated. All softness, all sweetness went to ground. The fishermen still plied the heaving ocean for its bounty but returned early, chilled and exhausted. Children were warned that the slick of ice on the Arum River was not to be trusted, and poor Nicolai Korsakov and his ferry were threatened by that river ice every day.

There were two rivers, actually, that fed Lunenfarne Bay. The two were as different from each other as foxes from foxgloves. The Arum River had its source on the slope of mountains that were more than fifty miles to the west. From there it wound lazily back and forth through a sheltered valley of long summer-green plains and farmlands that brought forth barley and potatoes and lush apple orchards. It widened and passed into Lake Arum, then purred gently along until it lapped at Mr. Korsakov's ferry dock on the edge of the bay.

The other river, the turbulent Nolta, was born in a spring-fed lake high in the Tomgat Mountains. The Nolta River dashed like a mountain goat through forests and over rocks and down the mountainsides, leaping and foaming and prancing. On its way, it spilled into two or three numbingly cold pools and burst over uncounted long drops before finally cascading into the bay more than half a mile north of the mouth of the Arum.

The people of Lunenfarne made good use of both of these rivers.

The Arum River carried barges of farm produce and charcoal into town, ore from the mines and lumber from the forests. The Arum was beloved by boaters and picnickers. Water taxis and pleasure boats poled up to the lake, until, that is, Dort Mynydd shocked everyone by closing the entire Lake Arum Park. The mouth of the Arum River had no bridge but was crossed many times a day by Mr. Korsakov's ferry. The Nolta, on the other hand, offered few pleasures. Refreshment to hikers, yes, and trout to fishermen, but it was not navigable. Its rushing waters did drive Mr. Forman's mill wheels and Mr. Guntram's forge before taking its last fall over the mill dam just before the Nolta bridge. This bridge was used all day long by anyone leaving or going to the town center. The river was too swift to be crossed without it.

Early in the decade that Vladimir Mynydd was chancellor, he had ordered the rickety Nolta bridge to be completely rebuilt, widened, and shored up with stout supports. Guard rails were added to prevent accidents in icy weather. At the time, some people complained that Mynydd was spending the town's money wantonly and going overboard with his safety precautions. The town magistrates were furious. But Mynydd knew the Nolta bridge was an essential link for almost everyone in the community. He made sure it was constantly inspected and kept in good repair. Indeed, if something should ever happen to that bridge, Guntram's blacksmith shop would be inaccessible. Farmers in the Arum Valley wouldn't be able to get their grains to Forman's mills, so there would be no feed for the animals. There would be no flour for bread. People wouldn't be able to get to the market, or to school and, crucially, the chancellor and magistrates themselves would not be able to get home at night. In order for them to leave the market square or the wharf and climb the River Road up to their mansions in the hills, they had to cross the Nolta Bridge.

But now Vladimir Mynydd was no longer chancellor and for the last two years, the bridge had been woefully neglected. The money that had been used for bridge maintenance must have gone somewhere but there were very few villagers who dared to ask where, and anyone who could answer that question would never speak a word. The bridge inspectors had been fired, too, and the repairmen let go. Their salaries were quietly channeled elsewhere. But this fall the townspeople had started to complain that there were planks on the bridge that needed to be nailed back down or replaced. Erosion had set in at the foot of the bridge, causing it to twist. Mr. Guntram himself had left his forge more than once to hammer boards back into place using his heaviest nails. But he could do nothing about the riverbank eroding and the footing crumbling from under the bridge supports.

Bridge maintenance was far from the purview of Lunenfarne's magistrates. Foppish in their satin trousers and heavy golden ankle bands, they turned a deaf ear to the complaints of the villagers. How could you listen to that riffraff? They were vultures, those people who lived down close to the bay. You couldn't trust them. They fed off the fat of the land and gave nothing back.

No repairs were done to the Nolta bridge for over two years.

So late in the unlucky autumn of the year that Gregor Treyse died, a tragedy on that bridge was yet another disheartening event. No one could have forseen this particular danger. The unanticipated event, the freaky accident, the worst case scenario – no one had bothered to anticipate them. Why worry about imaginary disasters when there were more pleasant things to distract one?

Besides, everything in Lunenfarne seemed to have settled into such a pleasant state of equilibrium.

Equilibrium, though, is hardly a permanent state. Ask any tightrope walker.

The Nolta Bridge was headed for trouble. It began with a bird. A bird and one lone spruce tree, way up in the mountains. This tree had bathed its roots in the Nolta River for a hundred years but one summer the activity of a hyperactive woodpecker, pounding holes in its trunk, encouraged an infestation of insects. The pests gradually weakened the tree and rot set in. Still, the tough old spruce withstood several more winters until Nature, hand-in-hand with her unstoppable accomplice Time, finally wore it down. A windstorm twisted its rotted trunk right off its roots and the river took it for its plaything. For days, this huge tree trunk slammed from one side of the river to the other, dropping through rapids, jamming itself against rocks, then working itself free the next time the river swelled with rain, and continuing to boom its way down the mountainside.

Early one fateful morning, Mr. Wunder the baker, all unaware, was at Forman's mill buying supplies. He loaded a sack of barley flour and heaved fifty pounds of ground oats onto his cart. He started back across the bridge. He had to go carefully. It was a school day and four children, dawdling along, had stopped ahead of him on the bridge. They had been startled by something, the sound of a mighty crash, and they stopped to gawk. Mr. Wunder heard it too. He stopped his horse. There was a woman crossing the bridge on her way to market. She stopped as well. The baker, his horse, the woman, and the four children all stared at the spectacle of a spruce tree being thrown wildly back and forth against the rocky banks upriver. Suddenly the tree was swept into an eddy. Swirling, spinning past the mill, it smashed against the wooden mill dam like a battering ram and burst it wide apart. At once, all the water that had been stored in the pond was released in a huge and powerful gush. It carried the tree away, flipping it end to end. Gallons and gallons of water carried the spruce onward, racing it toward the falls.

In a flash, everyone on the bridge saw what was going to happen. The four children stepped back from the rail and started to run. The market lady, all agape, backed away. She clutched her basket, turned, and scurried to safety, barely making it to the other end of the bridge. Mr. Wunder left his poor horse to fend for herself and leapt from his cart. He had just grabbed the hand of the smallest schoolchild when the tree hit one of the supporting legs of the bridge. In the old days, the bridge might have been sturdy enough to withstand such a hit. This morning though, loose boards groaned and snapped under the pressure and loose nails popped and the footing that had been eroding shifted and moved, and with a terrific and horrible moan the bridge started to lean.

The cart and its cumbersome load slid sideways and toppled into the frigid river, dragging the horse with it. Two of the children leapt for the shore. The other two, and Mr. Wunder as well, didn't make it across. They slid helpless into the river, into a maelstrom of broken bridge and mighty tree trunk and branches and swirling horse and cart.

Mr. Wunder was a strong swimmer. He kept tight hold of one child. He pulled the little body close and managed to drag himself and her to shore. That left the other child struggling alone in the whirling river. He never even had a chance. His head hit a bridge beam and he sank immediately. Mr. Wunder plunged back into the water to save him. He was able to rescue his body but could not save his life.

The bell tolled all morning for little Bobby Taptoe, and Lunenfarne had to bury another of its young.

Two days later, Ruslan Fairhedd was summoned by his boss. Dort Mynydd had called him into his office to address, Ruslan assumed, the issue of the ruined Nolta bridge. Two days had passed since the disaster, with not a lick of repair work begun. Mr. Korsakov had been ordered to run a boat back and forth so people could cross the Nolta River, but even he, Korsakov the intrepid ferryman, was complaining that it was dangerous to continue ferrying people across a river full of eddies and turbulence and the ruins of a sunken bridge. Something had to be done.

Nowadays when summoned, Ruslan Fairhedd no longer helped himself to a seat in Mynydd's office. He stood in front of Dort's desk, hands folded. His dislike for the young man, his son-in-law, was souring into genuine disgust. To get the meeting over as quickly as possible, he took the initiative and started the conversation.

"I spoke to Chapin at the lumber mill," he said.

Dort looked up, smiling artfully. "About what, may I ask?"

Ruslan Fairhedd was taken aback. "Why, about repairing the bridge as quickly as possible. People are getting fed up. They have to wait in line for a water taxi. And in bad weather, the water taxis can hardly manage the cross-currents and the ice."

"The water taxis are the least of my worries right now, Fairhedd. Here's the thing. You remember, I trust, that I told you that we have that slave ship landing here. Sometime in the next few weeks."

The slave ship. Of all Dort's hare-brained schemes, this was the most disagreeable. Why had the magistrates let it get this far? Because Dort had charmed them and wined and dined them and given them expensive gifts. "Yes, I – I do remember, but – "

"Well, we have to make some preparations, don't we?"

The thought of selling human beings here in Lunenfarne was

revolting, preposterous. In other towns, Bellesunde for example, it wasn't even legal. Fairhedd wanted badly to try to talk Dort Mynydd out of the idea. "You and I both know, my lord, that there is not a lot of spare cash available to some of our biggest families at this time. How can the mining families even afford –"

"You let me worry about the mining families, Fairhedd. That new mine they're about to dig will give everyone a tremendous boost."

Ruslan tried another tack. "It's getting very late in the year for traders to be coming this far north. I thought perhaps we should wait –"

"We can't wait. We have to get ready."

"Get ready?"

"You have to get things organized. Until we get a regular slave market going, we are going to need a temporary facility. Housing."

"Housing for –"

"The slaves! The slaves, Fairhedd. We have to keep them somewhere. They won't sell right away. We realise that, don't we? And, I admit, there will be people who have yet to get used to the idea."

"That will take some doing. Especially after Rex Botia kidnapped that little girl from the fishing village."

Dort glowered at this. "Now, just a minute. Why are you bringing this up? He didn't kidnap her. That girl is an orphan. He did her a favor."

"She's a child, working on one of his farms now, virtually his slave. It did not sit well with people, let me tell you."

"Water over the dam. A one-time occurrence."

"Her aunts are still upset."

"Upset fishwives, so what? Fishermen won't be buying slaves. Fishermen are not our market and we don't have to worry about what they think." He raked his fingers through his hair. "Anyway, I'm quite excited by all this. It won't take long for word to get around that Lunenfarne is bringing slaves up from the south. And precisely because selling slaves is not allowed in other places, we will have a corner on the market. People will flock to Lunenfarne to purchase household servants. Kitchen help. Farm laborers. We'll sell a lot of the men to ships that need crews. I myself am thinking about training a small cadre of slaves to be guards. Soldiers. My own army. This will turn out to be a very profitable venture, mark my words. And Fairhedd! You will profit by this, too, I promise you."

"But if you remember, sir, I did mention before that there might be some difficulties."

"Difficulties." Dort smiled, indulgent. "All right. All right." He sighed. "Let's hear it. What difficulties were those? And why should I concern myself with them?"

"For one, winter is not an ideal time to start selling men. Who needs to buy slaves when fields are buried in snow? Just something to consider."

"We don't know for sure when the slave ship will arrive. Besides, the mines are working. The lumber mills."

"I wasn't aware they had a shortage of labor."

"They can probably use more workers."

"Maybe we should check on that."

"Let me remind you how much employers prefer slave labor. These are workers who won't make any trouble. Docile. Subservient. And they don't have to be paid wages."

"But the mines aren't even working to full capacity –"

"That is going to change."

"Can we count on that?"

Dort slapped his hand on his desk. "All these complaints! Fairhedd, you're such a pessimist. Use some foresight. We're all going to make a bundle of money. Now then. Next year I plan to raise taxes to pay for a proper market building. Spacious, big enough for fifty slaves. For now though, our cash reserves are low. It will have to be something simple. We'll have to make do."

Ruslan spread his hands. "I don't know of any empty buildings at this time."

"No. We have to build something. Nothing elaborate. Basically four walls and a door."

"What about plumbing? Cots for sleeping? A woodstove?"

"Fairhedd, come on. Be realistic. We're talking about slaves. We don't need to put them up in grand luxury. They will be here for a few days and then sold off."

Ruslan opened his mouth, then shut it.

"A stable or some kind of pen is what we need. Like you'd build for animals. It should be in the middle of town. Near the farmers' market."

"There is really no room there. The farmers are complaining about over-crowding already. And if there is to be no plumbing, the smell alone would be most –"

"Can we hope to keep everyone happy? It's unfortunately not possible. Should we let a bunch of farmers ruin our chances for the good life? We have our families to think of, yours and mine. Tear out the fountain, if you need more room. That thing is butt ugly –"

"I must advise you, sir, that it would be unwise to tear out the fountain. For a few villagers on that side of the river, that is still their only source of water. They would raise holy hell."

"Well, then … figure out an alternative. What about that puppet theatre? It's an eyesore, taking up a prime location."

"The puppet theatre? No. That's – it's an institution here, my lord."

"Puppets! We're talking about pieces of wood, Fairhedd. Puppets are not profitable. They're completely useless."

"Your own son loves the puppet theatre, sir. And the renovations your father started were almost half done before he –"

"Do not mention my father to me."

"I'm sorry but he was –"

"He thought he was so enlightened. But his business sense was nonexistent." Dort gripped his stomach as a pang shot through it. "My father, I'm sorry to say, doesn't know his ass from a hole in the ground."

Fairhedd surreptitiously tried to stretch the stiffness out of his neck. "The puppet theatre has traditionally been one of our finest assets, I always thought."

"Asset? Does it bring money to anyone but a couple of ne'er-do-well idlers? No, and we can't go on without money. Do you see my point, Fairhedd? Do you see how important it is that we establish a lucrative trade in this town?"

Ruslan Fairhedd paused, then, with a tilt of his head, conceded.

"You're making me tired. You do understand, Fairhedd, that I have invested a good bit of my own personal money in this shipment of slaves."

"I realise that, sir."

"My plans are beautifully interconnected, one to another. And now … at present … it so happens that I'm running out of funds. Temporarily short of cash." Dort shoved a pile of ledgers to a corner of his desk. "I'm involved in something else, an enterprise up – up north. It's a big investment. I need cash. I'm sorry the puppet theatre has to go but there's only so much usable land between the bay and the mountains."

Ruslan felt the old fear, the old need to placate his boss before Dort's legendary anger surfaced. "I'll put some feelers out, my lord."

"Feelers?" Dort sagged forward and shook his head. "Bullshit! This has to be taken care of immediately. If anyone gives you trouble about this, I want you to be sure to let me know." He rapped his knuckles on the desk. "I want names."

"Sir. Yessir." Ruslan nodded, asking himself for the twentieth time how far he was willing to go to stay loyal to Dort Mynydd. How far?

Dort's tone hardened. "Any naysayers, Fairhedd, you hear me? I don't care who, rich or poor. Any naysayers, you give me their names. If I have to line a few pockets, I will. If we have to twist a few arms, we can certainly do that, too."

"Yessir."

"You understand that, Fairhedd?"

"Yessir." He understood completely. He rose. "Oh. Before I go, I should remind you that the little boy's funeral is today."

"What little boy?"

"The one killed when the bridge collapsed?"

Dort shifted suddenly in his chair. Some fisherman's kid. He had heard something about it. His stomach felt like it had been shot full of hot lead. Damn Fairhedd and all his negativity. "The funeral. Yeah." There was a long minute of silence. Maybe he should get rid of Fairhedd, fire his ass. Dort rubbed his hands up and down his thighs. He shouldn't let this guy get to him, but what a bastard Fairhedd was. Standing there staring. What was he waiting for? "Well? What do you want from me? Not much I can do about a dead boy. Is there?"

"I thought it would be in your best interest to go to the service, at least." Fairhedd waited. "To show a measure of concern for the townspeople."

"What's there to say? These things happen." Dort pressed his hand against his raging abdomen. "Accidents happen. I don't have the time to worry about funerals, do I?" He looked at Fairhedd. "Well? You can't expect me to be everywhere today, can you?"

"I'll go, then, in your place."

"No. I'd rather you start working on getting that building erected before the slaves get here."

In a show of defiance, remarkable for him, at the hour of the funeral, Ruslan Fairhedd slipped into the chapel for the service. For once, he didn't care whether Dort Mynydd found out or not.

The early shoppers in Mr. Basko's grocery, one fine morning, were the first to come across them. Only one page long, but free of charge! And who didn't like a bargain? There was a pile of a dozen when Basko's store opened. They were gone in two hours. Forman's mill and Guntram's forge carried a few copies. Those made their way back to the farms up in the valley, where they were passed hand to hand. When Rimsky Korsakov's ferry dock ran out of all but one copy, people shared that one during the ride across the river, then dropped into Wunder's bakery or the Bayside Inn to see if they could get their own copies.

Teron's new print shop was besieged that afternoon when the fishermen returned. What was this news sheet that everyone was talking about?

Squawk! Bou Bou the parrot, rattling his feathers, mightily resented all this customer traffic in the usually quiet shop. Coming and going, coming and going. How could a parrot get his beauty rest with all this coming and going? Chilly air, sweeping in every time the door opened. Oh ho, and wouldn't you know? Just look at who this was, coming in here.

Fishermen! Bou Bou bobbed up and down.

Blow it up your butt, me hearties!

Fishermen! Those assholes who refused to throw him so much as the fin of a fish a few years ago – yes yes, he remembered them. Well, it was actually quite a bit more than a few years ago, but Bou Bou did not, oh no, did not forget an insult. Nope, not this parrot. As proof, or maybe just to make trouble, Bou Bou put on, as it were, his metaphorical dancin' shoes and, swaying and swinging on his perch, resorted to obscenity, which was pretty much his only vocabulary, anyway.

Roll me over in the clover!

The fishermen shuddered. A frightening thing in itself, a bird who dances. But his singing voice? Holymother.

Roll me over lay me down and do it again!

This was too much! Don't go into that shop if you don't have to, the fishermen warned. That damned evil thing is in there. Poking only their heads through the doorway, they hollered to Teron across the shop. "Is it too late to get copies of your news sheet?"

The Lunenfarne News. Yes, people did sneer at the oxymoron. Nothing new ever happened in Lunenfarne! The news sheet, though, made quite an impact when it first appeared. Almost everyone in Lunenfarne could read, thanks to the nuns who ran the school. But only a handful of villagers had ever taken an interest in the political goings-on in the village. Why should anyone bother themselves with all that stuff, when everything was going smoothly? Or fairly smoothly.

Today though, they read in this news sheet that the men who maintained the Nolta Bridge had been fired two years ago. How did the powers-that-be let that bit of news leak out? Inspectors fired too? Very few people had realised. How shocking! No wonder that terrible accident happened when little Bobby Taptoe was killed, Thorfinn and Marie Taptoe's kid. It had taken a while but the bridge had supposedly been repaired. According to some observers though, the job had been literally thrown together. The Nolta bridge was not at all what it used to be. Everyone agreed that was true.

The next copy of the news came out a couple of weeks later and cost a penny. Gerbert, the boy who lived in a crate on the wharf, was hired to collect the cash boxes for Teron Adante at the end of the day. That job earned him enough to buy one of Tilda's dinners at the inn, the first hot meal he'd had in ever so long. And what's this latest news? The mining company had made an arrangement with the magistrates? Someone had purchased the peoples' park on Lake Arum. The whole town had wondered what was going on up there. Barriers had been erected to keep the public out. Now they read that their park would no longer be theirs.

The third copy of *The Lunenfarne News* contained an item far more grim. The puppet theatre would be torn down, never to be replaced.

Not replaced? Impossible!

Well, this was a revolting turn of events. Sometimes unpleasant things happen but you let them go because they don't impact your own life that much. Other things you can let slide, not a big deal. But this? Losing their puppet theatre? This was a terrible blow. This was the last straw.

Unfortunately, saying it was the last straw didn't make it true.

Now it was getting on toward the winter solstice. People were busy with decisions about their cattle and pigs, how many to slaughter, how many to continue feeding for an entire winter? Dog-tired fishermen would soon haul their boats into sheds and sort through the nets that needed mending.

The snow in town was knee deep already but there was no one to clear off the market place anymore because Petey the street cleaner had been fired by Chancellor Dort Mynydd two months ago. Trying to deal with this new development, shop-keepers shoveled their own walkways. The nuns asked for student volunteers to shovel the market square. Dock-workers had to clear the snow off the piers and wharves themselves or risk slipping and breaking a leg. More than one good mother, bustling home from market, had already fallen on the ice, scattering cabbages and rutabagas everywhere.

Ice rimmed the riverbanks on both rivers. Out in the sea, frozen bergs from the far north trolled the coast. The moon wore an icy halo that predicted more snow and the Aurora Borealis painted fiery curtains across the night sky. Cold nipped people's noses and little children's cheeks were red roses.

People said the *Lunenfarne News* that month had more to say about what wasn't happening than about what was. The snow wasn't shoveled and the lighthouse wasn't rotating and the bridge wasn't right, even yet. But most people were too busy at this time of year to do more than mutter complaints because the solstice was also the start of the Twelve Days of Christmas – twelve days when peasants didn't have to work on rich peoples' lands, when only a handful of fishermen bothered to go out, when Mr. Forman's mill ran in the morning hours only and complain all you want, it was Christmas holiday and even the miller wanted time off. It was twelve days of dancing! Dancing and cross-dressing and trickery and masks and music; feasting on pasties and sausages, fish pies, custards, cakes, tarts, and sweetmeats. For twelve days!

In the market square on Christmas Eve, the church gave out cocoa and hot mulled wine for everyone (even the slackers who hadn't attended mass). Mr. Wunder the baker sold sugared fried dough and pretzels as big as a child's head. Sister Angelica's children's choir sang their hearts out. It was too cold for the harp but Silvio Filvio brought out his guitar because he knew it wouldn't be Christmas without music and besides, he would do anything Sister Angelica asked of him. Literally anything.

Angelica had worked hard rehearsing her small singers, encouraging them to take breaths at the end of the word 'wassailing' instead of in the middle, and to pronounce "excelsis" without spitting down the neck of the child in front of them. That Christmas, though, her richest gift came from the most indigent person in all Lunenfarne, the grubby little orphan who couldn't attend school because he had to try to earn a living running errands for people, that ragamuffin boy known by an unsavory name. Two months previous, Angelica herself had been startled to see Gerbert sneak into one of her rehearsals. A dirty wraith that people called the wharf rat, he slunk to the back of the choir.

Then he opened his mouth to sing.

She waited for him afterwards. She arranged some lessons, fed him dinner on choir nights, and taught him the carols. She liked their times together. She loved seeing how a little tender care wrought changes in the boy. It was then that she started thinking to herself, very very secretly, about children, about babies, about the miracle of childbirth. It wasn't the Virgin Birth that was foremost in her mind, either. By the time she realised it should have been foremost but it wasn't, she knew she had a problem.

Anyway, on that frosty Christmas Eve with Silvio Filvio strumming quiet chords and arpeggios, Gerbert began to sing a solo, 'O Holy Night', in his high pure soprano. Something came over the town of Lunenfarne then. Something happened. Something in the best spirit of Christmas. People stopped in their tracks. The market square went completely quiet and

Gerbert's voice lifted high. Amazed, the moon pulled the clouds apart and gazed upon that shabby little town. The stars stopped their eternal humming, and mythical riders astride comets flew lower in their orbits to listen. No one breathed. All were hypnotized, transfixed by the beautiful voice of an outcast boy.

For several seconds after he finished, everyone, every single person, was held enthralled. Then a great sigh went up, the moon hid its face again, and the comet-riders flew on. Aye, wasn't little Gerbert's voice beautiful? A beautiful voice. A great revelation, was it not, to think there was such talent right here in Lunenfarne?

In that entire crowd, if there was one eye not brimming with tears, it could only belong to someone whose stone-hearted mother, say, gave him away in early boyhood to a cruel hermit, in exchange for a pet viper.

Meanwhile, along the Hill Road above town, among the second- and third-generation barons of the lumber and mining industries, there seemed to be a madness for parties like never before. Servants in their thin jackets were sent out to shovel the snow and to run before carriages with torches, leading them up the drives to mansions lit with a hundred candles, where ermine-swathed glitterati were welcomed to splendid dinners of tiny delicately-sauced fowl on beds of truffle, and for dessert, tall cones of croquembouche and snifters of brandy. Gowns shimmered with clustered jewels and men wore velvets and embroidered satins freighted with chains of gold and silver. Everyone was crazy for dancing and gambling, anything to spare themselves the frivolous conversation of the other guests, those shallow, tireless yappity-clappers with their vindictive gossip and exaggerated stories and obsequious lying.

Dort Mynydd dressed carefully for these occasions. On this night, he found his wife Florri at her dressing table, running a lackluster finger through the baubles in her jewelry box. Dort went into her room, sipping at some purported remedy for the stomach ache that always plagued him at evening parties.

"Wear the sapphires I gave you, would you, darling?" Dort suggested. She picked out the necklace and let it dangle it from her fingers.

Dort came and took it from her hand. "Let me." He set the jewels on her white neck, watching their effect in the mirror.

Florri kept her eyes off the mirror.

Dort liked seeing his wife dressed elegantly, her shoulders bare above the midnight blue gown he had chosen for her. He knew other men gazed at her with desire but none dared lay a finger her. Not on his wife. The pleasure this gave him was almost sexual. He almost had the urge to – but no, they were already running late. But maybe a night or two with Florri this week would make a nice change for him. Yes, maybe he would stay at home with her tomorrow night. He sipped some more medication.

Nearing now her eighteenth birthday, Florri was actually more beautiful than when he had married her. He had chosen well, hadn't he? There was the financial benefit of marrying her, of course, and much needed at the time. He had so manipulated her father with fears for her reputation that Ruslan Fairhedd would have paid any amount as a dowry. Surprisingly though, the mate he had chosen for practical reasons had turned out to be – yes, it was true, he was just realising – she had turned out to be the ideal wife. It came to him that, of all the women he consorted with, she was the only one he really felt – what? What he felt was hard for him to articulate. He felt he could relax with her. Maybe that was it. Why was that?

Dort rested his hands on either side of her neck. She was the only person who never pandered to him, or falsely flattered him. She never reproached him for staying out all night, either. It showed how much she respected him. Her father had trained her properly, to appreciate men in positions of power. She seemed to know, he told himself, that she should never stand in his way, because some of the things he needed to do were a little unconventional. And too, he was a man with urgent needs that could not be ignored. Florri knew that he was unique, that he couldn't be like other husbands.

It was odd, wasn't it, the way things turned out? He would never in a hundred years have thought that this marriage, formed on impulse, would turn out so well. He gave himself a lot of credit for that.

He pulled away from Florri and stood back.

"The earrings that go with the necklace would look nice." He watched her lovely head bending to left and right and seriously contemplated giving up his plan to seduce Lars Evindar's frisky little wife at the party tonight. He was only planning on doing that because he had to. Would he be able to get away from the clutches of his fawning syncophants for long enough to nail that little whore in some back room or other? He hoped that, after he softened up the man's wife, she would be willing to tell him, more readily than Lars would, exactly what schemes her husband was involved in. He didn't trust Lars. He wasn't as loyal as he should be. Yes, he'd have to get Ruslan Fairhedd to keep Lars entertained. Just as a courtesy to Lars. No need to embarrass the man at this point. Save that til later. Ruslan could keep an eye on Lars. His mother Natalia would keep an eye on Florri.

"Make sure you stay by Mother's side tonight. I don't want some sly fox sniffing around, taking advantage of my being out of the room for a moment." He ran his finger up and down the back of her neck.

Florri hid a shiver. She kept her eyes lowered, staring at the open jewelry box in front of her. All those gems, winking at her. Silent, she reached up and closed the box.

"I'll make sure Mother is ready. She'd better not be knocking herself silly with that useless medication of hers. Come down right away, Florri. It's getting late."

Dort walked out and Florri raised her eyes to meet her own in the mirror.

Humans, most humans, will stifle tender feelings toward another person in a moment, if that person threatens them or thwarts their desires. Dort Mynydd had surprised himself, that night, with a moment of tender feeling for the wife who never thwarted him. He hadn't felt that way toward another person in such a long time. He had, at one time, felt tenderness for his parents. He remembered distinctly how, as a little boy, he had looked up to his father. He liked the games they played, the stories his father told, the walks they took together. He remembered all that. He remembered far more vividly, though, how those warm feelings had been crushed. Devastatingly crushed.

Even when he was quite young, Dort had been overhearing arguments between his parents for some time. Usually it was his mother belittling his father. That was upsetting enough. He didn't know why that bothered him so much. But today it was something else. They were arguing about him.

"For god's sake, Natalia," his father was saying, "he's almost five years old."

Dort felt a wave of panic then. He didn't understand their argument, but it frightened him. He lurched restlessly back and forth outside their closed bedroom door, impatient. He needed his mother to come out of that room immediately, this minute, and take him tenderly to her breast. Fortunately the argument ended with Natalia doing just as she pleased, sweeping Dort into her arms, taking him to his room and locking the door. It was such a relief to snuggle against his mother, her soft hand tenderly caressing his brow. Sometimes, to get Dort to do what she wanted, she threatened to deny him their time together. She knew that particular punishment would reduce him to a snivelling baby. But today, he was getting what he needed. Yes, he had long known how important it was to stay in his mother's good graces. Against Natalia, when she had her hackles raised, even his father was helpless.

Then, one day Dort's father suggested the two of them take a walk down to the harbor to look at the ships. Dort took Vladimir's hand and skipped down the pier. His father even arranged for them to board one of the ships so Dort could watch the crew preparing to set sail. And then they did set sail. Away they went, past the big ghost island and away out to sea. Dort loved it.

Until he discovered that they were not going home again. Not going home that day, or the next or the next. He screamed at his father then, his wicked father who had tricked him, deprived him. He needed his mother! He screamed for most of two days straight. But his father refused to order the captain to turn the boat around and go home.

Finally, on the third day of their voyage, Dort emerged from their cabin. Hostile, sullen, he went up on deck. He refused to speak to his father but the ship's captain introduced himself. The man was so kind, so genial, so attentive to the anguished little boy that Dort tried to follow him everywhere. Here was a man who had but to say one word, Dort observed, and the ship's crew instantly obeyed him. After a day, Dort found out the crewmen were not obeying out of admiration.

One of the sailors, that day, had told an officer a lie of some kind. The captain ordered another sailor to cut off the man's ear. The man was forced to cook his ear over a pot of burning coals. Then he was forced to eat it.

Dort Mynydd, unbeknownst to his father, watched all this from a hiding place. Strangely, the torture didn't make as much of an impression on the young boy as did the comportment of the captain. Dort was fascinated. He watched him carefully, this man who coupled charming manners with absolute authority and ruthless cruelty. This was why people respected him. Dort had never seen that kind of silent authority. No arguing, no shouting. This confirmed something that Dort had begun to suspect about his own father, his sense that Vladimir Mynydd was a weakling. A pitiful weakling, just as Natalia always claimed. Dort was becoming ashamed of him.

He never forgot the Janus-faced captain. This was the man he wanted to be.

For two weeks they sailed on, down to Bellesunde where they stayed for endless ages with relatives. In all, they were gone for over two frantic months. All that time Dort suffered deeply. His mother was not there to give him the comfort he needed, and though he had cousins who were about his age, he alienated them almost immediately with his contemptuous ways. They were very rough on him, making fun of him, calling him a sissy.

He learned from this experience, though. He learned that he had yet to perfect the ship captain's ability to mask his real feelings, to ignore his real feelings. He did manage to enchant his aunts and uncles, though. They doted on him so gratifyingly. They thought he was a marvelous child, and beseeched their own children to be as polite and deferential. The cousins, in consequence, hated Dort all the more.

Dort deflected this hate onto his father. His father had pushed him beyond endurance. Dort had not been prepared for this trip. Every day of that two and a half months was torture. He was overwhelmingly relieved to arrive back in Lunenfarne. And then he received more devastating news, just in time for his fifth birthday. He discovered what else his father had taken from him. He had been forcibly weaned from his mother's breast.

So brief, his days of happy innocence. His father betrayed him. His mother refused him, and Dort, not understanding, saw her also as a betrayer, a conspirator. It was a heavy blow. Nevertheless, he let no one know of his defeat. Defeat must always stay hidden.

Forever after, child or man, Dort trusted no one, certainly no one who considered themselves superior to him. He looked for vulnerable people and locked them, his victims, to his side. He learned, and learned well, to put on a good face, to smile and cajole to get what he wanted. He knew his dark-haired good looks were another ace in his hand. He also learned to anticipate, sooner or later, some measure of betrayal from everyone he met. He watched carefully for the signs. He never failed to uncover them. He never failed, either, to mete out punishment, swift and cold.

Dort Mynydd grew up with many privileges in life. But despite being so blessed, every personal misfortune disturbed him profoundly. Personal set-backs were far more significant than any good fortune that ever came his way. Perhaps this was the cause of the crippling indigestion that plagued him all his life. Even his own body betrayed him.

Back at Christmastime, Lisabetta Button had decided on a way to explain Lily Treyse's presence at the lighthouse. The little girl could take a new last name. She could be Lily Button, daughter of an imaginary cousin, recently deceased. Only two people besides her sisters knew the truth. Ermentrude Treyse would be silent as a tomb, relieved that Gregor's name would not be involved. Florri Mynydd knew the importance of keeping secrets where children were concerned.

So Lisabetta took Lily to the festivities on Christmas Eve and they ran into Florri and little Gregor there. Florri asked if she could visit the lighthouse sometime. She wanted so much to see where Gregor had lived, and where he had died.

"How about tea some afternoon? I see a few patients now in the mornings."

"Do you? Then maybe you would be a good person to talk to Natalia, my mother-in-law."

"Does she have a problem?"

"I'm worried about her. She is so unstable sometimes that she scares me. I'm almost afraid for Gregor and I to be in the house with her."

"Mentally unstable?"

"I would say so. Physically, too. She claims she has a broken arm but I don't think it's being properly attended to. The man she consults has advised her to take all kinds of weird medications. Maybe you could convince her that he's just a quack."

"I thought there were no physicians in Lunenfarne."

"He's not a physician. He's a sort of wizard or shaman. Maybe a witch doctor. He gives me the creeps, but she puts all her faith in him. Will you talk to her?"

"I'll try, Florri. It would be a bad idea for me to have to confront her healer, though. Will he be there?"

"Come in the morning tomorrow, if you can. He never gets up before noon."

"Good. Then Lily and I can go to the puppet show in the afternoon."

"No, the puppet theatre has been closed."

"Closed? Not closed for good?"

"For good. My husband's idea."

The closing of the puppet theatre destroyed the livelihoods of the two worthy men who had been mounting puppet shows for years. They lost their incomes. They lost all sense of purpose in their lives, their very identities. They had no other marketable skills. Now they were drifters.

Behind every puppet theatre is usually a "professor", the person responsible for the primary puppet characters, and the plots too, feeble though they might be. Lunenfarne's professor, Silvio Filvio, was known to all and sundry by his stage name, Signor Bologna. His assistant was called Hahri Fahri. Hahri delighted in improvising little jokes of all kinds. In a performance, when Signor Bologna's puppet-character reached for a prop, say for example, the stick he needed for beating his puppet-wife, Hahri would hand him a wet noodle instead. Then, while the male puppet stammered and mumbled, trying to improvise lines, Hahri's lady-puppet would steal the show with some impertinent rebuttal that always brought the house down. Oh, all the world was a panoply of delights to Hahri Fahri.

Hahri and Silvio Filvio were both currently, and in fact pretty much perpetually, without romantic partners. So when Dort Mynydd destroyed their livelihood by closing down the puppet theatre, they had no one to turn to for financial support. They toyed with the idea of going to work in the mines but the thought was so repugnant, they decided to save it as a last resort. They were forced to beg Irina Francevili to let them stay in one of her rooms. They were more than willing, in fact they begged – oh please have mercy, Irina – to be allowed to do any job, anything at all that Irina wanted done. She gave them a room, practically a closet. Well in fact, it was a large closet. They barely had room to stow the puppets, Silvio's guitar, and their meager wardrobes on a narrow shelf. All this, in exchange for house cleaning in and around Irina's establishment. They became chamber maids, the two of them, a task at which, it turned out, they proved surprisingly adept.

Their lives had always been tenuous. Like most artists, they made just enough money to get by. During their careers, Fate had disrupted their lives more than once, but it taught them to keep their options open. They had learned to adapt. This current setback, though nothing new, was decidedly more severe than any in the past. They hashed over the idea of moving south, but couldn't afford to pay for their passage.

Then, just when the men felt as though they were hanging by their fingernails, they hatched a wonderful plan. Hahri and Silvio were sitting in their closet-boudoir one night, getting on each other's nerves. It was too late to clean anything and too early to lie down on the closet floor, head to foot, and try to sleep.

Hahri interrupted Bologna's cranky mutterings, sitting up suddenly with one finger pointed at the ceiling, and said, "I just had a thought."

"A thought."

"Yes. And, Silvio my friend, I would like to tell you about it."

"Yep. Sure. Sure."

"Listen to this. When I was last in exotic Siam —"

"Whaat?"

"When I was last in exotic Siam —"

"When were you ever in exotic Siam, Hahri?"

"Not recently, I grant you. But in days of yore, yes. Yes, I assure you I was there."

" Right. 'Not recently but in days of yore' is just short for 'never'."

"No no, my dear Signor. I speak only what is true. I was in Siam —"

"Doing what, may I ask?"

"Ah. You ask what was I doing in exotic Siam."

"What were you doing?" Silvio Filvio scratched at his armpit.

"You will doubtless say I invent stories, but trust me, there are more things in Heaven and Earth, Silvio, than are dreamt of in your coconut." Hahri tapped his pointy finger on his temple.

"Here comes a tale told by an idiot," Silvo muttered. He laid back on the floor and set his great large feet upon the closet wall.

"Lend an ear, Silvio. I am about to make a point."

Silvio belched, making a point of his own.

"Listen. While in Siam, I was pursuing," and here Hahri's eyes wandered dreamily toward a couple of brooms leaning in the corner, "I was pursuing a beautiful, sinuous, lithe Balinese dancer."

"A Balinese dancer."

"You know, one of those very supple types." Hahri sighed. "She wore a jewel in her navel, and that was only one of her attractions. A jewel! In her navel, Silvio!"

"I'd wager you never in your life laid your liverish lips on any jeweled navel. Am I correct?"

"I must confess you are correct, Signor. Sadly, yes, you are correct, but –"

"I'll wager you never laid so much as a finger on any Balinese dancer."

"Again, quite correct. You are quite correct, my dear sir. But what I did do," he waggled that pointy finger, "what I did do when I was in old Siam, was see a puppet show."

"Gaa! Spare me."

"What?"

"I don't want to hear about any pornographic Siamese puppets. My constitution couldn't take it. Not penned up, as I am, in this little closet with nobody but your swarthy self."

"But the Siamese have a beautiful puppet tradition, and in fact, in point of true fact, I am thinking that you and I, Signor, could just possibly implement some of these Siamese techniques."

"Siamese techniques. Are they immoral?"

"Not at all. We wouldn't even need a conventional puppet theatre."

Silvio Filvio snorted. "Siamese puppets would undoubtedly go over very big with the fisher folk and shopkeepers of Lunenfarne!"

"Yes! I think they would! My point exactly. Let me tell you about these puppets."

"I'd rather talk about jeweled navels, to be perfectly frank."

"Silvio Silvio Silvio. You mustn't let your mind linger on the subject of navels. This is your despair talking."

"I know. I am depressed. Nothing, mind you, that one lovely jeweled navel couldn't fix." He wondered, dangerously, if Sister Angelica – but no. No, of course she didn't.

"I am sorry I mentioned jeweled navels. It has sent your poor wretched mind into dangerous channels. Come now, let's be practical. Let us put our heads together and try to figure out what innovations we can implement, our penniless pecuniary position notwithstanding."

"Yeah sure. Let's you and I put our heads together."

"Good man, Silvio! Good man!"

"Once more into the breach," sighed Silvio.

"That's the spirit! To scheme, Silvio. To scheme! Perchance to dream!" chanted Hahri Fahri.

So those two dreamers schemed a scheme. And do you know, something did come of this, after all. We could make a long story short and reveal that Silvio Filvio, a.k.a. Signor Bologna, will achieve his new dream and indeed set sail for exotic Siam one day, searching for the truth about supple *danceuses* and jeweled navels. But that would be getting ahead of ourselves. Besides, it might not turn out to be true, and we would miss out on the amazing story of what Signor Bologna's World Famous Siamese Puppet Show accomplished in the town of Lunenfarne. Nobody would believe such a thing could be done if they hadn't heard the whole story. It turned out to be quite the show.

But first, we must follow Lisabetta and Lily Button on the day they visited a print shop. It was the only print shop for probably a hundred miles around. It had officially opened in the early part of this past winter, and of course it was run by Teron Adante, with the invaluable help of Poggio the book binder – oh yes, and Bou Bou the golden macaw, who on the day in question, hopped up to his perch when he heard the shop door open.

Slam! Bang! Thank you, ma'am.

Lisabetta stopped in her tracks.

Lily's eyes were wide. Her mouth hung open. "Is that a bird?"

Lisabetta arched an eyebrow. "I believe so."

"He talks."

"Yes. I can tell that."

"What did he say, Betta?"

"He's – welcoming us to the shop."

Be a good bird.

Lily laughed. "He's funny, isn't he?"

"Hmm. Adorable."

The printing press behind them went still and they watched Poggio carefully lift a pile of newly-printed sheets, tap them to even the pile precisely, and set them on a table. The shop was impeccably neat and clean. Lily was about to go forward to get a closer look at the press when the front door opened again and Florri and little Gregor came in.

Bou Bou whistled. *I'll be damned!*

"Lookit, Gregor. He talks!" Lily pulled the boy close to the bird's perch.

"Is he going to?"

"Mmm-hmm. Watch." The children watched. "Keep watching. He will." They stared up at him, waiting waiting waiting. Bou Bou stared back. Stubborn bird. Bou Bou uttered not a word, reveling in the depths of an exceptionally ornery mood.

Behind him stood Poggio the bookbinder, he of the willow-wand body and an improbably stupendous mop of fine-textured but ungovernable hair. Poggio was staring too. One look at Florri Mynydd, literally one look and Poggio fell in love on the spot. It happens in real life. It does. Not only in fairy tales. Poggio was instantly head over heels. Florri was busy greeting Lisabetta and didn't notice him.

Just then, Teron came out of a back room, accompanied by Silvio

Filvio and Hahri Fahri. "I'll be with you in a moment, ladies." The men shook hands. Silvio and Hahri looked triumphant and left with smiles on their faces.

"Can I help you?" Teron asked.

Florri gestured to Lisabetta, who carefully removed a large book from her bag. It was the handwritten work of Sister Rosemarie, containing everything she had ever discovered about fungi.

"I wondered if it would be possible to print a copy of this."

Teron took it from her and began to leaf through its pages. "Is this your work?"

"No. I'd like to get a copy printed to give the author as a gift. I may be able to get more of her books, as well."

"It's expensive to print something of this length. You would also have to pay someone to replicate these drawings. Yes, I agree. This book is definitely worth preserving."

"Can you give me an idea of the cost?"

"If you keep the same size and format?"

"Yes." Lisabetta blanched when he told her the price. Could she get her sisters to help pay for this?

"Do you mind? Could I?" Florri stepped forward with her hands outstretched. She opened the book and studied some pages. She looked up, biting her lip. She had rarely done anything very bold in her life. So she sounded quite timid when she said, "I could help."

"Pardon?"

"I could help pay for this." She looked anxiously at Teron and Lisabetta. "And maybe? With your permission? If you would let me try – maybe I could show you some – if you like what I do – I could maybe ...."

"What?" demanded Lisabetta.

"I could try to copy these drawings? You can just tell me if you don't like what I do?" She winced. "But I'd like to try?"

Teron nodded. "These aren't too complicated. They would have to be etched on copper plates. Poggio could help you with that."

There was a great crash behind the press. Poggio, in mid-swoon, had nearly dropped the ink ball he was replenishing. Black splatters now freckled his smock and his pointy chin.

"Florri, that would be wonderful," said Lisabetta. "The book is really useless without the drawings. I love your idea."

Florri was so overcome with the reception of her proposal, she couldn't answer.

Teron handed Lisabetta the book. "You two talk about it. Come back in a few days. We'll see what we can do."

"Thank you so much, sir."

"Oh, not sir. Teron is fine." He smiled and shook his head. "Pardon my manners. I'm Teron Adante."

"Thank you, Mr. Adante. My name is Lisabetta –"

"Ah. You're running the lighthouse, aren't you?"

"For the time being. I'm also working as a physician now."

"I'm pleased to meet you, Lisabetta."

They turned to go. Bou Bou, neglected, unnoticed, and unhappy, began swaying wildly on his perch.

Piss shit corruption snot!

"Snot? Haha! He said snot!" squealed Gregor.

Snot! Snot!

The children erupted in gales of laughter. Lily, having never heard the word, laughed because Gregor was laughing. "Snot snot snot!"

They were quickly herded through the door.

Piss, shit, corruption, snot. Ninety-nine assholes tied in a knot!

Teron shook his head and ducked into the next room.

Poggio hadn't moved. He stood in place for another minute, staring into space. Gone? Oh. Oh. She was gone? He had ink on his hands. He did not know it. Ink trickled down his arm. He did not notice, though he customarily worked with fanatical neatness. Drops of ink splashed onto his boots.

What was her name? Stupid stupid! He cursed himself, wiping, to unfortunate effect, his hand across his brow. He did not even know her name.

Lisabetta had promised to visit Florri's mother-in-law, Natalia Mynydd. An early-spring snow had fallen the night before. The day was cold, gray, and windy, so she was glad to see Florri's sleigh waiting to pick her up. They hadn't gone far before she started to wonder if it wouldn't have been better to walk. The drive was taking a long time. The road left the river and took a series of switchbacks up through the steep hills. The horse kept slipping in the heavy wet snow and stumbling into large pot holes.

When they finally drew up in front of the house, Lisabetta realised, from the size of the place, that Florri must lead a very comfortable life. Once inside, she began to change her mind. Though there seemed to be a vast array of treasures everywhere, the rooms were dank and gloomy. It was mid-morning but every window was heavily draped. Dark furniture loomed in the shadows because lamps seemed to be few and far between.

Florri led the way to Natalia Mynydd's apartments. She knocked.

"Sulman?" came the instant reply.

"No, Mrs. Mynydd. It's me, Florri."

"Unh."

"I've brought someone to examine your arm. Can we come in?"

The door opened. Lisabetta had seen colorfully-dressed bishops and potentates come as visitors to the convent during her time there, but rarely had she seen extravagantly dressed women. Natalia Mynydd was something of a shock. Her thick dark hair was swept untidily atop her head, or most of it was. Her face, possibly beautiful at one time, was smeared with make-up like a mask left out in the rain. She wore a velvet robe, open nearly to the waist. Natalia was a full-figured woman, probably at one time voluptuous. When the young women entered, she pulled her robe together and yanked the belt tight at her waist.

"Who are you?"

"This is my friend, Lisabetta, Mrs. Mynydd. Remember that healer that I told you about?"

"What is she doing here?"

"She came to look at your arm. We wanted to make sure it is not broken."

"It is broken. It is! How many times do I have to say that?"

Florri touched Lisabetta's shoulder. "I'll go check on the children while you two chat." She winged, at speed, out the door. It was an effort for Lisabetta to take her eyes off that door and turn to face her patient.

Natalia threw herself into a chair. "Well? Examine me, if that's what you came to do."

"Is it this arm that is giving you trouble?"

"No! It's the other, and it's not just giving me trouble. It's broken and it hurts like the devil."

Empathy did not come naturally to Lisabetta, but she knew she had to make the effort. "I'm going to remove these bracelets so I can see if there is any swelling." She lifted the arm gently, careful not to get scratched by the long red nails.

"Ow!" Natalia bellowed. "You call yourself a healer?"

"I'm so sorry. Does it hurt when I move the hand?"

"Everything hurts. You have no idea. Nobody does."

"I'm sure it must be painful. I don't feel any separation in the bones, thank goodness. Still, you might have fractured something."

"I know I did. No one believes me, but I know it's broken."

"At least the skin is not hot to the touch. That's a good sign."

"You think so? Really?"

Lisabetta replaced the arm tenderly on the chair. "If it is fractured there is not much I can do except make you a sling. It will protect your arm from bumps and take some of the weight off your shoulder."

"Well, at least someone understands what I'm going through. Nobody has any idea. This is all more than I can bear, really it is."

"Yes, I can see that. This sling should help ease the pain you're having. It must be very aggravating to have to put up with that."

"Let me tell you, as much as this hurts, it's nothing, believe me, to what I'm feeling here." Natalia put her hand over her heart. "Death will be my only solace. Life gives me no comfort."

Lisabetta knelt beside her chair. "Tell me why you say that."

"Oh, how can I make you understand what I have to go through? This heartache will kill me. I know it will be the death of me. Not that anyone cares. My son – I have a son, you know, a very prestigious man, a very prominent man. He has nearly broken my heart. He pays no attention to me at all. And of course you know that my husband deserted me."

"Oh no, I didn't know, Mrs. Mynydd."

"Yes, yes. I'm nobody to him now. Nobody. He has completely

forgotten all about me. He left me nearly penniless. So here I am, a widow, practically a widow, for all intents and purposes. All alone in this world." Natalia fingered an errant lock of hair. "Once I was considered beautiful, you know, but now what am I? An abandoned woman."

"I can sympathise."

"Oh, no you can't. You have no idea. Let me give you some advice." Natalia lurched forward in her chair to lean her face close to Lisabetta's. She shook a red nail in her face. "Don't ever let your husband take advantage of you. Never give him the upper hand."

"I don't have a husband."

"You don't? Well, if you get one, you've got to crush him under your heel."

"That's … a handy piece of advice."

"Crush him before he crushes you! Don't end up like me. I've been too soft-hearted. Now I have no one, no one to see me through these difficulties. And at my time of life, oh, it's hard."

"I'm so sorry."

"If it weren't for Sulman, I'd probably be dead by now. Sulman, he's my spiritualist, you know. He's the only one who can give me any relief. Where is he this morning, anyway? He is usually in here by now."

"Mrs. Mynydd, speaking of this healer, can you tell me what he says about this tremor in your hands? How long has it been going on?"

"You noticed? Look at me! I'm shaking like a leaf. I'm a mess."

"You're taking medications? If not, I'd be happy to leave you one or two of my remedies."

"Sulman gives me what I need, if he ever bothers to get himself out of bed. Where is he?"

"I'll leave these tinctures here. Try them, and if they help you, just let me know and I'll bring some more."

"I'm not paying you for those. I have no money to give you."

"All right. Let's say I'm doing this as a favor to Florri this time."

"Hmph," Natalia grumped, "Florri, that little minx. Well, you've seen me now. Go ahead." She waved a dismissal. "Leave me. You'll have to see yourself out. I can't get up."

"It was very nice meeting you. Take good care of that arm."

"Tell Florri to send Sulman to me."

Lisabetta closed the door carefully and turned to go down the hall but, startled, she immediately backed up, banging against the door. A small involuntary screech escaped her. "Augh!" There was a man, hardly a foot away from her, shoulders hunched like a vulture, his face inches from hers. A man in a dark cloak, mesmerizing her with his eyes, blocking her way. Dark hair cascaded halfway down his back. Black eyebrows were drawn together, frowning above glittering obsidian-black eyes. His cruel mouth was a red slash in his pointed black beard.

"Oh! Oh, excuse me. I didn't see you there."

"What were you doing? What exactly were you doing in there?" His voice was low, his tone threatening.

"I –"

"I introduced her to Mrs. Mynydd, Sulman."

Lisabetta breathed a sigh of relief and involuntarily reached for Florri's hand.

Florri moved forward and took her arm. "Her being here is none of your concern. Go ahead in. Mrs. Mynydd is probably waiting for you." She pulled Lisabetta down the hall.

"Who was that?" Lisabetta whispered when they were alone.

"That was Sulman, her witch doctor."

"He's rather terrifying."

"I hate having him lurking about this house," Florri said. "Anyway, what did you think?"

"About Mrs. Mynydd? She almost surely does not have a broken arm but I would be very concerned about her general health. She seems like a very unhappy woman. Has she always had this trembling in her hands?"

"I've only noticed it in the past few weeks."

"I'd like to know exactly what that man is giving her."

"I'll try to find out."

"He'll talk to you?"

"Good lord no. He is extremely suspicious if I ask anything. I'll try to get a look at the bottles she keeps near her."

"He is a very creepy man. Anyway, see if you can get her to take the remedies I left. They won't do anything for her broken heart, but they may calm her a little. It's too bad about her husband."

"She mentioned her husband?"

"Yes, she told me about him. What a despicable man, deserting her, leaving her with nothing?"

"Deserting her? He didn't desert her. She, well actually she and her son had him thrown in jail. They took all his money."

"Jail?" Lisabetta stared. "Her son, your husband? He did that to his father?"

Florri nodded.

"So she was lying to me."

"Her memories of actual happenings are very selective."

"Florri! If things like that are going on here – Don't you worry sometimes?"

"Worry?"

"I just have a bad feeling about this house. I worry for you and Gregor. I wish you didn't have to live here."

Florri bowed her head.

"All right." Lisabetta sighed. "All right. I won't say any more. Just — be wary, be careful, will you?"

Lisabetta hugged her, gathered her bag and coat, and dragged Lily away from Gregor's toy-mobbed nursery.

Stark white mountains of ice towered just outside the harbor. Grey fog, so heavy that nothing could pierce it, blew in from the sea. Maybe it was this persistent fog that produced in Lunenfarne villagers their stubborn determination, but to people up on the Hill Road it contributed nothing but despair. The clash between these two sensibilities would soon rear its head.

The market square was muddy and littered with blowing refuse. The waterfront was piled with unused crates and when the ice left the harbor, it also left one of the piers tilting dangerously. In the place where the puppet theatre had been, a heap of broken lumber was another eyesore. Before the winter was half over, though, that wood had disappeared piece by piece. People made off with boards to use as firewood or to make shelves for their pantries.

Then one day there was some encouraging activity to be seen there.

"What's going on, Valter?" someone asked a man who was raking the ground clean.

"No idea."

"They building something?"

"Dunno. Nobody said nothing."

"A new puppet theatre, finally?"

"None of my guys is building anything. Just hired to do some cleaning up."

The project collected passers-by all day. A load of new lumber was delivered there, but nobody knew what it was for. That afternoon, Teron Adante came out to see what was happening but could learn no more than anyone else. He went back to his shop where a young woman was waiting for him, the one who had offered to do the illustrations for Lisabetta Button's book. She showed Teron her sketches.

"These are very nice," Teron told her. "Forgive me. I never even asked your name."

"I'm Florri Mynydd."

Teron raised his head and looked at her. She looked back. "Are you Dort Mynydd's sister?" he asked, though he saw no resemblance.

"His wife," she said. She dropped her eyes. Poggio the book binder, lurking nearby, made a small bleating sound.

"Ah. Mynydd's wife. So maybe you know something about this project they are working on over beyond the bridge."

She blinked, looked away, looked back at Teron. "I do know what it is."

Teron waited. "What is it going to be?"

She let out a sigh. "It's going to be a slave market."

Teron nearly dropped the sketches he was holding. "You have got to be kidding me!"

She shook her head.

"Slavery is illegal."

"Not in Lunenfarne, apparently."

"Someone is bringing slaves to sell here?"

"Yes. My husband." Those words did not sit well in her mouth, even after almost four years of marriage. "Dort has purchased twenty slaves."

"Twenty. He thinks he can sell twenty slaves? Here in Lunenfarne? When does he expect them?"

"Soon. A Spanish ship is bringing them from Africa and the Caribbean."

Teron frowned, speechless.

"Don't ask me any more because that is all I know."

"I don't see how he thinks he can sell slaves up here."

"I'm told that my father tried to convince Dort of that. Without success."

"Your father has influence with Mynydd? May I ask his name?"

"My father? Ruslan Fairhedd, Dort's factor."

Teron couldn't figure this out. This pleasant young woman, involved up to her neck with such characters, the worst people in all Lunenfarne? He didn't know what else to say to her, what else he dared say.

She could tell he had lost interest in her sketches. "Don't think I am in favor of what they're doing, Mr. Adante, or that I am in any way involved. I am only telling you what I've heard Dort say at home. I probably should not have told you that much."

Teron thought for a moment. "I wonder, Mrs. Mynydd – "

"Please! If you don't mind." She hid a shudder and stopped him with a raised hand. "I really don't like being called that. Please call me Florri."

"All right Florri, I want to ask you something. I publish a broadsheet every week or so. It carries the local news. Such news as we ever get here. But the idea of a slave market in Lunenfarne is so – so startling, that I feel that people should know about it. How would you feel about me mentioning it in the next newsletter?"

"That could get me into trouble."

"If I promise I will not reveal your name, would you be upset if I wrote about it?"

Florri thought for a minute. "I'll worry. If my husband finds out that you heard it from me, I do not know what would happen."

"News of this slave market will get out eventually. But we can assume the magistrates have decided to keep it to themselves for as long as possible. Florri, I promise you that Poggio," Teron pointed to the young man slumped like a human cipher behind the press, "only Poggio and I will know where this information came from."

"I understand, Mr. Adante." Florri paused. She pressed her hands to her lips. "The more I think about this …. Yes. Go ahead and publish it. Maybe some action could be taken to stop it, if enough people are against it."

"That is brave of you, Florri Mynydd."

"No. I'm not brave at all. No. I'm just a little … getting a little desperate to … hoping to find …." She shook her head. "I don't know. Something."

The news was a shock. A slave market would be built where the puppet theatre used to be? The more people talked about it, the angrier they became.

"Slavery's illegal down in Bellesunde, I knows that for damn sure," said a fisherman.

"Selling slaves is illegal there. But they can own slaves."

"These rich people, see, slavery's a good thing for them. One more thing that's good for them but won't do us no good at all."

"What's going on in this town these days? First they close the park for no reason –"

"Oh, there's a reason. You can be sure about that."

"– and now they're bringing in slaves?"

"That don't sit right with me an' I'm not ashamed to say it."

"Why should you be ashamed? We all know slavery ain't right. Owning people? How is that right?"

A couple of older women, with no little ones to tuck into bed, heard from their menfolk that some talk would be going on that evening at the Bayside Inn. Those wives had thoughts of their own. They wanted to be part of the discussion.

"But girls, we can't go to that meeting. It's in a tavern."

"Yeah. I don't think they allow women there."

"It's two women what run the place. They should allow us to come in."

"Yeah, well. Women run whorehouses too and we're not welcome there."

"So we're not welcome. So what?"

"Yeah. So what!"

"Come on. This is no time to be timid. I'd like to hear what's going on."

Practically clinging to each other, they stepped into the Bayside Inn.

"What can I get you, ladies?" Freya called.

"Oh dear me. I, uh, oh, I'd like a cup of tea. Tea, if you have it."

"Us'n will have beers." They dragged chairs up to the table where the men were sitting.

"All right, listen," one of the men at the table was pointing out, "say – just say that some big wig buys a bunch of these slaves. Come spring, that guy ain't gonna be hiring my boys to work them fields no more."

"Nor me to do they washing."

"Nor me to fix their porches and windowsills."

"Besides, you gotta admit, folks, slavery don't feel right. It just don't feel right. Do it?"

"Selling people? Uh uhn."

"It's got to be illegal."

"The Lunenfarne News says it is legal here. Other towns, no. But here, it is legal."

"And all this time I thought we had some, I dunno, some good people here in our town."

"You talking about them magistrates? Look at them. A bunch of ninnyhammers in high-heeled booties."

"You know, I'm just thinkin'. One day – just thinkin' ahead a little – what happens one day when they rich people run out of Africans to buy? Who's to say they won't turn to us?"

"Turn to us?"

"If it's legal to own people, what's to keep them from taking you or me and making slaves of us?"

That thought silenced everyone for a minute.

"Eish."

"Yeah. You're right. What's to stop them?"

"If it's legal to own him, why not own you or you? Or make your wife a slave, or your children?"

"Yikes."

"Sure. Who's gonna stop 'em?"

"Good lord! How we gonna protect ourselves?"

"We can't. We got no say. Who are we?"

"Nobody ain't gonna listen to us!"

"We got no clout. That's the problem."

Freya Button came with a tray of tankards and one cup of tea.

"You don't actually believe that?" she demanded.

The women looked up. The men stopped in mid-slurp and stared at her.

"You think you have no clout? They can't fight all of you. Look, there are always things you can do," Freya said. "Just think about it for a minute."

The villagers looked at each other. "Know what? When it's time to unload the Spanish ship, if it ever arrives, all us dock hands can be off in the mountains somewhere."

"Before they get here, move the daymarks out on the reef so they run aground. That'll stop them cold."

"Or us pilots –"

"Yeah. Maybe it'll happen that none of us pilots ain't around to guide the ship up to the pier."

Freya nodded. "There are lots of ways to wield your influence, and it will work for one reason."

"What's the reason?"

"Because those people up there in the hills depend on you." She pointed. "All of you. They depend on you to do the things they don't know how to do. Oh yes. You do have clout."

"She does have a point," one of the women said.

"Gentlemen! Ladies!" Freya continued. "You think any of those magistrates even know how to pound a nail, much less dock a ship?"

Gentlemen? Ladies? Not one in this group had ever been referred to as such.

Who said there was never any news in Lunenfarne? The story in the Lunenfarne News the next week reported the simple fact that there was no progress on the building that was to house slaves. A sizeable pile of lumber had been delivered to the site. It disappeared one night, every last board.

One of the magistrates gave Dort Mynydd a copy of the most recent broadsheet, the Lunenfarne News. Mynydd absolutely never deigned to read that farcical rag. But he read it that week and he nearly blew a gasket. He was furious.

He swore several oaths too painful to repeat, not even here. He smacked the broadsheet he held with the back of his hand. "Where does this piece of crap come from?" he demanded of Ruslan Fairhedd. "Who wrote this?"

Fairhedd, who had absolutely never withheld anything from Mynydd, told a lie. "Hmm. No idea, my lord. No idea."

"I saw you with a copy of this paper a couple of weeks ago, Fairhedd."

"I have read a few issues."

"You lousy traitor!" Dort needed to yell at someone.

"Reading the local news sheet isn't traitorous. I thought we should be informed about what's going on, that's all."

"Since when do we care what the gutter rats are saying, Fairhedd?" Dort blew a loud hiss of breath. "The guy that printed this bullshit is going to pay for it. He can't go spreading this stuff all over town."

And you, you traitor, Ruslan Fairhedd, thought Dort, just because he felt particularly cantankerous. You'll pay for your disloyalty. I never could trust you.

Ruslan Fairhedd was stunned, soon after, to hear that he was being demoted. Suspected of disloyalty, they told him. His big mouth had flapped once too often.

Being demoted was humiliating. Then something surprising happened. Ruslan got used to the idea. He no longer needed to bend over backwards to be Dort Mynydd's most favored employee. Ruslan began to see the whole situation in a different light. He deserved this. Fate was pushing him to do what he should have done a long time ago.

He sat now at a rickety desk, elbow to elbow with two novice accountants. In his present frame of mind, he felt no compunction about sneaking a look at their books. He waited until after they had gone home one night, then took their ledgers out of their desks. He ran his finger down the columns on the pages. There were transactions here that he had known nothing about, though he should have. This deal with the mining company – he had heard only hints, and apparently, they were true: for the privilege of digging in Lake Arum Park, Botia Mines was paying a lot of money into a bank account Ruslan hadn't even known existed. A lot of money.

Ruslan wasn't sure this was a crime, but he did believe that Dort Mynydd had just made another bad decision. This, Ruslan predicted, will be the beginning of the end for Dort. This is the end for me, as well. I only wonder why it took me so long.

That evening, he walked out of the office for the last time, but it wasn't this that made him shake with dread. He had some old business to take care of before he did anything else.

He didn't know where to start looking. He'd heard a rumor or two about a woman at the Bayside Inn and decided to start there. It was five o'clock in the afternoon, so the place was filled with fishermen and dockworkers. Ruslan had never been in the Bayside Inn before. A blonde woman, wariness written all over her face, stood behind the bar, looking at him.

Freya Button watched him come in. A chewed-up man, he appeared to her, chewed up, eaten up, and sucked dry. She knew who he was. She looked at him with narrowed eyes, watched him hesitate, then come toward her. He moved in jerks, like he had a small knife stuck in his gut. Which, she thought, was exactly what such a person deserved.

He stumbled clumsily against the leg of a stool and clutched the edge of the bar. He coughed to give himself a moment to collect himself. "I – I'm looking for Vladimir Mynydd."

"You don't really think, do you, that Vladimir Mynydd would want to speak with you?" She knew who he was and what he had done, but seeing the way he flinched, she was sorry she had said that.

"No." Why had he – he shouldn't, he shouldn't have come. "No, I'm sure he wouldn't." He looked up. Vladimir, a sheaf of papers in hand, had just entered from another room. He came over to speak to Freya, then glanced in Ruslan's direction. He took a second look, drew himself up taut, raised his chin, and said nothing.

Ruslan bent his head. They were staring at him. "I've been an ass," he bleated.

"I couldn't agree more," Vladimir replied.

"I can't – I don't know where to start. There are things I need to say to you, and things that I know. About your son."

Vladimir and Freya looked at each other. Freya, fierce by nature but softened by experience, gestured with her head toward the beer barrel.

Vladimir sighed, took two mugs off the shelf, and poured. He waved the mugs at a table. "Sit over there."

They sat. They talked for a few wrenching minutes.

Ruslan rose like an old man, exhausted. "I'd like to talk again. I know some things that should be looked into."

Vladimir stayed seated, his eyes on the table.

Ruslan extended his hand. "I wish we could shake hands."

Vladimir rose slowly. "Now what will you do for a job?"

"I haven't the faintest idea."

Vladimir hissed softly through his teeth and shook his head. "All right. I suppose we could use an accountant in the warehouse."

"A job?" Ruslan's face wrinkled. He frowned, trying to keep his composure. He wanted to answer but couldn't make a sound. He nodded, holding his breath, teeth throat jaw clenched. Finally, finally they shook hands.

Ruslan stood in the doorway of the Bayside Inn a minute later, looking out over the bay. He reminded himself to breathe, breathe deeply. He turned and walked slowly along the boardwalk. He found a bench and brushed peeling paint from its seat. Had he known it, it was the bench where his daughter had first met Gregor Treyse in happier days. He sat down and put his head in his hands. It had been gut-wrenching, apologizing to Vladimir Mynydd. Years ago, he had lied about Vladimir. He had accused him falsely. He had seen him arrested. The apology this afternoon had felt like he was stabbing himself repeatedly. So awkward and pathetic, he had been so awkward. Then Mynydd offered him a job. Now he had to go home and admit his humiliation to Ludmila, his wife.

Another coincidence intruded. Across the way, Ermentrude Treyse was the last to leave the weavers' workshop for the day. She turned the OPEN sign face down and was locking the door when she noticed Ruslan Fairhedd sitting by himself, looking very lonely. Aww, a little greeting might cheer him up.

"Hello?" she said quietly. She smiled, hesitant.

He looked up. "Hello."

"We've never formally met, have we? Oddly enough. You know, seeing as how –" She wagged her head and smiled.

"No." He frowned. "I don't think we've met."

"I'm Ermentrude Treyse." She smiled some more. A little shrug. "No? Doesn't ring a bell? I'm Gregor's other grandma." She ducked her head with a little laugh. "It's a little strange that we've never met when, of course, I see Florri and the baby quite often."

"Gregor –?"

"I just adore that child. You can't know how I cherish him. I keep telling Florri that he is so like his father. How is he, anyway? I haven't seen him all week."

"Gregor?" Ruslan was mystified.

At the look on his face, Ermentrude stopped. Her smile drained away. "Oh." She closed her eyes. "Oh dear God."

"Mrs. Treyse, I don't know what you're talking about."

"No. Oh. No, of course not. I'm so sorry."

What had she done? It was Florri's great secret. Would he guess it? She would never be able to explain this to Florri. She certainly didn't have the courage to explain herself to Florri's father. Sick at heart and cursing herself, Ermentrude wished Ruslan a good evening and hurried away.

Ruslan walked all the way home. He needed time to sort things out. His thoughts startled and leapt like a field of grasshoppers. He didn't give even a glance at the cottage gardens sprouting their first spring snowdrops on the River Road, or the swelling buds on the trees. He acknowledged no passers-by. The farther he went, the more confused he became. What had that woman meant? Gregor's other grandma? Was there something they hadn't told him – his wife Ludmila, his daughter Florri? They were hiding something from him, deceiving him or – or betraying him in some way?

At the top of the River Road he stopped, stopped dead in the middle of the street. Deceit? Betrayal? He had the nerve to accuse them of betrayal? Look at me, he thought. Me, a beast. I practically wrote the book on deceit and betrayal.

It took all his determination to steel himself and turn up the Hill Road.

"Secrets?" Ludmila came to sit beside him on the sofa. He looked so drawn and despairing. She sighed. "There have been secrets, too many secrets between us. Yes, Ruslan, we have been pretending, all of us. You, Florri, me."

His heart almost stopped. Secrets. So. Ludmila was in love with someone else. This was happening to people he knew. Now it was happening to him, happening on top of everything else. The chatter in his brain would not stop. He closed his eyes and turned his face away. "Who?" he asked. He was afraid he would be sick.

"Who? All three of us. You feel you have wronged us. We have wronged you."

The words he tried to get out were strangling the air in his throat.

"Who is he?" He forced himself to face her. She frowned. "You have someone else, Ludmila? Tell me who."

"What?" She shook her head and laughed a little. "No, you fool. I'm talking about something between Florri and me."

Wait. He started to breathe again. It wasn't what he thought? Anything else, he could take anything else, or so he thought.

"We should have told you this long ago. I hope Florri won't be mad at me for finally saying it." She stopped to put her hand over his. "Your grandson, our little Gregor, is not a Mynydd. Dort thinks he is the father, but he is not."

He stared, shocked.

"Florri had a lover who she continued to see, with my help, for a short time after she was married. She is sure that the child is his."

Ruslan lurched in his seat. The heat in his chest burst up into his head. "I told you, Ludmila! I told you!" So Dort had been right about Florri's wanton behavior? "I told you that. Before she was married, I told you. Dort warned me that no-good gypsy boy was after her."

"No! Ruslan, no! That's not who it was."

"It wasn't?" Dort had told him – what? – a lie? "Then who was it? Dort told me she was whoring around with someone."

Ludmila pulled away. "How dare you say that? How dare you? Dort lied, Ruslan. He lied. You dare to call your daughter that name and yet you listen to the man who keeps at least a couple of mistresses? How could you be so stupid? Florri was still a virgin a month after they married."

Ruslan reeled back as if struck. "But he said – then why did Dort tell me – he convinced me she was – why did he do that?"

"That I don't know. To get the dowry we paid him, maybe? I don't know."

"Oh my god. I didn't understand, Ludmila. I didn't know."

"If you hadn't been so certain you were right, you might have listened. Neither of us could get through to you. We wanted to, we tried to tell you, Ruslan, but you wouldn't listen."

He felt so crushed he could hardly speak. She was right. Ludmila was right. He spoke barely above a whisper. "Well – who is it, then, this other man?"

"He was Gregor Treyse."

"Not – not that boy who committed suicide?"

Ludmila nodded.

"Did he – is that why?"

"We don't know why he did it. They had stopped seeing each other a long time before that."

"That boy who was crippled? The lighthouse keeper?"

"Yes."

"Florri loved him?"

"Very much."

"Before she was married? They were in love before she was married?"

"Yes, Ruslan."

"So is that why? Is that why she is so – so different, now?"

"Probably. I'm sure that's part of it, yes."

"And that boy? Did I – was it my fault that boy committed –? Oh my God, Ludmila."

Ruslan folded up until his head touched his knees. What kind of a person was he? He had turned into something he couldn't or wouldn't recognise.

Some people seem to be blessed in their relationships. Ludmila was determined to hold her family together. She arranged for Florri and little Gregor to visit the next afternoon. Florri was taken aback when Ruslan walked in. Ordinarily, she never saw her father from one month to the next, and here he was, at home in the middle of the day?

Ludmila took Gregor for a walk. Ruslan Fairhedd, sitting opposite Florri, was shaking with humiliation. His daughter, that always-obedient little girl, that little moppet who had so delighted in pleasing him. Now they had traded places.

Ruslan, abject, tried to apologize, halting, stumbling. It was difficult. Personal insight was a new thing to him, whereas Florri, barely eighteen years old, had wrestled with her demons for almost four years. She had certainly suffered her own regrets. She had also, long ago, come to terms with her father's devotion to men of power.

"How can I make this up to you?" he asked her, after they had talked for some time. He waited. Please, wouldn't she say something?

She thought for a minute, feeling it was vital that she come up with some answer. "I wonder if you know something about what is going on up in Lake Arum Park."

He looked at her, surprised. "I know a little. What I do know does not present your husband in a good light."

"I'm sure it doesn't. Maybe you and I could go together, one of these days, to talk to Teron Adante about it. He thinks it is something the whole village should know about. And maybe there are other things you could tell him?"

You and I? You and I together? Ruslan did not give a fig for Teron Adante or why he would want to know anything about the Botia mines. All he heard were her words "you and I together."

The next week, a citizen came into Teron's shop. Otto Wohlfahrt had run the chandlery in Lunenfarne for four decades. He sold ships' supplies: oil, candles, rope, paint, soap. His business had grown, expanding into the building of fishing boats and small ships. He had a hundred fifty acres of forest in the mountains that supplied him with lumber. He had managed his woodland very carefully. The trouble was, another lumber company had poached some of his largest trees. But that was not the reason he was speaking to Teron. He had something worse than that to reveal. He had made a visit yesterday to one of the lumber barons to complain about poachers, only to find out that the same company was also removing trees, all the trees, from the Lake Arum Park. And why were they removing these trees?

"Because," griped Otto, "those trees had to come down before the Botia Mining Company started work. Now they are ripping up the park. They think there is copper there, though apparently they haven't done the research to know for sure. You should visit the site."

"You've seen it?"

"I have. All that's left of that park is a gaping hole thirty feet deep. Not a vein of copper. But they're still digging."

Florri and Ruslan Fairhedd had already come to speak with Teron about this. "This confirms what I have heard elsewhere. That mining company must have paid someone a boatload of money."

"But who?"

"No one is sure. It looks like foul play."

"I think, Mr. Adante, that the townspeople should hear about this. It's too late to save the park but still, it's not right that this was done behind our backs. This whole town, our town, is going to hell and we have nothing to say about it?"

So the Lunenfarne News lived up to its name for the second time in a month. It told what everyone knew, that the slave market was being built under armed guard. And something only a few people knew, that Lake Arum Park was now a pit mine. No one knew what money had changed hands to make this possible.

More news appeared the following week. It was good news this time. There was going to be a special puppet show soon, even though there was no longer a puppet theatre.

Signor Bologna was putting on a puppet show again? Wonderful news for a change! Even adults were looking forward to it. No one could figure out how the puppets would work without a theatre, but Signor Bologna would surely find a way.

But first, the Spanish ship.

The day the Spanish ship came in, dark clouds oppressed the town and every beating heart felt the weight of them. Lily was the first to see the boat come over the horizon. She was standing on a chair up in the lighthouse tower, helping, in her way, to polish the prisms.

"Boat coming!" Lily declared. Lisabetta reached for the glass and pointed it to the horizon.

"You're right, Lily." She couldn't read the name of the ship. "Let's get our coats. We're going to see the aunts."

"Aunties!" Lily yelled. "Pie at aunties!" She loved Freya and Tilda.

Lisabetta took one more look through the glass. She could barely make out the ship's name. *Dragòn*? It sounded like a Spanish name to her. The slaver they expected was said to be Spanish. *Dragòn,* arriving now just outside the harbor, appeared to be dropping anchor. They were lowering a boat. Lisabetta rowed with all her strength to reach the wharf before they did.

She helped Lily ashore. She called to Mr. Francevili, the harbormaster, that a ship was on its way, possibly Spanish, possibly a slaver, possibly called *Dragòn*. Like morning mist, Francevili, dockworkers, pilots – they all disappeared, every one of them gleeful as could be. They had been waiting for this day. Freya Button had promised them a free lunch in an upstairs room at the inn on the day the slaver came in, as long as they agreed to stay away from the docks. Today, the only duty required of them was to eat and have a good time and do no work. There wasn't a man-jack among them who would shirk that duty.

The Spanish rowers pulled up to the dock but though they tried for an hour, they were unable to find anyone who would help dock their ship. They rowed back out to the *Dragòn* and, sweating bullets, tried to guide it into the harbor themselves.

The day the Spanish ship came in, the harbor was cold and deserted at first, except for a bank of clouds and the gusty north wind they dragged behind them. The ship fought the wind to get closer to the piers. Dort Mynydd and one of his assistants were the only men around. Dort had seen the ship struggling to get through the channel. Where were the pilots? And the dockworkers? There should be five or six stout-hearted men along the wharf who would help with the task of tying up a ship. Dort paced, frantic. What was going on? Someone was deliberately stirring up trouble!

That newspaper printer! Was this a vendetta? Revenge? Long ago, a long long time ago – Dort had been only an innocent child at the time – he might have given away a secret. He had never realised it would send Teron Adante off to Balgrim Prison. Had Adante found out? Was he still blaming Dort for that trouble, for that admittedly stupid boyish prank? Was that newsman holding that long-past incident against him, against his slave enterprise?

Dort's charming manners deserted him. He screamed at his aides. Why couldn't he get some answers about these dockworkers? Where were they? His assistants met his questions with excuses more numerous than bones in fried catfish, and exactly as irritating. Somebody has fomented this hostility against him! Him, the chancellor! Someone was going to pay!

Dort ran along the wharf, furiously angry. The *Dragòn*'s pilot boat was still trying to guide the ship closer to the pier. Men were bellowing at each other in Spanish. Someone threw Dort a line. He didn't know what to do with it. Though he had lived all his life beside the sea, he knew next to nothing about boats. He backed away and the line fell like a dead snake onto the dock. What did they expect him to do? What's this capstan thing they're yelling about? Capstan? Was that an English word, or Spanish? He couldn't understand a thing they said. That was fortunate because if he had known the dreadful names they were calling him, an apoplexy would have smote him like a rock from a siege engine.

The north wind made all maneuvers more difficult. When the ship was finally able to turn broadside to the wind, it was blown so hard against the pier that it knocked Dort right off his feet. The sailors had to rappel twelve feet down onto the pier in order to get the boat tied up.

The day the Spanish ship came in, the village of Lunenfarne watched in silence. Townspeople, mostly women and old men, began to collect on the boardwalk, but not a murmur could be heard from them. They huddled in their wraps against the cold and wind, and watched, their faces grim, squinting, frowning. Georgiana, the maids, and a couple of cooks came out from the Bayside Inn. Fishermen's wives left the markets, seamstresses and weavers came out of their workshops. After hearing stories of the way slaves were captured and dragged from their homes, the villagers wanted to see and yet they didn't want to see them.

Certainly none in the crowd had come expecting to hear their exalted chancellor, Dort Mynydd, slinging gross insults at the Spanish captain.

"I bought twenty slaves, you ignorant asshole! Where are they?"

"Many died on ship. So sorry." The Spaniard held up one hand. "Five come. Others dead." It wasn't true. None of the slaves had died. The captain had sold fifteen of the African slaves to sugar cane plantations in the Caribbean, though Dort had already paid for them and for their passage. They were not exactly constrained by morals, these slavers.

"You bring me only five? Five? As God is my witness, you are going to reimburse me, every single damn cent, for the fifteen that are missing, or your ship does not leave this harbor."

"Sorry?" Another shrug. A smile. "No unnerstan' the Anglish."

"I want my money back! I paid for twenty slaves!"

"Ah. Money!" The Spaniard shrugged. "I know nothing, signore. I know ship only. Know nothing about these –" He pointed to the ship's hold. "You must do –" the captain made a writing motion " – at man, Madrid man. Madrid man have you money."

By this time, Dort was overheated and wild-eyed. The villagers looked at each other in disbelief. This was their chancellor? Heaven forbid anyone's grandmother should hear the language he was using. He needed a good caning, that's what he needed, grown man or not.

And then, emerging from the ship's hold, came the five African slaves. They appeared at the top of the gangplank. Heads in the crowd came up. Fingers pressed against lips.

The day the Spanish ship came in was a sad day for Lunenfarne. Three Black men, one Black woman, and a boy of about ten years, possibly her son. Chained together, heavy iron cuffs on their wrists. They had been imprisoned in the stinking hold of a creaking ship for weeks. They huddled together, dressed in thin rags in the cold sharp wind of March, staring out at a bleak, unfamiliar land. Pushed, prodded, slapped, forced to walk down a narrow, bouncing gangplank, and up through the town to the new slaves' quarters. They stumbled with lowered eyes through a silent crowd of white people who separated to make way for them. Only one of the five dared to raise his eyes to the crowd. Only one harbored a shred of hope that someone would come to their aid and spare them this plight. It was the boy. Very young, that boy must have been, very young. He didn't yet know the world.

Dort's assistant held the door to the new slave quarters. They filed in to the windowless, unheated building. Dort ordered their chains removed. He didn't want the merchandise to be damaged. His assistant put a large padlock on the door, banged it smartly into place, and gave the key to Dort.

That night, the first of the fires occurred. A rock crashed through the window of Teron Adante's workshop. A flaming ball of rags followed. If Poggio hadn't been sleeping in a back room, the whole place would have been lost. Not only was Poggio there, he was instantly awake. Not only was he awake, he was prepared. His former master, for several reasons, had always insisted they keep fifty pound bags of sand here and there throughout the shop. They sometimes worked at night, and candles and lanterns could tip over. They often had braziers of fire going to heat copper plates, or to melt wax. The presses, the valuable presses, were made of wood, and the cupboards were full of paper. There were many fire hazards. Sand was their first line of defense.

Bou Bou the parrot, in his covered cage, knew something was going on, and he wasn't about to let it go without comment. He screamed every obscenity he knew. Poggio shouted up the stairs for Teron. Then he pulled his nightcap down over the voluminous headdress that was his hair and dragged a bag of sand across the floor. He flung handfuls, then dumped a mountain of it onto the blaze. By the time Teron flew through the door, the fire was out, though the place stank of smoke and burning oil. Poggio's white stork-legs were bare and, in his short nightshirt, he looked decidedly feeble. But he alone had saved the print shop.

He pulled off his nightcap and used it to wipe his face. His hair, exploding with static, was a vagabond haystack. He looked at Teron and shook his head.

Teron swore roundly. "See anyone? Any idea who?" he asked, panting.

Poggio shook his head again. "Somebody with a grudge against the newspaper."

"Somebody realised the truth hurts, I guess. You're in your bare feet, Poggio. Watch those glass shards."

They cleaned until four in the morning.

Teron took a bucket of broken glass and oily rags to the back porch. "Someone is going to be very unhappy to read the details of this in our next edition," he said when he returned.

"I'm sure they weren't expecting there to be a next edition," said Poggio.

Cover the cage. Poor bird. Poor bird. Cover the cage. The cage had not been uncovered, but Bou Bou, you know, had needs.

"Did you check on Bou Bou?"

"No, I forgot him. I hope he didn't get hit with anything." Poggio lifted the cover. Bou Bou was an eyesore of disgruntled feathers. He shook himself and hunkered down on his perch.

"That bird survives everything, but only because he is meaner than pusley."

"A bit bedraggled you are, aren't you?" Poggio cooed, leaning close to the cage. "But still a handsome bird. Such a handsome bird. Sleep tight, Bou Bou."

Tighter than a crab's ass! And that's waterproof.

Ah, Bou Bou. A bird of many words. No grasp of their meanings, but a repository of many, many words.

It was very inconvenient for a printer to board up a window. He needed all the light he could get to do his work, but it would be a while before Teron's shop could hope to obtain a new piece of window glass to replace the damaged one. The boarded up window did, however, transform the shop into a place for people to gather and talk without being seen and heard.

This was convenient, because Teron was devising a plan, a plan born of moral outrage and indignation. In his boarded-up shop, Teron assembled a few people he thought crucial to this plan. Signor Bologna's puppets were not at the meeting themselves, but they were the characters who would, if all went well, almost literally steal the show.

SISTER HOGAR

It was a Sunday morning, cold and grey and quiet. In the villas that were strewn across the hilltops, people were still sleeping off the effects of Saturday night's debauchery. Last night's gowns had been flung across chairs, tail coats had been dropped crumpled to the floor, jewels in rare colors tossed onto dressers, entwined with snakes of gold chains and pocket watches.

It was quiet, too, in the village below. Most everyone had risen early, donned clean shirts and Sunday frocks, and gone off to church. Those few who hadn't joined the congregation hid themselves instead in secret nooks where they could contemplate the universe in whatever way they deemed most satisfying.

Nicolai Korsakov had a little brazier going on the ferry dock. He was warming himself beside it, enjoying a moment of peace. Soon Father James would finish singing the mass and church would let out and people would line up to be ferried back across the Arum River. Korsakov felt his dock sway with a heavy tread. He closed his eyes. All right, all right, an early customer. Korsakov got up with a sigh. He took one glance at the person fishing coins from a large canvas bag, and forced himself to look away. Korsakov, usually more garrulous than a magpie, could not think of a word to say as he accepted his fee. Lunenfarne had some odd-ball people, but none as wackadoodle as the nun who just stepped onto his ferry.

Tongue-tied, Korsakov polled her across the river and deposited her at the dock on the other side. A little later, Korsakov's sometime-assistant Chilperic was walking to work. This same nun caught his eye too. That woman must be very devout, Chilperic mused, seeing her kneeling on the cold ground up in the old cemetery above the fishing village. Even kneeling, he could see she was of a remarkably ample height and girth. That backside, thought Chilperic. Whew, big as the broadside of a barn. Nuns must be eating well these days. She knelt with her forehead touching the cold mud, her arms outstretched on the ground before her. Then she rose, lifted the strap of her bag to her shoulder and, just as Chilperic came even with the cemetery gate, hastened down the hill toward him.

"Excuse me, sir! Excuse me," the nun called, her arm waving, her robes flapping.

Chilperic stopped in his tracks. The voice was deep, not really the voice he had expected of a woman. Actually, her deep baritone was not at all the voice he expected. Slowly he turned himself around and stopped again, stopped dead, mouth hanging open and working like a netted salmon. It was startling to see a woman even taller than he, but that was not what grabbed him. No, it was the beard that did it, the long full red beard that grew thick over the entire lower half of the nun's face.

Shockingly, this nun was cussing roundly. "What the bleeding *#^* piece of luck is this? Chilperic?" She stood with arms outstretched. "Chilperic, is that you?"

" 'Tis I indeed, but –" He took a couple of steps back, wary in the extreme.

"You don't remember – ah!" The nun pulled the habit from her head and a mop of plentiful red hair sprang up, long, thick as a bayberry bush. "It's me! Hogar Hanon!"

"Hogar? Hogar, as I live and breathe! I never would have known you. I mean, how could I, dressed like –" Chilperic hesitated, gestured. "Dressed as –" He shrugged. Why mince words? "Why the hell are you rigged up like that?"

Hogar laughed. "First, give me a hug, you anus-sniffing cur!" He threw his arms around Chilperic and clapped him hard on the back. Chilperic submitted with reluctance, patting his old friend lightly and extricating himself as hastily as possible.

"Your language hasn't improved much, Hogar."

"Hey, if life deals me a pile of shit, I'm not one to call it honey."

Chilperic rolled his eyes. "You be frank and I'll be earnest."

"Frank and Ernest! Good joke!" Hogar roared with laughter. "Still the same old Chilpy!"

"Heh heh, yup. So Hogar, you uh – we uh – haven't seen you in a long while. You – you doing good these days?"

"Oh, you know. There's good and there's bad. You?"

"Can't complain. So and uh you uh you ah – you jumped the fence, did you, Hogar?"

Hogar fished in his robes for his flask. "Jumped the fence?"

"You … you … you don't want to be a man anymore, or you …?"

"No." Hogar's delighted laugh was deep and loud. "Oh no. This is not what you think. Here, sit here a minute, old friend." He brushed a few of last year's leaves from a bench near the cemetery gate and motioned Chilperic to sit. "Damned if you don't look ready, more than ready to share a drop with me. And you bet your boots I've got something that'll stiffen that limp proboscis of yours on this chilly morning. So did I surprise you? I guess you thought I was dead, eh? Here, take the bottle. Go ahead. Try a swig. It's good for what ails you. Puts hair on the bottoms of your feet. Straight from the bishop's cellar, so you know it's quality swill."

Chilperic felt, by this point, entitled to a drink, very well entitled. He gulped a man-sized swig and was taken by a fit of coughing.

Hogar laughed. "A bloody peat monster this stuff is, eh?" He pounded Chilperic on the back.

"Like drinking liquid fire – gak! Woo!" Chilperic shook himself. "The bishop gave you that bottle?"

"Naw, you kidding? The bishop doesn't give anybody anything. Whenever I get the chance, I steal the keys for the special cabinet he's got hidden in a cellar up at the convent. St. Scholastica, I'm talking. Where I work." He raised his hand. "Used to work, I should say. I sneak his cabinet open, pour half a bottle of his Scotch into my flask. I refill his bottle with the nuns' cheap sherry – and that hooch of theirs is nothing but absolute weasel piss, I swear to you. Then I put the bottle back in his cabinet and the lame-brained old fart never knows the difference."

"Tricky."

"I'm one slimy son of a bitch, I tell ya." Hogar erupted in laughter.

"But how did you get to be a nun, is what I want to know."

"I ain't a real nun, Chilpy. It's a long story."

"I got time. I can't guarantee I'll believe you, but I got time to listen. If you don't mind, though, I'll just liquidate my tongue once more. Gimme another sip, wouldya please?"

They passed the bottle back and forth, liquidating their tongues to the point of dissolution. Then Hogar wrapped his meaty hands around his flask. He coughed delicately and spoke in a voice barely above a whisper. "I guess you remember Emma, don't you, Chilpy?"

"'Course I remember Emma. You took one look at Emma, and nobody never forgot her."

"That is God's truth, I swear it is. God's truth. She was a woman. Ah me." Hogar ran his hand over his beard and blinked several times, feeling like his throat was full of gravel. "You remember the fire? Her and the baby?"

Chilperic placed his hand on Hogar's knee. "I remember." He looked up toward the cemetery, up where he had first seen Hogar that morning. He patted Hogar's knee, then glanced up and down the lane and quickly withdrew his hand. "Of course I remember."

"Yeah. So you know how it was for me back then, I guess." How fleeting, the days of his marriage.

"I know. I know, Hogar. It was awful. So so young. We all felt terribly sorry."

"After the fire, I had no house. No family. I couldn't even bring myself to take the boat out and fish anymore. Just didn't have it in me. I couldn't stand coming back at the end of the day to nothing but a pile of ashes where our home used to be, our lives – ah, mercy me." Hogar's sniffle sounded like an elephant in heat.

"I can't imagine what it must have been like for you."

"So Father James sent me up to the convent. They needed a gardener so bad and none of the sisters up there could tell the difference between a rake and a hoe."

"Nuns can't even tell a lady from a ho', can they?" Chilperic liked his wordplay and giggled tipsily at his own joke, but Hogar was deep in memories and didn't get it.

"Susanna," Hogar went on, "you remember Susanna O'Malley, from, you know, in school? She was the Mother Superior back then. But she couldn't give me a job."

"Couldn't or wouldn't?"

"'Hogar,' she says to me, she says 'there are rules. I can't hire a man. They just will not allow it and besides', she says, 'the sisters wouldn't like it.'"

"Susanna said that to you?"

"Though she admitted there were times when the nuns could use some muscle about the place, she still couldn't bring herself to break that rule. She felt for me. I knew she did. But she couldn't help me."

"Eiy", Chilperic exclaimed. "Still, it sure don't sound like the old Susanna." He waggled his fingers toward the bottle. " 'Nother sip?"

"Sure. But here's what I did. I got that seamstress – what was her name, that skinny little mousy little thing who married –? Oh. Ermentrude. Remember her?"

"Ermentrude Treyse."

"I got Ermentrude Treyse to help me. She made me this outfit. I shaved off my beard and went back up to the convent. Susanna laughed her ass off. And I guess it gave her second thoughts. She gave me the gardening job."

"Well I'll be a horse's patooty."

"It took a little time, but they all got used to me by and by. I let my beard grow back after a while because I was sick of shaving, and everything was working out fine. A decade I worked there, more than a decade. Then Kunegunde took over the job of Mother Superior. Surely you remember Kunegunde?"

Chilperic hawked and spit. "That one! You ever heard of that smart-ass writer who said 'What a piece of work is man'? Never did that man know Kunegunde."

Hogar snickered. "No shit. She is a piece of work. Old Lumber Loins."

"Thorn-holed cow."

"Iceberg-crotch."

"Granite gr– Man, this fairy juice gots me cussing bad as you,

Hogar."

"Yep, elixir of the gods. Well anyway, Kunegunde took over and that was the end of my gardening job. She fired me. After all those years, she up and fired me. I don't know who they're going to get to grow their vegetables, and I sure as hell don't know what I'm going to do with myself from now on. But here I am."

"Gi' me one more li'l nip of that 'lixir juice, wou' ya, Hogar? Just one las' taste. Ahh. So wha' you aimin' now? What you aimin' to do?"

"I just come for a visit. You don't happen to know a girl named Lisabetta Button, do you?"

"Sh- sure. 'Course I do. She's ou' there on Pa- Parrot Islan', runnin' the li'- li'- li' house."

"The lighthouse? I noticed when I come in that thing is still standing. I thought the Furies would have torn it to pieces by now."

"There's them wha' thinks iss haw … haun'd … haunted out there, but still … yup, it sstill ssstands."

"I'd like to get out there to see Lisabetta."

"Sh-sure. I can row you. It'll be ssslow goin', you big ox, but I can row you."

"I've got no money to pay you, Chilpy. Not a centavo."

"No prollem. I ta- take it out of your hide one day, my frien'."

Lily stood up and stared at the red-bearded nun huffing up the hill and through the brown meadow. Hogar stopped next to where she was playing, trying to catch his breath. He set his bag down, squatted, and beamed at her.

"Well," he rasped. "Aren't you the prettiest little thing I've ever seen?"

Lily, studying his face, read kindness there. She did not strain herself to wonder at his nun's habit, at his unkempt hair. The beard didn't faze her. She liked this person immediately because of the smile in his eyes, simple as that. She rose, wrapped her hand around one of his immense fingers, and led him into the cottage where Lisabetta had her head in the closet, gathering coats and hats.

"We're just about ready to go, Lily."

"So! You left me only a few months ago, Betta, and already you're a mamma?"

Lisabetta heard the voice, dropped the coats, and threw her arms around him.

"Hogar! Hogar, I have missed you so!"

"Me too. I thought I'd come see what you were up to."

"How did you get away? This is always such a busy time of the year for you, getting the garden ready for planting."

"Ah. Kunegunde fired me."

"What? What? How could she fire you, of all people?"

"She did it. Without a moment's hesitation."

"Oh, I'm so sorry, Hogar."

"No use me staying where I'm not wanted. I thought I'd pass through Lunenfarne, check on you, see how things are getting on here." He bent down to Lily and put his hands on his knees. "So who is this little sweetheart?"

"This is Lily. She's come to stay with me."

"Hello, Lily. I'm Hogar. Can we be friends, you and I?"

Lily, clinging to Lisabetta's gown, batted her eyes and smiled winningly.

"Good!" He straightened. "Ah, almost forgot. I come with some sad news. I'm sorry to have to tell you, Lisabetta. Our Sister Rosemarie has been gathered to God." He handed Lisabetta the heavy bag he'd been carrying. "She asked especially that you take care of these."

Lisabetta's eyes filled when she looked inside. "Her books," she breathed.

"Original manuscripts. All the books she wrote and illustrated." Hogar blew his nose into a handkerchief that could double as a pup tent.

"One on wildflowers. Here's healing herbs, ferns. These are invaluable. Thank you so much, Hogar. We will miss her, won't we?" They hugged and patted each other again. "Well, since you're here, why don't you come with Lily and me today? My sister puts out a wonderful Sunday dinner, and you would be more than welcome."

Lily tugged on Hogar's sleeve and stretched her hand up so she could pull his bearded cheek down close. She whispered windily in his ear. "The aunties, they – they have pie."

"Say no more. Let's go."

It took Freya and Batilda Button a couple of blinks to absorb the image of the nun who sailed through their door, black robes billowing behind him. By the time they registered the contrast between beard and nun's habit, and possibly as much as a minute longer, but certainly no more than a minute after Lisabetta introduced him, he was accepted as part of the family. That being settled, they sat down to eat at the long table. Hogar had some blinking of his own to do when Georgiana and the other girls joined them. Ah, in all his years at St. Scholastica, he had not often, in fact had never seen such a bevy of pretty things. It set his poor heart going, but did not stifle his appetite.

Everyone agreed that a place should be found for Hogar in Lunenfarne. He was too good to let get away. Freya proposed that he join the crew of the *Wolf*, and he said, patting his lips daintily with a napkin, he would be honored to consider that option. Lisabetta begged him to instead take over her job at the lighthouse. She and Lily could move into town and she could open an office where she could more conveniently see patients. She had already patched up quite a few villagers who had been stricken by one mishap or another, and their families were beginning to trust her advice.

That Sunday dinner lasted so long that Lisabetta and Lily had to rush away to light the lamps before it got dark. Hogar was invited to spend a night at the inn. Tilda begged a suit of mens' clothes from Chekov, the Sunday cook, and by the next day Hogar, for the first time in a long time, looked like any other Lunenfarnian. A large, red-hairy Lunenfarnian to be sure, but no more bizarre than any other citizen. He was almost ready to feel that he belonged here again.

"Uh, Miss Button," he said to Freya quietly when he could get her alone, "there's one little thing. I hesitate to bring this up and I don't mean to be crude, but I have a small problem. See, it's that I'm just not used to pants anymore. I gotta – well, sorry to say – how can I put this? I gotta make some other arrangement. I don't know if you can help me, but I don't know where else I can turn." His face flamed red. His eyes were round and troubled.

"You need a better fit?"

"It's not that. It's a – I have a wee problem, see. Not wee, that's not a nice word. Oh, jayzis. I don't mean to – this is embarrassing."

"Wait." Freya thought for a minute. "How about a kilt? Would that be more comfortable?"

"A kilt! The very thing!"

"We'll see that you get one."

"I'm so relieved. So very obliged to you. To all of you people. Thank you. I'm going to try to be the best damned lighthouse keeper that island has ever seen."

"I'm sure you will be, Hogar."

"Personally," Freya told Vladimir later that evening, "I prefer Hogar's old look."

"The nun's habit?"

"It was much more intriguing, don't you think? Dramatic?"

"It was."

"We need more of that around here. Why don't you wear them, darling? Those robes would look well on you."

"I might, someday," said Vladimir. "Don't get rid of them. They may come in handy."

Teron had been scheming ever since he had heard that a Spanish slave ship was coming to Lunenfarne. He had put together some ideas and assembled a few people he thought crucial. Lisabetta Button, because she knew her way around Parrot Island. Thorfinn Taptoe, the fisherman who had lost his son when the Nolta bridge collapsed, because he had a donkey cart and a heart gone stone-cold with resentment. Hogar Hanon, the new lighthouse keeper, looked strong enough to make a rowboat fly across the bay. Chilperic could contribute a little false bonhomie. Vladimir Mynydd might help out. Key to the whole operation, and taking a bigger personal risk than any of them, was Florri Mynydd. But really, the whole plan hinged on

Signor Bologna's Fabulous Puppet Show living up to its name, just as it had done in days of old.

The five slaves had been confined near the municipal offices for four days now. It was the time of the Alder Moon, just before the vernal equinox. A small scrap of that moon was pinned to the heavens, a sliver of silver, aligned almost perfectly between the earth and the sun and therefore causing the highest tides of the month. So the ocean was a restless thing, and the people of Lunenfarne, ever in sympathy with their ocean, were restless too. They could hear it booming out beyond Parrot Island, roughed up by the lashing of an angry wind and throwing itself on the mercy of the beach. Was it this that gave everyone that vague feeling of uneasiness, or was it just weariness from the long winter?

Then, in a time of its own choosing, the weather turned warmer, hinting at imminent release of the bright days of spring. Heavy clouds still murked the skies but what snow remained lay only in patches here and there among the trees. Just as everyone had predicted, and half-dreaded, a sea change was in the air.

They wanted a dark night for their scheme. Darkness was crucial. Glimpses of clear sky that night showed stars glintering with cold fire, but most of the time a solemn convoy of clouds obscured everything. It looked like fortune was favoring them, at least this far. But no one should trust Lady Luck. Timing was the only thing that would save them. Timing tonight would be everything.

Tonight! Signor Bologna's Fabulous Puppet Show was tonight! People began to gather while it was still early. There was such an air of excitement and anticipation. Everyone was primed for a diversion. Of course, there was something of defiance here too, a cockiness, like the thrill of playing hooky when everyone else was at school. The villagers were, in their small way, defying the authorities. Those benighted magistrates had taken their village puppet theatre away. Well, tonight Signor Bologna was taking it back.

The man who Dort Mynydd hired to guard the slave quarters was patrolling nervously, clicking his fingers behind his back, strutting, peacocking up and down. He didn't like all this activity so close to his post, so many villagers streaming and eddying, and he all by himself out here. What if there were trouble? What would he do? What could he do, one man against an entire village? And now look, here comes some idiot driving a stupid donkey cart like he owned the place, coming way too close to that door that locked with the giant padlock! This was already getting out of hand and the puppet show hadn't even begun yet.

Villagers heard the guard yelling. Ah, he was angry at Thorfinn Taptoe, who had arrived with a cartful of benches. Benches made of nice new wood. Now, how could these poor fishermen afford all that wood? That question gave the guard a moment's pause, but before he sorted that puzzle out, he was jostled rudely aside like some junkyard dog by a crowd of men. Several of them came forward to lend willing hands, unloading the benches, placing them in semicircles under Thorfinn's direction. How was this makeshift theatre going to work?

Signor Bologna had set up a large screen of white sheets and pulled them taut across a tall wooden frame. Villagers milled about, curious. The screen was uphill from the edge of the bay, and crowded closer to the slave quarters than the guard would have liked. Fie! Fie on these troublesome villagers! He watched people begin to claim their seats, corralling their annoying children, trying to get them to sit and wait with some measure of patience instead of cavorting about in manic anticipation. Ermentrude Treyse gripped the hands of her three-year old charges, Gregor and Lily, lest they take flight in their excitement. Signor Bologna and his assistant were putting the final touches on this strange new theatre. Between the slave quarters and the back of the white screen, Hahri Fahri was building a pile of logs. Were they going to light a bonfire back there?

The crowd was dense now, the benches full, the faces eager. When was this going to start? The show had even attracted strangers, a pair of wool merchants passing through from Bellesunde. Docked overnight in the harbor, they were curious about all the activity and were waiting patiently on a bench. The children were ungovernable, couldn't wait much longer, and then BOOM! Their hands flew to their ears. BOOM! The screaming crowd stood as one being. What? A cannon? What was this? Wait! The unimaginable! Who had ever seen such a thing, such a wonderful thing? The sky was lit with a thousand little lights raining down in fountains of colors. Fireworks! Fireworks, here in Lunenfarne for the very first time! People sat again, watching in awe. It was beautiful! It was magical! You absolutely could not watch without shouting with pleasure. The crowd roared! Signor Bologna was outdoing himself tonight! Never in their lives had anyone seen such a display!

No sooner were the fireworks over when the logs behind the white screen burst into flame. It *was* a bonfire, and it illuminated the hanging white sheets from behind. Those sheets glowed golden in the dark night. And then, and *then* the new puppets made their debut. They were shadows on the screen, dancing silhouettes, two-dimensional, flat figures made of thick leather and manipulated with sticks behind the screen.

This night's puppet tale was all new. Of course there had to be the requisite amount of slapping and trickery and arguing and sword fighting.

It was expected! What was unexpected was an army of puppet soldiers and horses and, really special, the new princess character, a Balinese dancer that Hahri Fahri had fashioned his very own self all from memory, and a vivid memory it was, as we have heard heretofore. Her body was articulated and he moved her hips seductively by means of a pair of sticks. He had cut a small hole in her tummy exactly where a jewel might be placed, if one possessed such a thing as a jewel. The townspeople were not aware that she was Balinese and never in their wildest imaginings realised that the hole represented a jewel. Who could ever conceive something as strange as that? But they thought she was a beautiful princess and later, little girls and more than one matron almost put their backs out of joint trying to emulate her sinuous dance. Silhouettes of shadow-puppets cavorted and danced and fought back and forth behind the sheet-screen, backlit by the fire. Silvio Filvio turned himself inside out trying to be in two places at once. He worked puppets. He played his guitar, enchanting the audience with lush, seductive music whenever the princess came on, or thundering drums that announced a coming battle or invoked valorous mighty-man action.

The show was a tremendous success. The audience erupted with cheers and laughter. Children squealed with joy. Those two visiting Bellesunde merchants had never expected such artistry in Lunenfarne. Signor Bologna's Fabulous Puppet show was even more fabulous than the old puppet shows and it felt wonderful, even for the adults, to give themselves over to this childlike delight.

It ended too soon, but the entertainment, it appeared, was not over. What a night! More festivities! Everyone rose from the benches and flocked down the hill. Hahri Fahri marshalled them down the slope and the local shopkeepers went to work. Mr. Basko and Mr. Wunder lit the new torches that stood in a row along the edge of the bay. The crowd was seduced with popcorn balls and pretzels shaped like cats and mice. There was fried cheese toast and baked apples, cider and ale. Chilperic took up his fiddle, Silvio his guitar, and Mr. Guntram the blacksmith played the spoons and put a fiddlebow to his saw. Poggio Gomoggio was a new addition with his washtub bass. Hogar, returning, or so people thought, from lighting the lighthouse lamps, sang some lively tunes and the boy Gerbert surprised everyone when he joined Hogar with an improvised accompaniment, a little bit descant, a little bit harmony. Thorfinn Taptoe swung Marie off her feet and the dancing began. Plump little Charlotte Russe asked Poggio for a polka and nearly knocked the wind out of him as he tried to follow her dance steps and still keep track of all the bouncing parts of her that vied for his attention. Rather than wait for their stodgy husbands, Mrs. Wunder danced with Mrs. Basko. Out of the corner of his eye, Silvio Filvio saw Sister Angelica circling the edge of the crowd. She came to stand close to the band and when she smiled at Silvio, he completely fumbled two entire chord changes and almost missed the refrain. He so very badly wanted to ask Angelica to dance. But of course, you couldn't, could you? No, you could never ask a nun to trip the light fantastic. Everyone else was dancing – the old, the young, the merchants from Bellesunde, the tiniest children. The good folks of Lunenfarne hadn't had this much fun in, oh, ages.

All good things must end, but the tragedy that followed was at first, utterly heart-breaking. But wait now – rest easy. Something caught fire. Yes, another fire, but it wasn't quite what it seemed.

Fire! Fire leaping into the sky! What a terrible end to the night this was! It was the slave quarters! The slave quarters were on fire, practically bursting into flame all in a moment! Terrible, terrible sight! The dancers stopped, the musicians lowered their instruments. The crowd cried out in horror. Flames ate into the building, feasting, devouring, and growing. Those poor people inside! Help them! Was it too late to save them? The entire building was on fire now. Oh, how they must be suffering! Someone help them! Can't someone get them out? The guard was nearly assaulted by the crowd that demanded he unlock the door. But he could not! He had no key! He swore on his mother's grave that he had no key! No one had a key! No one but Dort Mynydd, and who knew where he was to be found tonight? Oh how terrible, to think of five helpless people being burned to death, one of them a mere boy. Pray that they go fast and don't suffer too long.

Silvio Filvio urged everyone to stay back, to stay calm. Don't even try to douse the flames. But no, they hollered, how could he ask that of them? That was unconscionable! It wasn't right! They had to try, at least try to save those people.

Then, two words were whispered. Two words, repeated, spreading like lightning. A message was passed and in a matter of minutes, people knew. The crowd quieted. They linked arms. Softly, Hogar started a *Dona Nobis Pacem*. Soft as a requiem, the whole crowd sang.

The slave quarters burned, burned to the ground. Nothing but ashes left. Only then did the entire spectacle of that evening – the fireworks, the bonfire, everything – make perfect sense.

Much earlier that same night, as twilight stole across the sky, Florri and Lisabetta were hurrying their two children down the lane to Ermentrude Treyse's cottage. Only a shard of moon rose into the lavender sky. One favorable omen, at least. They had wanted a dark night, hadn't they?

Little Gregor and Lily would have supper with Ermentrude, and she was to take them to the puppet show later. The two young women left the children at the cottage. By the gate, they wished each other luck. Lisabetta went her way and Florri, head bent with determination, went hers. Hogar rowed Lisabetta out to Parrot Island. Florri crossed on Korsakov's ferry and went along nearer to the center of the town and down to the edge of the bay. The temporary puppet theatre was getting its final touches. Hahri Fahri was arranging trunks full of puppets and props behind the screen.

Florri saw Teron Adante standing alone. She wished him a good evening and they stood together in nervous silence. Hahri came over.

"I think everything is about ready." He looked at Florri. "Are you feeling all right?" he asked her with concern.

"I'm a little scared." An understatement. It would be disastrous if any single part of their plan failed to work out.

Teron looked up sharply. "Don't worry. You'll be fine. We know we can depend on you, Florri."

"I know how much depends on me. If I get caught and my husband finds out, well, that I could bear. I don't care about that. But the people I'll be letting down, those five people – that's what I can't bear to think about."

"It cost us some money but we tried to arrange it so Dort will be having dinner at home tonight."

"Yes? Instead of with –?"

"She's busy elsewhere tonight. It will work, you'll see," Teron assured her.

"I'm just afraid –"

"My dear," said Hahri Fahri soothingly, stepping close and looking up into her pale face. "you'll figure it out. If a problem occurs, you'll work it out."

Florri's eyes fastened gratefully on Hahri's for a moment.

"It's probably time we got started, isn't it?" interrupted Teron.

Florri closed her eyes, said a prayer, and went home for dinner. If Dort failed to join her for the evening meal, all would be lost. What would she do then? Knock on Mistress Magnolia's door and ask to see him?

But Dort did come home. He changed his clothes and came down for a drink before dinner. Florri excused herself for just a minute, went upstairs to his dressing room, and pocketed his keys.

At dinner, which Florri only picked at, Dort said he was going out later and didn't know when he'd be back. She was trying not to let her nervousness show. She said she was taking Gregor to the puppet show. Abruptly, too abruptly, she rose awkwardly, swirled her cape over her shoulders, and hurried out to the waiting carriage before he could answer.

She had the key. Step One of the plan.

Back at the edge of the bay, Silvio Filvio and Hahri Fahri paced about nervously, watching for Thorfinn Taptoe's cart. Thorfinn was supposed to bring the benches that he and his neighbors had built in his barn, seating made expressly for this event from brand new wood. It might have been stolen wood, but no one wanted to talk about that. The benches were important, the cart even more so.

Thorfinn's cart finally appeared. He apologized and blamed Sheila, his famously stubborn donkey. He pulled the cart up beside the slave quarters.

"Hey! You can't leave that there," shouted the guard, waving his arm. He didn't like all these people around, all these people and those stupid puppet guys and all their trunks of stuff and the bonfire they had laid so close to the slave quarters. And now here was this jerk with a cart.

"I'm going to leave it here, just 'til we unload these benches." Thorfinn Taptoe informed the guard of the facts. "It will be no trouble."

The guard groaned. "You better get it out of here as soon as it's empty. I don't want it anywhere near here."

Thorfinn waved heartily. "Ah! A good suggestion! Will do. Thanks, man." They put the benches out in semi-circles, facing uphill and away from the bay.

Florri came back and stood beside Teron again. She waved at Gregor, coming in with Ermentrude and Lily. If the show didn't start soon, she would not be able to get the keys back to Dort's pocket before he discovered they were gone.

Chilperic materialized out of the darkness and Hahri Fahri came running over.

"We're about to start." He gave Chilperic the high sign.

"You have the bottle?" Teron asked Chilperic softly.

Chilperic nodded and went into his act. He sauntered over to stand a few feet from the guard. He popped open his bottle of whiskey and swirled it to release the bouquet. Heady alcoholic fumes rose like butterflies, fluttered into the air, and flirted with guard's lovely Roman nose. He sniffed. He looked at Chilperic, looked away, looked back. Chilperic sipped. The guard licked his lips.

"Nice evenin'."

The guard nodded.

Chilperic glugged some whiskey and wiped his mouth. The guard looked at him, looked away, shifted his feet. Chilperic glugged some more. He noticed the guard's eyes on him again. He held the bottle up and raised his eyebrows. "Care for a short snort?'

"Well. Maybe. Sure. Hey, thanks," said the guard, walking stiff-legged to take the bottle for a sip. Pretty friendly, after all, some of these townspeople. He shouldn't worry so much. He took a gulp and passed the bottle back.

Then darkness came and the drama began. Fireworks! Where had these come from? From the Button sisters, of course. They had stashed some away in a forgotten corner of a warehouse, "borrowed" a year ago from a Spanish trading vessel. Fireworks! Lunenfarne had never seen such a thing. Just imagine the screaming and cheering and awed faces tilted to the sky when that display began. And just imagine the noise!

Chilperic looked over his shoulder. A stern-faced nun was standing there alone, a back-up in case distraction was needed. He passed the bottle to the guard a couple more times and strolled away from the slave quarters. The nun was not far behind. Chilperic took up his appointed place behind two blonde women. As surely as night follows day, his whiskey was a magnet. As surely as day follows night, the guard felt the attraction. Some little profligate demon had seized him. He took a few steps, swaying along in Chilperic's wake and relishing – whoo! – the warm feeling of that liquor. They watched the fireworks and shared the bottle.

The guard leaned back once, checking the door of the slave quarters, worried about leaving his post. The nun turned his face away, in case he was recognized, because there had been a time when Vladimir Mynydd's face was well-known. Chilperic, worried that the guard would start feeling the weight of his responsibilities, gave the signal. He sneezed loudly. Two blondes, Batilda Button and Georgiana from the Bayside Inn turned around.

"Bless you, good sir." They smiled, two radiant blue-eyed beauties.

The guard's eyebrows shot up and he swayed on his feet. Whoa,

whoa-ee doe! These women. Tsk tsk! He giggled. No collars to their frocks! Their frocks had no collars at all, or no – what was the word? – necklines! Low necklines! He loved loved loved frocks with low necklines. They were smiling at him, too, those women, standing so near him. Incredible edible women. They were speaking to him. Half his body tilted to one side. His eyes fell half-closed. Half his brain shut down completely or dropped into his pants or wherever and the other half was blinded by love or whatever.

Chilperic watched him. The man was getting paid to do this job? This fool was nothing but a lump of putty. Putty in the hands of a pair of women. The guy was a goner.

Back by the door of the slave quarters, Florri quickly pressed a key into Teron's hand. Teron inserted it into the padlock, returned it to her, and she ran back to her carriage.

"Home, please, Burt. And hurry."

They tore back up the River Road, turned onto Hill Road. All along the way, all up among the mansions in the hills, people had come outside to see what the deafening noise was. Entire households stood out in the chill night air, mesmerized by the show in the sky over the bay. When her carriage pulled up in front of the Mynydd house, Florri saw that Dort, too, was standing in the courtyard.

"Where did this all come from?" he yelled over the noise.

"From the puppet show people."

"Puppet show people!" he scoffed. She paused. She couldn't think how to slip the keys into the pocket of the coat he was wearing.

"Look at that!" He had never seen such a display.

Florri clutched the keys, still in her pocket. She walked over to him and stood close. "Aren't you cold, Dort? I'll run in and get you a heavier coat."

He looked down, surprised, and saw her concern. He put his arm around her and held her tight. "Let's both go in."

She could feel her heart thumping. Her arms were pinned. Her hands were stuck in her pockets. She gripped the keys to keep them from rattling. "You said you're going out tonight?"

"I don't have to go, Florri. Shall we –"

"I just came back to get a warmer coat for Gregor."

"You could stay for a –"

"It's too chilly for him down by the water. I don't want him to catch cold."

"What about me?" pouted Dort. "I could use some warming up." He stopped and regarded his wife. Florri, sweet Florri. His latest girlfriend, Magnolia, had gone off somewhere without telling him.

"I'll get you a heavier coat, shall I?" Florri pulled away and started for the stairs.

"Wait. Florri, where are my keys, do you know, darling? I can't find them anywhere."

Dread swamped her. She was too late. "Your keys? I haven't seen them."

"This is ridiculous. I can't go out until I find them. I know I brought them home with me tonight."

Florri continued up the stairs. She tried to keep her voice even. "They must be around somewhere."

"Help me look for them, would you?"

"I have to find a coat for Gregor and get back to town." She hurried into Gregor's room. "Oh, Dort. Look." She came back to the head of the stairs and leaned over the bannister, holding up his keys.

"Ah! You've got them!"

"I found them."

"Where were they?"

"In – in here. Gregor must have been playing with them." She held her breath. Gregor couldn't possibly have taken Dort's keys. By the time Dort arrived home for dinner, Gregor had been gone for more than an hour. "I'm sorry, Dort." She might have known Gregor's absence wouldn't register with him. He paid Gregor so little attention.

"Florri!" Suddenly stern. "You can't let him do that. You've got to keep an eye on him. It's not like you to be so careless. You can't just let him get into my things like that. He could have lost these, and they're irreplaceable. He has got to learn …." His scolding went on.

He believed her story? She had made up a story and he believed her! Dort lectured away while she stood with her hands wrapped in Gregor's coat. She nodded, watching his mouth but not hearing, waiting for the moment she could slip away.

"Pardon?" She tried to focus. He must have asked her a question.

"Were you listening to me?"

"Yes. But –" She laughed a little, happy she had pulled this off. "Gregor needs his coat. I really have to go."

"But I'm talking to you."

"Shall we talk later?" She stepped forward and, feeling rather giddy, kissed him on the cheek. "Good night, Dort." Hadn't she learned, these past couple of years, how to charm a charmer? "I have to be off. Burt has the carriage waiting."

"I was kind of hoping you'd stay for a bit."

"Sorry. Have a lovely evening with –" She almost mentioned Magnolia by name, but decided this was not the time. Burt handed her into the carriage. She left Dort standing bewildered and alone in the drive. The carriage rolled away and she covered her pleased grin with her hand.

Step two of the plan, completed.

Meanwhile, under cover of the fireworks down by the bay, Teron had unlocked the door and entered the slave quarters. In the dark, five terrified slaves squeezed themselves into the corner, shaking their heads, no no!, hands out, no no! All Teron could see were the whites of their rolling eyes. He tried frantically to convince them to come out in spite of all that unearthly noise. It must sound like a war to them! He had to get them into the cart. They were shaking with fear but when they saw Vladimir the nun appear at the door, they calmed a little. Nuns weren't bad, were they? A nun would never hurt them, would she? Vladimir gently urged the Black woman out and the rest hurried after. He made them lie down in the cart. He and Teron threw a tarp over them.

"Go!" Teron yelled. Thorfinn shook Sheila the donkey's reins. Sheila, though, had royal blood in her veins. A donkey princess. You don't tell a donkey princess what to do. She did what she wanted, she did, and what she liked to do was to put on airs. She planted her feet and stuck her nose straight in the air. Oh boy. Thorfinn's donkey, the joke of the village.

Poggio stepped forward and saved the moment. He pulled an apple from his pocket and tried to lure Sheila into taking a step. She was not falling for that old trick. No. Fond as she was of apples, she had her principles. Move, Sheila! They had to get that cart moving before the fireworks ended. Sheila reconsidered. Principles could be abandoned if a better option presents itself. Even humans had figured that out. She reached for the apple, her lips working. Poggio pulled it back. Sheila gave him the stink-eye, but stepped closer. Step by step, the donkey started to follow Poggio down the hill. Then gravity took over and both Poggio and Sheila found themselves trying to outrun a runaway cart. The crowd was oblivious to all this. They sat with their backs to the drama. Their attention was on the fireworks, their shouting was boisterous, the whole place a cacophony of sound.

Hogar was waiting by the ferry dock in his rowboat, his kilt pulled over his hairy knees against the chill. He sat up when he saw the cart careening down the hill. There was Thorfinn standing in the driver's seat, pulling madly on the brake. Poggio, hero of the moment, turned in the face of danger. He stopped, one thin willow-wand of a man facing a bouncing runaway cart. Sheila the donkey stopped because Poggio's apple had stopped. She stumbled against the inertia of the braking cart. Then, with characteristic delicacy and ever so politely, she wrapped her lips around the apple in Poggio's outstretched hand.

Thorfinn jumped out. He threw off the tarp covering the Black people.

"Come on, come on! Get out!"

They didn't speak the language. He could not convince them to get into the boat, not with that hairy giant at the oars. In frustration, Thorfinn picked up the boy and carried him. His wails were drowned out by the fireworks. He handed him into Hogar's waiting arms. The boy's mother, frantically protesting, followed. The three men, scared to be left behind, hustled out of the cart, dropped awkwardly into the boat, and barnacled themselves to its sides. Hogar pulled mightily on the oars and rowed them all off into the night.

There they go. Thorfinn Taptoe watched the boat until it disappeared in the darkness. If the lamps in the lighthouse had been rotating as they should, Hogar's boat would surely have been spotted. But Dort Mynydd himself had commandeered all the mercury in the lighthouse. That's why those lamps weren't rotating, and there you have it. Dort Mynydd had defeated himself. No one else was to blame for his loss. That was the way Thorfinn Taptoe saw it. Dort had made this problem for himself months ago.

Thorfinn turned back to the festivities. No one would never find those slaves.

Step three of the plan, completed.

The fireworks ended and the puppet show began. In the blink of one inebriated eye, the guard lost track of Chilperic and his whiskey bottle. Those entrancing women had drifted away. The guard, disappointed, swayed anxiously back to his post at the door of the slave quarters. Ah, all was well. He leaned on the door, sodden and forlorn. Thank goodness there were no villagers hanging around to make him nervous. They had moved the dagburn cart. The big black padlock hung on the door, impervious, still bolted closed. He peeked around the corner of the new building. Where had those gorgeous women gone? He couldn't see them anywhere. Too bad, because they had apparently liked him a great deal. He sagged, warm and stupid with drink, back against the locked door.

The final step of Teron's plan was to get everyone away, far away from the slave quarters, which was accomplished easily enough. Musicians tuning, the smell of dough frying in a kettle of hot oil, torchlight reflected romantically in the waters of the bay, children begging for a penny to buy popcorn balls – it took very little to get a crowd moving. Hahri Fahri didn't join the festivities, though. Trunks of theatre supplies had to be moved. The sheets had to be taken down from the frame. He didn't want anything to happen to those, in case they could be put to use another time. That accomplished, he took a careful glance around to make sure no child was near.

Every single person was down by the waterside. Quick! Douse the wall of the slave quarters with lamp oil. A splash of oil on a rag, a burning stick from the bonfire, and make sure the one marries the other. Quick quick! Hahri stood back and watched a little curl of fire burst into a hungry flame.

So, the last step of the plan, nearly completed.

At about the same time, in Teron's old cave out on Parrot Island, another fire had been lit. Five Black faces shone in its light. Five hearts beating hard, wondering whether this fantastic good fortune was real. Could this be happening? They wore coats borrowed from here and there. Lisabetta served them soup and bread. One night soon, when the weather was right, they would be rowed out to the *Wolf* and sailed down to a settlement of Black people in Nova Scotia. The workers who raked through the ashes of the slave quarters the next day had been warned they would never find the bones of five people.

When questioned about this by the authorities, the workers explained, with the most somber faces they could muster, that it must have been a very hot fire.

In time, as years rolled on, Hahri Fahri might have proved unable to resist hinting, if given the assurance of complete secrecy, that the fire had not been a tragedy, but an opportunity. After all, a hero does like to be recognized. But if Hahri ever did let the cat out of the bag, it was long after the fact. For now, the tragedy of the fire affected Dort Mynydd to a greater degree than anyone else. It wasn't the five lives he assumed had been lost, but the profits he would never see, and the expenses he had incurred that would render no gain.

Dort went to the site of the fire the next day. The ashes had already been raked up and carted away. He never thought to ask about the bones that had been raked up as well. No thought of charred bodies crossed Dort's mind. One of the workmen handed him the sooty padlock, the only item that had been recovered. He watched Dort Mynydd to see if it registered with him that the lock had supposedly kept five souls trapped inside a burning building. Did he feel any guilt about that? He watched also to see if Dort's memory gave him a little nudge, as he held the lock in his hand, to remind him that his keys had been mysteriously lost the previous night?

Did it occur to Dort that his wife might be involved in some way in this? No. Dort had decided who was responsible and it never occurred to him that he could be wrong. Dort was not a person with a desire to get to the bottom of anything, anyway. His only goal, his guiding principle, was to stay on top, no matter what.

His staff milled around, afraid of the look on his face, afraid to be near him. They had seen that sunshine smile disappear before, quick as lightning. Standing next to the ashes, Dort beckoned to his new factor. He asked him, "What's the name of that person who owns the print shop?"

The man looked at him, trying to see the connection between the print shop and the blackened ground in front of them. "The print shop? I don't know but I can certainly find out, Lord Mynydd."

"He's going to have to pay for this."

"The owner of the print shop?"

"Exactly."

"I don't see —"

"He started all this, trying to turn everyone against me." Dort put on a rueful face. "Now someone has to pay."

"I – I'm not sure that would be appropriate, my lord. I heard this was all an accident. There was a bonfire, some say, and it got out of control."

"No." Dort's eyes were narrow slits. "No, this was revenge. He was wreaking his revenge, pure and simple."

"Revenge for?"

"He blames me for that fire in the print shop." Dort's voice hardened. "Do I have to draw a picture?"

The factor felt his insides tighten. He had not, until now, heard his new employer use that tone of voice. He looked at his toes and chewed his lip. "I wouldn't say that in public, if I were you, my lord."

"Say what? That this is revenge?"

"That would be tantamount to admitting guilt for vandalising the print shop."

Dort spoke softly. "I'll say any damn thing I please and no one will dispute me."

"I don't think you want to imply that you were responsible for the print shop fire. If you don't mind a little advice, my lord, you should forget the idea of revenge."

Dort said nothing for a moment. "They will not stop me."

"Stop you from?"

"I want to buy twenty more slaves." His voice was nearly expressionless. "I want you to find me another dealer. Not that Spanish swindler. Someone else. Do you understand?"

The man hesitated, then said in a near-whisper, "That would mean spending money you don't have, sir."

Dort turned on the man, suddenly furious. "Find it, then! Find the money!"

There was more bad news in Lunenfarne that month. The magistrates were restive.

"Don't worry," Dort tried to calm them. "Let's not call this a rebellion. The sheriff has himself all worked up, but I can deal with this, I assure you." He pressed his hand against his abdomen. "We'll hire a deputy. Everyone will feel safer and it will shut the sheriff up."

Bobert Notting had been sheriff for ten years and only this spring had the magistrates finally agreed to hire a deputy to assist him. A rather sorry excuse for a deputy he was, but Bobert Notting was now the boss of someone, and the new man had no choice but to follow his orders and play the part of second-in-command. Bobert was discovering how gratifying it was to have an underling.

Admittedly, Sheriff Notting really did need more help. There had been several unfortunate incidents in the recent past. No one dared mention the bridge collapse, of course, because that would bring up unsavory issues of blame. But then a shop had been vandalised. A fire had killed five people, all of whom were assets belonging to Lord Mynydd.

Now, this new problem. Theft. Thieves had broken into two of the mansions up on Hill Road.

Most of the homes on the hilltop were walled and well-protected, almost fortresses, but three of them were no longer inhabited. They were empty of all but their furnishings. The owners had moved out with incredible speed when the Botia Mine Company collapsed. Though all these people, and their fathers too, had been born in Lunenfarne, they were now forced to seek sanctuary elsewhere. One reason for this was that they had piled up a lot of debt with local tradespeople, villagers who were suddenly getting very cranky about their outstanding bills. Because paying these bills was just not possible, the Botia people fled Lunenfarne for their family seats in the south. Their homes were put up for sale. They couldn't even afford to move their furniture. It was all to be sold at auction. Disaster had come upon them so quickly that it had been quite demoralizing. Overwhelming, actually. No wonder these poor sad rich people couldn't spare a thought for the villagers' piddling losses.

Word got around: three large estates, abandoned. By the end of the week, first one, then two of those estates were missing several pieces of furniture. Vandalism, the neighbors screamed! We must get some protection up here! The town pandered to their demands with great haste. A small unheated sentry box and a gate was built. The unpleasant job of sentry was given, naturally, to the brand new deputy. Deputy Weebly spent his nights there now, armed and preposterously dangerous, freezing his bony buns off in the fight against crime.

If Thorfinn Taptoe, down in the fishermen's village, had not recently acquired a taste for perilous escapades, maybe these thefts would never have happened. Ever since they had so successfully tricked Dort Mynydd and set five slaves free, Thorfinn had been as eager as any boy for another adventure. Thorfinn wasn't a bad man. He just liked to thwart injustice. He liked taking chances. And he didn't mind wreaking a little revenge if the opportunity arose. If a new adventure would poke a thorn – or anything sharp – in Dort Mynydd's side or any other part of him, so much the better. Dort Mynydd's name was linked forever in Thorfinn's mind with the death of his little Bobby in the Nolta Bridge disaster. And forever is a long time.

Abandoned mansions? They were as attractive to Thorfinn Taptoe as plums to fruit bats. Hadn't he heard Father James preach something about rich men and camels? Thorfinn conferred with his friend, John Little, who had got some religion a while back, so he would know. John agreed. Yep, Father James, he remembered, had said something about "take up thy bed".

"Thy neighbor's bed, was it, John?"

"Yep."

"And don't forget the Ten Commandments," Thorfinn reminded him. "How did that one go? About bearing the false adultery, because, you know, an eye for an eye? Settle the score done unto you?"

"No, Thorfinn. That was in the Beatitudes, not the Ten Commandments."

Thorfinn looked at John, impressed. The Beatitudes? Well, there you go. John Little sure did know his Scripture.

The men felt they had scores to settle on behalf of several people. They proceeded with plans to plunder, absolved of guilt because more than a few villagers were owed money for work they had done for the Hill Road families. There were months-old bills outstanding to fishermen, to green grocers, laundresses, carpenters and repairmen, seamstresses, weavers, and gardeners. It irked everyone to think that they, who could least afford it, had been taken advantage of in this way.

So Thorfinn and John Little had called on Briar Tuck the locksmith, and late one night, those three drove a cart up the hill, broke into a mansion, took up thy beds, and settled some of those scores unto others. It had been so easy. Tuck picked the locks and they hauled out a cartful of goods. It wasn't a large cart and they weren't greedy, but it was stealing and it made the neighbors furious. And worried. What if these thieves, emboldened by success, broke into their homes? A few nights later, it happened again.

Now, with a third home recently vacated and another of the Botia

Mine families gone, temptation gnawed at Thorfinn Taptoe. The furor caused by the first two break-ins only made the prospect of another caper more compelling. Success had whetted his apetite, and the challenge of getting past a sentry was an added stimulant.

"Maybe it's not a good idea, boys. They just put up a gate across Hill Road, you know, and a guard," John Little told them.

"Who'd they get to stand guard?"

"Radovan Weebly. Sheriff's new deputy."

"Oh." The three men laughed. "Radovan Weebly."

"If Weebly's the guard, count me in. I'll do it," Tuck the locksmith declared.

"Let's take two carts this time," said John Little.

"Three," said Thorfinn. "We each drive a cart. We won't get a chance like this again."

"We need a fourth man. Someone to subdue Weebly." They thought hard.

"How about Hogar Hanon? He's strong."

"He can't leave the lighthouse at night."

"How about that guy who works in the print shop? Poggio."

"That scrawny excuse for a man? Come on. Not possible."

"He's good in a pinch."

"He did put out the fire in the print shop, they say."

Poggio Gomoggio had been trained as a bookbinder. He took his job very seriously. With the exception of a couple of men in Italy, there was probably no other bookbinder in the world whose work was as beautiful. When Thorfinn asked him to take on this new exploit, Poggio treated this job just as seriously. He found out where Deputy Radovan Weebly lived and strolled past Weebly's house of an afternoon, whistling, hands in pockets. He waved to Old Mother Weebly, who sat rocking on her front porch, surrounded by at least a dozen cats. Ah, here we go. Poggio had what he needed, his *modus operandi.*

In the late hours of the night, Radovan Weebly could not help but succumb to fatigue and boredom. He was leaning his stool back against the wall of his inhospitable sentry hut, snoring gently, when something stirred him awake. He cracked his eyes open, rolling them side to side without moving his head. Hmm, all quiet. Nothing happening. He shut his eyes, but then came that sound again. Meow. He straightened. A itty bitty kitty cat. He got off his stool and yawned and stretched. Again, gentle meowing, closer. Aww. He stuck his head outside and made kissy noises.

"Here kitty. Here Puss Puss –"

He received a hard blow across the back of his shoulders and fell to his hands and knees.

"Oww!"

"Stand up." His arm was wrenched behind his back. His gun was slipped from the holster. "Unbutton your jacket. Take it off."

Weebly couldn't see his assailant.

"I ain't taking this uniform – Oww!" His arm was wrenched higher. His hat was snatched roughly from his head.

"Left arm out of the sleeve." The shoulder of the jacket was pulled off, then his left arm pulled high up behind his back. "Other arm out." The jacket fell to the ground. Both hands were yanked behind him and tied tight with a very thin cord that cut into his wrists something awful. Bookbinder's string – incriminating evidence, if anyone had thought to investigate.

A blindfold was tied tight over Weebly's eyes, a wad of fabric thrust into his mouth and a gag tied behind his head. He heard noises, cart wheels creaking, low voices. Then Weebly felt the barrel of a pistol against his head. His own pistol. He was dragged out of the sentry hut.

"Get in." They almost threw him into a cart and it rumbled into motion.

At the courtyard gate, Tuck picked the lock in a matter of seconds, jumped back into his cart, and followed the other two inside. They tied Weebly to a cart wheel and left him there, bound and gagged and blindfolded. The front door lock took Briar Tuck only a little time, and they were in the house.

"Look at this place," said Thorfinn.

"It's a bloody palace," said John Little.

"Too bad the town can't buy it. Put it to some decent use."

"We're here for the loot, lads," urged Tuck. "You can chitchat later."

Loot! They went quickly through the place. Rugs, blankets, sheets, pillows – swans' down pillows! They took every one of those they could find, and small dressers and tables and chairs, nice soft chairs where some old grandfather could rest his weary bones. A few lamps and candlesticks, take those dishes too, but no, they didn't have room for huge mirrors, too gaudy for their taste anyway. John Little, though, couldn't leave behind the painting of the nude with the apple, it so appealed to his artistic eye, don't you know. Tuck found a small chest with a beautiful old lock that he wanted to duplicate. Thorfinn took a clock with a pendulum, and was pleased he could also find something that Poggio had asked for particularly.

Poggio, meanwhile, stood in the doorway of the sentry hut wearing the hat and jacket of the deputy's uniform. He heard the hinges of a gate creak. A figure appeared, a man, hands in pockets, ambling down the dark road, looking this way and that.

"Who goes there?" Poggio called into the night.

"It is I, Duke Treuberg. A neighbor." Duke – that was not a noble title. It was only a name he had taken for himself because it impressed people who had no real dukes in their lives.

"Good evening, sir."

"I thought I heard noise out here. Did someone pass?"

"Not a soul, sir." Poggio tried not to glance in the direction of the courtyard where three carts were parked, and prayed that they would not come lumbering through the gate even as he spoke.

It was the middle of the night, but the good Duke seemed primed for a chat. "So it's been pretty quiet tonight?"

"Oh yessir. Very quiet."

"You're out of uniform, aren't you, Deputy?"

"I put these pants on over the uniform, sir. My legs get so cold. No heat out here, you know."

"Really? No heat? Well, that will never do. And you, without a bit of fat on you. We'll have to get you something for tomorrow night."

"That would be much appreciated, sir."

Duke looked around. "Nice night, though. At least it's not snowing, eh Deputy?" Duke laughed, hahaha.

"Hahaha," laughed Poggio.

Duke was settling in, leaning affably in the doorway of the sentry box. "I suppose it's pretty boring when nothing happens out here, but maybe you're kind of glad about that."

"I envy you your warm bed though, sir." Poggio hoped the man would take the hint. "It sure would be nice to snuggle under a pile of soft warm blankets about now."

The power of suggestion. Duke yawned. "Yes. You know, as long as there's no trouble out here, I think maybe I'll go home and do some snuggling myself. Hahaha."

"Hahaha."

"Don't you fret now. It'll be morning soon and you'll have earned your bed. In the meantime, keep a sharp eye out for trouble. You have a firearm?"

"I do, sir." Poggio raised Radovan Weebly's pistol.

"Well don't be afraid to use it, if you must."

"I'm not afraid." Poggio coughed noisily to cover the sound of a gate opening. "Good night, sir," he said loudly, "and don't worry about a thing."

"Thank you, Deputy. Thank you. We can all sleep soundly, knowing a man of your caliber is on duty."

"That you can. Good night!" As soon as Duke turned his back, Poggio checked the gate across the road. He could see someone standing behind it, waiting. He held up his hand, motioning them to stay there.

He heard Duke shut his gate. Poggio waited to hear his front door close, then waved to his accomplices. They wheeled the carts onto the road and dumped Weebly back into the shed.

He sagged like a bag of oats into the corner. Oh, brother! If — *if* he lived through this, he was going to be in such trouble with his boss. Sheriff Notting would ream him out, up down and sideways. Weebly wanted to cry, but he mustn't. Mustn't cry. He sniffled. Deputies didn't cry.

Poggio spoke quietly to Thorfinn. "Did you find me an *objet d'art*?"

"A thing of lasting beauty." Thorfinn handed him a foot-tall ceramic figurine, a pert pink pussycat with rhinestone eyes and a lacy neck ruffle.

Without untying his prisoner or taking off his blindfold, Poggio left the figurine beside Weebly's feet. "This is for your mama." He took off the uniform jacket, arranged it around Weebly's shoulders, set his hat on his head and his gun in his lap, and went out to the waiting carts.

Meanwhile, March turned to April and performed the hat tricks April always manages to pull off, winter collapsing into late winter, just another variation on winter. Lunenfarne was drab as an old work boot. Slush-gray skies, disheartened people plodding through their days.

Vladimir Mynyyd, ever the agent of transformation, seized on this restlessness. A seachange! Everyone needed a change. He could picture it. If it didn't happen naturally, they would have to make it happen. Weren't they all ready for it? The caterpillar had been rotting in its chrysalis for long enough. It was the butterfly's time now.

One day, – a day when the maple leaves were the size of squirrels' paws, when daffodils unexpectedly trumpeted their arrival next to garden gates and roseblossom clouds puffed across a sky of powder blue, when the bay winkled with diamonds and forget-me-nots speckled the Parrot Island meadow that Hogar now thought of as his own – seemingly all in one day, there was a shift in the wind. It might have started with a single act: Hogar asked the homeless boy Gerbert to give up living in a crate on the wharf and move out to Parrot Island. Gerbert would assist Hogar with lighthouse duties. In return, Hogar would give him singing lessons. Then – which of them had the idea first? – they thought of forming a fishermen's choir. Hogar couldn't convince the men to come to Parrot Island to rehearse, not in the beginning. They still had an uneasiness about that place that couldn't be reasoned away. But that fall, when their choir won, hands down, a contest in Bellesunde, new recruits rowed out to the island willingly, confident that nothing soothes the savage beast (or was it breast?) better than music. The ghosts were exorcized and the meadow rang with song on summer nights.

Not long after, a visitor came to town. He had booked passage on a trading vessel going north because he had heard there was someone in Lunenfarne who ran a printing press. He owned a press himself but didn't understand how to put a book together, how to sew the book block, how to bind it in a cover. Could Mr. Adante and Mr. Gomoggio, he wondered, spend a few days with him? He would be happy to pay.

Vladimir Mynydd heard about this request. He watched choir people rowing back and forth to the island. The two circumstances gave him ideas. That seachange! If only to scratch his old itch for progress, Vladimir talked to Freya Button. He spoke with Teron Adante. They put some money together and purchased, for a rock-bottom price, one of the empty mansions on the Hill Road. It took only a little arm-twisting to get a couple of villagers to help paint rooms on the first floor and turn them into studios. People began to stop by out of curiosity and stayed to lend a hand. The place smelled of fresh-sawn pine now, and in the evenings, people hurried through their own chores at home because taking on some little task at the house on Hill Road seemed like fun. There was a cacophony of hammering and sawing up there, and each night, when they finished working, they all sat down to feast on tavern left-overs that Batilda Button sent up from the inn. Folks contributed the odd table, a few chairs, an old cupboard. Slowly, the house on Hill Road began to buzz with new purpose.

Teron moved his print shop up to the house on the hill and took over the back rooms. Silvio Filvio set up a studio for guitar lessons and played the accompaniments for Hogar's singers. Florri Mynydd started art classes for children. Sister Angelica gave music lessons, and she and Florri turned one of the rooms into a library and started soliciting book donations. Ermentrude Treyse installed a loom for making rugs and she gave lessons using the patterns Anne d'Inquierre had taught her. Rugs from Lunenfarne were instantly sought after by passing traders. Word got out that Poggio Gomoggio tutored book-binders. He showed them how to marbelize paper with the assistance of one of his students, Charlotte Russe, a creamy confection of a woman who, by night, loved his skinny body.

All of this took a little time, a few months, a year or two, but word spread surprisingly fast. Lunenfarne was the place to go, people said, if you want to learn skills that are hardly known outside of Europe. People came from all over, and there was hardly a family in the village who wasn't involved at the house on Hill Road in some way. No one was at all surprised that the most requested classes, far-and-wide the most popular, were the courses Hahri Fahri called "Living Puppets". People came up from the south just to take his classes. He taught not only puppet history, but also puppet-making, theatre building, script writing, and his secrets for convincing audiences that these dumb inanimate objects, bits of painted wood and remnants of discarded cloth, were actually living and breathing characters.

Dort Mynydd couldn't help but notice all the activity in the Hill Road house. For the past few weeks, he had been fooling around with some woman who, it turned out, was a little too tiresome and demanding for his liking. Why he took up with these women in the first place was a question he asked himself every time he ended one of these restless episodes. So he was glad to be back in his own home for a while, with a wife who made no demands on him.

"What is going on in the Botia's old house?" he asked Florri one day. "I keep seeing all these people going in and out."

"Lots of good things are going on. Everybody in the village is involved in some way." She was putting on a coat and hat, in somewhat of a hurry. Many a time, if Dort did come home, she went out.

"Everybody in the village? I never heard a word about it. Everybody in the village doing what?"

"Helping with renovations so we can hold classes there."

"Classes?"

"Music, art. That sort of thing."

"Who started all this?"

"Your father had a lot to do with it."

Dort's face darkened. "What is he –?"

"I'm on my way over there this morning," Florri interrupted, not daring to look at him, "to donate some books of Gregor's."

"You don't need to do that, Florri. Our family does not need to be part of 'everybody in the village'. We're above that, I should hope. This – whatever it is – is not something you want to be involved in." Especially, he thought, if his father had anything to do with it.

"I'm teaching drawing classes there. Gregor is taking music lessons."

"Music lessons? Not with those people?"

"Yes. With those people. He loves it."

"Well, I don't like it." Dort took her arm, trying to make her pay attention. "No, he's got to stop. I don't want Gregor mixing with that kind."

She backed away to look at him and smiled. "Wait a little bit." She gathered an armload of books. "You haven't had a chance to get used to the idea yet, Dort. You will, one day."

He reached for her again. His arm quickly encircled her waist and he tried to pull her close. "Darling –"

Florri, still smiling, pushed him away. "I'm in a bit of a hurry, Dort. Oh, you'd better let Cook know whether you'll be home for dinner. She's gotten used to cooking for one, lately."

"Mother doesn't eat dinner?"

"Yes, she does. She's been eating alone."

"Alone?"

He stared at the door for a long time after she closed it. Florri doesn't eat at home? He had a thought then, a thought he had never had before. It brought him up short.

He felt hollow all of a sudden. A bolt of acid hit his stomach. He went to the window and looked out, frowning at Florri's back as she disappeared up the lane.

Lunenfarne was becoming a busy place. Nowadays there was always a foreign ship or two in the harbor. Winter and summer, the place on Hill Road was a hive of activity. Down at the Bayside Inn, there was activity of another kind. For the last few years, the Button sisters had employed a group of four young women who had some very special skills. Freya called them her vixens. They were charming serving maids, bright and friendly and as pretty as could be. Their dresses, their hair, their manner of docile femininity made them great favorites with the clientele. They were sympathetic listeners and in half an hour could convince some lonesome sailor that he had just gained a bosom buddy, and that it would be fine, perfectly understandable if he needed to get anything off his chest. His every ill-gotten gain and every infidelity, every heart's desire and darkest deed would inevitably come pouring out, as well as the contents of his ship's cargo, its sailing plans, and the size of its crew.

This information was put to an interesting use. All four of these serving maids had lost a husband or a fiancé, a parent or a sibling, to kidnapping, or rape, or murder by Spanish pirates. All four of them, and the Button sisters too, had been shattered by that loss. Instead of self-pity, they chose revenge.

Just let a sailor from a Spanish ship come into the Bayside Inn, and one or more of these girls would be all over him like flies on a honeybun. You might wonder why men don't realise that falling for a woman's flattery was as stupid as trusting a politician's smile, but therein lies a mystery that no male in the history of the world has had the wherewithal to unravel.

While they were busy flirting and prying, these pretty serving maids often let slip some horrifying news. The ship belonging to the Black George was once again on the high seas. Oh yes, the Black George, that fiendish pirate who terrified crews into wishing they were anything but Spanish. He disemboweled, he mutilated, all with a smile on his face, while his men cleaned out ships' holds and off-loaded booty onto their own ship. Tales of the Black George, expressly meant to strike fear into Spanish hearts, were as effective as a sharp-edged weapon.

At any time of the year, no sooner was any Spanish ship out of Lunenfarne's harbor, and three or four of Freya's vixens would be ready to go after them. The swift little sloop *Vixen* would partner with the male crew on the formidable *Wolf,* one ship to lure and the other to attack. The *Wof's* men did the heavy fighting but those women from the *Vixen*? You would never believe it to look at them, but the moment they unsheathed their knives, their pussycat eyes transformed into the eyes of hellcats. Their only act of mercy was to give the Spanish sailors a choice: submit to being chained to the rails until help arrives, or be shark food, slashed with a knife and thrown overboard alive. Needless to say, Lunenfarne's ironmonger, Mr. Guntram, forged a quantity of chain for the *Vixen* every year.

This month, the *Dragòn*, the Spanish slaver, had just returned to tie up at a pier. Its crew spent an evening in the Bayside Inn. Georgiana and her friends hated particularly the slavers. On this trip, however, the *Dragòn* was not carrying slaves to sell. This time she was going to make her crew instantly rich, or so three or four sailors revealed separately, on the promise of deepest secrecy. *Dragòn* carried, the sailors boasted, furs and skins from the tundra, a large cargo of silver and copper from north of Ville-Marie, and three chests of ill-gotten Venetian gold.

Foolish sailors! Woe, woe be unto the *Dragòn!*

It should come as no surprise that, a few days later, the *Vixen* and the *Wolf* were laying in wait for the *Dragòn,* having discovered her plan to sail over to Vinland for more furs and then come west again and follow the coast south. As soon as they sighted her, the *Vixen* sailed out from a headland, tacking wildly, feigning a lack of control of the sails. The *Dragòn's* captain, seeing a bevy of ruffles and bosoms and curls through his monocular, lowered canvas and hailed the *Vixen.* Ladies in need of help? His specialty.

Georgiana asked permission to board and the captain said he would be delighted to give refuge to all four of them.

"Do I know you?" he asked, taking their little white hands one by one and helping them onto the deck. He spoke perfect English after all.

"I don't think so," Georgiana lied, "unless we met in Halifax at some point."

"I've never been to Halifax. But I'll make it my business to go there soon. Now what seems to be the problem, my little sweetcake, my little sugarplum?"

"Oh, good sir, I beg you to protect us. We are being pursued. Look!" Georgiana pointed to the *Wolf*, also making its way toward the *Dragòn*. "They have taken our crew. We got away but they are still after us. I don't know what they will do to us if they catch us." She blushed delicately. She batted seductively. She fluttered beseechingly. "Is there any way you can help us?"

"I can of course take care everything. It would be my pleasure, my beauties. We will simply lure them close and then blow them out of the water. You must go below, my darlings, to avoid harm."

That was exactly where Georgiana most wanted to be. Below, she and the other three dropped their skirts, pulled daggers out of their trousers and turned them on all crew members who weren't on deck. The Black George had struck! They forced the sailors to forfeit their weapons. They made them kneel down while they tied their wrists back to their ankles. It didn't take long. The women were very quick, from long experience.

One threat remained though, unbeknownst to Georgiana. They had tied up all crewmembers but one. The cook in the storeroom, hearing a commotion, was hiding behind the pickle barrel.

Meanwhile, visions of heroism clouded the captain's man-brain. He ordered a shot to be fired across *Wolf's* bow. This was but an invitation for the *Wolf* to fire back, come alongside in self-defense, then swing out of the rigging, and onto the deck of the *Dragòn*. A fight ensued, hand-to-hand, and no matter how much the captain bellowed for help, none was forthcoming from the crew below decks. No help for him, but he was shocked to see the fighting sailors of the *Wolf* joined by three of the women from below.

The Spaniards were outnumbered, not to mention outclassed. Foiled by a bunch of women? This was why no word of the *Vixen's* treachery ever got round. What Spaniard would reveal that he had lost his cargo, his sword, and his almighty pride to a woman?

Vladimir Mynydd was one of the crew of the *Wolf.* It hadn't taken long to subdue the Spaniards, but Mynydd marked one of them slipping down the companionway to find out why his mates hadn't joined the fight. Mynydd knew he must go after that man, as soon as he tackled his remaining opponent.

That Spanish sailor, going below, had to stop to catch his breath, shocked out of his mind at the sight of his helpless crewmates, tied up like roasted fowl and on their knees. A woman with a foot-long dagger turned on him, and Georgiana, when her blue eyes sparkled with challenge and she tossed her dagger from hand to hand, would make anyone's stomach turn over.

But the Spaniard had a sword, and as soon as he recovered his senses, he put it to work. He slashed and Georgiana parried. He thrust again. She sprang away and he missed. He stabbed and she jumped back, but not soon enough that time. His swordpoint ripped through her bodice. She looked down. It was her turn to be shocked. She had never, in all her years of piracy, been seriously wounded. The fabric of her bodice was already dark with blood. She managed weakly to duck the man's next thrust but the move made her dizzy and she tripped. He came at her. She tried to scream but he fell upon her. She hit her head hard as she went down.

She could not move. She realised dimly that the sailor was not moving either. His entire weight pressed her against the floor. In a thickening fog, she saw Vladimir appear in the companionway, and then she blacked out. She did not see who had felled the Spaniard, but Vladimir had seen: some Spanish woman, maybe the ship's cook, he guessed from the apron she wore. He moved to where Georgiana lay motionless, alarmed at the blood, trying to figure out where she was injured, trying to puzzle out why that cook had just beaten her fellow crewmate over the head with a cast iron skillet. Sheer spite? Sympathy for another woman in peril?

Vladimir was bending to push the unconscious Spaniard off Georgiana's body when the cook turned on him, ready to swing again.

"I mean you no harm!" he cried, gesturing because he didn't know how to say that in Spanish. He gathered Georgiana in his arms. She was badly injured. So much blood spouting, spreading red across her bodice.

The cook paused, still in fighting stance. Vladimir was on his knees, holding his handkerchief uselessly against Georgiana's wound.

"Can you get me a towel, anything to –"

The iron skillet crashed to the floor.

He started, and looked up. "Please! Get me something to –"

The cook sank to her knees in some kind of pain. Was she injured too?

He almost dropped Georgiana.

Distracted, he laid her back on the floor and turned to face the wretched cook.

Judging by the heavy iron chain around her ankle, he realised she was a captive. The woman was trembling visibly. Her body rocked in agony, her face contorted in some kind of distress.

Vladimir rose. He extended a hand. He realised he didn't have to speak to her in Spanish after all. "Get up."

He helped the woman to her feet. She hunched, miserable in front of him.

"If you're ready, we can take you home now."

She whimpered softly, a choking noise in her throat. Her voice broke. "It took you long enough."

He put his arms around her. He pulled her head to his chest and stroked her hair. "Just tell me one thing. Let me hear you say you're glad that you saved me from drowning all those years ago. Come on. I want to hear you say that."

Anne d'Inquierre leaned her face against his chest and sobbed aloud.

They slashed the rigging of the *Dragòn* to thwart pursuit, and the *Wolf* turned south with a load of booty to trade. One of the women stayed aboard the *Vixen* to crew for Vladimir, and they turned toward Bellesunde. Though it was two days' sail away, they hoped to find a physician there who could look after Georgiana.

Because Anne was told her son was also in Bellesunde, the two-day journey would be the longest of her life.

She spent the time, first, sitting for hours while Vladimir sawed at the chain on her ankle. It was a very thick chain, heavy enough to slow her down if she ever tried to escape her captors, or drown her if she tried to swim to shore when they were in harbor. Her ankle had been chafed raw for years. They found her some soft stockings and a pair of boots, and clean clothes to replace the filthy rags she was wearing. The luxury of being able to wash her hair and bathe, awkward as that was in a small tub, the pleasure of dressing in a clean cotton gown and walking unburdened by a chain – all this had come to her so suddenly that Anne spent a lot of the two days just sitting quietly on the deck and trying to convince herself it was all real.

They managed to patch Georgiana up so well that, if she didn't move about, the bleeding had nearly stopped. Thanks to the stays in her corset, the sword cut had not gone deep enough to injure her organs, at least not in Vladimir's assessment. But she needed to see a doctor and in Bellesunde they were sure to find the best.

When the city finally appeared on the horizon, gleaming golden in the late afternoon sun, Anne thought she would be ill from anticipation. It was terrible to be entering the city where her little boy lived and not have any idea where he might be. She wanted to run about shouting his name. She forced herself to curb her wild excitement and merely watched for him, hawk-like, from the moment they entered the bay.

They found a mooring. Now the city had turned rose-colored in the evening light. The water rippled deep pink and blue, ruffled by a light offshore wind. People lit candles at sidewalk cafes. None of them was Kai. People lingered on the bridges over the canals or strolled along the waterways. None of them was Kai. The windows of the university on the hill blazed in the setting sun. Anne wondered if he was up there on that beautiful campus, just where she had long ago imagined him being. Teron, too, had gone to that school.

Teron. They said he was still in Lunenfarne and had taken no other woman. How long would it be before she would find out whether he still cared for her?

The lamps along the streets were being lit by the time they found someone to treat Georgiana. The man was meticulous, carefully surveying the damage to her abdomen and cleaning and binding the wound. She was very lucky, he said, very lucky that everything was healing so well and without infection.

Anne tried to stifle her impatience. It seemed to take forever to find a carriage to drive them to the house that Freya Button still owned in town.

It was a big old place. Trees lined the street, their fleshy leaves ticktocking in the fragrant twilight breeze. Crickets murmured in gardens. A lone carriage creaked past. Anne, heavy with disappointment, took one last look up and down the street before following the others through the dark courtyard.

Silent, exhausted, they mounted the steps to the house and Vladimir unlocked the apartment on the first floor. Anne sank wearily into a chair, frustrated that everything had taken so long tonight, chafing that she had to wait another day to look for Kai.

Vladimir came into the room, talking with some landlord or a manager. Anne sat downcast, folding her hands in her lap to keep them quiet. She had no sooner settled them in her lap then she put her elbows on the arm of the chair and leaned her forehead against her wrists. She heard Vladimir say something but it didn't penetrate her agitated state. She sighed and pressed her hands into her lap again.

"Ema?"

She bolted upright. Her eyes darted everywhere. She gasped. What was this? This wasn't right. The warrior prince from her girlhood – how did he get here? He called her 'Ema'? Oh! Angels in Heaven! She flew out of the chair and threw her arms around her son.

On an afternoon a couple of weeks later, the only sound in the Parrot Island Print Shop was the clink of iron type and the occasional rap of a wooden mallet. Teron Adante was printing five sets of Sister Rosemarie's herbologies, hoping to sell them in Bellesunde. Poggio Gomoggio had designed singularly beautiful covers for them with marbelized endpapers. Florri Mynydd had etched Rosemarie's drawings onto copper plates.

Dust motes danced in a beam of sunlight. The two men leaned silent over their tables in the composing room. Poggio, with one eye on Sister Rosemarie's manuscript, chose a piece of type from the case. At another table, Teron concentrated on moving a justified line of type from a composing stick to the galley, tapping the letters with a mallet to guarantee an even surface for printing. They worked slowly, each intent on his own task.

The shop door opened. Its bell jangled loud in the quiet.

I'll be damned, squawked Bou Bou the parrot.

Poggio heard Teron call to the visitor to wait a moment. He selected another letter and was just adding it to his stick when he heard Teron's mallet and an entire iron chase of text crash to the floor. What? A whole afternoon's work? What a mess!

Poggio tried to set his composing stick down without spilling. He did a double-take. Who was that? Trying to swipe a hank of hair out of his eyes, he fumbled his stick and thirty cast iron letters plinked onto the floor. Poggio gawked at the sight in front of him, his eyes round as coins. His business partner? Wrapped in the arms of a woman? A brown woman. He couldn't see her face, it was pressed so hard into Teron's shoulder. Vladimir Mynydd and an unknown brown man stood behind them, grinning and blinking, dewy-eyed.

Bou Bou the parrot stretched upright in surprise and fluttered his feathers.

I got out and looked and there I tipped over.

What? That crusty old parrot, sounding prim as a grandmother?

Unbelievable. Inexplicable.

Well, one never knows, does one?

When Anne d'Inquierre returned to Lunenfarne, she was amazed at the transformation. Teron showed Anne and Kai around the Hill Road mansion. A house full of studios and workrooms, purchased by a group of villagers? Yes, with a lot of help from the Button sisters. They had bought it from a desperate mining family who had no more mines in the area to plunder. The workshops and classrooms, the small apartments upstairs, all were full of local children or visitors who came to study. The place swarmed with activity every month of the year now.

Anne peeked in at the studio that was in use by the present lighthouse keeper. Hogar Hanon was teaching a student to sing Handel's 'The Trumpet Shall Sound'. Hogar had decided, Teron whispered, that he was never cut out to be a fisherman after all. He claimed that coming to the Parrot Island lighthouse was the best thing he had ever done, and he planned to stay forever, which, as it turned out, he would do.

In another room, Sister Angelica was rehearsing the children's choir. Anne had known Angelica when the nun was a girl in her mid-teens, teaching at Kai's school. Now Anne was surprised to learn that Angelica had left the nunnery. Well, it had surprised everyone, Teron said. More surprising still was the apparent change in the woman. Angelica's new life seemed so suited to her that everyone wondered why she had ever taken the veil in the first place. There were rumors, of course there were, Teron told Anne, rumors of a jealous step-mother who hoped that the St. Scholastica monastery in the Tomgat Mountains was remote enough to isolate a twelve-year old who was much too beautiful for her own good.

Angelica herself was surprised as well, when she found out that Anne d'Inquierre had returned. For the rest of that day, she couldn't get the story of Teron and Anne's separations out of her mind. It affected her deeply, very deeply. It seemed so tragic, all those years spent apart, he in prison, she taken into captivity. So much time lost.

That evening, Angelica forgot to eat dinner. She was too overwrought to eat, but food was the furthest thing from her mind anyway. She sat on a stool in her empty rehearsal room, thinking. She thought about her life with the nuns, women who, as the poet said, wanted only to live "where no storms come", and "out of the swing of the sea". Angelica had recently chosen not to follow that path. It was a difficult choice, giving up the veil. Did she have the strength to make another? What if it was the wrong choice?

She thought about life's uncertainties. For a long time, she sat and thought. Then she got up and stepped into the hall. She didn't get any further. She stood out there, unmoving, a hive of uncertainty. She almost turned back. Her hand was on the doorknob.

She let it go. Something urged her to go on. Something drove her to do the hardest thing she had ever done. With tiny steps, she minced hesitantly down that hall. The only other sound in the building was a guitar, Silvio Filvio picking out a tune in a small room. She knocked on his door. Silvio put down his guitar and answered her knock. Angelica smiled by way of apology for interrupting. The hardest thing she had ever done turned out to be quite easy after all. One smile from Angelica, and Silvio Filvio, the infamous Signor Bologna, was lost lost lost.

They married next day and they sailed away in a beautiful pea-green boat. For a year and a day they sailed away, and very lucky for them that they did, as things turned out. The North Star, Polaris, the Sky Pin – they kept it always in their gaze because they knew they would return to Lunenfarne one day. Lunenfarne, the village that was transforming itself into something uniquely beautiful. They would be eager to see how it had improved.

It wasn't too long after they left that the sorcerer Sulman also felt the winds of change. He was certain he had reached the height of his powers. All the world, the whole entire world must discover how he was worshipped as a shaman, as someone who literally dominated the underworld, though an underworld of his own invention. He, Sulman, should be glorified as a man of wisdom and potent masculinity. Now was his time, time to prove his superiority through the ritual he called Spiritlight.

He told Natalia Mynydd she would be the first, first of many, to be honored as his spiritual partner through Spiritlight. He had collected all the elements he needed. Malachite, azurite, cinnabar, morphine, gold, and the key ingredient, mercury. He gloated over the contents of his chest of treasures. Today, this was to be the greatest spectacle Sulman had ever created. These elements, mixed together, would open doors to secret knowledge, and he, Sulman the Great, would have all of it.

A misguided man can sometimes carry on far longer than he deserves before the gods tire of him. But when they do, they deal with him swiftly.

In the full throes of lust for power, Sulman set the stage for his Spiritlight ritual on Natalia's rooftop patio. An angry sky for a backdrop, lightning flaring from distant black clouds, thunder his orchestral accompaniment. Thunder, lightning! Portents sinister and compelling! He lit a brazier of fire and watched it fanned into life by the wrathful wind. Fire was crucial for the moment of transmutation. He laid a rug from the Orient to cushion their bare feet. He poured a goblet of a magic elixir that would cure every pain. This drink cured anything, he promised Natalia, because it relieved everything.

Sulman and Natalia opened their robes and let them billow in the wind. Long tresses of hair writhed and swirled about their shoulders. From his teak box, Sulman brought out poisonous cinnabar for rubbing over their bodies. They were vermillion gods, bloated with power!

Now, now they were ready. Here, the ceremonial vessel, a bowl of nitric acid. Here, a vial of mercury. Pour in the quicksilver – oh! They gasped, choking, appalled at the cloud of thick red vapor that billowed up.

Stand back! Sulman was aghast, stunned at the reaction. Natalia tripped and fell against him. The bowl of acid tipped, splashing onto the carpet. The brazier fire licked at their robes. From there, it danced over the carpet, the spilled acid making the fire burn hotter.

Their transmutation began. Sulman and Natalia became human torches. They had both lost consciousness long before the burning roof caved in.

Fire! Someone in the village beat the big bell frantically. Up on the Hill Road! It was Chancellor Mynydd's mansion! Of course Dort wasn't there. No one assumed he was, but his wife and his child and his mother were! They had to be saved!

A crowd of villagers gathered at the gates. Flames were pouring from the second floor windows now. Soon the ground floor would be alight.

Dort Mynydd's carriage pounded up the River Road, turned, and pulled up at the back of the crowd.

"Get out of my way!" Dort screamed. He ran to the gate in the wall of his courtyard. "Out of my way!"

He had only one thought, and because it was the most unselfish thought he had ever had, one might find oneself suddenly wishing the gods would treat him kindly, just this once.

Men had gathered by the gate. Vladimir grabbed Dort's arms. "Dort, it's too late!"

"Let me go!"

He would never let Vladimir stop him. Dort ran across the courtyard. Hogar struggled to hold Vladimir back. "No, no!"

Thorfinn Taptoe had no love for Dort Mynydd, but he pushed past the two men. "I'll get him!"

"No, Thorfinn!" Hogar Hanon roared as only baritones can roar. He pushed Vladimir aside and grabbed Thorfinn's coat. He took him by the throat. "You have a family, Thorfinn! I don't." He threw Thorfinn to the ground and ran into the burning house after Dort, following the sound of shouting.

"Florri!" Dort was screaming. "Florri!" Not his mother's name, not his son's, but Florri's name was the last on Dort's lips when the ceiling came down around him.

They heard the crash. They felt it. It shook the ground. Whimpers and groans of sorrow rippled through the crowd. Then, a cry of joy! Hogar emerged. It was neither Florri nor Gregor in his arms. He was carrying Dort's smoldering body. Both of their clothes were on fire. Someone threw a bucket of water at them. Hogar laid Dort on the ground.

Florri and Gregor, all this time, had been down in the village with Lisabetta and Lily. The crowd parted for them, relieved, happy they were safe, afraid for them to see Dort in this appalling condition. Florri broke free of the crowd. Someone held little Gregor back and shushed his cries for his mother.

She knelt beside Dort's horribly charred body. His hair was gone. All but a few tatters of his clothing had burned away. Most of his skin had been seared, black, red, and raw.

He lived, though. Somehow, he lived.

Lisabetta took over his care in her house at the end of the fishermen's village. She made up a cot for him. Lily and Gregor were sent to stay with Ermentrude Treyse and Florri slept, when she slept at all, in Lily's bed. It was impossible to feed Dort because he couldn't swallow anything solid. It was impossible to treat his burns because they covered every inch of his body. Morphine was the only thing Lisabetta could give him, and still he hung on to life.

Hogar's burns had to be treated too, but his clothing had mostly protected him. His red beard and the enormous bush of red hair, everyone joked, were apparently incombustible. Lisabetta babied him and called him a foolish old goat for running into a burning house, but the town praised him as their greatest hero, the epitome of bravery. Everyone made so much of his new fame that never, for the rest of his life, did Hogar have to buy his own drink at the Bayside Inn. He didn't let on to anyone what it had cost him, as a widower, to run straight into that burning house, but after surviving fire twice, he was beginning to believe in his own immortality. He didn't realise how that offended the jealous gods.

Vladimir Mynydd came to be with his son every day, giving Florri a chance to try to sleep. Mostly, she sat beside Dort's bed for hours, day after day, reading to him or just sitting near because she dared not touch him. His eyes could move, only his eyes, and all he wanted to look at was Florri. Hour after hour his eyes begged something of her, but what he wanted, she either did not know or chose not to think about.

After seven days of this, Lisabetta pulled Florri away from Dort's cot.

"Granny Taptoe is coming here later this afternoon." Florri just looked at her with dull eyes. "It's time you took a little rest. Granny will look after Dort while we take the children to the new puppet theatre."

"No. I should stay with Dort," Florri mumbled.

Lisabetta stamped her foot. "Florri, he's barely conscious anymore and probably doesn't even know you're here. You have to think of yourself once in a while. It's noble, this loyalty of yours, but it's killing you. Look at you. You're exhausted. You haven't seen your son for a week. No! You are coming with us, if I have to drag you."

"I can't leave him."

"Yes, you can. It will be good for you. They're opening Kai d'Inquierre's new theatre up at Lake Arum with a new puppet show. The whole town is going there to celebrate. Get cleaned up. Change your gown, for goodness sake." Lisabetta raised an eyebrow. "And that hair. Do you want me to put it up for you?"

Lake Arum's park had been defiled by the hideous deep pit that Botia Mining Company had deserted because it never yielded a single ounce of copper. So Hahri Fahri had decided to take it over. None of the magistrates bothered to contest him. If they had, fingers would have been pointed and covert exchanges of money would have been brought to light.

Hahri conspired with Kai d'Inquierre to convert the pit into an amphitheatre. Kai had taken on the project eagerly, directing a simple Greek-style theatre to be built, right here in Lunenfarne, with wonderful acoustics and sight-lines, and seating for a multitude of people. The Button sisters, ever generous, loaned their own money to pay for stone masons to carve the sides of the pit into long rows of benches that looked down onto the stage. The villagers gathered to help polish the stone floor until it shone. Teron put up posters to advertise the premier occasion, the first-ever artistic offering in the new theatre.

Everyone – everyone was going! Two or three elderly folks said they weren't up to it, including Granny Taptoe. Chekov, the Sunday cook, decided to stay in the Bayside Inn to maul the dough for his so-so pierogies. And Hogar didn't dare leave the lighthouse for that long. All in all, on the day of the spectacle, there were so few people left in the village that, by five o'clock, it resembled a ghost town.

Hahri Fahri had built an all-new cast of puppets. They were modelled on something he had seen when he was in the Orient, large dolls worn on one hand and manipulated by people dressed completely in black. Black netting covered their faces too, and would render the handlers almost invisible in the low light of the torches at the foot of the stage. These handlers were apprentices who Hahri had trained to kneel together on the stage so they could manoeuver their puppets. In the dark of an autumn evening, with most of the light on the puppets and the handlers mere shadows, the illusion would be incredibly effective.

Lake Arum was a mile upriver from Lunenfarne and the new amphitheatre was on the other side of the lake. So people left the village early, many of them taking picnic hampers because, though it was October, the weather was calm and warm enough to be pleasant. Those who could afford it were poled upriver on Korsakov's party barges. Some drove up to the park in donkey carts, some walked. Many had not yet seen the wonderful new amphitheatre so, long before the sunset hour, quite a crowd of curious people had already collected in Lake Arum Park.

Then, at five o'clock, something startling happened. Hogar, at the top of the lighthouse, heard the chimneys on his lamps start to chatter. The floor shook and rattled.

Down in the village, Granny Taptoe's ball of yarn bounced off her lap and the teakettle on the stove began to dance. The bottle of morphine next to Dort's cot tipped over and she saw his eyelids flutter nervously. It was the strangest sensation, everything shaking like this, the weirdest thing that Granny, in all her long years, had ever experienced. The trembling went on for a full five minutes. The people in Lake Arum Park felt it too. Then, just as mysteriously, it stopped. Granny picked up her yarn and went on knitting, knowing everything was under control again.

But the sea will not be controlled. The sea sets all rules. And it was deep under the sea and a hundred fifty miles away that the problem originated. An earthquake had erupted from the sea floor. This was what had caused the tremors. That created a massive landslide across the floor of the ocean. The forces released formed huge waves on the ocean's surface, waves that gathered and began to move, traveling at unimaginable speeds, eighty-five miles an hour. It took those waves almost two hours, but by seven o'clock they were driving hard toward Lunenfarne's shore. By then, Hogar was sleeping like the dead, his alarm clock set for eight o'clock. Because Hogar always managed to sleep undisturbed even through his own tumultuous snoring, he might not have heard a certain long roar and then a huge boom. Or maybe he did hear it. We'll never know. But that boom did indeed pull Granny Taptoe from her chair. By the time she hobbled to the window, the view was an unbelievable sight to behold.

The water, all the water in the entire bay had been completely sucked away. The sea floor was bare, exposed clear across the harbor.

This? This had never happened! Terrified, Granny looked back at Dort. She wanted to move both him and herself out of the house, or upstairs, anywhere, but how could she touch his burned body? When she turned back to the window, an eighty foot wave was towering at the mouth of the harbor. She limped screaming to the stairs.

That wave, and the two that followed, should never have touched the lighthouse perched so high, a hundred feet above the sea. But the speeding waters would not be denied their prey. They found an opening, the hidden door to the cave beneath the island. The Celtic cross incised on its portal did nothing to stop the massive flow of water from pouring in. Water forced itself roaring into the cave, filling it completely, driving hard, hammering every fissure and crack. Far beneath the lighthouse, water bellowed and boomed against the cave walls. Tons of water, smashing and crashing against the walls and ceiling, pushing and pulling relentlessly. More water pounding to get in, more water than the cave could hold.

Looking from an upstairs window, Granny was the only witness to the unimaginable. Before her very eyes, Parrot Island, the entire island, was blown apart, destroyed. A geyser of water shot up, exploding a million pieces of rock and soil and lighthouse into the air, and then falling like rain into the sea.

Parrot Island had disappeared. Into the underwater gorge it sank, an entire island gone, except for the towering cliff wall that faced the ocean.

That rock cliff was one of the few things in Lunenfarne that remained standing.

Three waves hit Lunenfarne's shore in succession, each growing in strength and speed as they plunged across the harbor. Granny felt Lisabetta's house rock with the force of the first wave. She heard water smash through the windows downstairs. Water filled the first floor to the ceiling and slid along the upstairs hall. With the third wave, Granny felt the house rise and tilt precariously. It, and she in it, was dragged through the mouth of the harbor, right over the drowned island, and out to sea.

Happy crowds of people returning from the amphitheatre later that night stopped in their tracks on the riverbank, confused. What happened? The fishermen's village, the ferry dock? Missing? How could they be missing? Group after group came down along the Arum River. They gathered in stunned silence. They peered into empty darkness, not trusting their eyes because what they thought they were seeing was not what they had seen every day before.

Along the shore, not a single house remained standing. Completely covering the bay was a vast expanse of floating debris like giant broken matchsticks. A few sections of roofing rocked on the waves at the mouth of the harbor. Touched with moonlight, two masts of sunken sailing ships were just visible out in the middle of the bay. Huge boulders had been tossed up to settle where gardens used to be. No wharf, no boardwalk remained, no elementary school, no market square. The stone walls of the Bayside Inn were badly damaged. Most shocking of all, no lighthouse and not a trace of Parrot Island remained, except for a huge fang of rock that dominated the mouth of the harbor where the island used to be. Of all the buildings in the village, only Father James's church remained whole, though it had been lifted straight up off its foundations and deposited far uphill in a meadow, still upright and not a hymnal out of place.

Two days after the devastating trauma, one of the few boats left intact in the village was patrolling the wreckage and found Granny Taptoe, a shivering wreck, clinging to a windowsill of a partially submerged house that was floating away down the coast. From a weak and tearful Granny, the people of Lunenfarne finally heard what had happened on the night of the last puppet show, Hahri Fahri's Fabulous Puppet Show, the show that they credited with saving so many citizens, but not their village.

The bodies of Chekov the cook and two of the old people were dragged from the wreckage. They never found a sign of Dort Mynydd, not in the half-submerged house where they found Granny Taptoe, nowhere among the floating wreckage. Most heart-breaking, Hogar Hanon, town hero, lay either at the bottom of the bay or had been swept out to sea. It hurt, yes, everyone acknowledged that it hurt badly, not knowing where that man rested.

The house on Hill Road that, a couple of years before, the townspeople had labored so hard to convert into classrooms and workshops was now packed full with homeless families. Looms and wood-working tools and the printing press and musical instruments were dragged outside to make room for people. Every effort, every thought was channeled into finding food and shelter for an entire village. They salvaged what they could from the debris but the next few winters took a terrible toll on the population. Some died. Many people, anyone who had friends or family in the south, moved away. The mansions in the hills were soon deserted and, being much too large for villagers to heat, were torn apart and repurposed as bayside cottages.

No longer was there any beam of light shining over the nightblack sea. For a little time, the Parrot Island Lighthouse had pulled the world a little closer, a symbol of something to a few people. Then the light was gone, extinguished. Ships passed by and Lunenfarne's dark harbor faded into obscurity.

Decay and renewal continue seamlessly. Over the years, the physical village of Lunenfarne was rebuilt on a much smaller scale. Fishing and farming were, as of old, once again the main occupations. Though there was much that was never recovered, not everything was lost.

One day, far, far away and a long time later, a young student pulled a large dusty tome from a shelf in a used-book store. This bookstore had been through two owners since that book was purchased. No one remembered where it came from. It was a book about wildflowers. It appeared to have been written by a nun, Sister-someone, and was beautifully illustrated, bound, and printed by – well, the girl never could make out the name of the printer. But she treasured it always as the book that inspired her life's work as a botanist.

So. One spark. There was that one spark. Not everything had been lost.

CULMINATION

Well, the world comes and goes. Time walks backwards so its footprints deceive, turning yesterday's truths into today's errors. It wasn't until a hundred years after the Lunenfarne tsunami that a group of cartographers set out along the coastline of that country to sound its depths; to accurately chart the mouths of its rivers, its bays and inlets and islands; to clear up any discrepancies on the old maps.

Charles Hermon, fifty-four year old Chief Surveyor, was at the helm of the boat on a cold, drizzly March day. "It's late and I'm freezing. There should be a small island called Par Ou just past this headland," he said. "It shelters a deep-water bay. We'll pull in there and spend the night."

"I wonder if you will find an island –", began Andrea Andropolis, a young crewmember.

Her boss interrupted her. "I have it on three old maps. Par Ou. It has a lighthouse, clearly marked. We should sight it soon."

"Maybe not," Andrea contradicted him. "The name could be a joke. You know the scenario. One ancient mapmaker draws a nonexistent island for whatever reason, and others copy and recopy it. But I'll bet you it never existed. I'll bet you any amount of money."

"Do you have evidence or are you relying on woman's intuition yet again?"

She laughed. "That's right, Boss. Insult me."

"I've done the research, Andrea. Geez, count on a woman to refuse to look at the plain facts."

"Do we have a bet or don't we?"

"Dinner tonight," said Chief Hermon.

"Dinner for the whole crew, if we can find a place to eat. I hope you can afford champagne."

"One of these days you'll learn not to make unfounded statements. You lose every time."

"I won't lose because I happen to speak a bit of –"

The two other crew members, bounding up to lean over the railing, interrupted her. "Hey! Isn't anybody watching for the lighthouse?"

"I say there will be no island and no lighthouse," called Andrea.

"I have it marked on two different maps." One young man turned to the other who stood beside him. He sneered in *sotto voce* singsong. "Someone has not done her homework."

"Someone relies on her feminine insights." They rolled their eyes.

Chief Hermon stood up. "Look! That must be the town of Lunenfarne across the bay."

"You call that a town?

"What? No island?"

"I told you. No Par Ou."

"No lighthouse."

They stared at a giant slab of bare rock rearing up out of the water just at the mouth of the bay. It needled the sky a hundred feet into the air.

"Hmm. Champagne will be a real treat tonight, Boss."

"You think we'll be able get a decent dinner in this place? It looks pretty desolate."

"I refuse to eat peanut butter sandwiches on board again tonight," Andrea said.

The two male crewmembers, listening, elbowed each other. One of them muttered, "Would it kill this woman to cook us a meal now and then?"

A cold rain began to fall as they chugged into the bay and came alongside a dilapidated pier. Andrea threw a line to the only dockworker. "Is this Lunenfarne?" she called.

"It is."

"Can you tell me if there is some place where we can get a hot meal tonight?"

He pointed to an old stone building. "The Parrot Island Inn. Best food for miles around."

More elbow nudging. The two young men eyed each other sideways. "Uh, we have decided to stay aboard tonight, Boss. We'd rather eat peanut butter than risk getting food poisoning in that dump."

"But Boss is buying – "

"Shh." Chief Hermon hastily interrupted Andrea. "Suit yourselves, men. Miss Andropolis and I will give this inn a try."

"But Boss, you agreed to buy us all –"

"Let them stay here, Andrea. All the more champagne for us."

"Oh sure. Champagne in this godforsaken port? We'll get the local rotgut swill or nothing, I'm afraid." Andrea slid her oilskin hood over her head. "Hey, Boss. Do you think that inn rents out rooms? I would love sleeping anywhere that doesn't smell like dirty socks tonight."

The chief looked up at the building with its creaking red sign. He raised an eyebrow. "I don't know. I myself am not fond of bedbugs." He cocked his head. "I wonder why they call it Parrot Island Inn. Did we miss an island coming down the coast? If so, you might owe me a dinner."

It was pouring rain by the time Charles Hermon and Andrea Andropolis stepped gladly out of the cold and into the Parrot Island Inn. The building had to be at least, oh, eighty, a hundred years old. They were immediately struck with the strangest feeling about the place. And with good reason.

The first things to catch their eyes were the wool portieres hanging in the vestibule doorway. They were quite old, woven in the most unique pattern, much lovelier than anything they expected to find in such a place. A waiter took their wet outerwear and ushered them to a table near the windows.

They looked around the dining room. Dark wood-paneled walls and a ceiling of heavy beams. In the fireplace across the room, massive logs blazed on a bed of red coals. Its mantel was crowded with dolls slumped one against another, gathering dust. But when Andrea went closer, she saw they were not dolls, but very finely-crafted puppets. She didn't notice, at first, the raggedy old parrot crouched on a post near the fire. He eyed Andrea with suspicion, eschewed a hospitable greeting, and mimicked the sound of a whiplash.

Tchshooo! Get humping, you clods.

The strain of conversation being a bit much for such an old bird, he fell promptly asleep. But he was the only tawdry thing in the room, him and his thin dull feathers and his rather crude vocabulary.

The rest of the place – tables laid with ecru linen tablecloths and sparkling silver cutlery and candlesticks – was surprisingly gracious. The champagne and the crystal stemware came in an ice bucket. The two cartographers tried not to look disappointed when the waiter told them there was no menu to choose from. They would have to make do with whatever the kitchen was serving tonight.

"I think you might find dinner quite palatable," the waiter assured them. They finally agreed to try it, they were that hungry. The chef, could they have met him, was Thorfinn Mynydd, nineteen years old, neither a fisherman nor a farmer, and another puzzling incongruity. An entire wall of his kitchen was devoted to cookbooks. He had read every one, cover to cover.

And there it was again, that passion, lit by a spark that no one could account for, even the chef himself; passion that comes seemingly from nowhere, that talent, that blade of grass that grows right through concrete.

On this evening, the only item that Chef Mynydd could offer for the appetizer was smoked trout. It was dabbed with a piquant horseradish mayonnaise, made in-house, and served on petite rounds of toasted brioche, accompanied by a small bowl of radishes, sliced raw fennel, and pickled baby eggplant. This was followed by a wedge of warmed red cabbage glossed with an earthy dressing and studded with pine nuts, small pink shrimp, and a swirl of basil pesto. Then came a tureen of buttery golden seafood chowder with pencil-thin asparagus and baby snap peas.

"Where are you getting all these lovely vegetables so early in the year?" Andrea asked the waiter.

"We grow them."

"Here in Lunenfarne?"

"There's an old open-pit mine up the river. It's warm enough down in that hole that we can grow all kinds of things on the terraces, even in winter."

"Who would have thought? I mean, you're pretty far north here and, well, in this kind of town, you wouldn't think ...."

"Yeah, tell me about it. Not much happening in this place, but we kind of like it like that."

"What's the story with those puppets? They're beautiful. Did someone here make them?'

"I really don't know. They were some kid's toys, I guess." He shrugged and bowed. "Please excuse me. I'll be bringing your dessert out shortly."

"Dessert?" they chorused. Shortbread squares, baked with slices of tart little apples and dabs of warm Aram River cheese; a thimble-sized glass of limoncello.

"Well, I'm happy as a pig in mud," said Andrea.

Chief Hermon sat back. "Now tell me. Whatever made you think that Par Ou Island was a joke, Andrea? I had it marked on three different maps."

"I was sure Par Ou must be a Greek name."

"Really? It means something in Greek?"

"Well, 'par' could mean 'beside', or 'beyond'. 'Ou' means 'not', or 'not at all'. Roughly, it could mean something like 'no beyond', or maybe 'nowhere'. I thought that was the joke."

"Ha, interesting. So some Greek mapmaker claimed he had located Nowhere."

Andrea nibbled a shortbread thoughtfully. "It almost feels like that, doesn't it? You ask where we are tonight? I don't know – nowhere. We're nowhere."

"Wherever we are, I have to apologise. You were right about the island and lighthouse. You realise I'm eating humble pie right now, don't you?"

"Are you saying you're not going to tease me about feminine intuition anymore?"

"I promise to give at least some small credence to your opinions."

Fine words! Yessirree bob!

They looked up.

Fine words butter no parsnips!

This, accompanied by a flutter of pathetic feathers, made them sit upright. "Was that the parrot?"

"Quite the philosophical fellow, isn't he?"

"I wonder what other words of wisdom he can offer."

Apparently not a one. The bird promptly tucked his head beneath his wing and, I'm rather sorry to report and you may or may not be sorry to hear, he passed into legend and was never heard from again.

"You know, Boss, you could almost turn this place into a tourist destination. People would come, I bet. Like sport fishermen. Or artists. They would come for the food alone."

"Really, Andrea? All the way up here? I'd say that's pretty far-fetched."

"You're never going to listen to my ideas, are you?"

The waiter came to take their plates. "You wouldn't happen to have two rooms vacant for tonight, would you?" Charles Hermon asked him.

"*Two* rooms?" The waiter's eyes flicked from one to the other. "I, uh, yes, certainly. I'm sure we do. We're never very busy this early in the year. We're never very busy at any time of year. Anyway, you'll be glad not to have to sleep on your boat tonight." He pointed to the window. The storm was belting the village with wind and rain. The waves in the bay were sea monsters, determinedly tugging the boat back and forth on its lines.

In all, the weather kept them in Lunenfarne for two days. They worked on their maps and in the evenings they were entertained at the inn with the locals' version of the history of the area. The owner of Parrot Island Inn, a grand matriarch named Lily Taptoe, was one of Lunenfarne's most elderly residents. She came downstairs to join them, and the young chef Thorfinn

Mynydd personally delivered her nightly glass of Irish whiskey. He stood by her chair while they asked her about Par Ou and its lighthouse.

"My great-grandmother," mewed old Mrs. Taptoe, "always claimed there was once an island with that name at the mouth of the harbor." From a crystal glass she sipped her whiskey and her memories. "She said no one believed her. But I always did."

"An island? Did it have a lighthouse?" asked Andrea.

"Maybe," Mrs. Taptoe mused. "Maybe she did say something about a lighthouse. I can't remember."

"Granny!" one of the locals scoffed. "Don't go spreading that guff. Everyone knows there was never any island called Par Ou. You're dreaming, old girl. It was a myth, nothing but a tall tale."

"It might be true, Uncle," said chef Thorfinn Mynydd.

His uncle waved the idea away. "Ah Thorfinn. You're such a dreamer, you'll believe anything."

"Hmm." Thorfinn leaned his head back and gazed upwards, seeing, instead of the ceiling, whatever it is that dreamers see.

No sign then, nary a trace of that small node of invincibility that, on ancient maps, once huddled between the deep upswelling sea and a land of balsam-scented mountains? No lighthouse, no beacon to guide mariners across the nightblack sea?

Total fabrication, the villagers insisted. Nothing like that ever existed in Lunenfarne. Some mapmaker got it all wrong.

Well, sometimes histories do get it wrong, and it has been posited, now and again, that the annals of mankind may be full of tall tales. But there's nothing wrong with that. People love stories, true or not, and hold onto them like favorite socks that aren't holey enough to throw away.

When they asked Granny about the monolithic rock formation at the mouth of the harbor, even old Lily Taptoe could not tell them, because no one alive remembered, the story of why it was called Hogar's Tombstone.

I guess that tale has all, all been lost.

ACKNOWLEDGEMENTS

I hope you enjoyed reading *Parrot Island Tales*. As a favor to a self-published author, if you can find it in your heart to leave a review on the book site of your choice, it would help immensely.

I'd like to express my gratitude to early readers and cheerleaders Dan Welcher, Heidi Weimer, Dorian Kincaid, Henry Zielinski, and Marg Dilmore. Without your encouragement, Parrot Island would have joined Atlantis and Lyonnesse in the most obscure depths of the sea. Thank you also to endlessly accommodating photographer Hermon Charles for several images, including the lighthouse image on the back cover of the book. Who knew he was also an excellent marketing wordsmith? Photographer Kris Kuszajewski kindly allowed me to use his image of a golden macaw that put a face on a leading character in this story, though he would probably have denied permission if he had actually met Bou Bou.

For a larger view of the bona fide map of Lunenfarne Bay, you can visit my website at kmdelmara.com.

People who spend two years wandering aimlessly in the mythical far north must be fed and cared for by someone. I am, as always, grateful that I have a husband who knows his way around the real world. Without him, I'd have drifted away in my beautiful pea green boat, lost forever on the heaving bosom of a nightblack sea.

K.M. del Mara

lives within spitting distance of the Delaware River,

if the wind is in the right quarter.